There are Rivers i

'Make place for Elif Shafak on your bookshelf. Make place for her in your heart too. You won't regret it' Arundhati Roy

'A great, sweeping, enthralling novel – Elif Shafak's narrative vision is as remarkable and astonishing as ever. Wonderful' William Boyd

'Elif Shafak's beautiful and moving new novel bears the reader along on its marvellous currents. Here, rivers twine with other rivers and lives with other lives across centuries and cultures, as the fate of a single drop of water weaves an intricate tapestry of love and loss' Robert Macfarlane

'Literature on a grand scale, mythic and timeless' Nadifa Mohamed

'Another mystical novel from Elif Shafak, in which time dissolves in the timeless water of two rivers and the characters who live beside them. The story flows like the rivers from ancient Nineveh to present-day London, with characters of the distant past as bright and vivid as those of today' Philippa Gregory

'A brilliant, unforgettable novel, which raises big ideas of "who owns the past" with nuance and complexity. Elif Shafak ties together diverse time periods and places in a way that seems both natural and wonderfully unexpected' Mary Beard

'Elif Shafak is a unique and powerful voice in world literature' Ian McEwan

'One of the best writers in the world today' Hanif Kureishi

'Shafak finds the world in a drop of water. She discovers the epic in the tiny, the global in the local, the love in the loss, the history in the momentary. An extraordinary novel, fresh and cleansing, like the rain bouncing off the metal roof of our lives' Colum McCann

'It will surprise no one that this is a brutal, elegant and incredible book. Amazing what Elif Shafak has done here – again! Magic' Evie Wyld

'A book that is astonishing, ingenious and beautiful. A modern classic. Elif Shafak is one of the great writers of our time' Peter Frankopan

'A writer of important, beautiful, painful, truthful novels' Marian Keyes

'A deep and satisfying sweep of a story, combining intellectual pleasures with a transformative empathy. Particular, universal, with head and with heart in perfect balance, this is surely a landmark novel' Laline Paull

'Elif Shafak approaches the world with grace, lyricism and courage. Confronting societies riven by conflicts over gender, religion, sexuality, nationalism, memory, ideology, and more, Shafak wields the novel's artistic power to cut through complacency and orthodoxy with ruthlessness and beauty. Her words and works – compelling and provocative – leave us in a space of light, a clearing from where we can see this world anew' Viet Thanh Nguyen

'From its bravura opening through to its final pages, *There are Rivers in the Sky* is a dazzling achievement. Shafak's imagination is a wonder: bold, capacious, beautiful and wise' Katie Kitamura

'*There are Rivers in the Sky* is an enchanting epic, told through the vantage of a single raindrop, where the sacred mysteries of water, science and poetry collide. In this gorgeous and riverine novel, water is poetry, water is memory. This is a love song to the keepers of our stories and histories, a resounding tribute to the wise women who know the poetry of our rivers' Safiya Sinclair

There are Rivers in the Sky

ELIF SHAFAK

VIKING
an imprint of
PENGUIN BOOKS

VIKING

UK | USA | Canada | Ireland | Australia
India | New Zealand | South Africa

Viking is part of the Penguin Random House group of companies
whose addresses can be found at global.penguinrandomhouse.com

Penguin
Random House
UK

First published 2024
002
Copyright © Elif Shafak, 2024

The moral right of the author has been asserted

Permissions: images © The British Museum; *The Epic of Gilgamesh*,
translation copyright © Andrew George, 1999

Typeset by Jouve (UK), Milton Keynes
Printed and bound in Great Britain by Clays Ltd, Elcograf S.p.A.

The authorized representative in the EEA is Penguin Random House Ireland,
Morrison Chambers, 32 Nassau Street, Dublin D02 YH68

A CIP catalogue record for this book is available from the British Library

HARDBACK ISBN: 978-0-241-43501-4
TRADE PAPERBACK ISBN: 978-0-241-43502-1

www.greenpenguin.co.uk

MIX
Paper | Supporting
responsible forestry
FSC® C018179

Penguin Random House is committed to a
sustainable future for our business, our readers
and our planet. This book is made from Forest
Stewardship Council® certified paper.

To a beloved writer, who, when asked to speak about 'women and fiction', sat down by the banks of a river and wondered what the words meant.

Dripping water hollows out stone,
not through force but through persistence.

– Ovid

Come away, O human child!
To the waters and the wild
With a faery, hand in hand,
For the world's more full of weeping than you can understand.

– W. B. Yeats

There are different wells within us.
Some fill with each good rain,
Others are far, far too deep
For that.

– Hafiz

In those days, in those far-off days,
In those nights, in those far-off nights,
In those years, in those far-off years,
In olden times . . .
Did you see the sons of Sumer and Akkad?
I saw them.
How do they fare?
They drink water from the place of a massacre.

– Tablet XII, *Epic of Gilgamesh*
(translated by Andrew George)

Contents

I

Raindrop

𒁹

By the River Tigris, in olden times

L ater, when the storm has passed, everyone will talk about the destruction it left behind, though no one, not even the king himself, will remember that it all began with a single raindrop.

It is an early-summer afternoon in Nineveh, the sky swollen with impending rain. A strange, sullen silence has settled on the city: the birds have not sung since the dawn; the butterflies and dragonflies have gone into hiding; the frogs have abandoned their breeding grounds; the geese have fallen quiet, sensing danger. Even the sheep have been muted, urinating frequently, overcome by fear. The air smells different – a sharp, salty scent. All day, dark shadows have been amassing on the horizon, like an enemy army that has set up camp, gathering force. They look remarkably still and calm from a distance, but that is an optical illusion, a trick of the eye: the clouds are rolling steadily closer, propelled by a forceful wind, determined to drench the world and shape it anew. In this region where the summers are long and scorching, the rivers mercurial and unforgiving, and the memory of the last flood not yet washed away, water is both the harbinger of life and the messenger of death.

Nineveh is a place like no other: the world's largest and wealthiest city. Built on a spacious plain on the eastern bank of the Tigris, it is so close to the river that at night babies are hushed to sleep not by a lullaby but by the sound of the waves lapping at the shoreline. This is the capital of a mighty empire, a citadel protected by solid towers, stately battlements, defensive moats, fortified bastions and colossal walls, each rising ninety feet or more. With a population of 175,000 souls, it is an urban gem at the junction of the prosperous highlands of the north and the fertile lowlands of Chaldea and Babylonia to the south. The year is sometime in the 640s BCE; and this ancient region, which is lush with perfumed gardens, bubbling fountains and irrigation canals, but which will be forgotten and dismissed by future generations as an arid desert and abject wasteland, is Mesopotamia.

One of the clouds advancing towards the city this afternoon is bigger and darker than the others – and more impatient. It scuds across the sky's vast canopy towards its destination. Once there, it slows to a halt and floats suspended thousands of feet above a majestic building adorned with cedar columns, pillared porticos and monumental statues. This is the North Palace, where the king resides in all his might and glory. The mass of condensed vapour settles over the imperial residence, casting a shadow. For, unlike humans, water has no regard for social status or royal titles.

Dangling from the edge of the storm cloud is a single drop of rain – no bigger than a bean and lighter than a chickpea. For a while it quivers precariously – small, spherical and scared. How frightening it is to observe the earth below opening like a lonely lotus flower. Not that this will be the first time: it has made the journey before – ascending to the sky, descending to *terra firma* and rising heavenwards again – and yet it still finds the fall terrifying.

Remember that drop, inconsequential though it may be compared with the magnitude of the universe. Inside its miniature orb, it holds the secret of infinity, a story uniquely its own. When it finally musters the courage, it leaps into the ether. It is falling

4

now – fast, faster. Gravity always helps. From a height of 3,080 feet it races down. Only three minutes until it reaches the ground.

Down below in Nineveh, the king walks through a double door and steps on to the terrace. Craning his head over the ornamented balustrade, he gazes at the opulence of the city, which spreads out before him as far as the eye can see. Manicured estates, splendid aqueducts, imposing temples, thriving orchards, charming public parks, verdant fields and a royal menagerie where gazelles, deer, ostriches, leopards, lynxes and lions are kept. The sight fills him with pride. He is particularly fond of the gardens, which are brimming with blooming trees and aromatic plants – almond, date, ebony, fir, fig, medlar, mulberry, olive, pear, plum, pomegranate, poplar, quince, rosewood, tamarisk, terebinth, walnut, willow . . . He does not just rule over the land and its people, but also the streams and their tributaries. Directing the River Tigris through an intricate network of canals, weirs and dykes, storing water in cisterns and reservoirs, he and his forefathers have turned this region into a paradise.

The king's name is Ashurbanipal. He has a well-trimmed, curly beard, a broad sweep of a forehead over thick eyebrows and dark, roundly arched eyes lined with black kohl. He is attired in a pointed headdress studded with jewels that glow like distant stars each time the light strikes them. His robe, deep blue and woven of the finest linen, is embroidered with threads of gold and silver, and embellished with hundreds of shiny beads, gemstones and amulets. On his left wrist he wears a bracelet with a flower motif for good luck and protection. He reigns over an empire so immense that they hail him as 'The Emperor of the Four Quarters of the World'. Someday he will also be remembered and renowned as 'The Librarian King', 'The Educated Monarch', 'The Erudite Ruler of Mesopotamia' – titles that will make people forget that, whilst he may have been highly learned and cultured, he was no less cruel than his predecessors.

Tilting his head to the side to scan the cityscape, Ashurbanipal inhales. He does not immediately notice the storm brewing in the distance. The delightful fragrance emanating from the gardens and groves absorbs him. Slowly, he raises his eyes towards the leaden sky. A shiver passes through his sturdy frame, and his thoughts are ambushed by stark warnings and sombre portents. Some soothsayers have predicted that Nineveh is fated to be attacked, sacked and burned to the ground, even its stones borne away. This magnificent city will be wiped off the face of the earth, they said, and beseeched everyone to leave. The king has made sure these doom-mongers were silenced, ordering that their lips be sealed shut and sewn with catgut. But now a sense of foreboding tugs at his insides, like the pull of a river's undercurrent. What if the prophecies were to come true?

Ashurbanipal shakes off the ominous feeling. Although he has enemies aplenty, including his own flesh-and-blood brother, there is no reason to worry. Nothing can destroy this glorious capital so long as the gods are on their side, and he has no doubt that the gods, however capricious and inconsistent in their dealings with mortals, will always come to Nineveh's defence.

Meanwhile, the raindrop is about to arrive on earth. As it gets closer to the ground, for an instant, it feels so free and weightless it could almost alight anywhere it pleases. To its left is a tall, branchless tree – a date palm – whose fronds would make a lovely landing place. To its right is an irrigation canal running through a farmer's field, where it would be welcome, helping this year's harvest grow. It could also come to rest on the stairs of a nearby ziggurat dedicated to Ishtar – the deity of love, sex, beauty, passion and war as well as thunderstorms. That would be an apt destination. Dithering, the droplet has still not resolved where to fall, but that does not matter, for the wind will decide in its stead. A sudden gust lifts and carries its tiny mass straight towards the man standing on a terrace nearby.

A heartbeat later, the king feels something wet plop on to his scalp and nestle in his hair. Annoyed, he tries to wipe it away with one hand, but his ornate headdress is in the way. Frowning ever so slightly, he glances up at the sky one more time. Just as it starts to pour in earnest, he turns his back to the view and retreats to the safety of his palace.

Through the long galleries Ashurbanipal stalks, listening to the echo of his own footsteps. His servants kneel before him, never daring to look him in the eye. On either side, flaring torches tremble high up in their cast-iron sconces. The eerie light they emit sweeps over the bas-reliefs that are mounted on the walls – carved from gypsum and painted in the brightest colours. In some scenes, the king holds a bow and shoots winged arrows, hunting wild animals or butchering his foes. In others, he drives two-wheeled ceremonial chariots, flogging horses harnessed with triple-tasselled decorations. Yet in others he pours libations over slain lions – offerings to the gods in return for their support and protection. All the pictures depict the splendour of the Assyrian Empire, the superiority of men and the grandeur of the emperor. There are almost no women to be seen. One exception is an image in which Ashurbanipal and his wife are drinking wine and enjoying a picnic in an idyllic garden, whilst from the boughs of a tree nearby, amidst ripe fruits, dangles the decapitated head of their enemy, the Elamite king Teumman.

Oblivious to the raindrop still cradled in his hair, the king keeps walking. Briskly, he passes through richly furnished chambers and arrives at a door adorned with elaborate carvings. This is his favourite part of the palace – the library. Not just a random collection of writings, it is his greatest and proudest creation, his lifetime's ambition, an achievement unrivalled in scope and scale. More than anything he has accomplished, even more significant than his military conquests and political victories, this will be his legacy for future generations – an intellectual monument the likes of which has never been seen before.

The entrance to the library is flanked by two gigantic statues: hybrid creatures – half human, half animal. *Lamassus* are protective spirits. Hewn from a single slab of limestone, such sculptures have the head of a man, the wings of an eagle and the hulking body of a bull or a lion. Endowed with the best qualities of each of their three species, they represent anthropoid intelligence, avian insight, and taurine or leonine strength. They are the guardians of gateways that open on to other realms.

Most of the *lamassus* in the palace have five legs, so that when viewed from the front they appear to be standing firm, but seen sideways they are stomping forward, ready to trample on even the most fearsome adversary. In this state, they can both confront unwanted visitors and ward off any evil lurking in the shadows. Though he has not told this to anyone, the king feels safer and more at ease with them around, and that is why he has recently commissioned artists to chisel a dozen more sculptures. One can never have too much protection.

With such thoughts in mind, Ashurbanipal enters the library. In room after room, the walls are lined with floor-to-ceiling shelves that hold thousands of clay tablets, arranged in perfect order, organized by subject. They have been collected from near and far. Some were rescued from neglect; others were bought from their former owners for a pittance; but a considerable number were seized by force. They contain all kinds of information, from trade deals to medicinal remedies, from legal contracts to celestial charts . . . For the king knows that in order to dominate other cultures, you must capture not only their lands, crops and assets but also their collective imagination, their shared memories.

Quickening his steps, Ashurbanipal bypasses the sections of the library dedicated to omens, spells, rituals, cures, curses, litanies, lamentations, incantations, hymns, fables, proverbs and elegies, gathered from all corners of the empire. He wends his way through an extensive collection on the use of the entrails of sacrificial animals to divine the destinies of humans and the intrigues of the gods. Although he sets great store by the tradition of haruspicy, and regularly has sheep and goats slaughtered to have their livers and gallbladders read by the oracles, he won't be studying the auspices today. Instead he heads for a room tucked at the back, half hidden behind a heavy curtain. No one may enter this secluded area apart from the king and his chief counsellor, who is like a second father to him – a deeply learned man who has tutored and mentored Ashurbanipal since he was a boy.

There are bronze lamps set in alcoves at the entrance to this private area, burning sesame oil, sending up coils of smoke. The king selects one and pulls the curtain behind him. It is morbidly quiet inside, as if the shelves have been holding their breath, waiting for him.

The raindrop shivers. With no windows or braziers, the room is so cold that it fears it could harden into ice crystals. Given that it has only recently changed from vapour to liquid, it has no desire to solidify just yet, not before making the most of this new phase of its life. But that is not the only reason why the droplet trembles. This place is unsettling – neither of this world nor of the netherworld, a lacuna betwixt the earthly and the unearthly, somewhere midway between things that are plain to see and things that are not only invisible but are also meant to remain that way.

His movements purposeful and practised, Ashurbanipal strides into the room. There is a table in the middle and, on top of it, a cedar box. The king puts the lamp by his side, and the light chisels shadows across his face, deepening the creases at the corners of his eyes. As though in a dream, his fingers stroke the wood, which still exudes the aroma of the forest whence it came. Conifers of such high quality being rare in Mesopotamia, it needs to be felled in the Taurus Mountains, and, from there, lashed to the decks of rafts and floated down the River Tigris.

Inside this box is a poem. A section from an epic so old and popular that it has been recited again and again, across Meso-potamia, Anatolia, Persia and the Levant; passed down from grandmothers to grandchildren long before it was written down by scribes. It is the story of a hero called Gilgamesh.

Ashurbanipal knows the entire poem like the lines on his palms. He has studied it since he was a crown prince. As the third royal son, the youngest heir, he was not expected to become king. So, whilst his older brothers were instructed in martial arts, war strategies and diplomatic tactics, he was instead offered a great education in philosophy, history, oil divination, languages and lit-erature. In the end it came as a surprise to everyone – including himself – when his father favoured him as his successor. Thus Ashurbanipal ascended to the throne as the most literate and cul-tured ruler the empire had ever known. Of the many written works he has pored over since he was a boy, his favourite was, and still is, the *Epic of Gilgamesh*.

The king opens the box, which contains a single tablet. Unlike every other tablet in the library, this one is brightly coloured – the blue of restless rivers. The words have been incised not in red-brown clay but in a slab of lapis lazuli – an extraordinary stone that the gods reserved for themselves. The script is neat and per-fectly executed. His touch of the marks is so careful and gentle that it is almost a caress. Slowly, he dips into the verses he has read over and over again but that still stir his heart as if for the first time.

> *He Who Saw the Deep . . .*
> *He saw what was secret, discovered what was hidden,*
> *He brought us a tale of the days before the Flood.*

Some kings are fond of gold and rubies, some of silks and tapestries; still others of pleasures of the flesh. Ashurbanipal loves stories. He believes that, in order to succeed as a leader, you do not have to embark on a perilous journey like Gilgamesh. Nor do you have to become a conquering warrior of brawn and sinew. Nor do you have to traverse mountains, deserts and forests, from which few return. All you need is a memorable tale, one that frames you as the hero.

Yet, as much as the king treasures stories, he does not trust storytellers. Their imagination, unable to settle in one place, like the Tigris in springtime, changes course in a manner most unpredictable, meandering in ever-widening curves and twisting in haphazard loops, wild and untamed to the end. When he built this library, he knew there were other versions of the *Epic of Gilgamesh*. Copied and recopied by scribes throughout the centuries, the poem emerged in new renderings. Ashurbanipal sent off his emissaries to bring tablets from far and wide with the intention of gathering every possible variation under his roof. He is confident that he has achieved this staggering task. However, the tablet he keeps in the cedar box is different from all the others in his collection – not only because it is written on precious stone instead of clay but also because it is tainted by blasphemy.

Holding the poem up to the lamp, the king inspects the familiar text. The scribe who has produced it, whoever it was, has done his job as one might expect – save for a note at the end.

> *This is the work of a junior scribe,*
> *One of the many bards, balladeers and storytellers who*
>   *walk the earth.*
> *We weave poems, songs and stories out of every breath.*
> *May you remember us.*

This is a rather unusual thing for a scribe to add, but it is the dedication that follows that is even more disturbing:

Now and always,
Praise be to Nisaba

The king's expression hardens as he takes in these last words. He frowns, his pulse throbbing angrily in his temples.

Nisaba – the goddess of storytelling – is a numen from a bygone age, a name consigned to oblivion. Her days are over, even though she is still revered in remote corners of the empire by a few ignorant women who cling to the old lore. She was supplanted by another deity long ago. Nowadays all tablets in the kingdom are dedicated to the mighty and masculine Nabu instead of the ethereal and feminine Nisaba. That is the way it should be, the king believes. Writing is a manly task, and it requires a virile patron, a male god. Nabu has become the official custodian of scribes and the guardian of all knowledge worth preserving. Students in schools are instructed to complete their tablets with an appropriate inscription:

Praise be to Nabu

Had the blue tablet been old, a relic of the past, the postscript would not have been controversial. But the king is certain that it is a contemporary piece – the penmanship is new. By insisting on revering a forgotten and forbidden goddess and brushing aside the authority of Nabu – and therefore the orders of the king – the scribe who copied this section of the *Epic of Gilgamesh* has knowingly defied the rules. Ashurbanipal could have had the tablet destroyed, but he could not bring himself to do that. That is why the offending object must be kept hidden in this room, isolated from the rest of the library, lest the unenlightened masses should catch a glimpse of it. Not every written word is meant for the eyes of every reader. Just as not every spoken word needs to be heard by every eavesdropper. The public must never know of the blue tablet, for they, too, may be led astray. One man's rebellion, if left unchecked and unpunished, can embolden many dissidents.

As the rain continues to fall on Nineveh, the king stays sequestered in his library, absorbed in the blue tablet. For a while he forgets about everything – the conspiracies of his elder brother in Babylon to usurp the throne, the intrigues at the imperial court, the uprisings raging within and beyond the borders of his kingdom in Anatolia, Media, Urartu, Egypt, Syria, Cilicia and Elam . . . They can all wait. Nothing can disturb him once he has buried himself in the adventures of Gilgamesh. But something unexpected does today.

There is a sudden ruckus in the gallery – alarming, jarring sounds. Grabbing the handle of his dagger with one hand, still clutching the tablet with the other, Ashurbanipal darts out.

'Who dares disturb the king?'

'My lord, my sun, forgive this intrusion.' The military commander, a man of few words, bows his head.

Behind him, four soldiers drag a man clad in a coarse cloth stained with dried vomit and fresh blood. He is sobbing and wailing incoherently into the sackcloth hood pulled over his face.

'Speak and explain this gross transgression,' orders the king.

'My lord, we have caught the traitor we have been seeking for so long. He has confessed his evil deeds.'

One of the soldiers pulls back the hood from the prisoner's head.

A trace of sadness crosses Ashurbanipal's countenance, disappearing as fast as it appears. The king narrows his eyes as if looking at something that is fast receding into the distance, all the while keeping a steady gaze on the captive – his former mentor, his tutor, his confidant, who was closer to him than his own father. The man has been beaten and tortured so badly that his face is deformed, and there is an ugly gap, crusted with pus and blood, where his teeth used to be. He can barely hold himself straight.

'My noble king,' says the military commander, 'by the gods Ashur, Ishtar, Shamash and Nabu, the chief counsellor is a spy. He was the one who was passing vital secrets to your brother. At first he did not want to admit siding with the enemy. He kept denying his crimes. But we confronted him with unassailable evidence, and he could spew no more lies.'

The commander digs into the bag on his shoulder and produces a tablet. He shows it to the king. It is a letter addressed by the chief counsellor to Ashurbanipal's brother, pledging allegiance and offering support – a letter that proves beyond doubt the extent of his betrayal.

'Where did you find this?' asks the king, his voice dry as driftwood.

'It was amongst the possessions of an enemy soldier seized whilst crossing the border. He carried the seal of the chief counsellor and confessed he was doing his bidding.'

Slowly, Ashurbanipal turns to the captive. 'How could you?'

'My king . . .' the chained man rasps, his breath rattling in his chest. His left eye is swollen shut, and his right eye, bruised and bloodshot, quivers in its socket like a trapped bird. 'Remember, you were merely a boy when you were brought to me. Did I not instruct you in literacy and numeracy? Did I not teach you how to enjoy balladry and compose poetry . . . mercy, for old times' sake –'

'I said, how could you!'

Silence gathers in the air.

'Water . . .' murmurs the captive. For a moment they think he is asking for a drink, but then they hear him say, 'It is a gift from the gods; it gives us life, joy and riches aplenty. But you, my lord, turned it into a deadly weapon. No more fish left in the River Ulai: you choked it with so many corpses that it flows the colour of dyed-red wool. First the drought, then the famine. My king, your subjects are starving. The plains of Susa are strewn with the dead and the dying. Now, I hear, you will do the same in Castrum Kefa . . .'

Castrum Kefa, the 'Castle of the Rock'. The large walled city, north of Nineveh, on the banks of the Upper Tigris. A flutter of recognition registers in the king's eyes. He asks: 'Wasn't your father from a village near there?'

'My people . . . You planted guards at every fountain to deny them water. You poisoned the wells. Families are slaughtering their animals and drinking their blood to quench their thirst. Mothers have no milk to give their babies. My king, there are no bounds to your cruelty.'

The military commander lands a punch below the captive's ribs. The man doubles over, coughing blood. He straightens up surprisingly fast. His one open eye now notices the object the king is holding.

'Ah, the blue tablet . . . the little blasphemy,' the captive says, the ghost of a smile lifting the corner of his mouth. 'We studied it together for the first time when my king was a young prince. My lord was always fond of it. Did not our readings of poetry leave unforgettable memories?'

If Ashurbanipal, too, recalls the tranquil afternoons of his boyhood, reciting poetry with his tutor, he does not comment.

'Gilgamesh . . .' says the captive. 'He wished to conquer death and so he travelled to the ends of the world – but he failed. He did not see that the only way to become immortal is to be remembered after you have gone, and the only way to be remembered is to leave behind a good story. My king, why is it that you chose to make your story such a heartless one?'

The military commander steps forward, awaiting orders to kill. But Ashurbanipal raises his hand and stops him. Bowing his head, the military commander asks, 'Would my lord like to deliver the final blow?'

The captive begins weeping – a quiet, dignified sound, one that rises from deep inside his chest, and that he cannot control. The soldiers on both sides shift their feet, anxious to hear the king's decision.

But Ashurbanipal will not kill his old teacher. He has never been keen to lead charges into battlefields, preferring to direct massacres, demolitions, plunders and rapes from the safety of his throne – or, as often happens, from the quiet of his library. He has overseen the sacking of cities and the starvation of entire populations, leaving people no choice other than to eat the corpses of their relatives; flattened towns, reduced temples to naught, scattered salt over newly ploughed fields; flayed the skins of rebel leaders and hung their supporters from stakes, feeding their flesh 'to birds of the heavens, fish of the deep'; gored the jaws of his rivals with dog chains and kept them in kennels; desecrated the graves of his enemies' ancestors so that even the ghosts could not sleep in peace – all these acts and many more he has conducted from his reading chamber. He won't dirty his hands. He is an erudite king, after all, an intellectual who has studied celestial and terrestrial portents. Unlike his regal forebears, he can read not only Akkadian but even obscure Sumerian texts that most would find impossible to unravel. He can debate with oracles, priests and philosophers. He is not a man of brute force and raw rage. He is a man of ideas and ideals.

Sensing the king's reservation, the military commander clears his throat and says, 'Should my lord hand over his noble dagger, or allow me to use my own blade, I will pierce his treacherous heart.'

'No need,' says Ashurbanipal. 'We won't spill his blood.'

In that moment the faintest gleam of hope flits across the prisoner's battered features.

Ashurbanipal does not look at his mentor. His stare stays fixed on a bas-relief on the wall behind him. For a while he inspects the image, a hunting party out on the plains of Nineveh: the king is riding a horse at a gallop, clutching a spear that is about to impale a lion trying to escape its fate. As if pulled by an invisible string, he walks towards the impression. Once there, he takes a flaming torch from its mount and holds it close. The figures on the bas-relief come alive in the shifting light – the hunter, the spear, the prey.

Glancing over his shoulder, still clasping the blue tablet with one hand, the king passes the torch to his military commander. In a voice meant to be obeyed, he utters a single word:

'Burn!'

All the colour drains from the military commander's face. He hesitates but only for a second.

A man in flames is running down the galleries of the North Palace in Nineveh. His body ricochets off the murals that decorate the walls, and his screams, loud and piercing, echo down the corridors, reverberating off the high-vaulted ceilings and sending chills down the spines of the servants. Spilling outside the great gates, his desperate cries can be heard as far away as the plantation fields, where wheat and barley grow in profusion, and the sandy coves, where fishing boats unload their daily catches. Disturbed by the terrifying sounds, the seagulls that had fallen quiet earlier in the day take flight at once, wheeling over the city in confused circles.

If the captive could make it to the banks of the Khosr, the tributary of the River Tigris that meanders its way through the centre of the city, or get as far as the Mashki Gate nearby, where there are plenty of water-carriers, there is a chance that he could be saved. But, as he careens back and forth inside his own growing inferno, he crashes into a *lamassu* that guards the royal library, slamming up against its right-front hoof, whilst the fire consumes him with intensifying fury.

Once, it was poems and stories that brought joy into his life, reading as much a part of his being as the instinct to breathe. Nothing gave him more pleasure than mentoring the young prince, the two of them reclining on plump cushions discussing literature, reading the *Epic of Gilgamesh* and marvelling at the beauties of the world – did he create a monster from that softly spoken boy with the gentle smile or was the monster within the boy all along? He will never know. Now his entire body is a furnace scorching words to cinders, turning all the verses he has studied to ash.

This afternoon, as Ashurbanipal – the leader of the wealthiest empire in the world, the last of the great rulers of the kingdom of Assyria, the third-born son of Esarhaddon but the chosen heir to the throne and his father's favourite, the patron and founder of a magnificent library that will change the course of history – sets fire to his erstwhile teacher and burns his childhood memories along with him, the raindrop remains ensconced inside the king's hair. Alone, small and terrified, it does not dare to move. It will never forget what it has witnessed today. It has been changed – forever. Even after centuries have passed, a trace of this moment will remain embedded in its elemental form.

As ripples of heat rise into the air, the raindrop will slowly evaporate. But it won't disappear. Sooner or later, that tiny, translucent bead of water will ascend back to the blue skies. Once there, it will bide its time, waiting to return to this troubled earth again . . . and again.

Water remembers.

It is humans who forget.

H_2O

Water . . . the strangest chemical, the great mystery.
With two hydrogen atoms at the tips, each bonded to a single oxygen at the centre, it is a bent molecule, not linear. If it were linear, there would be no life on earth . . . no stories to tell.

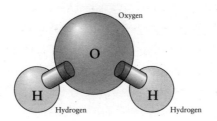

Three atoms join to form water: H–O–H.

Three characters connect across borders of time and place, and together they make this story . . .

—o—

ARTHUR

By the River Thames, 1840

Winter arrives early in London this year, and once it presents itself it does not wish to leave. The first flurries of snow descend in October, with temperatures dropping day by day. The lichen growing on the walls, the moss blanketing the rocks and the ferns pushing out of the crevices are all covered with rime, glistening like silver needles. Ready for the cold spell, caterpillars and frogs gently allow themselves to freeze, content not to thaw until next spring. Prayers and profanities, as soon as they leave their speakers' mouths, form into icicles that dangle from the bare branches of trees. They tinkle sometimes in the wind – a light, loose, jingling sound. Yet, despite the frigid climate, the Thames does not set firm as it did a few decades ago, when it turned into a sheet of ice so hard that an elephant was marched across for fun and games of hockey were played from bank to bank. This time it is solely the shorelines that solidify, and thus water continues to flow in between stretches of white crystals on either side.

Whether it is chilly or warm, blustery or calm, makes little difference to the smell emanating from the river. Sharp, acrid and vile. A stench that seeps into your pores, clings to your skin, penetrates your lungs. The Thames – 'Tamesis', 'Tems', 'Tamasa', 'the dark one' – though once famous for its fresh water and fine salmon, nowadays runs a dirty, murky brown. Polluted by

industrial waste, rotting garbage, factory chemicals, animal carcasses, human cadavers and raw sewage, never in its long life has
the river been so neglected, lonely and unloved.

A pall of dust, soot and ash hovers over the bell-towers, spires
and rooftops of London – the most crowded city in the world.
Every week another wave of newcomers turns up with their bundles full of dreams whilst the chimneys pump out more nightmares
into the sky. Like stuffing bursting out of an old cushion, as the capital grows and expands beyond its confines, its refuse, excrement
and debris spill out through the cracks. Whatever is unwanted is
discarded into the river. Spent grain from breweries, pulp from
paper mills, offal from slaughterhouses, shavings from tanneries, effluent from distilleries, off-cuts from dye-houses, night-soil
from cesspools and discharge from flush toilets (the new inventions enjoyed by the rich and the privileged) – all empty into the
Thames, killing the fish, killing the aquatic plants, killing the water.

Yet the river is a giver, and no one understands this better than
the people known as *toshers*. They are restless scavengers, foragers
of the shorelines. Patiently and purposefully, they wade through
miles and miles of fetid sludge. Sometimes they walk the laby-
rinth of sewers that criss-crosses the city, sifting through rivulets
of effluent. Other times they rummage in fluvial deposits, combing the riverine banks. Scouring a liquid world, they search for
valuable items, both beneath and above the ground.

They usually set out to work when the tide is low and the wind
has subsided, the surface of the stream dull and smooth like a tarnished mirror that no longer reflects the light. Always there will be
something of value hiding in the recesses of the turbid waters –
scraps of metal, copper coins, silver cutlery, and, occasionally, a
crystal brooch or pearl earring – prized possessions that have been
accidentally dropped in the streets and parks of London, and then
swept down into the gutters, embarking on a long and stinking
course into the ripples of the Thames. Some of these objects will
keep travelling towards Oxford and beyond, whilst others will
become stuck in the mud, buried under the thick, slippery gloop.

You can never predict what the river will offer each time, but you can rest assured that it will not send you away empty-handed. A skilled tosher can earn up to six shillings a day.

The job is not only disgustingly filthy but also fraught with danger – particularly inside the sewage tunnels. Always it is wiser to work in groups, since one can easily get lost in London's intricate underground passages and never be able to emerge again. There is the risk of a nearby sluice gate being lifted without warning whilst you are groping around down there, releasing a flash flood through the drains, and if you have nothing to hold on to, or no one to grab you by the collar, you can be washed away and drown, your lungs full of excrement. It is also possible to plough into a pocket of gas that may have been building up under layers of debris – a most unfortunate encounter that can spark an explosion, as if gunpowder ignited, delivering you to an instant death or, worse yet, a life of agonizing injuries. The river is a taker. No one understands this better than the toshers.

On this icy morning in late November, a party of eight trudges along the Chelsea shore, on the north bank of the Thames, their boots squelching in the slime. They carry long poles, which they jab through the muck every now and then to check if there is anything useful underneath. The lanterns tied to their chests paint golden ribbons ahead and lend their faces a ghostly pallor. Around their mouths they have wound scarves to ward off noxious smells – not that this helps. They are swathed in capacious velveteen coats with oversized pockets and thick gloves to shield themselves from the filth – and attacks from rats, some of which are as big as cats. But the last person in the group, a young woman with a shy smile and freckles scattered across her cheeks, has been able to pull her cloak only halfway over her large belly. Although heavily pregnant, she still needs to work. Besides, the midwife has assured her that the baby is not due for at least another month.

The group approaches a bend in the river where an oak tree has extended its branches over the water, lying almost prostrate on the ground. Whilst the others sift through the mire, the young woman stops to catch her breath. She wipes her forehead, where beads of perspiration have formed despite the biting wind.

Her gaze follows the deep grooves and ridges along the bark of the oak. How unusual it is for a tree to contort itself in this way, as if it is having a heart-to-heart with the Thames. What could they be gossiping about? The thought makes her smile. Just as she is pondering this, she feels a pang shoot through her. Sharp, unexpected. Her heart accelerates, but she tries not to dwell on the pain. So far the day has not been kind to her; she has found but one small ring, whose worth she cannot be sure of until she cleans off the grime and takes it to a pawnbroker. Regardless, she has slipped it on her finger, afraid of losing her only treasure.

Another spasm – this one so piercing that it almost knocks the air out of her. Dragging herself away from the water, she plods wearily towards the tree. Her chest heaving up and down, she reclines against its trunk, grateful for its unusual shape. The stabbing cramp subsides, only to return in a little while with even more intensity. She presses her hand to her stomach, unable to keep from groaning out loud.

'Oh, Lord!'

One of the toshers – a short, stout elderly woman with translucent blue pouches beneath her eyes – hurries to her side.

'What is it, Arabella? Are you all right?'

'The baby – do you think it might be coming already? Isn't it much too early?'

They both glance around, one in sheer panic, the other with concealed concern.

Surely not now, not here. No baby would want to be born in a damp and stinky place such as this, by a stream overflowing with refuse and sewage.

'Shall I send someone to call your husband, love?' asks the old woman, dropping her voice, for she already senses the answer.

Arabella lives in a slum tenement not far from here, in a part of Chelsea called the World's End, with a carpenter so skilled that he was once commissioned by Buckingham Palace to build a chest of drawers for the royals – although nowadays the man's drinking habit makes his hands shake to such an extent that he rarely works any more.

'My husband?' Arabella says. 'Haven't seen him in weeks.'

'All right, then, we will manage ourselves,' says the old woman, trying to keep the sadness from her voice. 'Let us first take you home and make you comfortable, lass.'

Arabella nods in agreement, but her breathing is coming in increasingly shallow gasps. As she attempts to stand up, she staggers, losing her equilibrium for a moment. Her face crumples more in shock than in pain. A warm burst of liquid gushes down her legs. She stares down at the puddle by her feet in horror.

'Oh, God, oh my stars . . . it is too soon!'

The other toshers, having all stopped working, are watching from the river's edge. One yells over the noise of the current: 'Oi, everything all right over there?'

To which the old woman replies with a swift shake of her head. 'We are in trouble. Lord help us.'

'What are you babbling about?'

'I'm saying, you had better get out of there and give us a hand. Come here, you lot, be quick! Her waters broke!'

The toshers who rush to help and selflessly spread their coats across the muddy banks of the River Thames cannot possibly know that just then another expectant mother in London has gone into labour with her first child. Queen Victoria, only twenty-one years old, is having contractions in a cosy chamber inside Buckingham Palace. That Her Majesty hates being pregnant is a well-known secret. Resentful at having to forgo dancing and riding, she cannot wait for this delicate phase of her life to be over. The young queen, nicknamed 'Good Little Wife' by her husband, hopes to deliver a male heir today so that she can be done with childbirth once and for all. Prince Albert is by her side, holding her hand and murmuring words of comfort, until he joins the Cabinet ministers waiting outside. In a corner, the infant's cradle – made of high-quality mahogany and padded with emerald-green silk – is designed to look like a seashell. The naval reference is perfect for the firstborn of the Ocean Queen, indicating the glory and splendour of England, whose symbol, the white rose, is embroidered on the coverlet.

When, after excruciating hours, the royal baby arrives, the doctor smiles apologetically. 'Alas, Your Majesty, it is a girl.'

The queen, though equally dismayed, lifts an exhausted hand. 'Never mind. The next will be a prince.' Thankfully, she has an array of nurses to choose from, all with excellent credentials.

When, after excruciating hours, the river baby arrives, one of the toshers yells gleefully, 'Glory be, Arabella, it is a boy!'

The young mother, rising up on her elbows, cranes her head to look at her son. His tiny fingers, rose-pink toes, rounded cheeks . . . he is beautiful. She breaks into tears. What chance does such a sweet, innocent being have in a world full of sin, sorrow and suffering?

'Cheer up, lass. What are you so worried about, eh?' reprimands the old woman. 'You should be proud of yourself: the boy is alive and well.'

But Arabella is crying so hard she can barely talk.

'There, there, you will be fine. Now, tell us, what will you name him?' asks the old woman.

Still no answer.

That is when the other toshers chip in helpfully.

'Call him Thames – most appropriate to the occasion,' someone suggests.

'Yes, he will be Father Thames when he grows up.'

'And if he lives that long, he'll be Grandpa Thames someday.'

'How about Thomas – it's close enough to Thames.'

'Nah, just name him Jack,' another man interjects. 'I've been Jack all my life – it's not too bad.'

'Seems pretty bad to me!'

'How about Albert?' someone else says. 'If it's good enough for the Queen's husband, surely it's good enough for the tiny tot.'

'Oh, do shut up! What bosh you are talking.' It is the old woman who objects this time. 'Lily-livered and hen-hearted . . . that's the kind of man he is, Prince Albert, what with his namby-pamby ways and all! He didn't even propose to Victoria, remember? It was she who asked him to marry her. Not the best husband for our Queen. Not even a fit hubby for me!'

They all snigger and jeer – until Arabella's reedy voice pierces the clamour. 'Throw him into the river!'

Someone chuckles loudly, assuming it is yet another joke about royals whose lives cannot be more different from theirs. But everyone else has fallen quiet. A discomfort gathers in the air whilst the implication behind these words sinks in. The toshers exchange guilty glances, as if by merely hearing the unspeakable they have become part of something tainted and unfathomable.

Into the ensuing silence the old woman asks in a murmur, 'What are you saying, lass?'

'Chuck the baby into the water. I cannot take care of him. Let the Thames look after my son.'

'Hush now! Don't speak in that sinful manner.'

The young mother covers her face with her hands and lets out a strangled, guttural cry. She can barely believe what she is about to say but nor can she stop the words from gushing out. 'I cannot afford to keep this little 'un. I can hardly get myself enough cop-pers for my own food. I am starving hungry most of the time. My husband . . . he's no use at all – he's fallen in with the worst types! Always angry, never sober, never works. If he passes out, it's a blessed relief – you think a man who beats his wife ain't going to hurt his son? My poor babe . . .'

The old woman raises her chin and shakes her head. 'Now you listen to me, lass.'

'You don't understand –'

'I do, every word, and I am telling you, this boy is going to brighten your life, you hear me? I feel it in my bones. You give him a bit of grub and a morsel of love, and he will give you much more back. He will lighten your burden and make you proud. You shall see: all will be well.'

Arabella is crying louder now. Her shoulders shake with each sob, and the cold and worry set her teeth chattering.

The old woman sighs. She has heard midwives complain about a mysterious condition called 'puerperal insanity'. It is said to afflict new mothers, robbing them of their senses and plunging them into a despair so bottomless that they may never emerge. She knows the treatment calls for purgatives, cupping, bloodletting and lots of opiates.

Turning to the others, she asks quietly, 'Does anyone have something to lift her spirits? The poor thing, she's got the morbs.'

'Aye, give her some of this,' says a man, producing a murky-brown bottle.

Laudanum. It helps to soothe the nerves and dull the pain, and besides it is said to ease women's troubles. Although it tastes extremely bitter, the smell is sweet and strong – being made of cinnamon, saffron, alcohol and extract of opium from poppy seeds.

They urge Arabella to take a sip, then a couple more for good measure. She complies. Her head drops on her chest, her arms go limp. Exhausted and distressed, it does not take long for the young woman to tumble into a deep, dreamless sleep.

But now the toshers are left with a quandary they did not expect. With the father nowhere to be seen, and the mother half comatose and half crazed, who will name this baby? The matter cannot be postponed. They are dangerously close to the river. Since time immemorial the eddies of the Thames have accommodated ghosts, ghouls and other ghastly creatures. Demonic spirits, hovering over the water and hunting for vulnerable souls, may at any moment swoop down and snatch the newborn away. Even if the spirits were to decide for once on a softer tack, the spectre of William Kidd will most likely loom out of nowhere. Everyone knows that the notorious pirate is incandescent with rage after he was coated with tar, bound with chains and hanged from a gibbet, his corpse left rotting for three years. It has been more than a century since his public execution, but, his fury unabated, he continues to haunt these shores.

Given the gravity of the situation, the toshers conclude that the task must fall upon them. The old woman lifts the baby in the air and looks into his grey-blue eyes. Oddly, he stares straight back at her. All this time he hasn't cried even once.

'What a strange wee mite you are!'

'Why not call him that, then?' someone proposes. 'That's some handle. "Strange" will be his first name and "Wee Mite" his middle. There you have it!'

'Nay, that won't do.'

The old woman reckons that this hapless child who clearly lacks a caring father and a stable mother, and who has the misfortune of having been born beside a stream of waste water and excrement to boot, deserves a helping hand. They are bound to bestow an august name on him, a sweetener to help him through the difficulties of life and not drag him down even further. So she gives the matter some more thought and then she announces, 'I think it should be something rather brave and grand. Yes, that's right, a name worthy of a noble.'

'Well, why don't we call him Your Majesty?'

'His Serene Highness?'

'Most Exalted Eminence?'

'How about King?'

'King is nice,' says the old woman. Her face brightens up as a new thought occurs to her. 'King Arthur would be even better!'

'Aye, King Arthur it is!'

'Praise be!'

'Glory be to God!'

'Just like King Arthur of the Sword in the Stone?'

'More like, King Arthur of the Sewers, I'd say.'

'And . . . and Slums.'

'That's been decided, then,' declares the man who produced the laudanum. To raise a toast, he takes a swig from the bottle of gin that he carries inside his coat; then wipes his mouth and passes it on to the others.

'King Arthur of the Sewers and Slums!'

And that is how the boy born on a secluded stretch of the Chelsea waterfront, under the low-lying branches of a bankside oak tree, will someday come to be known to all. A child of the river he is, and so he will remain all his life.

They place the newborn on his mother's breast, though the woman is still sound asleep. Under the gaze of everyone, Arthur suckles slowly, as if out of courtesy. Lying on a pile of coats spread across the cold and muddy earth, without a cradle to hold him or a roof to shelter him, his face puckers, but he does not cry. Instead he remains motionless, listening to the sounds around him. A thin trickle of milk streams from the side of his mouth.

It starts to snow again. Frantic flurries drift down from the skies in long, slanting curves, shimmering luminescent against the muted light. As they approach the earth, they take on a bluish hue, whirling in circles that neither overlap nor make them dizzy. They dance playfully, like an evocation of wandering spirits. Watching them with wide open eyes from where he lies, the baby breaks into a smile, dazzled by the beauty of this world.

In a little while, one of the snowflakes pirouettes in the wind, veering fast towards the ground. Water in its solid form. A weightless pearl formed in the depths of a vast celestial shell. From so small and slight a presence, can a whole universe be conjured?

That snowflake was a raindrop once upon a time, in a land far away. It passed through a sumptuous palace with a magnificent library, and witnessed exquisite gardens, extravagant fountains and unspeakable cruelties. It carries within the memories of its previous lives. The aura of an Assyrian king is impressed upon it, like an invisible fingerprint. Gently, it alights on the baby's face, dropping between his open lips.

In that instant the baby feels on his tongue something cold, crisp, faintly metallic and hugely exciting. He clenches his fingers and stuffs his fist into his mouth, trying to seize this marvel – and failing. He cries then, for the first time. It is his first disappointment in life, his earliest sorrow, not being able to hold on to a beauty that has touched him briefly and, just as suddenly, melted away.

A drop of milk, a flake of snow. The two will blend in his mouth – and in the deepest recesses of his memory. Someday, when he is much older, someone who has never seen snow will ask him how it tastes, and he, without even missing a heartbeat, will reply, 'Like mother's milk.'

King Arthur of the Sewers and Slums will remember the moment of his birth. He will remember it with exceptional clarity and in astonishing detail: the roar of sewage rushing nearby, the bark of a crooked oak tree, the coarseness of the coats piled beneath him, their edges frayed and gnawed away by rats and mice, the locks of golden hair cascading on to the shoulders of the woman who brought him into this world but then wanted to throw him into the Thames, and, above all, the feel of icy crystals dissolving on his tongue . . . Shards of memory that he will be able to piece together no matter how many years have passed and no matter how painful the reminiscence. For this baby, who shares the day of his birth with Queen Victoria's firstborn and is named after a legendary hero by a band of good-hearted toshers, is a most unusual child.

Arthur Smyth is gifted with an extraordinary memory – visual, verbal and sensory. Just as a drop of rain or a pellet of hail, water in whatever form, will always remember, he, too, will never forget. What he sees or what he hears or what he feels, even once, he retains forever. A remarkable talent, many will argue. A blessing from God, others may hasten to add. But also a terrible curse, as he will soon find out.

H—
NARIN

By the River Tigris, 2014

O n the banks of the Tigris in south-east Turkey, beneath
the canopy of a clear blue sky, a group of mostly elderly
Yazidis are gathered one afternoon in late spring. They
form a semicircle, facing a girl in a white dress. She is being baptized
with sacred water brought over from the Valley of Lalish in Iraq.

The child's name is Narin. Nine years old this month, she has
delicately carved features – a wide forehead, straight nose, arched
eyebrows over large, strikingly bright sage-green eyes. As she listens to the sheikh reciting prayers on her behalf, she notices a bird
swoop low overhead, darting towards the bushes, but she cannot
tell what species it is. She glances at her grandmother standing
proudly by her side. The old woman knows all about birds and can
accurately mimic hundreds of avian songs, but this is not the right
moment to ask her. Focusing her attention back on the ceremony,
Narin waits quietly, respectfully. She lifts her gaze again only when
the holy water is sprinkled on her forehead.

The first drop falls on her brow and slides down gently, resting
on her eyelashes – thick, copious and straight, their tips bronzed
by the sun. Narin wipes it away and smiles.

'Lamb of faith,' says the sheikh. 'May your path always be blessed.'

The tufts of milkweed by their feet shiver in the sudden breeze
that gusts in from the river. Into the descending quiet, Narin hears
her grandmother speak, her voice tinkling in a loving echo.

'Lamb of faith, *dilê min*.'

Dilê min – 'my heart'. That is how Grandma expresses her affection, by turning her own body into an anatomy of love. When she misses Narin, she says, 'Come and sit next to me, the corner of my liver'; when she wants to raise her spirits, she says, 'Cheer up, the pulse of my neck'; when she cooks her favourite food, she says, 'Eat up, the light of my eye; if your tummy is full, then mine rejoices'; and when she wishes to advise her that there is a hidden blessing in every trial, she says, 'Don't forget, my soul, if God closes one door, He opens another. That is why you must never despair, the air in my lungs.' Heart, liver, stomach, lungs, neck, eyes, soul . . . It is as if love, by its fluid nature, its riverine force, is all about the melding of markers, to the extent that you can no longer tell where your being ends and another's begins.

'May life be kind to you, child, and when it is not, may you emerge stronger,' intones the sheikh.

The second drop lands on Narin's collar; a pale, round shadow forms over the white fabric, like the centre of a moonflower.

Shifting her weight from one foot to the other, the girl looks around, half expecting to find the world altered somehow, now that the ceremony is almost over. But everything seems to be the same – the brambles that catch at the hem of her dress, the jagged rocks by the shoreline, the patches of sun-scorched grass pushing through the grit, the muddy smell that rises from the silt of the river and lingers in her nostrils . . . They are all exactly as they used to be. So are the expressions on the faces of the adults present, both happy and worried for her. Grown-ups are not good at masking their concerns, although they can hide their delight and curiosity surprisingly well. Whereas with children it is the other way round. Children can tactfully mute their anxiety and conceal their sorrow, but will struggle not to express their excitement. That is what growing up means, in some simple way: learning to repress all expressions of pure happiness and joy.

Narin is good at hiding her worries – and she has many. Today she is upset that her father was not able to attend her baptism.

A highly popular and sought-after *qanun* player who performs at weddings and circumcisions across the region, he often needs to be on the road for days on end. He travels widely not only in Turkey but also across Iraq, Lebanon and Syria, returning from each trip with funny stories to tell. Then he is gone again. Narin understands that, as much as he loves her, Father cannot stay for too long in one place. People say this has been the way with him ever since he lost the love of his life – in the same afternoon, in the same hour, the door of life opened for Narin and closed for her mother. From that day forth, despite all attempts to find him a suitable match, Father refused to remarry and the child was raised by her grandmother.

Grandma is everything to her.

'May this consecrated water bring goodness and kindness into your life, protect you from troubles.' The sheikh raises his hand, about to sprinkle the third and last drop. 'May it –'

A deafening rumble, as if rising from the bowels of the earth, drowns out the final incantations. Startled, they all turn in the same direction.

A bulldozer. A mud-splattered, dirty yellow, mechanical behemoth. The vehicle, its engine having roared to life, rolls into motion across the clearing, belching puffs of black smoke into the clear air. It creaks and groans into forward gear and lumbers towards them, making the ground shudder, its heavy metal blade suspended ready to strike.

They are everywhere these days. Ever since the land around has been earmarked for a major dam-building scheme by the Turkish government, the vast plains of the River Tigris are filled with an unbearable racket – an endless hammering, banging, drilling, boring, tempering and hewing. It is a controversial operation, protested by ecological activists and local farmers alike. Foreign companies, initially interested in a lucrative enterprise, have withdrawn their support over concerns about human rights, cultural heritage and environmental destruction. Yet the construction has not slowed. Every morning, all along the riverbank, earth-movers, tip lorries and bulldozers rumble away, hauling heaps of basalt, clay and limestone to form the foundation of what will someday become the largest hydropower plant in the country.

By the time the Ilisu Dam is completed, over eighty thousand people will have been displaced, more than two hundred villages and forty hamlets evacuated. When the work began, the peasants, most of them Kurdish, were forced out of their homes, their fields and orchards expropriated, leaving them in despair. The government deposited token payments into their accounts in return for the confiscated lands. Many families, like Narin's, have not touched the money, refusing to agree to such a miserly deal. Some are planning to sue the authorities, but people in this area are poor, and the state simply too powerful. Court cases take long years and don't necessarily end in favour of the plaintiff. Either way, the construction is going ahead.

Hasankeyf, an ancient settlement along the River Tigris – once known as *Castrum Kefa*, the 'Castle of the Rock' – will be inundated, as soon as the water level rises to 60 metres. Its limestone cliffs and man-made caves, its unexplored historical sites and unplumbed secrets, will disappear under an artificial lake. A 12,000-year-old history will be obliterated by a dam that will last 50 years – the lifespan of a mule. This region – home to churches, chapels, mosques, monasteries, synagogues and shrines – has already lost so much of its heritage. Most local populations have migrated to cities, near and far, where they have been swallowed by the currents of urban life, severed from the traditions that always sustained them. It was usually the elderly who stayed behind, delaying leaving until the last moment possible; they were the ones who found it hardest to part with their memories.

The bulldozer stops in front of the group, barely a few centimetres away from Narin. The driver, a man with a drooping moustache, pulls up the brake lever, pops his head out of the window.

'Why are you people gathered here? Move! Government orders.'

'*Effendi*, we were about to finish,' the sheikh says. 'If you could kindly give us a few minutes.'

'Finish what?' the man asks, a look of suspicion crossing his face. 'What are you doing here anyway?'

The sheikh purses his lips, not wanting to tell a stranger that they were in the midst of a baptism ceremony. He only says, 'We live here.'

'Not for long, though. Why haven't you left yet? You've been ordered to move to the cities. The project will move faster with you people out of sight. You're slowing us down.'

Grandma takes a step forward and crosses her arms. 'Can't you go dig over there, son?'

'No, I can't! This is where I feel like working today,' replies the man, annoyed at being challenged by a woman.

'Does it make any difference where you start?' Grandma insists, a determined set to her jaw. 'You're going to excavate the entire area anyway.'

'I'm not moving, woman. You'd better leave, all you lot, go now, scram – or I'll file a complaint that you're preventing a government official from doing his work. Then you'll get into trouble.'

Without waiting for a response, the man draws in his head. As he is about to turn on the engine, he mutters something under his breath, too quietly for anyone to hear – but Narin, standing closest, reads his lips.

'Filthy fucking devil-worshippers!'

A second later the roar of the machine fills the air, the sound overpowering after the initial lull.

For a confused moment the group remains rooted to the spot, watching the bulldozer scoop away at the earth, hauling out chunks of alluvium from the shores of the Tigris, disturbing the bones of antediluvian animals and dormant rocks that witnessed thousands of years of Mesopotamian history. The machine veers back and forth, and catches underground tubers, dangling like monstrous tooth extractions, in its maw, and rips out the roots of long-ago-felled trees.

'Let's move a bit further up,' says the sheikh over the din. 'We don't want trouble.'

They follow him silently, trudging up the river in single file, searching for a spot where the noise may be a bit less intense.

'How about here?' suggests the sheikh, pointing to a clear patch. 'This seems good enough.'

They form a semicircle again, all the while feeling the gaze of the bulldozer driver burning through his window, scrutinizing their every move.

'We'd better hurry,' says the sheikh, unable to hide his nervousness. Holding up the bottle with the remaining sacred water, he resumes his position. 'My child, may your –'

No sooner has the holy man uttered these words than he halts, his face paling. The bulldozer is coming towards them. The powerful machine drives disturbingly close, lowers its scoop and begins digging, making it impossible for them to hear each other speak.

Once again, they walk away.

'I'm afraid that man is not going to leave us in peace,' says the sheikh. 'He's doing it deliberately; he wants to intimidate us.'

'We shouldn't have come here. It clearly wasn't a good idea,' says a neighbour. As far as he is concerned, this ritual could just as well have been held in the village; there was no need to drag themselves to the banks of the Tigris, since they do not require full immersion in flowing water, like the Mandeans – the disciples of John the Baptist – but Narin's grandmother insisted they stay close to the river, and, as anyone will attest, she is a headstrong woman.

Ideally, they all acknowledge, the baptism ceremony, *Mor Kirin*, should be performed in Lalish, the holiest temple of the Yazidi faith, tucked away in a peaceful valley surrounded by undulating hills north of Mosul in Iraq. Narin should wear a wreath of flowers around her head – daffodils, periwinkles, gardenias. She should drink from the sacred fountain of Zamzam and then be baptized at *Kaniya Spî*, the 'White Spring' – the only place on earth that remained safe and clean when God sent down the Great Flood. Miraculously forming a whirlpool, the spring never mixed with the muddy, dirty floodwaters, staying forever pure.

Yet until now their circumstances prevented the family from taking the child to Iraq. Money was tight; it was never the right moment. Besides, for quite some time, Narin's health has been deteriorating. So this year water from the venerated Valley of Lalish – sealed in a bottle and entrusted to a *qawwal* – was brought over instead. One should be baptized as early in life as possible, girls sooner than boys, but it isn't uncommon for children to be initiated into the faith when they are older, if they are sick or unable to travel.

'We can return later in the day,' says the sheikh. 'Or we can continue in the village.'

'Or perhaps it is a sign,' remarks Grandma. 'It was not meant to be.'

The lines on the sheikh's forehead deepen. 'What are you saying?'

'Maybe the last drop was not meant to fall.' Grandma shakes her head. 'The time or the place was not auspicious.'

'Do you wish to delay the ceremony, Besma?'

Grandma responds with a slight nod. 'I do, most respected sheikh.'

A shudder of unease ripples through the group.

'But don't you know your granddaughter is getting older?' a neighbour interjects. 'She should have been baptized long ago.'

Another neighbour says, 'That's right. Besides, if you put it off, even for a couple of weeks, maybe you won't find us here next time. Things are bad already. Who can tell which one of us will still be around come tomorrow?'

People across the region, from every sect, creed and tribe, have been affected by the construction of the dam. But for the tiny

Yazidi community, added to the sadness of losing their ancestral land is the fear of being subject to discrimination in the places where they are to be resettled. Leaving home is never easy, but it is much, much harder when you have nowhere to go.

Over the past decades, their village has dried up and shrivelled, crumpling at the edges, like scorched parchment. Many families migrated to Europe, becoming immigrants in countries where the sun does not raise its golden head for months on end. Some come back to visit in the summer to help repair the fountains and shrines, but none of them plan to return for good. In hamlets and villages where their ancestors once thrived in their thousands, only a handful of Yazidis is left. Grandma always says she will be one of the last to go. She cannot abandon her pistachio trees. But primarily it is the river she cannot part from. Every so often she walks to these shores, lamenting that the ground under her feet is about to be flooded, thousands of years of history gone, knowing that these are her last prayers to the Tigris.

Once upon a time there was a large, flourishing Yazidi community in and around Hasankeyf, connected by custom and faith as much as by stories and songs. Their numbers dwindled with every decade of deprivation, migration and forced conversion. Today only twelve Yazidis are left in their village, and tomorrow, they, too, will be gone.

'I was just thinking,' says Grandma, her expression both fierce and loving. 'Narin is the beat of my heart, the light of my eyes. God knows what she means to me. I always wanted her to be baptized in the holy Valley of Lalish. Not over here, when the earth is being hollowed out and the Tigris is in distress . . .' She waves her hand towards the river, leaving the sentence hanging in the air.

The sheikh inhales. 'You want to take the child to Iraq?'

'I do, venerable sheikh. We were not able to travel all these years. But my son-in-law received invitations to sing at three big weddings in Mosul this summer. Maybe he could take us with him. I will speak to him – let's see what he thinks. If he agrees with me, we can make things work. Just the same, I'm very grateful that you all came here today.'

Thus saying, Grandma opens a bag. Inside there are sweets wrapped in colourful foil, which she distributes to everyone present, thanking them for attending the holy occasion.

'God bless your feet, neighbours. May your toes never stumble over a pebble.'

'You, too, old soul,' says the sheikh, sighing.

Taking turns, they hug Narin, and, even though the ceremony has not been finalized, they give her gifts – a sachet with dried rosemary, a vial of oil distilled from clove buds, a pot of rose salve, a jar of apricot jam, a garland of fragrant flowers . . . Lastly, the sheikh hands her the bottle from the Valley of Lalish, and, aware of its significance, the girl carefully places it in the front pocket of her dress.

'We'd better be on our way, then,' says a neighbour. The village is not far, but the heat of the afternoon, now noticeably stronger, may slow them down.

'You walk ahead of us,' says Grandma. 'We'll catch up with you.'

No one is surprised by her words this time. They all know that Besma loves being near the Tigris and will never miss an opportunity to spend time by the river, as if pulled towards the waterway by some unseen force. Whenever she visits the area, she takes Narin with her. She teaches the child the names of the native plants alongside their medicinal and culinary uses. Together they collect tree resin, which they apply to wooden trays and bowls as a varnish. They search for roots and leaves and bark that can be used for dye.

'We'll take the gifts to your house so your hands will be free,' says the sheikh. 'Just be careful, though. Don't be late.'

'We'll be fine, honourable sheikh, don't worry. I might teach Narin how to collect cat's-tails – it's the season.'

A neighbour leans in close, her voice dropped to a whisper. 'Besma, dear, are you sure you want to go to Iraq? You're old, Narin is unwell, poor thing . . . and the roads aren't safe, I hear.'

'Yes, but when was it ever safe? Not in living memory. When were the troubles of Mesopotamia over? There has never been a good time to travel,' Grandma says, her face concentrated in thought. 'Don't you think the child should fully experience the holy Lalish while she still can?'

When Narin was born, she was a placid and healthy baby. As yet unaware that she did not have a mother, she approached life with an endless curiosity and an appetite for discovery. Raised on goat's milk, sour yogurt soup and herbal concoctions, she would grab the beads suspended over her cradle, hung there to ward off evil spirits; giggle at her father making silly faces; and, later, chase the chickens in the yard or jump gaily over ditches. But, whatever the illness was that struck her before she started school, it progressed quickly, and, since last year, her auditory world has been retreating behind a periodic buzzing and ringing in her ears. Her faculty of hearing is fading. The transition from sounds to silence will be slow and gradual but irrevocable.

The doctor they visited at the university hospital in Diyarbakir told them they should prepare themselves. In as little as eight months' time, Narin will have gone completely deaf. A rare genetic disease. She will first lose her ability to detect high-frequency sounds. Soon after, she will struggle to understand when several people speak at the same time. It will happen not at once but bit by painful bit; her range of hearing will contract from the outer margins, like curtains closing on the last act of a play. Some day before long, Narin will wake up to discover that the early-morning chorus of long-tailed tits, crested larks, barn swallows and white wagtails has fallen silent. She will no longer be able to catch the delighted squeal of an infant or the whistle of a train receding into the distance, nor the bleating of newborn lambs; she will hear only those that remain in her recollection.

Before that day arrives, Grandma believes, the girl should hear the birds, susurrations and prayers of the sacred Valley of Lalish for the first and last time. Narin should behold the one place on earth where despair turns into hope and even the loneliest souls find solace.

After the others leave, the old woman and the child walk by the river, their shadows following beside them. They pass stands of thorny sedge and pick their way through dense thickets of reeds and rushes. In lulls between the steady rhythm of their footsteps, they can hear the croaking of frogs, the whirring of insects. Every so often they pause to examine the flora. Across the rich alluvial soils of the Tigris, a variety of vegetation flourishes. Grandma guides Narin's fingers, teaching her how to recognize plants solely by touch. Leaves are complex things, the child learns. Some are leathery with sunken veins; others smooth and waxy; yet others covered in a fine downy hair, like a teenage boy sporting an incipient moustache.

'Grandma?'

'Umm?'

'When I go deaf, will I forget your voice?'

'How is that possible? The ear never forgets what the heart has heard.'

'I don't know what that means.'

'It means my voice will always be by your side – even after I'm gone. Because I'm impressed here . . . and here . . .' Grandma touches the girl's temples. 'That is what happens when you love someone – you carry their face behind your eyelids, and their whispers in your ears, so that even in deep sleep, years later, you can still see and hear them in your dreams.'

Tilting her head, Narin considers. It is a comforting thought, though a bit baffling, but by now she has no doubt Grandma is always wonderfully baffling. For a peaceful instant, which lasts no longer than a breath, she forgets all that has been troubling her, suspended in the warmth of the old woman's compassion. Then the moment passes, and the child says, 'That bulldozer-driver . . . He was not a nice man.'

'He was not, my heart.'

'He called us a bad word.'

Grandma stares at the girl, puzzled. Narin is biting her bottom lip, the way she always does when confused or worried.

'What are you talking about, child?'

'He called us devil-worshippers.'

A shadow passes across the old woman's face. 'Don't utter those words.'

'But why did he say that?'

'Maybe he meant something else?'

The girl shakes her head. 'No, I don't think so. And it wasn't the first time. It happened at the hospital, too. While Baba was speaking to the doctor, they asked me to wait in the corridor. A cleaner walked by, and he said, *What are these filthy, fallen devil-worshippers doing here?* He was talking about us.'

A quail calls in the undergrowth – a solitary succession of chirrups. When the bird falls quiet, Grandma asks, 'Did you tell your father?'

'No, I didn't want him to be sad.' Narin folds her hands on her lap. 'Why do people call us that?'

'Listen, my soul, there are those who say wrong things about us. They utter harmful lies and hurtful slanders. They've no right to do this, but they do it anyway. They vilify us not because they know us well. Quite the opposite: they do not know us at all.'

'But that doesn't make any sense. I don't go around saying horrible things about people I don't know!'

'Of course you don't; that's because you're wise.'

Narin is not satisfied with the answer. She does not want to be wise. She wants to understand why people are the way they are and if they can ever change.

Sensing her disappointment, Grandma opens another bag. Inside, wrapped in a cloth to keep them warm, are flatbreads – each spread with sheep's milk butter and filled with herbed cheese. The old woman makes these every morning at the crack of dawn, settled on a stool in the courtyard. She pats the dough into round pieces, slaps them against the tandoor and bakes them until they are crisp and puffy. She knows how much the girl loves them.

'Eat, Narin. When the belly is light, the heart will be heavy.'

The child bites into her flatbread, the taste of herbs and butter mixing on her tongue.

As she chews slowly, she says, 'I just don't understand –'

'Well, this world is a school and we are its students. Each of us studies something as we pass through. Some people learn love, kindness. Others, I'm afraid, abuse and brutality. But the best students are those who acquire generosity and compassion from their encounters with hardship and cruelty. The ones who choose not to inflict their suffering on to others. And what you learn is what you take with you to your grave.'

'Why so much hatred towards us?'

'Hatred is a poison served in three cups. The first is when people despise those they desire – because they want to have them in their possession. It's all out of hubris! The second is when people loathe those they do not understand. It's all out of fear! Then there is the third kind – when people hate those they have hurt.'

'But why?'

'Because the tree remembers what the axe forgets.'

'What does that mean?'

'It means it's not the harmer who bears the scars, but the one who has been harmed. For us, memory is all we have. If you want to know who you are, you need to learn the stories of your ancestors. Since time immemorial, the Yazidis have been misunderstood, maligned, mistreated. Ours is a history of pain and persecution. Seventy-two times we have been massacred. The Tigris turned red with our blood, the soil dried up with our grief – and they still haven't finished hating us.'

Reaching into the pocket of her dress, Narin takes out the bottle brought from the Valley of Lalish. She holds the glass up to the sun, feeling the caress of the light reflecting off its surface. Then she turns it upside down, waiting for the last drop to fall. Water in its liquid form. This she cannot know, but that drop was a snowflake once upon a time, in a land far away. It passed through what was then the world's richest and largest city, its chimneys belching clouds of smoke and sulphur. It witnessed the birth of a boy, the force of another river. Ephemeral though it is, it carries within the memories of its previous lives. Gently, it alights on the girl's hand, quivering.

Holding the drop in her palm like a precious pearl, Narin feels a wave of sadness descend on her. It seems like everything is coming to an end. Hasankeyf will soon be flooded because of the new dam. She will no longer be able to forage for herbs and roots with her grandmother. Someday her hearing, too, will disappear – just like the land she has always known as home.

The child falls silent. So does the old woman. Beside them the river flows, fast and furious, rolling its pebbles like dice.

—O—
ARTHUR

By the River Thames, 1852

King Arthur of the Sewers and Slums is an eccentric child, though it is a long while before anyone pays much attention to him. By the time he turns five, the boy knows the names, ages and ailments of every person who lives on their street, and he can mimic their accents and mannerisms with uncanny perfection. The following autumn, he astonishes his mother by speaking Yiddish, having picked it up listening to a Jewish–Russian family that has moved to the building. Aged seven, he will glance at a shuffled pack of cards splayed open on a gambler's stall and repeat the complete sequence without pausing. Aged eight, he will draw with closed eyes an exact depiction of the whole neighbourhood, down to the obscure alleys and narrow lanes where more immigrants have taken up residence. When he reaches the age of nine, he is enrolled in a school by some respectable ladies from the Charity for the Uneducated Poor, who have visited the slum tenements looking for children in need.

School is a drab red-brick building with a tall clock tower, surrounded by a lofty garden wall and separated from the rest of the city by a pair of wrought-iron gates that creak in the slightest breeze. It was founded, just a few years back, to provide free education to the poorest of the poor. A brass plate mounted at the entrance announces:

The students are a mixed bunch. Children so destitute and deprived they have no chance of receiving an education elsewhere. They span various ages and stages of development but come from similar backgrounds: the sons and daughters of paupers, prisoners, addicts, thieves, murderers, fugitives, beggars, forgers, swindlers, pimps, procurers, prostitutes . . . Amongst them are orphans or the otherwise abandoned. Some are so malnourished that their bodies are deformed, their growth stunted; others sport cuts and festering sores that will leave permanent scars. Whilst their counterparts in private schools are attired in smart uniforms – dresses and pinafores for girls, and ankle boots and tailored jackets with waistcoats for boys – the pupils here wear hand-me-downs, most of which are mere rags.

Many of these children will attend school for a few days and then stop coming, but some will stay on. It is better than being on the streets overall. The classrooms, though bare and draughty, are not as freezing or as dangerous as the world outside. Besides, food is provided once a day. It does not hurt to study the Bible in return for a bowl of gruel. They are also taught the three *r*'s: reading, 'riting, 'rithmetic. It is this solemn institution that Arthur attends six days a week, along with 425 others.

At first glance, there is nothing remarkable about the boy. He looks just like any other pupil, only quieter and perhaps more shy. He is too dreamy and too distracted to be popular. This month he turned twelve, though everyone assumes him to be younger. Slim and nimble, he has a wide forehead, jutting ears and dark eyebrows over cerulean-blue eyes that appear green in a certain light. His lips, dry and cracked, peel like old paint. His hair is the colour of chocolate sponge – a delicacy he has heard people rave about but never tasted himself.

On this bleak day in late November, as Arthur rushes to school, having already missed the morning lesson, he dashes past small shops, each with its own distinctive sign. He does not need to look at them to know where they are located. Even with closed eyes he can recall every thoroughfare he has ever wandered; every baker, butcher, cheesemonger, glass-blower, hat-binder, butter-carver, tallow-chandler, toy-maker or confectioner he has walked by but could never afford to buy from. Yet, as he crosses the street now, stepping aside to avoid an oncoming hansom cab, his mind is crowded with other thoughts. He is worried about his mother. Arabella is unwell – again. People tell him something is the matter with her head, an excessive sentimentality strains her fragile nerves – a quintessentially female condition, they say. But Arthur believes that if only his mother could eat better and not have to be cold and in penury all the time, she could be cured. She could be happy. Last night she spent hours pacing up and down, mumbling incomprehensibly to herself, because she was not able to sleep; and, therefore, neither was the other family with whom they share their room. If such behaviour continues, Arthur fears, they may soon find themselves homeless – he, his mother and his twin baby brothers. As for his father, he comes and goes as he pleases – mostly, he just goes.

Sniffling, the boy pulls up his collar and rubs his hands. It is no good. The wind pierces through his frayed garments, chilling his bones. He does not mind the cold as much as the hunger. Hunger is a beehive inside his abdomen, one that has been stirred with a stick, buzzing day and night, jostling, irritated and frantic. He reckons the bees need a distraction, something to keep them busy and out of mischief. So he seeks help from mathematics. Whenever he feels worried, he does sums and multiplications in his head. He takes a gander at a lady with a parasol strolling along the park or a gentleman in a top hat sprinting across the square, and he sets himself the task of calculating how many ruffles are on her skirt or how many lines pattern his frock-coat. Numbers, with their unwavering reliability, comfort him and make him forget the pangs in his belly.

Hearing the snap of a whip now, Arthur instinctively recoils. As he has reached a busy high street, he needs to be extremely watchful. Last winter on this very spot a man was trampled to death by a hansom cab. The horses slipped in a rut in the road, pulling the carriage at full tilt even as they charged on over human flesh and bones. No sooner does the boy reflect on that day than the word 'accident' flashes through his mind, leaving a curious taste in his mouth. Words always come to him with their distinctive flavours. 'Accident' is gamey, like burning fat and stale sausages, bags o' mystery, whose ingredients no one really knows. 'School' has a pungency that lingers on the tongue, like licking old boots. And 'mother' is buttery, warm and sweet, though with an acidic undertone, reminiscent of an apple pie gone sour. For years, Arthur assumed it must be the same for everyone, that other people also experienced similar associations, until he realized this was not the case. Since then he has been careful not to mention it to anyone. A quiet boy by nature, there are lots of things he keeps to himself.

It is past eleven when he reaches the school gates. He hopes that the teacher, Mr Hopkin, will not be cross with him. For Arthur is a good student. The best in his year, if the truth be told. In a classroom whose population fluctuates between seventy and eighty-eight depending on the season, he is the first to complete each assignment, no matter how difficult the subject. So quick is he on the uptake that the teacher has chosen him as his chief aide. Several other boys are appointed to assist Arthur. Together they are called 'the monitors'. To facilitate teaching in a room this crowded, Mr Hopkin often beckons the monitors to the board to study every new exercise and then they return to their seats to instruct the others. Each is responsible for a group of about ten pupils. Arthur always does his best to support those who are lagging behind, not only to ease the teacher's load but also because he genuinely likes helping people. In the past, more than a few times, he had an inkling that Mr Hopkin was fond of him, though the man has never said as much.

As he crosses the schoolyard, the boy slows down. Running on the premises is strictly forbidden, as are jumping, whistling, humming, singing, swearing, sulking and grinning. Careful not to make any noise, he enters the building and climbs the stairs, his hand closing around the worm-eaten banister, cracked and discoloured in places. At the end of a long, ill-lit corridor is his classroom. The door is closed. From inside he can hear a male voice – thick, throaty, unfamiliar.

He knocks, waits a heartbeat and walks in. A broad-shouldered man is standing by the board, addressing rows of students, his back turned to the entrance. Arthur feels his stomach drop. This is not Mr Hopkin. It is someone he has never seen before.

The child makes a mistake then. Instead of walking up to the new teacher and apologizing for his tardiness, he tries to sidle into an empty seat, hoping not to draw attention to himself.

'Someone is sneaky!' The man swivels on his heel and scowls.

'Beg your pardon, sir,' Arthur says, blushing.

'Why were you late? Enlighten us.'

'My mother was unwell, sir. I had to stay home and take care of her.'

'Oh, spare me the deceit! You surely do not expect me to fall for such a pitiful fib.'

Arthur blinks. 'I am not lying, sir.'

'Enough, be quiet. I will make an allowance this time. Do not, I am warning you, let it happen again.'

A high-pitched ringing filling his ears, Arthur sits back, uncomprehending. He knows that his words, which he uttered honestly and with conviction, correspond to the truth, so why won't the teacher believe him?

In the following hour, the students parrot the formulas on the board, chanting in unison the same sentences over and over again, like a music box churning out the same old melody until it winds down completely.

There are 4 farthings to a penny. There are 12 pennies to a shilling. There are 20 shillings to a pound . . .

What they repeat out loud they are instructed to write down on a sand tray with the help of a stick. Arthur awaits his turn, wishing he had a quill pen instead. He has seen one in the window of a shop on the high street, the feather so soft and bright it still sang of the bird it had graced. Smiling at the thought, he completes the exercise, flattens the sand and passes the tray to the next boy.

'All right, everyone!' The teacher claps his hands. 'Now listen carefully for I shall not say it again. A gentleman left his four heirs a substantial inheritance. He gave his eldest son 488 pounds and 5 shillings more than the youngest. The middle two received 300 pounds and 10 shillings. The third child was granted 60 pounds more than his youngest brother, who received a quarter of that bestowed on the eldest brother. Calculate the total amount bequeathed by this benevolent father to his sons.'

The pupils, many of whom are so poor they risk frostbite from sleeping in cheap lodgings, groan as they set to calculate wealth the likes of which they have never known and never will.

'Looks like you are struggling. Clearly your previous teacher didn't get very far with you, did he?' The man scribbles a number on the board, which he then circles with a flourish. 'This is the answer you ought to arrive at. That's enough help. Now get on with the work!'

The children fidget in their seats. Those holding the trays scratch in the sand, pretending to work out the sums, whilst others look vacantly at the ceiling, hoping not to be called upon. Meanwhile Arthur sits still, staring at the sum written on the board. The numbers squirm and wiggle in front of him, flopping their tiny bodies, like fish trapped in a net. They look miserable in each other's company. The boy realizes with horror that the teacher has got his calculations wrong.

Arthur knows he must hold his tongue. But he is sleepless, tired. His breath smells of hunger and his hands of the laudanum that his mother has been taking each day without fail since the day he was born. He tries to distract himself by scrutinizing his surroundings, not that there is much to explore. A world map, worn at the edges, dangles from a crooked nail. Next to it hangs an abacus, the beads of which are greasy from the touch of many fingers. There is a dunce's cap in the opposite corner – dirty, tattered and pointed – which the children who are slow to learn are made to wear. A symbol of ridicule and shame. Feeling increasingly uneasy, Arthur glances towards the windows through which rays of light trickle out. The windows have deliberately been built too high for any passer-by to see inside the classrooms and, most importantly, the students cannot see what is outside.

'Right, time is up. Have you all arrived at the figure I've provided?'

The monitors, eager to earn praise, nod . . . all but one.

Arthur lowers his head. If he can keep quiet and let this moment pass, later in the afternoon a different teacher will come to instruct them. They will learn a bit of carpentry. He can whittle a bird out of a slender branch, and he adores the way solid wood takes on a new shape beneath his hands, although he has no desire to follow in the footsteps of his father. No, he will not become a carpenter. He wants something different for himself, though what that may be he cannot tell.

He wishes he were in the girls' section now. It seems to him that girls study more useful things than boys – how to repair a dress that has been mended too many times, how to prepare a meal on a tight budget, how to prevent milk from curdling, how to weigh sugar and measure flour and which substitutes to use when these ingredients are unavailable. He would have loved to learn these things. Instead here he is biting his bottom lip so as not to blurt out the solution to an arithmetic problem posed by a joyless man.

'All right, monitors, stand up,' orders the teacher. 'It's your duty to demonstrate to all these dullards how to arrive at the answer I have provided.'

'But it can't be done,' Arthur mutters to himself.

All heads turn towards him. The boy pales, appalled that he has voiced the thought loud enough to be heard by everyone.

'Who said that?'

Silence falls into the classroom, sudden and irretrievable, like a stone dropped into a well. The students at the front point fingers at Arthur. They will not miss an opportunity to snitch.

The teacher takes a step forward. 'What was it you were saying?'

Slightly shaking, Arthur stands up. 'I was just doing the numbers in my head, sir.'

'Well, it was not in your head, was it? Or we would not have heard.'

'That is right, sir.'

He can sit down now; with a display of contrition and a bit of luck the danger can be averted. There is still a chance. But his eyes slide towards the board. The numbers, penned in a circle, trapped in a mistake, look miserable, begging to be put right.

'However, that figure on the board is wrong, sir.'

The expression that crosses the man's face is one of mere shock; there is neither anger nor annoyance in it . . . not yet. He does not move for what feels like a long moment, his eyes bulging.

'Are you trying to humiliate me, lad?'

The boys at the front cover their mouths to suppress a snigger. Those at the back chuckle.

'No, sir. I'd never do such a thing,' Arthur says, his heart beating fast. 'I just corrected your error.'

The entire classroom ripples with nervous laughter.

'You shameless, impudent rascal! You are coming with me to the headmaster,' says the teacher, his eyes narrowing on the last word. 'Right now!'

Arthur shivers as if touched by an icy blast of air. He has heard the stories, of course – stories about boys crammed inside baskets hanging from the ceiling, beaten so hard that it takes them days to be able to walk again. Since he has been enrolled in this school, he's had his fair share of caning and smacking, mostly because of the misdeeds of others, but he has never had reason to visit the headmaster's office, which is not a place anyone ever wishes to go.

'Move!'

His eyes on his shoes, Arthur follows the teacher outside. As soon as the door closes behind them, a hubbub erupts inside the room. A maelstrom of raucous shouts and obscenities. In stark contrast, out here in the corridor there is only silence. They march on, the man in front, the child trailing behind. Their footsteps echo along the walls darkened by years of woodsmoke, mould and boredom. Even when they reach the end of the corridor, they can still hear the rumble from the classroom. Arthur has never left London, but he has read a bit about other lands, distant shores, and it occurs to him now that this is what it must sound like when you hold a seashell to your ear and hear the ocean roar.

The headmaster is a hefty man with drooping eyelids and a waxed, ginger moustache whose ends he likes to twirl. Arthur stands in a corner whilst the teacher offers a summary of his version of events. No one asks the boy for his account.

'Such unruly behaviour is utterly concerning and unbefitting of our values and principles,' says the headmaster. 'Leave him with me.'

The teacher, not wanting to be excluded from a spectacle he has unilaterally initiated, pauses. He must have been hoping to watch the punishment being administered. 'I would not mind staying longer if I could be of further help.'

'No need,' says the headmaster. 'You may return to your students.'

The teacher departs without so much as a glance at the boy. On his way out, he pulls the door shut with considerable force.

Alone with the headmaster, Arthur feels even more afraid. In an attempt to calm his nerves, he sneaks a glance around the room, looking for anything – a sequence of patterns – that he can count or calculate. The contrast between this study and his classroom cannot have been sharper. This place is sumptuous, brimming with expensive objects and trinkets. A massive mahogany desk

with hand-carved legs, a cabinet with glass shelves full of porcelain figurines and snuff boxes, a silver tray bearing tumblers and
decanters, high-backed chairs with velvet upholstery and anti-
macassars, and one draped with an oriental rug, a spinning globe
that glows in the light of a brass gas lamp, portraits of important
personalities glowering from their gilded frames . . . The walls are
covered from floor to ceiling with wallpaper in marigold yellow
and vivid crimson. In a flash, Arthur detects their patterns – the
vines, the roses, the thorns. He finds it odd that in a school with
pupils so poor the headmaster is surrounded by such visible luxury.

'Go stand by the window,' says the man. He opens a drawer
and extracts a rattan cane with a leather-wrapped handle. 'Lower
your trousers and bend forward with your palms flat on the desk.'

'Sir, please, I was only –'

'Be quiet and do as I say, now!'

Slowly, as if in a dream from which he cannot wake, Arthur
shuffles towards the window, unties the string that holds up his
breeches and waits. Silence expands in all directions.

A slackening to his jaw the only change to his expression, the
headmaster eyes the boy's naked buttocks. His hand holding the
cane goes still. He raises his other hand aloft, the fingers plucking
the air, as if picking imaginary wool from a thornbush. Then, fur-
tively, he bends forward and paws the boy's crotch. Arthur winces
instantly, flinching aside. Once again the man tries to fondle him,
but the boy, more agile, twists away. This time the headmaster
stands frozen, as if considering what to do next. Then, with an
abrupt movement, he shoves the pupil down towards the edge
of the desk. A second later the child receives the first blow on his
upper thigh. The pain is excruciating.

'Count!'

And for once in his life Arthur cannot. Numbers have abandoned him.

'Count!' the man orders, as he takes a step forward, lifts the
cane and hits again, harder.

'Two . . .' Arthur manages.

'Louder!'

'Three . . . four . . . five . . .'

On the desk – which the child is clutching so hard that his knuckles have turned white – there is a book. Bound in green cloth with gilded edges, it has debossed lettering in a delicate, cursive script on the cover, and a red silk ribbon bookmark peeking out from its middle. For Arthur it is a thing of exquisite beauty that shines amidst a fog of pain. Despite his tortured flesh, he focuses his gaze on that spot and nowhere else.

'Six . . . seven . . .'

The book is by someone called A. H. Layard. The boy can make out its title: *Nineveh and Its Remains*.

'Keep going!'

'Eight . . . nine . . .'

Underneath the title, there is a lengthy description. Arthur reads the first line, just as he receives another blow: *An Inquiry into the Manners and Arts of the Ancient Assyrians . . .*

'I cannot hear you!'

'Ten . . . eleven . . .' Arthur's shoulders curl forward, his breath falters. 'Twelve . . . thirteen . . .'

Forcing himself to concentrate on the publication in front of him, the boy glances at the next line: *And an Account of a Visit to the Chaldean Christians of Kurdistan . . .* Bizarre words, but the more bizarre the better, as he needs to take himself out of here, find a way to leave his body in this room whilst his mind escapes, and so he clings to this strange book, like a drowning person seizing driftwood floating past.

'Carry on counting, Smyth!'

'Fourteen . . . fifteen . . . sixteen . . .'

It takes the effort of every muscle in his body not to collapse. Yet the boy manages to read the last words of the subtitle: *And the Yazidis, or Devil-Worshippers.*

And the rattan cane continues to strike.

The headmaster stops at thirty-five, panting hard. He tosses the cane aside as if he can no longer stand the sight of it.

'This will teach you to respect your elders. Bear in mind, I have been lenient with you; others would not have been so kind. A strict disciplinarian might have given you fifty, or even sixty strokes! I am too soft on first-time offenders; it's an irredeemable weakness of mine. When you have healed, come and visit me. You will need my guidance to stay on the straight and narrow. I'll take care of you. Now stand up, lad.'

Arthur tries to do as he has been told, but his knees buckle and he staggers sideways. He would have keeled over if he were not still holding on to the desk. Taking shallow breaths, he manages to pull up his trousers. His legs are heavy as though they have been replaced by sacks of wet sand.

'I'll give you some valuable advice,' the headmaster says. His back turned to the room, he is staring out of the window. He does not sound furious any longer. Whatever wrath possessed him to thrash a twelve-year-old boy is gone, replaced by something akin to boredom. 'Are you listening?'

Arthur does not respond.

'You'd better get along with this new teacher. Mr Hopkin has left the institution. He won't be working here henceforth.'

Still, Arthur says nothing.

'Before he went away, Mr Hopkin wished to speak to me in private about you.'

'About me?' Arthur asks in a whisper, incredulous that a grown-up might show any interest in him.

'That's right. Would you like to know what your teacher said about you, Smyth?' The man surveys the boy from the corner of his eye. 'Or should I call you King Arthur of the Sewers and Slums – that's the ridiculous name you have been given, I believe.'

The child compresses his lips. He never imagined the head-master might be aware of his presence, let alone know the circumstances of his birth.

56

'Mr Hopkin thinks you are extremely intelligent – adept at numbers, patterns, languages . . . He says you have an uncommon ability, perhaps even a talent.' The man casts a suspicious look at the boy. 'Have you?'

'I wouldn't know, sir.'

'Well, your former teacher seems to believe so. He claims your memory is extraordinary and you can remember even the smallest things from the past with miraculous clarity.'

Arthur's chin quivers as a tear rolls down his cheek. Cruelty has not broken him, he is used to it, but this unexpected compliment, however indirect, has thrown him off balance.

The headmaster pulls a handkerchief out of his pocket – crisp white with embellished corners and crocheted edges. He offers it to the boy.

'Take it.'

Arthur stares at the precious thing. He can sell it for a penny and buy food for his mother.

'You may keep it,' says the man, as though he has read Arthur's mind. But the boy looks away.

'Oh, I see, you are upset. Petty, churlish behaviour.' The headmaster replaces the handkerchief in his pocket and consults his pocket watch. 'I don't have much time – let's see if your memory is as good as Mr Hopkin claims. Tell me, two years ago . . . say, the 10th of June. Which day of the week was it and where were you?'

Arthur closes his eyes. On the tenth day of the sixth month of the year before last, which was a Monday, he was with his mother. His father was there, too. As though emerging from a curtain of fog, the day appears to him, vivid and distinct. He recalls how his father, having been commissioned by a merchant to build a chest of drawers and the deposit paid that very morning, seemed a different man – less angry and accusatory. His mother, too, looked happier, a touch of colour tinging her waxen pallor as she pulled him close to her swollen belly and let him listen to the mystery growing inside. Late in the afternoon the three of them went to the zoo to see the creature everyone was raving about. An exotic beast named

Obaysch – a hippopotamus, the first in Britain since prehistoric times. A present from an Ottoman pasha in exchange for English greyhounds. Captured in the River Nile, the animal was loaded on a boat to Cairo, and from there sent on a steamer to England.

Arthur, always eager to learn new things, had been rattling on about the hippopotamus for weeks, and his parents did not decline his request, even though the trip cost more than they could afford. Months later his father would finish the chest of drawers and engrave his mark on it – a hammer and anvil to signify 'smith'. The day the piece was due to be delivered, the merchant would suddenly pass away and the payment would never materialize. But on that unusually jovial day they had every reason to believe that money was on its way. Cloaked with the warmth of this promise, off they went to the zoo. Whilst his parents enjoyed themselves, Arthur left the place feeling deeply sad for the captured animal with its small ears, soulful eyes and shiny skin sweating the colour of blood.

Now, as he blinks away the memory, Arthur purses his lips. He has no intention of telling the headmaster any of this.

'No response?' says the man with a sigh. 'I am not surprised. You can't possibly remember. Mr Hopkin was clearly misguided. You may leave now. Go and beg your new teacher's forgiveness and do not misbehave again. Next time, I won't be so indulgent.'

Arthur raises his chin, still saying nothing.

'Here is another piece of advice, Smyth. You may be clever, but vanity is a terrible sin. If you manage to avoid becoming a thief or a murderer or a layabout, like most of your kind, a surfeit of which the Lord knows we have in this city already, one day, you, too, might teach in this institution and lead boys such as yourself into the right path. Understand? Now thank me and leave.'

'Thank you . . . sir.' Arthur swallows, the words leaving a bitter taste in his mouth, like globules of bile.

Dragging his feet, the boy lurches on unsteady legs towards the door. The pain has intensified, searing like hot irons pressed into his flesh. Just as he is about to see himself out, he hears the head-master say behind his back: 'That old fool, Hopkin, what was he thinking? No genius ever came from the slums.'

Arthur stops. His breathing quickens as he stares at the door-knob. 'Sir, there is something I wish to tell you.'

'Go on, Smyth. Hurry up!'

'You were appointed headmaster,' says the boy without turn-ing around, 'three years, four weeks and four days ago precisely. The 25th of October, it must have been. It was a Thursday. You arrived with your wife. She had wrapped a lace shawl over her dress – teal blue with a matching bonnet. Her hair was parted in the centre with ringlets on both sides of her head. You were wear-ing a paisley tie, and there was a drop of blood on the collar from a nick on your left cheek. Perhaps you had shaved in a hurry. Your wife noticed a boy with a swollen ankle, limping. She said, "Oh, you poor little thing," and she wished to speak to him. But you rebuked her. "I would advise you not to touch any of them, my dear. They are all covered in fleas like stray dogs" – that's what you said. You pulled your wife by the arm, and the two of you left shortly after, just as the clock chimed eleven. You were dastardly then, and you are dastardly now.'

Arthur lets himself out, closing the door behind him. He walks down the empty corridor, past the classrooms from which he can hear the voices of hundreds of pupils reciting times tables by rote. He listens, taking in every little sound and sigh. When he reaches his classroom, he halts for a moment, his eyes lingering on the threshold he knows he will never cross again.

Outside, the fog has dissipated into mere gossamer. Shafts of amber light streak across the sky, the sun peeking from behind the clouds in a welcome surprise. The boy gives a moan of pain as he tries to fall into step with the other pedestrians and fails. His stomach growls.

It dawns on him, with sharp dread, that by insulting the head-master and leaving the school he has given up the only food he would be having today.

Striding with what little energy he can summon, he darts glances at shop windows displaying treasures beyond his reach. He can hear customers playing a game of Skittles in a corner pub; a knife-grinder singing as his wheel whirrs round, sending sparks into the air; a tinker shouting for trade, 'Any pots, pans or kettles to mend?' The pavements are crowded with costermon-gers selling fruit and vegetables from their barrows and carts, and hawkers with every kind of delicacy imaginable – jellied eel, sheep's trotters, hot green peas, stewed mussels, pickled oys-ters, baked potatoes, boiled meat, crumpets, toffee apples, kidney puddings . . . The smell of food clings to his hair and tickles his nostrils. He hobbles away, still doing his best to hurry. When the wind shifts, he catches a whiff of the stench rising from the Thames. Somewhere behind these streets, the river coils like an ailing serpent, its breath rank and rotten.

Wincing inwardly with every pace he takes, Arthur passes a heap of rubbish. Two children, no older than him, are scaven-ging through the refuse. A third boy, grubbing around in a pile of manure with bare hands, lets out a chuckle. Something is reflect-ing light in the filth. He has found a button, which he holds up proudly with soiled fingers, as though it were a trophy of war. Arthur turns his head away, feeling sick to his stomach. He does not like to be out on the streets. Given the chance, he would have loved to stay inside the headmaster's office, on his own, sur-rounded by all those pretty objects and curious books.

He needs to be home before the gas lamps are lit, but he is not ready to head back. So he keeps walking and promises himself he will not drift any further than the end of the road where the British Museum heaves into view, silhouetted stately and majestic against the crepuscular sky. He has never been inside the building and always wondered what mysteries it guards.

★

As he approaches the museum, Arthur is surprised to notice that a crowd has gathered at the front entrance. Although by nature cautious, curiosity gets the better of him and he edges closer to take a look. People are tumbling over one another to catch a glimpse of something on the other side of the iron railings. The boy joins them, trying to squeeze in. At first, he cannot see much – only the shoulders of grown-ups, blocking his view. A man in the front yells with excitement, but it is impossible to fathom what he is saying. In the ensuing commotion, an elderly gentleman faints and has to be carried away.

'Move aside! Make room!'

The crowd presses forward, pushing and jostling for every inch of empty space. Swept off his feet, Arthur is lifted up, as if he were airborne, almost weightless. His head spins and his battered haunches throb. When he manages to stand upright, he finds himself by the main gates, and that is when he sees, just a few feet away, inside the yard of the British Museum, something the likes of which he has never in his life come across.

It is a massive stone beast. A creature plucked from another world. Spectacular, breathtaking, frightening. It has the head of a human, the body of a bull and the wings of a mighty bird. It has been lashed to a huge wooden frame that sits on a wheeled platform. More than two dozen workers are straining to tow it up the staircase and pass it through the doors of the museum.

Arthur gasps. When he and his parents visited the hippopotamus at the zoo, there was no doubt in his mind that the animal, however exotic, was part of God's Creation. But this statue, albeit lifeless and inanimate, exudes so much vitality and mystery that it must have descended from another universe altogether.

The boy is still reflecting on this when he notices, about thirty feet away, to the left of the courtyard, another beast of similar proportions waiting to be hauled. There are two of them! A pair of giants!

Such is the child's sense of wonder and delight that, unable to contain his excitement, he turns to the nearest person. Eagerly, he

taps on the arm of a man with a silvery beard that reaches down to his waistcoat, a wealthy gentleman by the looks of him, even though it is a dangerous thing for the boy to do, as he may be taken for a beggar or even a pickpocket.

'Sir!' Arthur exclaims.

The man glances down at the child, and a mixture of surprise and suspicion collide across his broad face.

'Please, sir. Could you tell me what these things are?'

The stranger's mouth, drawn into a line, breaks into an amused smile. 'You like them, lad? They are very important archaeological discoveries.'

Although he does not understand what that could possibly mean, Arthur is unwilling to give up. 'Are they . . . are they monsters?'

'Monsters?' The man chortles. 'Not at all. They are protective spirits – that's what the Ancients believed them to be. The guardians of the palace. They're called *lamassus*.'

'*La-mas-sus*,' Arthur repeats.

'That's right. The pair you see here were guarding the royal library – built by a great king named Ashurbanipal.'

What a curious name! The boy's face puckers as the word leaves a pungent taste in his mouth.

The man, intrigued by the child's enthusiasm, carries on. 'These monumental statues were buried under the ground for thousands of years.'

'Pray, sir, why did the Ancients put them in graves?'

The man chuckles again. 'No, not like that. The whole city was destroyed by its enemies. It was tragic: everything Ashurbanipal built was reduced to rubble. Nothing remained, only ruins. Precious artefacts were covered under hills of sand. Until we British arrived and rescued them from oblivion. Well, the French were excavating, too, but never mind them. This was solely our discovery!'

Arthur listens, leaning in close.

'Each *lamassu* you see here is about sixteen feet tall and weighs more than thirty tons. These things are extremely difficult to transport. How do you move them across continents? That, my boy, is an extraordinary achievement. We managed to bring them over in one piece. Indubitably, Austen Henry Layard and his team have accomplished a marvellous task.'

Upon hearing this, the boy flinches. As the book in the head-master's room bursts into his mind, he blurts out, 'I know that name! He's the author of *Nineveh and Its Remains*.'

A look of surprise flashes across the man's features. 'And how do you know that?'

'I saw the cover of the book, but I have not had a chance to read it yet,' says Arthur truthfully, and adds, '*An Inquiry into the Manners and Arts of the Ancient Assyrians and an Account of a Visit to the Chaldean Christians of Kurdistan and the Yazidis, or Devil-Worshippers*.'

The boy pauses, unsure whether it was appropriate to utter these last words. He has no idea what kind of people the Yazidis might be and if they really worship Satan, and, if they don't, why they have been described so disparagingly, but he worries that it might have been disrespectful to introduce the Angel of Darkness into polite conversation.

The man surveys Arthur with renewed interest. 'You saw the cover once but you remember the full title? You are a strange boy, I must say.'

Arthur shrugs, not knowing how to respond to that. 'So these statues, then . . . are they from King Ashurbanipal's library?' he ventures.

'Indeed, son.'

'And this library is in a place called Nineveh?'

'Indeed, son.'

Nineveh . . . Arthur rolls the three soft syllables on his tongue, like a boiled sweet. Where exactly is this arcane capital, he wonders. He is certain he has not seen it on the map that hung on the classroom wall.

'Pray, sir, could you tell me where Nineveh is in relation to the River Thames?'

The man smiles at the boy's naivety. 'Mesopotamia is far away. These *lamassus* have been worn away by the waters of another river called the Tigris.'

Arthur's eyes grow wide and then narrow. An insight that he has long suspected dawns on him with startling clarity: that the world, too immense and untravelled for any one human mind, is full of exciting places.

'There is not much of value in the region any longer, I'm afraid. Backward, primitive tribes. The locals are simple villagers.' The man pulls a watch out of his pocket and checks the time. 'Anyway, it's good to see young people take an interest in biblical archaeology. What is your name, lad?'

'Arthur, sir.'

'Nice to meet you. I work at the museum. Do come visit us sometime. You can observe the statues close up.'

'I could do that?'

'Of course – they shall be on display to the public. If anyone asks where you are going, tell them I have invited you – Dr Samuel Birch is my name, and I am the Keeper of Oriental Antiquities.'

'I shall remember that, sir.'

'I am sure you will. Well, I must be off now. Good day, my boy.'

Arthur knows he, too, has to be on his way, but he can barely tear his eyes from the ancient statues. He wishes he had asked the man why the sculptors of olden times gave them five legs or, for that matter, imagined them as human, bull and bird in one. He has so many questions about the creatures from Nineveh and the people who once upon a time both respected and feared them.

In a little while, dusk paints the horizon bright orange, until the smog, back with a vengeance, blots out all colours with its dull brush. A lamplighter passes by whistling a tune. In his hand he carries a long pole with a burning wick. One by one the gas lamps along the street come alive, casting a brave glow into the gathering darkness. Tomorrow morning, the same man will appear again to snuff out each one. An unwavering pendulum swings between day and night. Light and shadow. Good and bad. Perhaps it is the same with past and present – they are not completely distinct. They bleed into each other.

A church bell, not far off, strikes the hour. Arthur thinks about his mother – the pale crescents under her eyes, the raw cracked skin of her hands. She will have started to worry about him by now, fearing that he has come to harm, perhaps having fallen under a carriage or been set upon by a cutpurse. That is the last thing the boy wants, to add to her anxieties. Still, he finds it hard to leave. Alone, starving and aching in a gradually thinning crowd, he holds on to the railings, pushing his face through the bars to peer at King Ashurbanipal's protective spirits.

Something peculiar happens then. The giant sculptures from the banks of the Tigris, though still majestic, begin to seem less intimidating, somewhat defenceless, almost vulnerable. The boy feels a surge of empathy for the bound stone beasts as he watches them being hauled with hemp ropes through the lofty doors of the British Museum, where they disappear into perpetual exile. Creatures of the river trying to adapt to dry land; lonely and lost in this grinding city, just as he has been all his life.

—H

ZALEEKHAH

By the River Thames, 2018

A young woman walks along the Chelsea Embankment, watching the Thames as it bisects London west to east. In her hands she carries a cardboard box, its base slightly damp. Inside there are books, a china teapot and mismatched cups, some randomly selected clothes and a Tiffany-style desk lamp, its domed shade poking out from under her arm. It has been drizzling since the early hours, clouds hanging over the city the colour of a neglected fish tank. She does not have an umbrella, but in her distracted state she does not seem to notice that she is getting wet. Drops of rain alight on her hair, which is abundant, curly and a chestnut so deep it looks black. Both her hair and her large, roundly arched, dark brown eyes are gifts from her ancestors, who belong in another land, by a different river.

Gripping the box close to her chest, she turns her back on the flats and houses where some of London's wealthiest reside. She recalls reading in a book that parts of this exclusive neighbourhood were slum tenements and hovels at one time, though, looking at the manicured gardens and luxury developments, it is hard even to begin to imagine this. The river, once so polluted that it was called the 'monster soup', nowadays offers a coveted view for which plenty are happy to pay excessive premiums. But she is not interested in the high-priced mansions and blocks towering all around her. What she is interested in are the houseboats docked by the shore.

Anchored along the historic Cheyne Pier, bobbing up and down, they come in various sizes and colours, each with its own name. There are twenty-four of them on this side of the bank, though the moorings stretch all the way to Battersea Bridge, covering 3,500 metres of river frontage. It is an entirely aqueous settlement – a village buoyed on water. Some of the houseboats are no larger than a bicycle shed, others stunningly spacious with spiral staircases and rooftop lounges. All have pots of flowers on their foredecks, and a few seem to have managed to squeeze in chaises longues for the occasional ray of sun. Lined up neatly, they look peaceful and remarkably solid in contrast with the undulating waterway in front of them and the stream of traffic coursing behind. This, from now on, will be her new address. Although she cannot quite believe it yet, she is moving into a houseboat today.

The woman is called Zaleekhah – or, as she is known to her colleagues and students, Dr Z. Clarke – and it would be no exaggeration to say that she spent a considerable proportion of her life spelling out her name for others: at school to a teacher reading out an attendance list, in a coffee shop to a confused barista taking her order, or on the phone making an appointment. From nursery to university and throughout her career as a scientist, she has felt compelled to clarify and correct her name every step of the way, distinctly enunciating each letter and syllable, knowing that in the end people will still get it wrong. As recently as last month she heard the new lab manager say, with a casual shrug and a nonchalant smile, 'I think I'm going to call you Zany instead. Your name is too difficult to remember.' In that instant, Zaleekhah knew she ought to object and stand up for herself, but she let the remark pass, trying to keep away from the man as much as she could afterwards, though not so completely as to avoid being referred to in public as someone she is not.

It does not get any easier when people ask her what her name means, and someone always does. Then she has to bring up the story of Zuleikha. A conniving she-devil, as described by all Abrahamic faiths. The salacious wife of Potiphar, fiery and tempestuous; a combination of virago, witch and whore, if there ever

67

was one. A seductress who lusted after the handsome and virtuous Joseph and, propelled by feminine wiles and unholy desires,
tried to lure him into her bed. For her sins, God turned her into
an ugly crone and wizened widow, and kept her like that until she
repented of her ways. When sufficiently docile and obedient, she
was rewarded with her former youth and beauty and given permission to marry Joseph, after which she never erred again.

Zaleekhah does not, and never did, like this parable. In her
mind she traces her finger over Zuleikha's wrinkles, each etched
on her face as a punishment, branching out like the tributaries of
ancient rivers, and she always imagines her as a liquid woman –
assertive, bold, impatient, desiring something different, something
better, until, diminished and defeated, she could desire no more.

What makes her name all the more complicated is the profusion of its regional, ethnic and cultural variations – Suleika,
Zulaikha, Zalikha, Zuleika, Zuleikha, Zulaikhaa, Züleyha,
Zuleikhah, Zulekhah, Zulekha, Zoleikha, Zuleyka, Zuleica,
Zuleykha, Zoulikha . . . One will struggle to find two Zaleekhahs
from different parts of the world who spell their names alike. It
can all be a bit overwhelming. Sometimes she just wants to be Z.

It was her mother's idea, this name with its complex combination of letters. It was her mum who wanted her to be called
something that showed that, even though their family tree has
grown and blossomed in rainy England, their ancestral roots are
elsewhere, in the soil of sunny Mesopotamia, burrowed under
the date palms of Nineveh, tethering them to a motherland they
have not visited in decades but that still has a hold on them. Her
father – a gentle soul, proud of his own Irish heritage – went along
with his wife's wishes, as usual. So they named their only child
after a biblical femme fatale, all charm and wild passion.

The irony never escapes Zaleekhah. Whenever she glances in
the mirror the woman that looks back at her is the opposite of
the seductive Zuleikha. With her oversized cardigans, flat loaf-
ers, baggy shirts, loose-fitting trousers, absence of make-up and
slightly chipped glasses that she never finds time to get repaired or

replaced, she could not be more unlike her namesake. Did her parents never notice the incongruity? But she does not blame them. It is hard to blame the dead.

Speeding up, Zaleekhah now approaches the waterfront, the ground wet and slippery beneath her shoes. Upon reaching the pier, she pushes open a rickety gate that leads to a narrow, wooden walkway straddling the entire dock. With every step she takes, the bridge shakes a little, and the porcelain cups in the box clatter, as if they have things to say. As she passes houseboats tugging softly at their moorings, she casts furtive glances, hoping to catch a glimpse of other people's lives, but then she quickly lowers her head, not yet ready to meet any of her neighbours. Thankfully there is no one outside.

Her boat is berthed at the river's edge, tethered next to an aged oak, whose crooked trunk throws its canopy out over the water. Zaleekhah knows that trees bent in this way often snap or break from their roots, but this one has managed to survive, despite its quirky shape and inhospitable location. She wonders how old the tree is, and what strange things it may have witnessed in its long life – but, then again, she is used to asking questions that have no apparent answers.

Tearing her gaze from the warped oak, she inspects her houseboat, which is visibly smaller than all the others and painted in a shade of blue so saturated that the Thames pales next to it. On two sides of the wooden hull in large, curved, white letters it reads:

She Who Saw the Deep

It is this unusual name that charmed her the first time she visited the property with an estate agent in tow. Zaleekhah has no idea what it means, and has not tried to find out; she just happened to like the sound of it. It prompted her to imagine that the houseboat is female and has experienced its – her – share of storms and doldrums, which it – she – survived with considerable damage

69

but perhaps improved resilience. It warmed her up to the idea of moving here. Not a logical deduction in any way, but, after being invariably rational and mostly predictable all her adult life, she felt entitled for once to deviate from reason.

Having never lived in floating accommodation before, Zaleekhah was surprised to discover how expensive it is to rent a houseboat in London. Early this week she signed a contract and paid a hefty deposit, which blew a hole in her budget. Orphaned at an early age, she has learnt that she needs to be frugal, but now she is dipping into her savings, amazed at how easy it is to spend what has taken her so long to accumulate.

There were more than three thousand houseboats on the River Thames in London, the estate agent had informed her. She was lucky to have found a place, as demand outstripped supply, he hastened to add. In the past few years there had been a sharp rise in the number of people inquiring about renting or buying water-borne homes. Thousands of Londoners were taking up residence on the border between river and land, putting down roots in liminal spaces. From now on, she will be one of them, he commented cheerfully. She will have to learn the movements of the tides, the habits of the winds and the variations of weather patterns. She will have to secure all her appliances, including the TV. Floating moorings are affected by tidal fluctuations. Her house may shake a little when large vessels sail past in the distance, rocked by the waves they leave in their wake. All the while Zaleekhah listened quietly. She didn't have the heart to tell him that she didn't own a TV and was not planning to purchase one. And, as for walking on unstable ground, she was used to that.

'Maybe it wasn't such a bad thing after all that we didn't have kids. God knows how they would have ended up.'

That is what her husband said to her last week – hours before she thrust a few belongings into a cardboard box, left the house key on the kitchen table and walked out.

'So you think I'd be a bad mum?'

'Honestly? Don't act so offended. You never even wanted to be one!'

'Yes – but, if I had, if *we* had . . . Can you tell me why you think I'd be a bad mum?'

'Do you really want me to spell it out?'

'I do, actually.'

'Because . . . cheerfulness isn't your strong point. You just don't have the capacity for happiness.'

It has been a long, messy break-up, months in the making. And maybe it isn't over yet – maybe they're still breaking. When she closes her eyes, she can hear a noise like the cracking of ice, the fracturing of bones. The past few months have been either excruciatingly quiet or embarrassingly loud – the hurtful words that once said cannot be unsaid, the slamming of doors and banging of cupboards in silent rage, the crash of a wine glass hurled at the wall, leaving slivers so tiny that, even after being hoovered up, they still find a way to cut.

Colleagues before they became lovers and long before they got married, they both dedicated their lives to scientific research. It was not only a profession they shared but a passion. She always believed that nothing – not even great sex or fiery love – could bring a couple closer than having a common ideal to fight for, and that is what they had. They were both devoted to the study and conservation of the earth's water. While it might not sound much to others, for them there was no stronger bond. How their relationship had soured like this, Zaleekhah cannot possibly say. All she knows is that at some point in their marriage she looked back and realized they had long since left the track they had set out upon, like a tram that derails on sharp corners. Although they had found their flat together and split the rent and expenses equally, when it became clear that they were parting ways, neither had any doubt as to who would stay and who would leave. For the past few days she has been sleeping in the office.

Her face concentrated in thought, Zaleekhah strides the remaining distance to her new home. She balances the cardboard box against her hip and reaches for the key in her pocket. The rain has slackened to a sprinkle, and there is a faint stir in the air as the tide rises and the river swells. It crosses her mind, and not for the first time, that her uncle will not be pleased when he finds out what she has done. Not about the money – Uncle Malek is always embarrassingly generous and God knows what a rock he has been to her ever since her parents passed away. He is the only relative she has in England, and, since she has never met her distant kin, scattered all across the Middle East, South Asia and North America in a global diaspora, as far as she is concerned he is the only family she has in this world. When he hears the news he will worry about her choice of residence, arguing it is not safe for a single woman, which she now is. Uncle has never been fond of her husband, wishing she'd married someone wealthier and more famous and generally more exciting, but he will be sad to learn that her marriage, however dull in his eyes, has dissolved.

As Zaleekhah steps on to the front deck her phone begins to buzz. Her whole body goes tense. She has no intention of speaking to her husband. Maybe later but not just yet. What can they say to each other that hasn't already been said? What good can there be in talking, when all this time, their words, like waves lapping at a castle of sand, eroded the foundations of their marriage, leaving behind a crumpling heap? But then it occurs to her that it may be her uncle calling. He had tried to reach her repeatedly earlier in the week, recording anxious messages. Zaleekhah can let it pass, ring him back later when she's had a chance to settle in, but she already feels guilty for not having answered any of his previous attempts.

Carefully, she puts down the box, hearing the teapot rattle against the lamp. A quick glance at the screen reveals that it is indeed Uncle Malek.

'Hello?'

'Oh, thank God and all His regiment of angels, there you are!'

'Hi, Uncle.'

'Hi, my dear. Your aunt and I were starting to get worried. I called the lab several times. I was about to contact the police. Didn't you get my messages?'

'Sorry, I was going to ring you back. I got sidetracked.'

'I tried your landline, too,' Uncle carries on. 'I managed to get hold of your husband. He sounded sleepy, at this hour? You guys need to start going to bed earlier; it's not good for you to be working so late.'

Her jaw tightens. 'What . . . what did Brian tell you?'

'He said you weren't at home. I asked him when you'd be back, and he said he had absolutely no idea. Not very helpful, is he?' Uncle pauses, a hint of suspicion entering his voice. 'Why, what was Brian supposed to tell me?'

'Oh, nothing. I'm glad you two had a chat.'

'Well, if you can call it *chatting*. It's like pulling teeth with that man.'

In the background, a River Thames sightseeing boat full of tourists passes by, blasting its horn. Zaleekhah covers her phone with her hand to block the sound, but it is too late.

'Where exactly are you, my dear?'

Zaleekhah sucks in a lungful of air. 'I'm in Chelsea – by the river.'

Uncle chuckles. 'Having a stroll in this gorgeous English weather?'

'Actually, I was . . . I'm moving into a houseboat.'

'A what?'

'Remember those lovely boats by the Embankment? I've rented one of them.'

Silence descends, lying as heavy as a water-logged blanket.

'I was going to tell you,' Zaleekhah says, the words rushing out now. 'It just happened so fast, I didn't get a chance to mention it earlier.'

'A houseboat, for God's sake! I thought you guys were fond of your place. What was the problem? Was it the neighbours upstairs –'

'Oh, no . . . it's not like that,' Zaleekhah interjects, a softness to her tone, like she's explaining something complex to a child. 'It's only me moving out. I'm renting the boat on my own.'

'As an extra office?'

'As my home.'

A sharp intake of breath is heard at the other end of the line, then a sigh. 'Are you telling me you two broke up – after three years of marriage?'

'Three and a half,' Zaleekhah says. 'I'm sorry.'

She does not know to whom she is apologizing: to her uncle, for not sharing the news with him until now; to her husband, for not trying harder to save their marriage; or to herself, for not leaving him before.

When Uncle Malek speaks again, there is a tenderness to his voice. 'Listen, *habibti*, let's talk. Will you join us for dinner?'

'I really can't.'

'Please don't say no. Come have a bite with us, my dear. How about tomorrow at seven – is that good?'

'All right,' Zaleekhah says, yielding.

She carries her sense of gratitude to him like a long-held breath inside her chest, one that she cannot fully release but can let out only in occasional short bursts.

'Excellent!' Uncle says. 'See you soon, my dear.'

Zaleekhah tucks the phone back in her bag. Suddenly, she has a sense of being watched. Upon looking up, she meets the stares of an elderly couple standing on the deck of the next houseboat, wearing matching yellow raincoats. Lifting their hands in tandem, they wave at her, and, not knowing what else to do, she returns the gesture.

'You must be our new neighbour,' shouts the woman.

'Yes, hi.'

'Blimey, you're young,' says the man. 'We were expecting someone older when we heard a scientist was joining our riverside community.'

'Don't be rude,' says the woman, before fluttering her ringed fingers in Zaleekhah's direction. 'Will your husband or partner be joining you, dear?'

'Now look who's being rude,' the man says.

'No, it's just me,' replies Zaleekhah. Eager to change the subject, she rushes to ask, 'Have you lived here long?'

'Twenty-two years,' says the man, straightening his shoulders. 'People come and go, like the tides, but we've stayed put. Cast anchor!'

Zaleekhah nods, acutely aware that she cannot say the same about her own life.

'We know pretty much everyone around here – don't hesitate to ask,' says the woman. 'Including the owner of your boat – such an odd fish! Runs a tattoo parlour.'

Zaleekhah's eyebrows shoot up. 'A tattoo artist owns this place? I had no idea. I did everything through the letting agent.'

The man says, 'Apparently it can be quite the money-spinner. The shop's just opposite the British Museum, we've heard. It's not somewhere we ever go, frankly. Far too many tourists! Doesn't feel like London any more.'

Sensing a rant coming on, Zaleekhah bends down to pick up her things. But as soon as she lifts the cardboard box its now completely sodden bottom gives way, sending all the items inside tumbling out.

'It's okay. I've got it!' Zaleekhah says, louder than she'd intended.

She stares at the mess by her feet. Thankfully the porcelain teapot and mugs are unscathed, but the books are not so lucky. Some are lying open, face-down, with their pages getting soaked; others have damp covers. *The Science of Water*; *Aquatic Ecosystems and the Uncertain Future*; *New Concepts in Hydrogeology and the Earth's Waterways*; *Chemical and Isotopic Groundwater Hydrology*; *The Global Water Cycle and Climate Change*; *The End of Water: Environmental Destruction and the Implications for the Hydrological Cycle* . . . She notices the couple are also peering at the soggy heap.

'Oh, is that what you're working on?' asks the woman, pointing at the books with her chin. 'Are you a water scientist?'

'It's called a hydrologist,' says the man.

Zaleekhah nods. 'Yes . . . right . . . sorry, I'd better get this lot inside.'

She grabs the lamp and gathers up as many books as she can into the crook of her arm. Under the last book, lying in a puddle, is a little porcelain figurine. An Ancient Mesopotamian creature – it has the head of a human, the body of a bull and the wings of a bird, one part now broken off. A *lamassu*, a protective spirit, a childhood birthday present from her uncle. She has always liked the look of it. Quickly, she collects the pieces, and, with a curt nod to her neighbours, she stumbles towards her new home.

'Use a hairdryer to fan out the pages,' yells the man behind her.

The latch, stiff with damp, does not yield immediately. On the second attempt she wrenches open the door and hurries in, closing it behind her. She knows she should go out to fetch the rest of her items, but she has no intention of doing so under watchful eyes.

She enters the small space that will from now on be her living room, dining room and kitchen. Her sleeping quarters are below deck – a single bed, and a tiny bathroom with a compact shower. There is no furniture save for a wooden stool and a single, turquoise velvet armchair left by the owner. Dropping the books in a heap, Zaleekhah sets down the lamp.

Carefully, she puts the *lamassu* on the kitchen worktop, its chipped wing next to it. Maybe she could glue it back on. Maybe it won't be visible, the fracture.

The tap in the kitchen is leaking, which she did not spot when she visited this place earlier. Rust stains cloud the basin, and these, too, she failed to notice previously. A pot of rosemary is wilting in the corner, and next to it is a mug with a missing handle. She washes the mug, fills it with water and drinks it in one draught, realizing only now how thirsty she has been. It tastes earthy and slightly metallic, with an aftertaste of iron. The flavour has less to do with its intrinsic qualities than with its biophysical environment, the set of conditions that brought it about. Water hardens in adverse circumstances, not unlike the human heart.

Out of nowhere a memory surfaces – the words Uncle Malek uttered the day she had graduated from university with honours. *I'm so proud of you,* habibti. *I want you to be very successful. Remember, people like us cannot afford to fail.*

'People like us' . . . immigrants, exiles, refugees, newcomers, outsiders . . . Too many words for a shared, recognizable sentiment that, no matter how often described, remains largely undefined.

Children of uprooted parents are born into the memory tribe. Both their present and their future are forever shaped by their ancestral past, regardless of whether they have any knowledge of it. If they flourish and prosper, their achievements will be attributed to a whole community; and, in the same way, their failures will be chalked up to something bigger and older than themselves, be it family, religion or ethnicity.

While the journey of life may be full of reversals of fortune, children from displaced families can never allow themselves to fall below the level at which their parents started out. Yet she is doing precisely that. Falling. Failing. She cannot help but feel that, in letting herself down, she is letting her ancestors down.

Zaleekhah sinks into the lone armchair. She runs her hand through her hair, which springs up in frizzy, dark curls now that it is dripping wet. For a moment, she sits still, watching the Thames. A ship passes on the horizon, bright red as in a child's drawing, sending its wake in her direction. As she waits for the waves to hit the hull of her boat, her new home, she starts to cry.

A tear falls on the back of her hand. Lacrimal fluid, composed of intricate patterns of crystallized salt invisible to the eye. This drop, water from her own body, containing a trace of her DNA, was a snowflake once upon a time or a wisp of steam, perhaps here or many kilometres away, repeatedly mutating from liquid to solid to vapour and back again, yet retaining its molecular essence. It remained hidden under the fossil-filled earth for tens if not thousands of years, climbed up to the skies and returned to earth in mist, fog, monsoon or hailstorm, perpetually displaced and re-located. Water is the consummate immigrant, trapped in transit, never able to settle.

The tear has disappeared, but it will find a way to emerge again, in some other manifestation. It will take a while, though. Smaller droplets vaporize more slowly than their larger counterparts. Even after all these years of studying it, water never ceases to surprise her, astonishingly resilient but also acutely vulnerable – a drying, dying force.

There is a tautness in her throat that makes it hard to breathe. Her chest constricts; a swelling pressure inside her ribcage struggles to break free. She has tried so hard to be someone else, a happier and lighter version of herself. It hasn't worked. Melancholy, an invisible noose that periodically loosens but never fully relaxes its grip, tightens round her neck, yet again.

She has not exactly planned it this way, but it makes sense the more she thinks of it, and thinking of it is all she has been doing lately. It makes sense that someone like her would want to die by water. A part of her is tired, and it is this part that keeps telling her it doesn't have to be this way, that she doesn't need to feel so drained any more. She can stay in this houseboat for about a month – one day for each year of her life. Then she will do what she needs to do – calmly and without a fuss. She will numb her mind with pills. She will stuff her pockets with stones, like her mother's favourite author. Being a good swimmer, she has to find a way not to rise to the surface. She trusts the currents of the Thames will help her succeed, the way they have helped so many others.

She hasn't made up her mind and maybe she doesn't have to, just yet. Certainty is neither needed nor something she would

78

trust. A month is long enough to prepare. It can be a humble and uncomplicated death – she will finish the article she has been secretly working on for so long, a controversial paper about 'water memory' that she was too scared to share for fear that it might draw harsh criticism and ridicule from the scientific community. Now it doesn't matter any more. She will settle a few outstanding debts, eat in her favourite restaurants and probably drink a bit more than usual; spend more of her savings and donate whatever remains to charity . . . It will be especially hard to leave Uncle Malek and Aunt Malek, the people who raised her, and their daughter, Helen, who has been like a sister to her. She can only hope they will not blame themselves.

Dr Zaleekhah Clarke does not wish to live. She wants to excuse herself from a world where she often feels like an outsider, a confused and clumsy latecomer, an accidental guest who walked in through the wrong door at the wrong time. Unlike her namesake, the Qur'anic Zuleikha, she is not, and has never been, assertive. She is not a fighter. She does not even like to argue – not with her husband, not with herself, not with colleagues or friends or strangers, and certainly not with a God that as a child she has been repeatedly instructed both to fear and to love, even though He never cared to explain to her why He took her parents away; a God that punishes women with old age and ugliness, and rewards them with pretty looks and attractive spouses when they prove themselves to be sufficiently submissive; a God she could easily be furious with, yet whose existence she does not even believe in. All she wants, right now, is to retreat, a silent admission of defeat for someone tired of trying to survive – less a departure than a homecoming, a return to water.

—o—

ARTHUR

By the River Thames, 1853

L ondon is shrouded in a blanket of fog this morning. There
is an unusual stillness to its streets and parks, an uneasy
silence that closes in on itself, like a purse pulled tight by
its drawstrings. Even though the bells from a nearby church have
just tolled ten o'clock, it feels like dusk has already descended.
Neither grey nor white, the air is a soupy ochre that glows green
in places. Particles of soot and ash float above, as domestic coal
fires and factory chimneys belch sulphur-laden smoke, clogging
the lungs of Londoners, breath by breath.

Arthur – thirteen years of age, pale skinned, gangly after a
recent growth spurt, with a trace of down on his upper lip – turns
a corner into a narrow alleyway of cobblestones. The brume is
so dense that the boy can barely see beyond a few paces. He takes
care not to step in anything nasty whilst keeping sight of his father
striding ahead of him.

'Stop dawdling, lad!'

'I am trying.'

'Well, you're not tryin' hard enough – dragging your feet like
a damn'd infant. Get a move on.'

The boy accelerates his steps. After months of absence his
father has returned home, having lost weight and what little
tenderness he had in him. Work is scarce, and the few odd com-
missions he managed to get when sober have gone unpaid. He

constantly complains about the lack of money. This morning he pulled Arthur out of bed, saying the child has been sponging off his parents for too long, and that it is time he found an apprenticeship to learn a trade.

Not that Arthur has been at all lazy. Ever since he left school he has taken on all kinds of odd jobs. He goes scavenging in the sewers with the toshers who gave him his moniker, collects horse manure to sell to tanners, gathers old clothes to trade with rag-pickers, helps a chickweed-vendor to feed pet birds, and, at times, wades into filthy ponds with a team of women, using his bare legs to catch leeches. With two small children on her hands, his mother cannot work long days as before. Although his father pretends otherwise, the boy has already become the breadwinner of the family.

A part of him misses school. The predictability of the daily routine, the joy of solving a mathematics problem or losing himself in a passage of history, the prospect of learning something new and exciting – these are the things he most longs for. There is a great deal he is glad to have left behind, too, especially the fear of setting foot in the headmaster's study. Yet this is of no consequence. His days of schooling are over. He has joined the droves of adolescent workers in the capital. There are plenty of children across the country, many younger than he is, grinding away in shipyards, cotton-spinning mills, nail factories and coal mines; out on the streets catching rats, sweeping night-soil or crawling up chimneys too narrow for adults. Arthur knows how exhausted they are, their eyes lustreless and sunken in their sockets. He has come across girls employed in matchstick factories, their jaws disfigured by the white phosphorus they use every day. He has heard terrifying stories about railway boys torn to pieces by oncoming freight trains or dressmakers inhaling particles of fibre so fine that they do not grasp how ill they are until it is too late. He is aware of all this. What he does not know is where exactly his father is taking him now. Every time he raises the question he receives a curt response. He tries once more.

'What kind of work is it?'

'Told you, son,' his father says, his voice muffled through the fog. 'They're printers. They have big machines to publish stuff. All kinds of stuff. It's a serious job – stable and respectable.'

'If it's so important, why would they want to hire me?'

''Cos they need an errand boy. Every business needs one. Why d'you ask daft questions?'

'An errand boy to do what?'

Abruptly, the man turns around. He grabs the child by the collar and pushes him against the wall.

'You bastard, you think you can leech off me for the rest of your life? Bleed me dry?'

Arthur struggles to free himself from the man's grip. Even as his stomach clenches in fear, he says, 'It is my mother who looked after me. She is the one who raised me, not you.'

A smack across the face. The force of the blow sends the boy tumbling sideways. Arthur climbs to his feet with a quiet intensity.

They walk on without exchanging another word. Somewhere inside the fog a dog barks, a baby whimpers, voices multiply.

In a little while they enter another alley not far from New Oxford Street. The fog is thicker here, oppressive. Holding out his hands in front of him, the boy takes careful steps into the murkiness stretching out on all sides. He can hardly see beyond his wrists. The air is bitterly cold.

'Stay close to me, lad.'

Arthur senses why his father suddenly sounds concerned. Further down the road is St Giles, one of the roughest rookeries in the city, notorious for its forgers, pickpockets and prostitutes. Recently the authorities set out to clear the slum by joining Oxford Street to Holborn but little has improved for the people who live here.

Father and son plough on, picking their way through the maze of lanes. All around is the acrid stench of rotting vegetables, mouldering rubbish and stale urine. Every now and then, when the curtain of haze parts, Arthur catches a glimpse of the inhabitants: children so skinny that the rags they wear hang from their bodies; men with sunken cheeks and gaunt expressions; and women too busy with their chores to notice him, whilst others are ready to offer themselves for a pittance, even to a boy of his age.

'So you brings your son for his first time, do you, then?'

Turning his head, Arthur sees a figure half hiding in a dim passage, almost camouflaged against the soot-stained bricks. Her skin is scarred by smallpox, her hair matted and uncombed, her face pale and pinched. An old wound runs down one side of her mouth, making her look as if she is smiling even when her gaze remains full of despair. The boy feels embarrassed, not so much by the woman's remark but by the helplessness in her tone. In his distraction he does not notice the bemused expression spreading on his father's face, until he hears him say, 'Now why would I bring my boy to an ugly wench like you?'

The woman tries to make light of the affront. 'Come, sir, if you was to get me some nice clothes, I could look pretty.'

'Nay, miserable maid – who would waste a ha'pence on a wretched hussy like you? No one can make a silk purse out of a sow's ear.'

Arthur stares at his father in astonishment, unable to believe he has said such a horrible thing. A deep sense of shame chokes him, lodging in his throat like a fishbone. He wants to apologize to the woman for his father's rudeness, but what can he possibly say to her that won't sound like ridicule and cause even more hurt?

'Move on, lad.'

His face burning, his eyes down, the boy follows the man, feeling increasingly small. Even as they turn a corner at the end of the street, he can still hear the prostitute muttering under her breath, cursing the two of them.

After they leave St Giles behind, they walk for a while eastwards towards the river. They stop in front of a two-storey building. A brass sign hangs above the door:

> *Bradbury & Evans*
> *Publishers Extraordinaire to the Queen*
> *Engraver and printer of postage stamps, certificates, newspapers,*
> *periodicals, pamphlets and exceptional books*

The sign creaks on its hinges, the sound reminiscent of a branch about to snap in the wind. Arthur listens, his gaze fixed on the words, and he would probably have stayed rooted to the spot had his father not started yelling again.

'Hurry up, lad! We haven't got all day.'

A few minutes later, Arthur finds himself in a spacious room with framed prints on the walls. Flames crackle in a fireplace; a large mahogany desk sits on either side. Behind them sit the owners of the company – the junior partner, Mr Evans, and the senior partner, Mr Bradbury.

By the window, hanging from an ornamental brass standard, is a birdcage housing two budgies, their breasts a vivid blue. These birds have become very popular ever since Queen Victoria was given a pair as a present. The craze, for that is what it feels like, has spread fast. Each week fresh cargo is brought from South Australia to England, and, from there, transferred into homes and aviaries across the country. The boy is so captivated by these two that it takes him a moment to focus on the conversation going on around him.

In rapid speech, his father is explaining that a customer of his, an apothecary, delighted with the quality of the cabinet he built for him, promised to help find a job for his lad. The chemist suggested that they pay a visit to Bradbury & Evans, a place he happens to know well, as this is where he has his advertising printed; he promised to put in a good word for the boy. Given the blank expressions of Mr Evans and Mr Bradbury, he has clearly done no such thing.

'I'm afraid there must have been some misunderstanding,' Mr Evans says, with a suspicion he feels no need to hide. 'We were not expecting you.'

'My good sir, I don't know why my customer has not kept his promise. He assured me he was going to speak to you.'

Mr Bradbury shakes his head. 'Even so, that would not have changed anything. We are not in need of hiring anyone at this moment.'

Arthur watches his father blanch. The man who berates his wife, rains blows and curses on his children, and has callously insulted a poor prostitute on the way here now looks utterly servile. Even his voice has changed.

'Please, sirs . . . why don't you give my son a try?'

Arthur senses his father has no chance, no matter how much he toadies before these well-dressed gentlemen with their brocaded waistcoats and silk cravats. They look at him with obvious disdain; in their eyes there is only contempt. Witnessing this makes the boy sad. We never want our parents' weaknesses to be seen by others. Their failures are our own private affair, a secret we would rather keep to ourselves; when they become public, for everyone's consumption, we are no longer the children we once were.

'I fear you have come all this way for nothing,' says Mr Evans, setting his fingers into a steeple under his chin. 'We are not in need of an errand boy.'

'Come on, Father, let's go,' says Arthur as he motions towards the door without looking at anyone.

But the man does not budge. 'Sirs, you do not understand. I have good reason to insist. My boy is a genius!'

Arthur halts, startled. His father never has words of praise for his children – or anyone, for that matter.

'Come here, lad. Show them what I mean!'

Arthur stands still, too mortified to move. Grabbing him by the shoulders, his father pushes him towards the two proprietors.

'You also print calendars, don't you, sirs? Ask my son a date from times gone by – pick any you want.'

'I do not understand what you are trying to do,' says Mr Bradbury.

'This boy of mine is a curious child. He has an extraordinary memory. It never fails, I can assure you. Give him a chance and he'll prove it. You won't regret this. Choose any date from previous years, ask him what day it fell on.'

The two publishers glance at each other, a shared concern passing between them. Mr Bradbury nods, musing. 'Fine, we'll indulge you. How about this very date last year?'

The three men stare at the boy. Arthur blushes under their scrutiny. He has no intention of telling them about this day last year, which was a Tuesday. Arriving home, he found his mother on the floor, having consumed a full bottle of laudanum and then vomited all over herself. The awful smell, settling into everything it touched, did not disappear for a week. He screws his lips shut and looks away.

A flicker of apprehension appears in his father's eyes. 'Come on, boy . . . so what day was it? Tell these good gentlemen. Do not embarrass me.'

Arthur says nothing, his gaze growing intense and distant.

'You are doing this deliberately to annoy me! How dare you!'

Mr Evans interjects, 'I think we should not pressure the child.'

'No, no! I don't understand why he's acting so. Ask him another date, one more chance, I beg of you.'

'All right,' says Mr Bradbury. 'How about 1849, the 12th of October?'

Arthur inhales and speaks in a slow, steady voice. 'That was a Friday, sir. It rained all afternoon. They carried out the bodies of five labourers. In Pimlico, that's where the accident happened. They were poisoned by sewer gases. I saw the corpses; I was there. The police came. There were journalists, too.'

The boy closes his eyes for a moment, recalling the faces of the dead, glazed as if made of bronze, and their hands, smudged and smeared with mud and clenched into fists, even though drained of all the fight in them.

Mr Bradbury clears his throat. 'My boy, you should know that we also print newspapers here. If you are making this up, it would be easy for us to refute what you just said. Now tell me, do you actually remember this happening?'

Arthur lifts his chin. 'I am not lying, sir.'

'All right, we'll see about that.' Mr Bradbury turns to his younger partner. 'Would you mind checking what the lad just said?'

An awkward silence descends after Mr Evans leaves the room. As they wait for him to return, they listen to the sounds of the street – a carriage drives by, dangerously fast. Hooves echo on cobblestones, muffling the cry of a vendor peddling ginger cakes.

Eventually, Mr Evans strides back in, waving a newspaper in his hand. He is smiling. 'It's exactly as the boy said!'

'Very strange,' mutters Mr Bradbury with a new interest in his eyes. 'Let us try another date. The 13th of June 1851?'

Arthur cocks his head to one side, his face brightening with the recollection. 'That was the day of the costume ball at Buckingham Palace. I waited outside the royal gates, hoping to catch a glimpse of the outfits. I heard they were going to be dressed as historical figures, but it was too crowded to see anything. The weather was good, though windy. That, too, fell on a Friday.'

'Shall I go to check?' asks Mr Evans, clearly enjoying himself.

'No need,' says Mr Bradbury. Peering over his spectacles, he studies the boy. 'You have a peculiar talent, young man. I must say I am impressed.'

Arthur notices his father straightening his shoulders, as something like relief crosses his face, and he says, 'I told you, didn't I?'

Mr Bradbury ignores the remark. 'Fine, we'll give it a try. But only for a week. If, by the end of the week, we are not satisfied, for whatever reason, we shall part ways in a civilized manner. In that case, I would not want to see either of you again. Is that understood?'

'Most certainly, sir. You have my word. He's a fast learner, my son.'

Mr Evans, his eyebrows raised in mild amusement, claps his hands. 'Well, well! Young Smyth, welcome to the world of engravers and printers.'

Arthur smiles shyly. 'Thank you, sir.'

'When would you like him to start?' his father interrupts, making sure he is not overlooked.

'Actually, he may start right away,' replies Mr Bradbury. 'You, my dear fellow, may therefore take your leave now. I am sure the boy can find his way back home.'

'Oh, in that case . . . I hope, most esteemed sirs, you will appreciate that I had to sacrifice my day's wages to bring my son here. I'm sure gentlemen such as yourselves would not want me to be out of pocket . . . and you might see your way clear to advance a little of his wage?'

'You are asking for money?' Mr Evans chides. 'For the boy's sake we will pretend not to have heard that. Good day to you.'

Arthur watches his father, his forehead puckering into a frown and his jaw set, walk out, without so much as a glance at anyone.

A heartbeat later, Arthur feels a friendly pat on his shoulder. It is Mr Bradbury.

'They are called Lapis and Lazuli.'

'Pardon, sir?'

'The birds – I noticed you looking at them earlier. Those are their names. Together, they make a precious stone.'

The boy blinks.

'Oh, you are not familiar with the bright blue rock? *Lapis* from Latin, meaning "stone". *Lazuli* from Arabic and Persian, meaning "heaven, sky, dark blue" . . . This lovely gem was treasured by many civilizations – Egypt, Greece, Rome, China, but especially Mesopotamia.'

Arthur listens, spellbound.

'You have a lot to learn, young Smyth. I hope you like learning.'

'Oh, I do, sir,' Arthur says, his eyes brimming.

'Good. In that case, come give me a hand.' The publisher opens the door and walks into the hall.

Arthur follows Mr Bradbury into a room in the basement, where an extraordinary scene greets him. Before him lies a bewildering proliferation of books, pamphlets and magazines, piled high on the floor and stacked higgledy-piggledy on the shelves. At the centre of this paper kingdom sits a machine – squat, pitch-black, steam-powered and massive. It has automated rollers, cylinders and metal plates.

Mr Bradbury smiles. 'A remarkable piece of engineering, don't you think? What do you say, do you like it?'

'What . . . what is this, sir?'

'It's a printing press. Everything you see in this room came out of this invention.' Mr Bradbury gestures towards a wooden tray with dozens of compartments, each containing letters, numbers and symbols. 'We compose these by hand on a metal plate. We get our type from the best foundries and we use the handsomest fonts. If you work hard, we'll teach you how.'

Gingerly, Arthur approaches the machine, though he does not dare touch it. There is a page at the other end, recently printed. Mr Bradbury picks it up and reads out a line: *Let the great world spin forever down the ringing grooves of change.*' The man surveys the boy. 'Do you recognize these words?'

Arthur shakes his head.

'Poetry, my boy – Tennyson. Are you familiar with verse?'

'I am not sure I would know what it is, sir. At school we sang hymns and memorized mathematical formulas and studied the Bible. No one said anything about poetry.'

'What a pity.' Mr Bradbury reaches out for another page.

'Ah, my Belovèd, fill the Cup that clears
Today of past Regrets and future Fears:
Tomorrow? Why – Tomorrow I may be
Myself with Yesterday's Sev'n thousand Years.'

Arthur's eyes widen. 'Is that poetry, too?'

'It is indeed. This one little known yet, by Omar Khayyám. My friend Edward FitzGerald, a poet and writer himself, is translating from the Persian. It is taking time, though. All being well we shall publish it soon.'

Tennyson . . . Khayyám . . . FitzGerald . . . The boy ponders. There is a great deal he does not know. How frightening it is, but also how strangely invigorating to realize that the world he has experienced is only one of many possible worlds.

Watching him, Mr Bradbury offers an encouraging smile. 'Don't worry, you have plenty of time to learn. Remember, Arthur, life is full of surprises. Who knows, you, too, may be seduced by the joys of verse. One day, you may even be known as a connoisseur of poems and a lover of the written word.'

It is in that moment that Arthur's gaze, scanning the room inquisitively, alights on the cover of a book. He recognizes the words that have haunted him ever since his eyes first fell upon them – *Nineveh and Its Remains*. The very same title he encountered in the headmaster's study, emerging in his life again, like a meandering river that winds its way alongside him and reappears just when he thought it had dried up.

'Sir,' says Arthur, 'are you also printing that book?'

The man turns to see what the boy is pointing at. 'Why, yes. It has proved highly popular – sold more than twenty thousand copies! We are charged with the second edition, which will be shorter and cheaper for wider distribution. I venture we shall be hard pressed to satisfy demand. The public are eager to learn about biblical archaeology – they are also rather keen to know about the devil-worshippers, I must say.'

'But who are they, sir? I have been wondering myself.'

Mr Bradbury winks at him as if they are old friends. 'Well, you will need to read the book to find out, dear boy.'

'Oh, thank you, I would be most happy to. Provided both you and Mr Evans are satisfied with my work, might I be allowed to borrow a copy when it is printed?'

Not anticipating that he will be taken at his word, the man regards the child. 'Are you genuinely interested in a scholar's account of his journey to Mesopotamia and discovery of an ancient Assyrian city? That is indeed unexpected. Perhaps you could explain to me the source of your enthusiasm?'

'It's merely that . . . to me Nineveh sounds like a dream of a place, unlike anything I have known or seen before,' says Arthur, after a heartbeat. 'That's where the massive winged bulls came from – the *lamassus*. I saw them outside the British Museum. And ever since I have been intrigued by them.'

His expression unchanging, Mr Bradbury listens.

'I have also been wondering about all those people mentioned in the title – especially the Yazidis,' Arthur carries on with conviction. 'Do they really worship the devil, or have they perhaps been mistaken for something they are not, accused of things they have not done, because, you see, sir, I . . . I think I kind of . . .' The boy stumbles a little then, but manages to finish his thought: 'I do know what it is like to be misunderstood and treated unjustly.'

H—

NARIN

By the River Tigris, 2014

'Grandma, those who say awful things about us –'

'What about them, my heart?'

'It's just I wish they had met you. If they only truly knew you, they would love you! How can anyone not love you?'

'Narin, joy of my life.'

The breeze from the Tigris tousles the girl's hair and the ends of the old woman's headscarf, loosely knotted around her neck. They have been making their way along a narrow trail up the hill, gathering sorrel, wild garlic, coltsfoot and spotted dead nettle. As the temperature scales up another notch, they stop to catch their breath. They sit in the shade of a rocky outcrop, from where they can observe the yellow bulldozers and tipper lorries roaring down below.

'Will you tell me a story, Grandma?'

'Which story do you want, my soul?'

'The one about how God created this world.'

'Again? I've told you many times.'

Narin is worried that, when she goes deaf, it is not only her father's music that she will miss but also the stories of her childhood. Grandma is illiterate and innumerate. She can scrawl her name on a piece of paper, but she cannot write down the words she carries within her. And so, before Narin loses her power of hearing, she wants to listen to every tale the old woman knows, so that she can still hear them when all else is silent. That is why she now pleads, 'Once more – will you?'

'All right, then. *In those days, in those far-off days . . .'*

Grandma's stories usually begin the same way, words that have been recited like an incantation for millennia.

Narin cannot help chiming in: *'In those far-off years, in olden times . . .'*

'Olden times it was indeed,' says Grandma placidly. 'Long before the earth came into being, there was only God – *Xwedê* – and nothing else. Back then everything was calm and peaceful. All around there was pure stillness, because sounds had not been invented yet. Not even a whisper. Then one morning, God decided to mould a pearl from His precious essence and fill it with divine light. A pearl so shiny He could admire His own reflection on its surface.'

Narin clasps her knees together in anticipation of what comes next.

'God entrusted the pearl to a magical bird called *Anfar*, and the bird kept it in his nest as if it were an egg. There the gem remained, unseen, untouched, unharmed. That blissful state lasted for forty days – or, perhaps, forty thousand years. It would not make any difference, because time, too, was inside the pearl. It was not yet born. It was not divided into years, months, weeks or hours. Time was whole, and the pearl was part of the whole, like everything else.'

Narin holds her breath. This is the bit of the story she likes best, when God starts to act in strange ways.

'But then, for a reason we will never know, God stepped on the pearl with all His might, smashing it to pieces. This is how Xwedê brought into being the mountains, the forests and the valleys. From the scattered shards He chiselled the sun and the moon. He hung the stars in the firmament like ornaments. He drew water from the core of the pearl and filled the fountains, streams and oceans. He created the seven angels from His own divine light – *sur*. That is why we call them "Seven Lights" – *Heft Sur*. He made them as if lighting seven candles from one. On the first day, Sunday, He created the angel *Azra'il*; on Monday,

Darda'il; on Tuesday, *Israfil*; on Wednesday, *Mika'il*; on Thursday, *Gibra'il*; on Friday, *Shimna'il*; and on Saturday, *Nura'il*. God chose the benevolent *Melek Tawûs* as the leader of the archangels. He is the peacock angel. Then He made the seven heavens and –'

'Wait, which language did the angels speak?'

'The language of silence.'

'What does that mean?'

'It means they did not need words to understand one another. They communicated through glowing light.' Grandma smiles longingly, as if wishing to be with them now. 'After that, God made humans – Adam and Eve. Christians, Jews, Muslims and everyone else in this world have sprung from this couple, but we Yazidis, my love, descended from Adam alone. No Eve involved.'

'How is that possible?'

'Well, Adam and Eve quarrelled one day. Each believed they were more important than the other. To find the answer they put their seeds in a jar and waited for a month. When Eve opened her jar, there wasn't anything in it. But when Adam opened his, inside he found a boy and a girl. These are our ancestors. We are the only people who descended from Adam alone.'

'Was Eve upset?'

'No, not really – later on Eve gave birth to many children of her own. She was a busy woman.'

Grandma passes her palm across her eyebrows, touching the tattoo on her forehead. The ink is made from soot, ash and mother's milk. Drawing patterns on the face – *deq* – used to be common among the women of this region, but the custom is fading. Some people have stars or moons or suns on their chins; others diamonds to attract strength and ward off the evil eye. Yet others have tiny honeycombs so that their words will always be sweet. Grandma's tattoo, which she inherited from her own grandmother, is three wedge-shaped vertical marks:

94

Narin, too, wants the same design someday. It is not fair that they won't let her, considering that Grandma got hers when she was a little girl. But times have changed, and they advise her not to rush. A tattoo is like a promise, they say, an oath inscribed into your skin, and you need to be sure you can keep it before you commit to it.

Her head bent in thought, Narin sighs. 'I just don't understand why God smashed that beautiful pearl.'

'Well, I think Xwedê did this for our sake. Otherwise human beings would not exist. None of us. There would be no rays of sun to greet every morning, no eggs to paint in bright colours on Red Wednesday, no doves cooing in the eaves, no lovers secretly holding hands . . .'

Narin giggles.

'Imagine, there'd be no stories to tell,' Grandma says. 'God destroyed His beloved pearl for us. And also maybe . . . because He wanted company.'

'Are you saying God is lonely?'

'Not any more, my heart – now that we are all here on earth. Every time we utter His holy name, He hears us. Every day we must pray to God, who is merciful, full of love and compassion. He is the judge of kings and beggars; the sovereign of the moon, the sun, the fire and the water. Prayer is not about asking for things. It is a conversation. When God is less lonely, we are less lonely.'

Pressing her lips together, Narin contemplates. Although she does not intend to question the ways of God, she cannot help wondering what would have happened if He had not done what He did. If only Xwedê had not smashed that lovely pearl, the universe would have remained as it was – complete, content. Then there would be no pain, no sorrow, no fear.

Grandma comes from a long line of healers. For generations, women – and several men – on her maternal side have relieved the suffering of the sick and the dying. Healing, she often says, resembles kite-flying. While a kite may aspire to drift freely in the skies, flying in all directions at once, its strings need to remain tethered to a fixed point. One can therefore master only a particular field, two at most. Some healers exclusively minister to victims of scorpion stings and snake bites, which are becoming more frequent these days, as the construction of the dam accelerates and the water level drops downstream. In times of drought and famine, venomous animals exhibit bizarre behaviour and start to attack humans in swarms. The lack of water, Grandma says, addles their brains and drives them wild, and who can blame them?

Other healers, like the descendants of Sora-Soran, ease creaking joints and repair broken hips. But Grandma's speciality is of an entirely different kind. She treats those who are afflicted by anxiety, depression and maladies of the mind. She relies on the potency of plants, preparing concentrated tinctures that are widely sought across the region. Yet the key element for her is, and always has been, water. She says it washes away disease, purifies the mind, calms the heart. Water is the best cure for melancholy.

Whenever there is a prolonged dry spell or an invasion of locusts ravaging the crops, the villagers gather in a ritual prayer to summon rain. They walk in a silent procession until they reach high ground, where they line up and call the dark clouds. It works, sometimes. But when it doesn't, they go to Besma. She can discern the locations of lost rivers, hidden canals and forgotten creeks – aquatic sources tucked away in the most unlikely places, even under barren hills.

At times she uses L-shaped brass rods that pull towards each other when she approaches a vein of water. At other times, she lightly holds a twig and walks around until she senses the tug. Occasionally she chooses a pendulum, waiting for it to swing. Ultimately, Grandma says, the implements are just a medium – rod, twig or pendulum; it is the human body that responds to sources in nature. The water inside us communes with the water outside us. A good diviner can tell the depth of an underground stream, and even whether it is contaminated or clean.

Grandma is a water-dowser.

Grandma is a spring-finder.

A bird swoops towards them and lands on a rock nearby. It is a small, olive-brown chiffchaff. A migratory passerine with a sweet song. They wait for a moment, hoping it might sing. When it does not, the child asks, quietly, 'After the dam is built, what will happen to your pistachio trees?'

'They will drown, I'm afraid.'

'I didn't know trees could drown.'

'Just like humans – if they are left without vital air. We cannot save our grove, but I'll take a cutting before we leave. I'll make sure at least one tree comes with us wherever we go. Would you like that?'

'Yes, please,' says Narin, comforted by the thought of a travel-ling tree. 'But what about the birds? They will be safe, no?'

'They will be safer, but they will have nowhere to build their nests. So they will have to leave.'

'The marbled duck –'

'She'll go elsewhere to lay her eggs. The willow-warbler, the red-wattled lapwing, the bluethroat, the kestrel, the eagle that soars high above – they won't come back to Hasankeyf.'

'I wish we had a huge ship,' says Narin. 'Then we could take all the animals and plants with us and sail away.'

'Like Baba Noah,' says Grandma. 'He built an ark and invited his family and friends on board. He brought two of every animal, and he did not forget to take pistachios so they could grow into trees someday. And when the flood rose, the ship drifted away. They rode the waves for a long time, until the timbers scraped dry land. With a bone-jarring jolt they stopped at the peak of a mountain – Sinjar.'

'Where is Mount Sinjar?'

'It's in Iraq. When we travel to Nineveh with your father, before you're baptized in the holy Valley of Lalish, I can tell you more about it.'

Narin beams.

'Listen, that was not all,' says Grandma. 'When the ship crashed into the mountaintop, a hole opened up in the hull. Flood-waters poured in. They were all going to die – humans, animals and plants. But then, out of nowhere, a black snake appeared! It coiled and coiled like a thick rope, plugging the breach. Thanks to the serpent, everyone was saved. For this reason, we Yazidis respect serpents and depict them at the entrance of sacred buildings. In our village, we also remember the great *Shahmaran* – "the Snake Queen". She has a woman's head and a snake's body.'

'How can something be both human and animal at the same time?'

'Oh, it's possible. We aren't that different. All over Mesopo-tamia there were hybrid creatures once upon a time. In fact, my grandmother Leila saw one in her youth. It was a giant with the head of a man, the torso of a bull and the wings of a mighty bird. It had five legs! She knew what it was called: *lamassu*.'

'*Lamassu*,' Narin repeats. 'What a funny name. Was Leila scared?'

'She was not, my heart. She knew they were harmless.'

Narin sighs pensively. Her great-great-grandmother Leila sounds like an amazing woman. What a pity she will never get to meet her. The world would have been a much more interesting place if everyone was given a chance to meet their ancestors at least for an hour in their lifetime.

To their right on a slope lies a cemetery – many of its stones broken and crumbling. Although originally arranged in separate sections according to faith, its internal boundaries have been eroded over the course of time, mixing up the tombs of Kurds, Turks, Armenians, Arabs, Yazidis, Arameans, Zoroastrians . . .

Now, turning in that direction, the child asks, 'Grandma, when they finish the dam and water covers everything, the graves will be submerged. Not even Baba Noah could have rescued cemeteries from the flood.'

Not expecting this comment, the old woman's shoulders droop a little. 'Well, the government says they'll relocate all the graves.'

'Do you believe them?'

'Not really.'

'What about my mother's . . .' Narin leaves the question hanging in mid-air.

Grandma pulls the child close and kisses the top of her head. 'I promise, the pupil of my eye. We'll do everything we can to make sure all our family graves are carried somewhere safe and dry.'

Grandma says that, just like a puff of vapour ascends to the skies, only to return as rain, hail or sleet, every Yazidi will come back to earth at least seven times. While it is true that the body is mortal, the soul is a perennial traveller – not unlike a drop of water.

'Don't forget, for us, death is more a hiatus than an end.'

Narin listens, gazing down at the backs of the old woman's hands, as if trying to commit them to memory – weathered and intersected with raised veins. She likes to touch these veins, blue and green, running beneath her grandmother's skin like underground streams. As she traces them with her finger, she asks, 'What about the Englishman?'

'What about him?' says Grandma, her tone suddenly changing. They seldom talk about the foreigner buried in this land.

'Well, he is of a different faith. What will happen to his grave when the dam is built and this area is flooded?'

'It will disappear below the waters,' Grandma says flatly. 'His grave has been neglected for as long as I can remember. No family or friends ever come to visit. Perhaps they aren't even aware that he is here – his people, I mean.'

Narin is surprised at the hardness in Grandmother's voice. She asks, 'Did you ever meet him?'

'No, he died long before I was born. My grandmother Leila had known him.'

'What was he doing here? You never told me.'

'There is not much to tell,' says Grandma. 'Some people are restless like rivers.'

'But there must be a reason why he came.'

'Well, they say he was looking for a poem.'

'A poem?' echoes Narin.

Grandma glances away. 'The Englishman travelled many miles from his home to find the missing verses of an ancient poem and to take what was not his to take. But they say he also left something behind – his heart. So he returned and he died here. He perished of thirst on the banks of the River Tigris. That's all you need to know.'

'Why did he die of thirst when –'

'That's enough chatting for today.' The old woman rises to her feet, too hastily for her age. Her knees creak. 'It's getting late; let's go back now. We don't want people worrying about us.'

Slowly, Narin gets up. This isn't like Grandma, cutting her off mid-conversation.

They walk in silence, their shadows pacing beside them. The grass beneath their feet gives off an ancient smell. Another bulldozer belches a gust of dark smoke into the air. Another pistachio tree sighs before the floodwaters arrive. The earth around Castrum Kefa is a canvas of scars.

By the time they reach the old Yazidi village with its shrinking population, Narin has all but forgotten about the Englishman buried by the River Tigris.

—O—

ARTHUR

By the River Thames, 1853–4

If, as the poets say, the journey of life resembles the march of rivers to the sea, at times meandering aimlessly, at others purposeful and unswerving, the bend in the flow is where the story takes a sudden turn, winding away from its predicted course into a fresh and unexpected direction. Becoming an apprentice at one of England's leading printing and publishing houses is the twist that changes Arthur's destiny forever.

In the beginning they give him random tasks of trivial importance – mopping floors, dusting shelves, removing cobwebs, blocking mouse-holes, scrubbing off the muck that clings to the windowsills . . . The air outside is so dirty that by the time he finishes cleaning the soot off the windowpanes, they are once again coated in a film of grime. His employers watch his every move, noting how he rises to each demand and challenge. Little by little, they allow him to approach the machines. Printing is a dangerous profession, Arthur discovers. The ten-cylinder rotary steam printing press – well-built and sturdy but also clunky – is not easy to operate. If you are not careful, you could lose a limb.

Dangerous, yes, but fascinating! The boy is spellbound as he observes how a single machine can not only transfer letters and images on to blank paper but also make thousands of identical copies. The company produces a variety of books, gazettes and periodicals – including *Punch* magazine, which sells more than forty thousand copies each week by poking fun at the pompous and the powerful – and a steady din reverberates throughout the shop all day long, like dozens of blunt stones grinding against one another.

This place is nothing like school. There are no canings, no beatings, no dunce's caps and no punishment baskets where students are forced to sit suspended from the ceiling. Although some of the workers give the boy a hard time for no reason – once tying his bootlaces together as a prank while he is watching the pages spool out and causing him to fall – there is no one as cruel as his old headmaster was. The job is onerous and the routine exacting, but Arthur does not mind. Determined not to disappoint his bosses, he works tirelessly. The mechanical clatter, though constant and loud enough to rattle the brain, does not trouble him either. Nor does the scent of damp ink, which is so pervasive that when he lies down in bed at night he can still smell it in his hair. His fingers may be permanently stained, his ears full of the thrumming of engines, but he is charged with a strange sense of purpose. For the first time in his life, he feels part of something important.

Bradbury & Evans has recently opened more premises across London to specialize in several fields at once. Arthur is asked to spend some time in each location before it is decided where he will be of most use.

His first assignment is to help to make postage stamps. The boy finds the letterpress with its hard cut-out image charming, but what mesmerizes him is how a tiny piece of paper can hold such artistry, value and meaning. After that, he learns about the technique of embossing and debossing. Creating raised or recessed designs on surfaces, for so long the preserve of the privileged few, has become more affordable of late. These days every self-respecting firm in London is keen to have their own personalized stationery, and demand is growing.

Arthur also delights in lithography. The limestone slabs are heavy, the acid water burns his skin, and the ink is so viscous and greasy that it leaves nasty marks on his clothes, but the outcome is astounding – he is exhilarated by seeing a drawn image come alive, both a reflection of the original and still unique, like a vivid sequel to a fading dream. Thanks to new methods of mass production, people across the country can now decorate their homes with black-and-white prints made from engravings of famous works of art, while books and newspapers can be printed faster and on a vastly larger scale.

'Words are like birds,' says Mr Bradbury. 'When you publish books, you are setting caged birds free. They can go wherever they please. They can fly over the highest walls and across vast distances, settling in the mansions of the gentry, in farmsteads and labourers' cottages alike. You never know whom those words will reach, whose hearts will succumb to their sweet songs.'

Arthur is also taught to engrave steel by cutting designs into metal plates. He discovers the oil sketches of the French painter Eugène Delacroix and studies the prints in *Faust*, by the German writer Goethe, produced a few decades earlier. He admires the engravings of the Spanish painter Francisco Goya, which leave a deep impression on him. He gets to know the craftsmanship of the French sculptor and cartoonist Honoré Daumier, who used his immense talent to satirize the powerful, including the king himself – an act of *lèse-majesté* for which he was sentenced to prison. He pores over the illuminated paintings of William Blake, riveted by their imaginative power and mystical intensity. Biblical scenes and Greek myths appeal to the boy most, whether woodcuts, engravings, etchings, aquatints or simple prints. More and more, he comes to realize that people fall into three camps: those who hardly, if ever, see beauty, even when it strikes them between the eyes; those who recognize it only when it is made apparent to them; and those rare souls who find beauty everywhere they turn, even in the most unexpected places.

The day he receives his first wages, King Arthur of the Sewers and Slums leaves the office with a quiet sense of achievement. As it is a Saturday, most of the shops have stayed open late – the gin halls, the oyster saloons, the tobacconists, the confectioners, the tripe-sellers . . . This being the day working men and women receive their pay, more money changes hands on this one evening than in the whole of the rest of the week.

He walks fast, checking over his shoulder every few steps to see if there is anyone following him. The city, canopied under a fog like smoke from a thousand fires, hides pickpockets and cut-purses. But that is nothing new. The only thing that has changed is that he has something to lose now. How strange that having money makes one feel less safe.

Rounding a corner, he sees a dustman collecting ashes and cinders. He knows that ash can be sold to brickmakers. As for cinders, they are good for fuel. The streets are full of refuse that can be collected and traded for a few pennies, even dead cats, which are soon snapped up by furriers. White cats are especially sought after, earning as much as sixpence each. But Arthur has never been able to bring himself to deal in dead felines.

He notices a hansom cab with a liveried driver, pulled up in front of cordwainer's shop. As he edges past it, he glances inside the open carriage door. A young woman, not that much older than he is, sits with her skirts spread neatly around her, a silk fan resting on the velvet seat, waiting for the sales girls to bring her samples of finely crafted shoes. Their gazes meet briefly. In that moment Arthur sees himself through her eyes, taking in his shabby bowler hat and worn jacket, ill-fitting and mud-spattered. He feels acutely the difference between them, as the wealthy lady looks through and beyond him, as though he were invisible.

If poverty were a place, a hostile landscape into which you were deliberately pushed or accidentally stumbled, it would be an accursed forest – a damp and gloomy wildwood suspended in time. The branches clutch at you, the boles block your way, the brambles draw you in, determined not to let you out. Even when you manage to cut down one obstacle, instantly it is replaced by another. You tear the skin off your hands as you work doggedly to clear a path elsewhere, but the moment you turn your back the trees close in on you again. Poverty saps your will, little by little. But, just now, with coins jingling in his pocket, Arthur feels hopeful. One day, he will get out of this city and travel far, to the ends of the earth if need be, where the margins of water and land seamlessly merge, and people will never know from what abject penury he came.

From a vendor nearby he purchases two meat-filled pies, *coffins* – one for him and his mother to share, the other for his twin brothers. He holds the package close to his chest, the smell tickling his nose like a feather.

In a haberdasher's window on Broad Street, he sees a pair of white kid gloves, lined in deep blue satin and trimmed with lace. He stares at them for a long moment, admiring the exquisite patterns and the delicate leatherwork.

Arthur has heard there is a glove-language spoken on the streets of London. Smoothing them out gently means 'I wish to be with you', while dropping the pair signifies 'I love you.' Turning them inside out is another way of saying, 'I hate you, stay away from me.' As interested as he is in the particulars of this language, what he really wants is to touch the soft hide, feel the subtle texture between his fingers. He wonders what his mother would do if he bought them for her as a present. He can almost see the smile blooming on her face – incredulous, pure. He promises himself he will one day get those gloves for her.

When he arrives home, it is his father who opens the door. 'Did you get paid today, boy?'

Arthur gives a slight nod, wary of what might follow.

'Hand it over, then.'

'I bought a couple of meat pies on the way home.'

'Begging your pardon? Why would you do such a foolish thing?'

Arthur looks away. 'A treat for the little ones.'

'You bloody cretin! What gives you the right to do that?'

The boy shrinks back but his voice doesn't. 'It's my money.'

'Your money, did you say? Bilge! It's me who found you the job. Show some gratitude, you bonehead!'

Arthur flinches at the undisguised malice in his father's voice. How can a man hold so much loathing in his heart for his own flesh and blood? He wonders, and not for the first time, what his father sees when he looks at him. Does he despise him because they are very different? Or is it just the opposite – is it because he cannot bear to recognize himself in his son?

'Speak, boy! Answer me.'

A flush stains Arthur's cheeks. He does not like confrontation. If only he could live without hurting anyone and without ever getting hurt. He turns his face away, but he is too proud to concede defeat.

'I work hard,' he says. 'I slog my guts out every day while you're at some godforsaken den drinking yourself senseless. I owe you nothing. Nothing.'

Swift as an arrow winged from a bow, his father punches him in the stomach. The boy doubles over, but, yanked up by the hair, he is forced to stand, and that is when he receives the second blow, this time to the face.

That evening Arthur lies supine on a mattress that his mother rolls out for him in a corner of the room. He speaks to no one, his head throbbing. To take his mind off the pain, he tries to think of the books in the office. Steadily, he recites the titles, the names of the authors and the dates of publication, in the precise sequence in which they are arranged on the shelves. And, although sleep does not come easily for quite some time, putting things in order soothes him, as it always does. Curling into himself, he manages to get some rest before dawn, finding a crevice of comfort between the dark of the night and the promise of a new day.

On Monday morning, he is the first to arrive at the printer's place. He sits on his haunches at the edge of the pavement as he waits for someone to come to open up the building. Around and above him

London wakes up – the scullery maids, the crossing-sweepers, the fish-curers, the dog-killers, the caddy-butchers, the costermongers, the coffin-makers, the rat-catchers, the long-song-sellers . . . Noise escalates, movements multiply; the city gushes forth, like a fountain that never runs dry. People pass him by without a glance, even though they can see he is weeping. He is just another sad, penurious boy, one of many in this great capital.

In the office, Mr Bradbury is the only person who pays attention to him. 'What happened to your face, son?'

Arthur averts his eyes. 'I had an accident, sir.'

Mr Bradbury's brow crumples. 'Tell that Accident if he goes near you again, we will not be able to pay you. If we see so much as a scratch on you, the money will swiftly drain away. Mr Accident wouldn't want that, would he?'

Arthur stares at his employer, his mouth hanging open. Is it that obvious that it was his father who did this? Swallowing his surprise, he says, 'I cannot tell him that, sir.'

'No, of course you cannot,' concedes Mr Bradbury. 'I am sorry, didn't mean to upset you further. Perhaps I should have a word with your father.'

'I appreciate your consideration, sir, but I would rather you did not.'

'Why do you say that, my boy?'

'Because I like working here. I don't want trouble.'

The man's expression remains grave, though his eyes soften. Whatever he makes of the situation, he does not raise the subject again.

Everything they print, King Arthur of the Sewers and Slums eagerly reads. Each time he is allowed to take a break, he sits on a stool in a corner by himself, nibbling on a crust of bread smeared with lard as he pores over some publication. This is how he finds out from a newspaper article that a second hippopotamus was sent to England by the same Ottoman pasha who gave Obaysch in exchange for English greyhounds. A female this time, named Adhela. She makes the same exhausting journey on board a steamer up the River Nile and arrives in London. The two animals have already met, but they do not seem keen on each other. Everyone is hoping they will grow closer and that there will soon be a calf on the way.

From the *Englishwoman's Domestic Magazine* to the *Boy's Own Magazine* to gentlemen's weeklies and socialist pamphlets, Arthur absorbs each text with unwavering attention. He hungers, almost with an excruciating desire, for knowledge – the only treasure in this life that, though not exactly free, has no price tag attached.

Mr Bradbury, for his part, never fails to observe how willing the boy is to expand his learning in all directions and how far-reaching the tentacles of his curiosity.

'Would you like to take a book with you home every now and then, young Smyth?'

'May I, sir?'

'Well, it is not something we usually allow our workers, but in your case we might make an exception – provided you return them unharmed the very next day. What do you say?'

'Thank you, sir!'

The boy cannot bring himself to tell his employer that reading at home will be nearly impossible, not only because he has chores to do every evening but also because his family can afford neither a candle nor a gas lamp. Instead he tries to make things work.

On nights when the moon is bright and the stars are shining, Arthur sits cross-legged by the windowpane, a blanket wrapped around his thin shoulders, absorbed in infinite worlds beyond his own. As he reads he can taste the words, the tip of his tongue tingling with flavours – buttery, oaky, zingy, spicy, herbaceous . . .

Reading is a feast he can never have enough of, and he tucks into each page with relish. But when the sky is cloaked in layers of smog and there is insufficient light, as there often is, he has to imagine the rest of the book inside his head.

Once again, Mr Bradbury understands more than he says aloud. One morning, he hands the boy two large tallow candles to take home. Arthur is speechless. No one has ever given him a present before.

And thus he starts reading in earnest – not only everything they print but also the volumes stacked in Mr Bradbury's personal library. He devours novels by Charles Dickens, William Thackeray, Jane Austen and Charlotte Brontë; fairy tales and bedtime stories by Hans Christian Andersen; cookbooks extolling the finest ingredients and exotic recipes; philosophical treatises by John Locke, David Hume, John Stuart Mill, Jeremy Bentham and an ingenious Dutchman called Baruch Spinoza; geological accounts by Charles Darwin from his *Voyage of the* Beagle; *The Communist Manifesto* by Karl Marx and Friedrich Engels; poetry by Lord Byron, Elizabeth Barrett Browning, Samuel Taylor Coleridge, Alfred de Musset, Friedrich von Schiller and Omar Khayyám, that Persian polymath, equally adept at both mathematics and verse. He discovers an exiled French writer by the name of Victor Hugo, a debut novelist from Russia called Tolstoy and a giant white sperm whale known as Moby-Dick, and he is enthralled by the memoirs of Frederick Douglass, an escaped American slave and abolitionist.

There is no limit to the range of his inquisitive mind, and he even reads literature written for the fairer sex: *Complete Etiquette for Ladies*, teaching women how to comport themselves; *The Mother's Mistake*, advising new mothers how not to raise children; *The Letters of a Fallen Woman*, on the ills and vices of prostitution; *House and Home and Happiness*, instructing housewives how to excel in domestic skills; *Counsel to Parents on the Moral Education of Their Children in Relation to Sex*, providing exactly what it purports to offer.

Every evening, as the glow of Mr Bradbury's candle throws flickering patterns on the walls and his twin brothers sigh in their sleep, or his mother, under the influence of laudanum, speaks to shadows that only she can see, or his father has his way with her under a thin blanket, the boy turns his back on his family and reads. Whenever he lifts his gaze, the face that looks back at him from the windowpane seems both familiar and somehow deeply changed.

'I've been observing you,' says Mr Bradbury. 'You are diligent and capable, quick to learn, but what I particularly like is your attention to the smallest detail and how considerate you are towards others. Mr Evans and I had a talk; we both would like you to work with us permanently.'

Arthur stares at the man with astonishment and then breaks into a smile – the first in quite a while.

'Tell me, do not be shy, to which area of the business do you think you would be best suited?'

'I'd be equally happy embossing paper or making stamps, sir. But I'd be most obliged if you placed me in book publishing.'

'Why is that?'

'Because with all the others – the stamps or the pretty, shiny paper – you can use them only once or twice, then they are gone, but books, it seems to me, do not end, even when we are finished reading them.'

'That's a brilliant answer, and timely, too. Do you know why?'

Arthur cannot say.

'Well, the world is changing faster than minds can grasp. It's picking up speed like a steam engine. All these smartly turned-out people with their polished boots and affected airs, you look at them and you think they must know everything, educated and cultured as they are, but I'll let you in on a secret: when times are confusing, everybody is a little lost. No one is as inwardly confident as they present themselves to be. Hence the reason we must read, my boy. Books, like paper lanterns, provide us with a light amidst the fog. That is why this is the perfect time to be in the business of publishing!'

A week later Arthur leaves the office with a package tucked under his arm – a title the company has just that day finished printing: *Nineveh and Its Remains*.

What a book it turns out to be! Austen Henry Layard – traveller, collector, diplomat, archaeologist and discoverer of Nineveh – recounts his peregrinations, as numerous as they are adventurous, into Mesopotamia, where he meets Arabs, Chaldeans, Kurds, Turks, Persians, Jews, Palestinians, Armenians, Roma, Mandaeans . . . He writes extensively about a persecuted people called the Yazidis, frequently and erroneously labelled as 'devil-worshippers'. Although wary of them at first, Layard seems to have grown increasingly fond of them over the course of his stay.

Arthur is captivated. Never before has he heard of anyone who has left England to venture into such remote lands. It excites him to think that in that vast region called Mesopotamia there are people so diverse in their customs and manners yet united in the secrets of the land. And deep under the ground somewhere is an ancient city – a legendary capital, once the envy of everyone, now mere dust and bones – with a royal library guarded by the majestic *lamassus*.

Such is the boy's fascination with Nineveh that, inspired by his readings, he starts sketching fantastical figures with lion's claws and bull's hooves. He draws palaces of impossible grandeur, gardens with perfumed fountains and, above all, the Tigris. The river in his imagination is not foul and polluted like the Thames but a limpid paradise, shining bright and blue as its waters glide through canals and over aqueducts.

And all the way through Mr Bradbury encourages him to keep reading, keep imagining. Taking the adolescent under his wing, he becomes a mentor to him, and a good one at that, though the man has a melancholic disposition that can flare up from nowhere from time to time. Yet his support is genuine and continuous. He tells everyone that this unusual boy from a slum tenement who never had the chance of a proper education but undoubtedly possesses an outstanding mind is destined to become one of England's greatest publishers.

These are the happiest days in the life of King Arthur of the Sewers and Slums, although he will come to realize it only once they are gone.

—H

ZALEEKHAH

By the River Thames, 2018

Shortly before dawn Zaleekhah opens the door and steps out on to the deck. Inadvertently, she glances at the next houseboat, half expecting to see her new neighbours lying in wait for her. But everyone is asleep at this hour, including the river. Dark and satiny, the Thames folds itself into pleats, dreaming of its previous lives.

Wrapped in a fleece, trainers on her feet and her hair swept back into a tight ponytail, she crosses the gangway quietly. Running is a need, like breathing. She has done it her whole adult life. Her husband used to joke, in their moments of tenderness, that she wasn't running so much as running away.

What are you trying to escape from, sweetheart?

As she sets off at a steady pace, her nostrils resist the cold air; her hamstrings protest. The first few minutes she always finds the hardest, as if her limbs need persuading. But the human body is good at adapting, more liquid than solid, and soon she is whizzing down the Chelsea Embankment.

She skips over dry leaves, cigarette butts, dog mess, broken glass. The city glides past on both sides, brick after brick, stucco after stucco, concrete after concrete, still beautiful. A double-decker bus coasts by, withdrawn faces at its windows. It is the hour of the day when different lives overlap, unlikely stories intersect – early risers and late nightclubbers, people with little in common, cross paths.

Zaleekhah is not the only one out running at this hour. A tall, hefty man is rapidly approaching from the opposite direction. As he nears, noisily gulping air, rings of sweat on his shirt, he passes uncomfortably close. He does not look at her. It does not occur to him that he might frighten her with his proximity, having never had cause to feel such fear himself.

A few metres ahead, Zaleekhah notices an elderly man carrying a bucket and a spade, in search of mitten crabs. There are many along the Chelsea shore, she knows, their numbers having swelled in the last decades. Digging their burrows into the mud, they block water outlets, threaten native species, cause erosion and damage riverbanks, increasing London's flood risk. She and her colleagues have examined dozens of shore and mitten crabs living in the Thames. In every single crustacean they inspected they encountered harmful plastics, their stomachs and intestines clogged with pollutants. More than a few times Zaleekhah found traces of sanitary pads in their alimentary canals. When crabs consume contaminants, they cannot easily flush them out of their system and hence these will be passed up the food chain. No one can tell how many die every year as a consequence of their poisonous diet. They are not the only marine species suffering. Just like dolphins in other parts of the world retain the residues of long-banned chemicals, the eels of the Thames are receptacles for high concentrations of coffee and cocaine.

The Thames is a zombie. The river that returned from the dead. Once declared no longer capable of sustaining life, a watery corpse decomposing in its bed, today it is home to more than 125 species of fish and no fewer than 400 invertebrates, as well as seahorses, seals and even sharks. Now considered one of the most handsome and cleanest natural streams in the world, it nevertheless continues to ingest the waste of a city of millions.

In the last ten years, her team has partnered with institutions in various countries. Covering a vast area from the Arctic to the Mediterranean and the sub-Sahara, they observed the way water responds to physical pressures, increases in temperature and other stress factors, all of which have a detrimental impact on food chains and trophic levels. Conducting joint experiments, they examined both freshwater and saltwater ecosystems – geothermally heated Icelandic streams, groundwater extracted from springs and boreholes in Italy, the canals and dykes of the Netherlands, farmland salinization in Bangladesh, meltwater lakes in Siberia . . . Cases that, though seemingly unrelated, were profoundly connected. The researchers came from a range of disciplines but shared a single understanding: climate crisis is essentially a water crisis.

It always surprises Zaleekhah how little thought and even less research humanity has devoted to water – the oldest and most common substance ever known. Older than the earth. Older than the sun. And millions of years older than the solar system itself. Given all the advances in technology, people assume that science understands water, but, in truth, only a small number of scientists specialize in the field and much remains to be discovered. Water is still the biggest mystery. Studying how it responds to growing threats – overpopulation, chemical pollution, habitat alteration, acidification and biodiversity loss – has brought Zaleekhah to the conclusion that every drop of rain that emerges through the aquatic cycle is, in its own way, a tiny survivor. If she'd had a streak of spirituality, she would have called it *sacred*.

Breathing deeply, the breeze at her back, Zaleekhah streaks along the winding path by the Thames. She moves effortlessly for a while, the ground pleasantly resilient under her feet. She does not like to listen to music when she is out running, only the rhythm of her heart against her ribs, and the sounds of the city that change with the season – hushed in winter, exuberant at this time of year. She can feel her leg muscles straining but keeps going.

A sharp pain stabs her in the lower abdomen, then mercifully eases, only to return in waves. Her appendix complains but instead of slowing down she speeds up, determined to bear down on the discomfort for as long as she can. Ahead of her, the embankment stretches out. She can feel sweat dampening her shirt as she drives herself harder, panting. Her mind numbs, arriving at an emptiness that allows her to hold every fear and sadness without hurting. In that liminal state in which the border between the present and the past disappears, memories, no longer contained by gravity, float like feathers in the air around and above her. She remembers things she wanted to believe she had forgotten. Before she knows it, the feathers are smothering her, covering her mouth, blocking her nostrils. She gulps air, chest heaving. She knows that if she does not run fast enough, she will drown in her past.

Zaleekhah closes her eyes. Inside the darkness behind her eyelids, she is seven years old again. A summer's afternoon in Turkey, the last light of the day brushing the tops of the trees. Cicadas buzz in the bushes, the hypnotic sound mixing with the tramp of hiking boots.

It's hot, very hot. On both sides of the dusty trail are rock formations in fascinating colours and stripes, their shapes so unusual they could have been sculpted by invisible hands. Someone is walking ahead, carrying a large backpack. Her father. Every now and then he glances back over his shoulder. When he smiles, a dimple appears in his cheek. Behind him is her mother, a burnt-orange bandana wound round her head. The two of them move in tandem, their shadows blend, like water molecules clinging to each other. Up ahead clouds of flies rise and fall along the track, as though above a corpse.

Zaleekhah stops, gasping. As soon as she opens her eyes, she winces, shocked to discover she is merely centimetres away from the spot where the embankment peters out. Another few seconds and she would have crashed into the wall.

After that she runs more slowly, watchfully. She will not allow her mind to go there again. She must compose herself ahead of the dinner at her uncle's house, given that she could not come up with an excuse to turn down the invite.

'Normal,' she mutters to herself, without realizing she is speaking out loud. 'Just be normal.'

At seven o'clock Zaleekhah arrives at Uncle Malek's address in The Boltons – a well-preserved part of South Kensington and one of the richest areas of London. The residents of this exclusive enclave include old-money British families and several of the wealthiest émigrés from the Middle East, Asia and Russia. Some pay extra tax every year to keep their ownership of these often-empty homes secret.

Overlooking an oval communal garden with an Anglican church at its centre, Uncle's house is a five-storey, white-stucco-fronted mansion of handsome proportions. Behind an ivory balustraded wall lies a front garden with a neatly trimmed hedge, flowering bushes and a weeping Japanese cherry tree; steps of Portland stone lead up to an imposing portico flanked by Tuscan columns supporting a first-floor balcony. With ten bedrooms, nine bathrooms, a gym, sauna, cinema, indoor pool and large south-facing garden, Uncle's house is the epitome of opulence. Zaleekhah knows every square inch of the property, as this is where she lived after her parents died.

She punches the code into the keypad and waits for the double gates to open. The scent of mimosas and the smell of freshly mown grass fill the air as she strides into the manicured garden. An Andalusian fountain tinkles in one corner, commissioned from an artisan in Spain, one of the last practitioners of a dying craft. Under the artful floodlights, the place looks like it has been designed to be photographed for lifestyle magazines – polished and perfect.

A feeling of unease creeps into her belly. During the years she spent here, Zaleekhah has always felt out of step with her surroundings, a guilty discomfort following her wherever she went, as though she were leaving muddy footprints on expensive carpet. An old awkwardness that she thought she had long outgrown hits her with surprising speed. Her pulse quickens, and for a moment she almost turns back and leaves. The last time she felt this nervous before having a conversation with Uncle was when she was eighteen and about to move to a student hall of residence in East London. It had taken her months to make up her mind and even longer to work out how to break the news that, instead of studying international economics and finance, as he had hoped, she would be studying for a degree in Environmental Sciences.

'Science, really, darling? I mean it's an admirable choice, but is there a future in it?'

The younger Zaleekhah did not know if there was a future in science, especially if 'future' meant money. All she knew was that she loved the vastness of the field, its infinite possibilities, the discoveries waiting to be made. Starting with Conservation Biology, she later went on to switch to Aquatic Resource Management and Hydrogeology. Despite the years that have passed, she senses that her choice of profession never ceases to bewilder Uncle, though he has done his best to hide his disappointment.

Time is circles within circles. It neither dies nor declines but whirls in epicycles. Like a wheel that continues to spin even after its power is turned off, family conflicts live on long after the individual members have passed away. Although he would never put it in so many words, Zaleekhah senses that, deep within, Uncle worries she will turn out to be just like her mother – a small-town teacher married to another small-town teacher on the outskirts of Manchester, indifferent to the trappings of wealth and status, intensely critical of the world and its inequalities but content with her own humble place in the universe.

Uncle often says that, while others can decide on a simple and unassuming life, those who come from troubled regions or difficult backgrounds do not have that luxury. For every displaced person understands that uncertainty is not tangential to human existence but the very essence of it. Since one can never be sure what tomorrow will bring, one cannot trust Dame Fortuna – the goddess of destiny and luck – even when she seems to favour you for once. One needs to always be prepared for a crisis, calamity or sudden exodus. Being an outsider is all about survival, and no one survives by being unambitious; no one gets ahead by holding back. Immigrants don't die of existential fatigue or nihilistic boredom; they die from working too hard.

Reaching the house now, Zaleekhah rings the bell. The door opens instantly and the family's long-standing butler appears.

'Zaleekhah! How wonderful to see you! You've been neglecting us.'

'It's wonderful to see you too, Kareem. Is this a bad time?'

'For you there is never a bad time.' He takes her jacket and handbag – swiftly evaluating and dismissing both as non-designer items.

'Are they at home – Uncle and Aunt?' asks Zaleekhah, and immediately finds her own question absurd. They have invited her over for dinner – where else would they be?

But Kareem looks unfazed. 'Lord Malek is upstairs in his study, and Lady Malek is getting ready. She'll be downstairs shortly.'

'I'll go check on Uncle, then.'

Slowly, Zaleekhah walks down the black-and-white chequerboard marble hallway, her shoes squeaking against the glossy floor as though in protest. There is a buzzing in her ears, throbbing in a low pulse, a frequency only she can hear. Gripping the banister tightly, she makes her way up the curved staircase. A Chinese reverse-glass painted mirror is mounted right across from the entrance – women in silk robes drawing water from a well and armoured warriors wielding their swords. Portraits of illustrious figures glare down at her from their elaborate frames along the wood-panelled walls. Some pose with horses, others with hounds, and one has a blindfolded falcon perched on his shoulder. They are not ancestors. None of these people are related to the Malek family in any way. Uncle purchased them simply because he liked the look of them – and probably because he thinks they confer on him a kind of sophisticated respectability. He is also fond of bird paintings, especially by the Dutch artist Melchior d'Hondecoeter. A keen buyer of Japanese woodblock prints and *netsuke* – those exquisitely fashioned ivory or wooden toggles – which he adores for their delicate and witty carving. Uncle collects art and antiquities from all around the world. 'Under this roof,' he likes to say, 'East meets West, and they never wish to separate again.'

Upstairs, Zaleekhah stops in front of the first door on the left. Her childhood bedroom. The one opposite belongs to Helen – Aunt and Uncle's only child. The two girls – merely ten months apart – grew up together in this house. They used to be very close back then, sharing secrets, exchanging clothes and always covering for each other. At night it was their habit to keep their doors open, so they could talk to each other as they drifted off to sleep. When people mistook them for siblings, they would never correct them. That was how they once saw themselves: not as cousins, not as friends, but as sisters.

After Zaleekhah moved out to go to university, something shifted. Not a sudden falling out but a gradual estrangement so subtle and slow as to be almost imperceptible. They still spoke regularly on the phone, and grabbed a coffee every so often, but it was never the same. And when Helen got married and had three children in quick succession, the differences in their lives became too great to ignore. The mutual affection was still there, but there was just never enough time together. Zaleekhah still feels the loss of that sisterhood like a missing limb.

Pushing open the door, she sidles into her old room. Every item inside is both familiar and foreign: the four-poster bed with its peach-pink headboard, the bookcase where she would display her school certificates and incense sticks, the Persian rug where she would sit perusing science magazines . . . the place has been left largely untouched, although the mess is gone. On good days, she finds it moving that her childhood existence has been so carefully preserved, as if time's flow has ceased and she could always pick up where she left off. But, on gloomier days, she wonders whether her aunt and uncle keep her room ready for her inevitable return, defeated by the outside world.

She sits on the edge of the bed. The room is strangely odourless, thoroughly sanitized, as if after an accident. A Barbie lolls back on a shelf, one hand raised in a plastic salutation. It has a shiny tiara, silver gown and straight, golden blonde tresses that cannot have been more different from her own unruly, dark brown curls. When she was a girl, Zaleekhah owned many of these dolls, despite showing barely any interest in them. It was Helen who was fond of them, but, since Uncle and Aunt were scrupulous about treating both children in identical fashion, each present was always duplicated. Yet, whereas Helen's Barbies were fastidiously combed and dressed, and prominently displayed, Zaleekhah's remained half hidden under the bed or forgotten in a shoe box, resentful of the mistreatment they received.

As she rises to her feet, her eyes alight on a shelf where a Noah's Ark toy set languishes. Animals grouped in pairs wait patiently on the jetty, while Noah gazes down at them from the deck, his expression grim as if the floodwaters are already rising.

Uncle Malek's study is at the end of the hallway, the door slightly ajar. Zaleekhah knocks and waits. Just as she is about to knock again, she hears the sound of a soft snore coming from inside.

Quietly, she tiptoes in. When she was a child, this room was her favourite place in the entire house. A veritable cabinet of curiosities, the scent of enticing objects always emanated from it – leather-bound books, floating candles in crystal bowls, trays of chocolate truffles and marzipan sweets, antique tobacco pipes, diffusers in porcelain holders . . . Glancing around now, she takes in the vintage magnifying glasses, the silver wick-snuffers, the framed maps on the walls, the revolving globes, the roses arranged neatly in ceramic vases. Her fingers trace the smooth surface of a glass paperweight with a fossilized eel encased inside. Petrified remains, frozen in time.

Uncle has fallen asleep in an armchair, his head tilted back and his reading glasses halfway down his nose. A faint wheeze escapes regularly from his mouth, his lips quivering with each shallow breath. On his lap is an open book, slowly sliding from his grasp. Careful not to make any noise, Zaleekhah reaches to rescue it. She turns it around and checks the title: *Nineveh and Its Remains*.

There is an image on the cover. A massive *lamassu* – man, bull and bird – is being heaved out of a trench by Arab workers tugging on ropes, while a man in European dress stands high up on a stone platform directing their efforts. Zaleekhah does not like the image. She does not like that the Westerner is set above the locals, or that the stone creature is being woken from its slumber. Even so, intrigued, she opens the book. It is an old edition. A second printing, published in 1854 in London by a company called Bradbury & Evans.

She riffles through the pages until her gaze lands on a line: *It is to be regretted that proper steps have not been taken for the transport to England of the sculptures discovered at Nineveh . . . several of the most valuable specimens are missing . . . once destroyed, they can never be restored, and it must be remembered that they are almost the only remains of a great city and of a great nation.*

'Oh, hello, darling, I didn't hear you come in!'

Startled, Zaleekhah shuts the book with a clap. 'I'm sorry, Uncle. Did I wake you?'

'Nonsense, I wasn't sleeping, I was just resting my eyes. When did you get here? I didn't hear the bell.' Uncle Malek pushes his glasses back up and smiles. 'Are you really moving into a houseboat, my dear? Tell me it was a moment of madness and you've forgotten it already.'

Zaleekhah leaves the book on a coffee table. As she lifts her eyes, she meets her uncle's inquisitive gaze. She says, softly, 'It's a nice boat.'

'You're too young to be going through a mid-life crisis. You know that, don't you?'

'I'm almost thirty-one.'

'At thirty-one you're barely an adult! Thirty-one still means scraped knees and scuffed elbows and a snotty nose. Besides, even when you are sixty, you'll always be that little girl with scruffy hair to me.'

Zaleekhah inhales, feeling her chest caving in. She was seven years old when her parents died. She remembers the summer her uncle, who became her sole guardian, welcomed her into his family home – the summer she kept scratching her legs, searching for invisible mosquito bites, drawing blood; and she recalls one morning in front of the bathroom mirror, when she hacked off her braids so unevenly that her scalp showed in places and it took months for her hair to grow back. She was loved, supported and given every opportunity to advance herself in this house. If she had been capable of belonging anywhere, it would have been here. Yet she left this sanctuary as soon as she turned eighteen, unable to settle anywhere for long.

'Please don't worry about me,' Zaleekhah says, her own voice sounding distant in her ears.

Uncle heaves a sigh. 'So how big is this houseboat?'

'Big enough for me.'

'I don't get it.' Uncle throws up his hands. 'Is this some kind of delayed rebellion? Your solo Arab Spring? Because, I hate to break it to you, but you're not that young any more.'

'A minute ago you were telling me I'm not that old,' says Zaleekhah, offering a smile – a lame attempt to lighten the conversation.

'Exactly. You're at that stage when you're too old to rebel, too young to admit defeat.'

A chill runs down her spine, as if she has been caught out. Words sting like the tips of needles. There is a thickness in her throat she cannot swallow away.

Unawares, Uncle continues with his usual elan. 'Look, this probably is the last thing you want to hear, but in every marriage there are two sides to the story – his and hers. They never match up. My recipe for matrimonial bliss? Voluntary blindness! Cover your eyes. Pull down a sleep mask. Voluntary deafness! Use ear plugs. She said that? I didn't hear! She did that? I didn't see! Peace of mind. Unless, of course, he's done something serious and you're not telling me.'

It takes Zaleekhah a few seconds to realize what he is talking about. 'Did he hit me, do you mean? No, nothing like that!'

'Thank God . . . and, umm, I don't mean to pry, but is there another woman?'

'Oh, no! I mean, not that I know of.'

'Good. If that's not the problem either, why on earth can't you work it out? I hate to see your marriage fail.'

She wants to tell him that she does not necessarily view the breakdown of her marriage as a failure. She has loved, and been loved. What more could one want? It would be naive to assume that love can go on forever – sooner or later, it is bound to wither. She wishes to explain this viewpoint, which sounds wise in her head, and, if not wise, at least sensible, but she struggles to put it into words and what comes out of her mouth is completely different.

'I just don't understand why we can't fail like everyone else.'

'Because we can't,' Uncle says briskly. 'We keep our scars to ourselves. We don't show them to anyone – even to our nearest and dearest.'

'And why is that?' Zaleekhah insists – something she rarely does.

Uncle Malek gives her one of his long, assessing looks. 'Why trouble them with things they cannot comprehend?'

A stab of sadness passes through Zaleekhah. It never occurred to her before how lonely her uncle might have felt in his own marriage from time to time. She knows that he adores his daughter, and she has no doubt that, despite all his grumbling, he is devoted to his wife. But something essential separates him from them.

Uncle is from elsewhere. Born in another culture, shaped by a different river. He may have become British, and turned his life into a success story, but there is something about him that eludes even those closest to him.

The only son of an established Levantine family from the Middle East, Uncle Malek came to England as a boy. In no other part of the world has he grown roots as strong. He has made English friends and English business partners; he married an Englishwoman; he speaks English every day and dreams in English at night; he supports an English football team with a passion bordering on obsession; he earns English money and donates to English charities; he is a member of several English gentlemen's clubs and has been honoured by the Queen; he has even taken English seaside holidays – and yet he is, and always will be, a foreigner. It is still there, his otherness, under the varnished image, like a splinter that cannot be prised from beneath his flesh.

'You must stop worrying about me,' says Zaleekhah. 'You've done so much for me already, I'm forever grateful.'

Uncle looks up at her over the rim of his glasses. His smile, when it arrives, doesn't quite reach his eyes. 'Why're you speaking like that, my dear? You're not planning to sail away on that boat, I hope. Tell me, is it even furnished?'

'It has a few things,' says Zaleekhah.

'Well, you must buy furniture – and a burglar alarm!'

'It's a safe place.'

'Is anywhere in London safe any more?' Uncle gestures towards the cabinet. 'Do you mind opening the first drawer for me?'

Zaleekhah does as he asks. Inside there is an elegant silver paper knife and an envelope in Uncle's monogrammed stationery. She does not need to break its seal to know that it contains a cheque.

'Take that, my dear.'

'I really don't need it – thank you, though.'

If Uncle Malek is disappointed, he does not show it. His voice stays bright as he tries, one more time. 'Consider it a house . . . a houseboat gift.'

Gently, Zaleekhah closes the drawer, leaving the envelope untouched. Her gaze falls on the book she put on the coffee table.

'What's this you're reading?'

'Oh that . . . I'm done with it.' Uncle's expression hardens. 'Just some research for an approaching auction. I might be bidding. Something exceptional has come up – an item from Nineveh.'

'I don't remember you ever buying from Iraq before.'

'Well, this one is special. A tablet from Ashurbanipal's library, thousands of years old.' Uncle lifts his head, looking out of the window. 'It's blue. Lapis lazuli. An extraordinary traveller through time.'

Zaleekhah waits for him to explain more, and, when he doesn't, she says, 'I broke the little *lamassu* you gave me.'

'You broke a protective spirit? That's not good. We must get you a new one.'

'I think I can glue it back together.'

'Oh, yes, that's a thing, isn't it?' says Uncle. 'Japanese *kintsugi* – displaying flaws and revealing failures for everyone to see. Very noble – except I'm not a fan.'

This, Zaleekhah knows, has always been the way with her uncle. He once described himself as an 'upholsterer of imperfections' – covering stains, padding hard surfaces, softening edges, hiding cracks and holes. Almost as if every mistake were correctable, nearly every loss replaceable, and what remained rough, raw or ruptured should never be seen by others.

Uncle picks up *Nineveh and Its Remains*. Instead of putting it back on the bookshelf, he deposits it in the top drawer, next to the envelope.

'Now I hope you're hungry. Your aunt made poached salmon *mousseline* in your honour or was it *messaline* – a recipe from the *Titanic*. It's a fad, apparently, re-creating famous last meals. If she keeps going like this, one of these meals will be my last.'

'But you hate fish,' says Zaleekhah with a pensive smile.

'Exactly! Thank you for noticing – and you're the only one. The last time I enjoyed eating anything with fins and gills I was a boy. My father would take me to these restaurants by the River Tigris. Oh, the *masgouf* – the grilled carp. Now that was divine, believe me. But ever since I've loathed limbless water creatures – except your aunt refuses to accept that. She thinks that if she steams and souses and douses it in some sauce with a French name I can't even pronounce I won't realize what I'm eating.'

Zaleekhah falls silent. What she knows about her uncle's past she has gleaned from oblique comments and overheard conversations, picking up crumbs of information dropped inadvertently over the years. It is at moments like these that it dawns on her how little she has actually managed to learn.

The light in the room shifts then as Uncle steps in front of a brass table lamp – Victorian and newly reconditioned, with a cranberry shade of stained glass shaped like an inverted tulip. When he turns around, his face seems more sharply drawn.

'Anyway, if you don't like what's on your plate,' Uncle says, 'just toe the line – that's what I always do. I've learnt not to upset your aunt.'

With that, Uncle Malek opens the door and ushers Zaleekhah into the corridor and down the stairs.

—O—

ARTHUR

By the River Thames, 1854

The year Arthur turns fourteen he gets to see the Great Exhibition of the Works of Industry of All Nations. The glass-and-iron behemoth, known to all as the Crystal Palace, was first opened in 1851 in Hyde Park by Queen Victoria, accompanied by Prince Albert and a phalanx of royals, diplomats and politicians. Since then it has been visited by more than six million people. Although desperate to witness this wonder that everyone has been raving about, the boy was not able to afford the entrance fee until now.

Recently the entire exhibition has been taken down and rebuilt in Sydenham Hill, overlooking London from the south. The entrance fee has been reduced, at first from a pound to five shillings, and then to one shilling. Once the rich have satisfied their curiosity and enjoyed the spectacle, and the middle classes have had their chance as well, it is finally time for the poor to be admitted. Today, at long last, Arthur's turn has come.

On a warm day in early summer the boy begins his journey south. The cerulean sky glows, and the sun casts intricate dappled shadows on the pavements. Arthur clutches his shilling, worried that a pick-purse might snatch it from him. As he approaches his destination, a convoy of carriages passes by in an unbroken stream, the clatter of wheels and hooves ceaseless. All around him, people scurry in the same direction, leaving a trail of chatter behind them.

Arthur does not like crowds, and, now that he finds himself in the midst of one, his palms sweat and his breathing becomes shallow. To quell his racing heart, he starts multiplying twelves in his head. At school he was taught to write down multiplication sums on a board from right to left, and only up to two digits each time, but he has his own method, calculating from left to right. This way, he can easily reach higher amounts. If he multiplies fast enough, numbers spin before his eyes, emitting glints of light, like sparks from a grindstone.

Finally, amidst the plane trees, he catches sight of the Crystal Palace. Massive and majestic – a towering mass of plate glass, cast iron and bold ambition. On both sides of the building are fountains that soar to a height of two hundred feet. The boy looks up, squinting, his jaw slack. Never in his life has he thought such a thing possible. Water flowing against gravity! Water so abundant it takes on every shape and colour, and so effortless that it seems to grow out of the earth like mighty plants.

Before he can collect his thoughts, Arthur is shoved towards the main entrance along with hundreds of others. It takes him a while to wriggle through the queue, pay the fee and pass the turnstiles. With every step he can hear a vibrating din, ever-increasing, like the flutter of a thousand wings steadily getting closer. His sense of bafflement grows as he scans the colossal space. It is filled to the gills – every gallery and passageway swarms with visitors. Dazed, Arthur surveys this vast array of men, women and children. Do all these people live in the same city as he does, looking at the same patch of sky every morning?

Inside, the building is spectacular. Displayed on two massive floors, a hundred thousand exhibits are spread beneath this high glazed canopy; a cornucopia of products, crafts and machines are showcased from Britain and all around the world – a mishmash of imperial pomp, national pride, colonial rapacity, scientific achievement, technological progress and cultural discovery. The eclectic nature of the enterprise makes it appealing to individuals who otherwise have little in common. There is something here for everyone – from the devout believer to the atheist, the reactionary to the liberal, the utilitarian to the freethinker.

'Ladies and gentlemen, come get a map! Don't lose your way!' cries a salesman.

'Is it free?' asks Arthur, clenching the hand where the shilling had nestled until a moment ago.

'Free?' The man repeats the word as if it is new to him. 'What are you, a halfwit? Everything worth having has a price, lad.'

Blushing up to his temples, Arthur walks away. Without a map to consult, he will have to follow his instincts. Ahead of him, as though emerging from a dream, materializes a crystal fountain. It glistens bewitchingly in front of tall elm trees, and its sparkling water, perfumed with eau de cologne, gives off a heady scent.

A kind of urgent power in his limbs, the boy stalks down the aisles. To his left and right appear pavilions representing places he has met only in books: China, India, Spain, France, Portugal, German Zollverein, Russia, Sweden, Canada, United States of America, the Ottoman Empire . . . In each is displayed a plenitude of objects – spices, minerals, textiles, jewellery, pistols, tapestries, agricultural products, surgical tools and stuffed animals with eyes that gleam like marbles . . . A coruscating kaleidoscope of colours and patterns. There is a foldable piano with a collapsible keyboard, a machine that produces the brand-new uniform cigarettes and a steam-hammer that can gently crack an egg. There are artificial teeth fashioned from hippopotamus tusks.

In the American display, draped with stars and stripes, are portraits of presidents, farming implements, cotton-gin machines from Connecticut, soap from Philadelphia, sailcloth from New York and a range of firearms. But the centrepiece is a sculpture of extraordinary beauty and finesse called *The Greek Slave*. She stands naked and chained on a rotating pedestal beneath a canopy of red velvet, a young woman sold into captivity by the Ottomans. As Arthur approaches, he notices people gathered around the statue, most of them observing it with open admiration, while some others – a group of abolitionists – are holding up signs and pro-testing. One man waves a copy of *Punch* magazine, pointing to a scathing comment piece recently published, asking why a white woman from another country was chosen to depict the horrors of slavery and not a Black woman from Virginia.

In the Tunisian quarter, Arthur sees skins of leopards and lions; and in the Persian section, he touches rugs so soft he suspects they must have been woven by angels. In the India Gallery, he admires fine mats, silks and tiles. There are specimens of ostrich feathers, elephants' tusks, ox horns, tortoise shells . . . He joins the throng of people admiring the Koh-i-Noor diamond, and then the Daria-i-Noor, with its pale pink colour. He gawps at a massive vase from Sweden, a suit of Cossack armour, a malachite urn from Russia, a ceramic jar from Portugal, optical instruments from France and elaborate machinery from the Zollverein. He marvels at a carved ivory chair, presented to Queen Victoria; a Singer sewing machine whose needle does the stitching for you; a bed that sets the sleeper upright when it is time to wake up; a hydraulic press that enables one man to move thousands of pounds of iron; and he blushes at the sight of marble statues with their genitals dangling close to eye level.

In every hall, he is greeted by the latest inventions and the newest technology – locomotives, telegraphs, cameras, air pumps, mechanical toys, hydraulic jacks, horticultural machinery; tele-scopes that pull the Milky Way into your lap and microscopes that reveal organisms invisible to the eye. Arthur examines himself in the gilded mirrors that line the pavilion – a skinny adolescent looks back at him, painfully shy.

He cannot exactly say what thrills him more – being in the pres-ence of so many exquisite objects under one roof or finding himself amongst them. For a boy who has known nothing but destitu-tion from the day he was born, the experience is exhilarating and unsettling in equal measure. Something wells up in his chest – a new desire. The world is immense, and the life he has tasted but a mere speck in the spectrum of possibilities and destinies available to human beings. Beyond the shores of the River Thames, there are other capitals, old and modern, each with its own tempests and tides, meandering, flowing. He is seized, and not for the first time, by an urge to travel far and wide, a frightening impulse for an introvert like him. He longs to see distant kingdoms and provinces whose tongues are foreign and customs different, not just to read about them in books.

In the next section, there are tea rooms where visitors can enjoy refreshments and cakes, but the boy steers clear, unable to pay for such indulgences. Nor can he afford to use the new-fangled public toilets, however curious he is to see one. Each visit costs a penny.

In a showroom bursting with light, he finds globe lanterns, gilt candelabra and pendants dripping with crystal lustres. He stares for a long while at a brass lamp with a cranberry-coloured stained-glass shade that curves gracefully downward like the petals of an upended tulip. The aura it radiates is so soft that entering its bounds feels like sliding into a warm bath.

Arthur gapes at a chandelier adorned with white lilies and green leaves that extend tendrils of such fragility that the slightest breath of wind could break them. How lucky must be the man who could afford to have all these pretty things in his home, turning night to day. If he had one such lamp or chandelier, he would read from dusk till dawn and never go to sleep.

Towards the end of the afternoon, desperate to relieve himself and no longer able to tolerate the crowd, Arthur threads his way through a final anteroom, anxiously looking for the nearest exit. That is when he arrives at an area bordered by carved stone blocks. He stops in his tracks. There before him, towering over everything and everyone, their eyes piercing like flaming arrows, are the *lamassus*. They must be on loan from the British Museum. A host of visitors is clustered around them, murmuring in hushed tones, as if fearful that they might wake the giants from Mesopotamia.

A stone arch curves between the two statues, and on it is a sign that reads:

The Nineveh Court
Come and marvel at the infamous biblical city of
sin, avarice and annihilation!

Arthur's eyes turn into grey-blue pools of sadness. Sin, avarice and annihilation are not what he sees when he looks at these hybrid creatures. They are haunting and woeful and unimaginably old but also calm and peaceful, as if nothing can surprise them any more.

Ignoring the sign's censorious tone, the boy approaches one of the *lamassus*. He studies the exquisite craftsmanship that has gone into its feathered wings, its long, curly beard, its cloven feet, the legs skilfully carved to show muscles and veins. He notices the front right hoof is scarred with a dark brown mark, as if it has been singed in a blaze. He touches the patch gently, wondering about its origin. What terrible inferno could have discoloured the alabaster like this? Has it survived a fire in Ashurbanipal's palace – but, if so, how did the rest of it remain unscathed?

Arthur glances left and right, making sure no one is paying attention to him. He whispers: 'What happened to you? Did someone hurt you?'

The boy waits. The statue waits.

'One day, I shall visit the place you come from. They say you guarded a royal library and it was built on the grandest scale. That must have been fascinating! Did you meet King Ashurbanipal? Was he nice?'

The boy waits. The statue waits.

'I must go now,' says Arthur, sighing. 'I know you are a protective spirit. I beseech you, please keep my mother and my little brothers safe when I make my way to Nineveh.'

As he moves away from the *lamassu*, a tiny sphere next to the colossal statue, Arthur lifts his head to look at it one more time. The hair on the nape of his neck stands up. It is the strangest feeling, but he cannot help it. In that very moment, he could swear the creature is returning his gaze.

The next day, after everyone has headed home, only the boy and Mr Bradbury are left in the office. The man has been unusually quiet all afternoon and there are dark crescents under his eyes.

'Young Smyth, come over and take a peek at this.'

It is a print of the Thames, reproduced from an original water-colour made a century ago. But the river in the picture looks nothing like it does now. It is bright azure, joyful, clean. There are ships nosed up to a dock in the background, a sense of calm.

'You like it?'

'Beautiful,' says Arthur. 'It's hard to believe it's the same river.'

'Imagine.' Mr Bradbury sighs. 'All too often, we humans destroy nature and call it progress.'

The boy is startled by the sadness in his employer's voice. But whatever melancholy has descended upon the man, he does not wish to discuss it. Instead he says, with a thin smile, 'You have learnt so much in so little time. It feels like only yesterday that you arrived here with your father and surprised us with the power of your memory. You've been an excellent apprentice – honest, assiduous, reliable. You will go on to achieve amazing things in life.'

Not knowing how to respond to such gratifying remarks, Arthur blushes. 'Thank you, sir.'

'I have always set great store by you,' says Mr Bradbury, his gaze filled with compassion. 'Tell me, did you enjoy the Great Exhibition?'

Arthur's face brightens. 'Oh, it was fabulous! I cannot stop thinking about it. I saw a *lamassu* in the Nineveh section. I even touched its hoof!'

'Nineveh,' repeats the man dreamily. 'Yes, of course, I had forgotten your fascination with ancient civilizations. You must also visit the British Museum and see the tablets.'

The only tablets Arthur knows of are slate pieces that school pupils write on with chalk. He senses his employer must be referring to something very different, and if it has anything to do with Nineveh he is more than happy to find out. There is, however, a hurdle he cannot reveal. He needs to save up money to buy a decent jacket first. He fears they will not allow him to enter the grand museum in his threadbare garb.

As if he senses the boy's thoughts, Mr Bradbury asks, 'Are you able to keep some of your wages?'

Arthur lowers his gaze. There is no point in saying that his father pockets whatever he earns, and on those rare occasions he can spare a shilling or two for his mother he feels lucky, retaining nothing for himself.

'You are a good boy,' says Mr Bradbury. He extracts two half-crowns from his pocket and places them on the table. 'Will you oblige me, son? Buy yourself something. A little treat from me.'

'Oh, sir, you are most generous, but I could not possibly accept.'

'I insist, get something for yourself. When is your birthday, do you know?'

Arthur has heard that some families have a queer custom these days, celebrating their children's natal day by eating cakes and drinking cordials, though he neither understands why nor knows of anyone who follows this practice.

'I was born in wintertime, sir. It was snowing. I remember snowflakes dancing around in the air and one of them falling on my tongue.'

The man draws in a breath, nodding his head. He has long ceased to be surprised by Arthur's oddities.

'Wintertime, eh? Still, let's imagine it *is* your birthday, shall we? Now run along and find yourself a present.'

King Arthur of the Sewers and Slums leaves the office soon after. But he does not rush to see if there are any shops still open. Instead he decides to save the money until he can think of the perfect gift to buy. Despite his excitement, there is a nagging feeling in his heart, and for a moment he almost stops and turns back. But he keeps walking. For as long as he lives, he will rue this decision. He will regret not having stayed with his employer to help the only man in this world who had ever looked out for him, instead of walking out into the damp night.

The following morning, picking up the iron key from under a stone by the entrance, Arthur unlocks the door. By now he is used to being the first to arrive in the mornings, and they trust him enough to open the office.

No sooner has he walked in than he is assailed by a smell – putrid and pungent, as if the damp of the river has seeped through the walls overnight. Drawings and engravings are strewn all over the floor. A chair has been knocked over, and beside that lies a bronze candelabra with candles burned down to nubs, lying in a puddle of wax. His first thought is they have been burgled, but a cursory scan reveals that nothing has been stolen. Quickly, the boy tidies the place, arranging the books and magazines into piles, organizing the woodblock prints, collecting up the imprints scattered here and there.

That is when he notices the empty cage.

'Lapis! Lazuli! Where are you?' Arthur calls, glancing around.

A muffled flapping is heard from the office at the back, where the publishers hold meetings with clients. As soon as he enters this room, the birds flutter through the open door.

'Oi, what's wrong with you two?'

On a table by the window there is a jug of wine and some left-over cheese. Mr Bradbury must have stayed late, the boy thinks to himself.

He opens the shutters. In the altered light, he makes out a shadow by the bookshelves. If it weren't for the familiarity of the figure, he would have screamed. Mr Bradbury must have fallen asleep on the armchair, his body bent at an awkward angle.

'Sir . . .'

Arthur takes a step forward . . . and then he understands. It is not the silence but the man's pallor that makes him grasp what is too awful to put into words. Mr Bradbury's skin has turned grey, the colour of the Thames on a stormy day. A line of foam trickles from the corner of his mouth, some of which has dripped on his collar and dried there. By his side is an empty bottle of prussic acid.

The boy starts to shake. It is not as if he has never witnessed death before. In his brief life he has already seen more than his fair share. But this man was not killed by a pitiless murderer or a terrible illness. He has chosen to end his own life. The one person who has been kind to Arthur is also the one who has not been kind to himself.

When his trembling subsides, the boy brings a washbasin. He wipes Mr Bradbury's chin and scrubs his collar. He hides the wine and brushes the crumbs from his lap. He wants him to look clean and dignified, as elegant in death as the engravings he has immortalized. He feeds the birds and tempts them back into their cage. With nothing left to do, he sits beside the dead man and waits for the others to arrive.

Nothing changes and everything does. Arthur neither stops coming to work nor neglects his duties, but he no longer takes delight in learning new printing techniques. He still looks after the birds and makes sure their cage is well kept, yet he has ceased to chat to them. Already a contemplative boy, he withdraws into the shell of himself. His usually pensive face is set fast in worry lines that make him look older than his age. It is the senselessness of it all that eats at him. Mr Bradbury had everything – an adoring wife, beautiful children, a lovely house and even his own carriage, a profession that earned him a decent salary and a respectable position in society. Why would anyone so successful, wealthy and accomplished want to end their life? Arthur understands poverty;

he even understands crime and delinquency; but the malady of the mind, an ailment that also hounds his own mother, puzzles him more than anything.

Mr Evans, moved by the boy's grief, keeps a close eye on him, and the other workers, even those who used to have a laugh at his expense, tread carefully around him. But Arthur barely notices. Unless it is absolutely necessary, he does not converse with anyone, carrying out his tasks silently. He is still the perfect apprentice.

H—
NARIN

By the River Tigris, 2014

'My grandma is a healer. She cures people who can't help feeling sad.'

Narin's cousins are visiting Turkey from Germany. A branch of the family moved to Hanover in the early 2000s, and they always come back around this time of the year. Narin is delighted to see the two children, who are older than her and speak fluent German. She wants to impress them a little.

'And how does she do that?' asks the boy, crossing his arms.

'I don't exactly know how she does it, but she uses water to treat her patients. She's a water-dowser.'

'What is that?' asks the girl.

'It's a special talent, and it runs in our family,' says Narin proudly. 'Grandma can find underground streams, even when they're hidden. I've seen her do it. Her fingers twitch and curl when she gets close to a source. Sometimes she uses rods. She has to whittle them at dawn, so they can catch the first rays of sun. It's something she learnt from her grandmother Leila. One day she'll teach me how to do it, and then, when I'm grown up, I'll pass on the secret to my grandchildren!'

'Why haven't we ever seen her dowse?' asks the boy.

'Because she's getting old and she doesn't do it much any more – and you two are away anyway.'

Although they sometimes quarrel, Narin is delighted to have her cousins' company. As an only child, she often wonders what life might have been like if she'd had siblings, and these are the moments when she can inch ever closer to finding the answer. When her cousins speak Kurdish, it is peppered with words in Turkish, and when they speak Turkish they almost instantly switch to German, which is their strongest language. Narin knows that her aunt and uncle are not wealthy people, and they work hard to earn a living, but they never fail to bring her the most amazing presents – rucksacks with shimmering front panels, pencils that smell like strawberries, chocolate bars and hazelnut wafers that taste divine . . . She wants to eat the treats in one go, they are that delicious, but Grandma rations them.

In honour of the guests, breakfast is a feast today: fried green peppers with yogurt sauce, sour-cherry jam, sweet-chilli marmalade, glazed halloumi and dried figs, bulgur-stuffed aubergines with tamarind, currants and pine nuts, pistachio tahini halva, hummus with flatbread, scrambled eggs with red pepper, cheese with wild garlic, and the first batch of honey from the beehive, topped with clotted cream . . . In a corner a samovar hisses away on a bed of coals that glows like rubies. Grandma loves the strong tea from Russia, which she drinks with a cube of sugar squeezed between her teeth. She says if you drink tea this way, the words you speak will be sweeter.

Next they take their guests to the cemetery on the outskirts of the village. It is important that ancestors be properly honoured. You cannot simply amble over to their graves. You first need to wash your body, polish your shoes, comb your hair. It does not matter whether your clothes are old or new, cheap or expensive. The dead do not care about such trivialities. But it matters that you are clean – inside and out.

When they enter the graveyard with its dilapidated tombstones, overgrown weeds and turf-covered mounds, Grandma spearheads the group. The women and children form a circle, while the men remain close at hand, observing quietly. Narin knows that whenever there is a memorial gathering, it is an elder female who must lead the way. Mourning is a woman's job – and so is remembrance.

Afterwards the adults walk ahead, chatting to each other, and the children linger behind.

Her girl cousin flicks a sideways glance at Narin. 'I hear your father is taking you to Iraq – will you visit the holy Valley of Lalish?'

'Yes,' says Narin, beaming. 'It's going to be wonderful. Grandma is coming, too, of course. We're all travelling together.'

The boy chips in, 'Is it true what they say about you?'

'What are they saying?' asks Narin, even though she can guess the answer.

'That soon you'll go deaf.'

Narin lets out the breath she did not know she was holding. 'It won't happen right away; I have several more months, I think – maybe a year.'

'That's terrible,' says the boy. 'I'd hate to be you.'

'Shut up!' the girl shouts at her brother. 'You're being rude.'

'What? It's not like she doesn't know what's going to happen!'

'I said shut up!'

Leaving them to their quarrel, Narin swerves to the edge of the cemetery. She heads towards the oak tree under which the Englishman is buried. The tombstone is weathered by years of sun and wind, and covered in patches of moss, glistening like green velvet against the dull background. A heartbeat later her cousins catch up with her.

'Who is this?' the girl asks.

'The Englishman,' replies Narin. 'You never heard of him?'

The cousins shake their heads.

'Grandma says he was looking for a poem. He travelled from England, and he died here of thirst.'

The boy chuckles. 'He died of thirst by the River Tigris? That's some ending!'

Narin says, 'I don't know how it happened. Can you read what it says on the stone?'

The boy shrugs. 'It's not German.'

The girl draws closer. 'It's in English. Let me have a go. I learnt a bit at school.' Her finger strokes the air as she reads out loud: 'King . . . Arthur . . . of . . .' She clasps her hands. 'Oh, how amazing! This man was a king!'

For a moment the three of them stand still, studying the fading inscription. 'Can you translate the rest?' asks Narin.

'Not sure. What does "sewer" mean?' The girl squints as if a clearer view might help. 'King Arthur of something and something . . . His date and place of birth; and then, his date and place of death.'

'That's it?' asks Narin.

'That's it,' says the girl firmly.

'But it doesn't make sense,' says the boy. 'Wouldn't an English king have a stately grave – with marble and gold?'

'Maybe he was toppled,' suggests his sister. 'Like the French king in the Revolution.' She raises and drops her hand, imitating the fall of a guillotine.

'What was he doing here anyway?' says the boy.

'Probably some colonizer,' says his sister. 'Why do they ever come?'

Narin purses her lips. She does not know what 'colonizer' means, but does not want to admit it.

'Come on, I'm bored, let's go!' declares the boy.

With that, the siblings run off towards the grown-ups in the distance. Left alone, Narin touches the tombstone, her fingers tracing the letters.

King Arthur of the Sewers and Slums
Born by the River Thames 1840
Died by the River Tigris 1876

'Hi, Arthur . . .' she says. 'I'm sorry you'll be submerged in water when they finish building the dam. Our houses and grapevines and fig groves, even Grandma's pistachio trees, will drown . . . Hasankeyf is going to disappear. It's very sad, but there's nothing we can do about it. The government wants us all to leave. You won't be seeing our community again.'

'Narin!'

The girl does not hear that they are calling her, until Grandma, walking back, enters her field of vision.

'I'm coming, Grandma!'

Narin glances at the grave, drops her voice. 'But I've good news, too. We're travelling to Iraq. I'll be baptized in the holy Valley of Lalish. After we return to Hasankeyf, I'll visit you again. I promise.' The wind, picking up, tears loose her braid. She pushes her hair away from her face. 'Then we need to move to a big city. It's all a bit scary. Were you also scared when you left your home?'

'Narin, hurry up!'

The child nods at her grandmother.

'Bye, Arthur. I'll come and see you again soon.'

Yet, just as she is leaving, something distracts her; an impulse she can scarcely define makes her look towards the family plot on the opposite side, where her mother and many of her relatives are laid to rest. She notices a detail she has missed on all her previous visits to the cemetery.

The grave of her great-great-grandmother Leila is situated diagonally across, pointing east towards the sunrise as is the custom, but in such a way as to directly overlook the English-man's resting place. It is as though, in her afterlife, she is keeping a watchful eye on him. By her grave, too, there is an old oak tree.

Later they have dinner in the garden – relatives and neighbours sitting around large copper trays carrying a panoply of succulent dishes. This is not just any dinner but a mortuary feast, organized as much for the living as for the dead. There are three parties to this gathering: the hosts, the guests and the deceased. Food is a language that brings them together beyond the borders of time and place.

Stuffed vine leaves, fried *kibbe* balls, chargrilled chicken kebabs, roast lamb with spices and a large plate of rice *tahdig*. They eat not only for themselves but also for the *miriyan* – those who are no longer of this world. As Narin chews the bread of the dead, *nane miriyan*, she reflects on the souls of her ancestors. Her mind keeps looping back to one in particular: Leila. Is it true that she was a healer far superior to all others, a seer who could read minds and speak the language of birds?

Narin eats heartily, as she is fond of *tahdig* – 'the bottom of the pot' – with its crispy crust at the base of cooked rice. Amid the din of easy chatter, the child misses some sounds but not Grandma's laughter, which washes over her like fresh water.

That evening, Narin goes to bed early, sleeps fitfully. She wakes up with a queasy feeling in the pit of her stomach, as if she were falling from a great height. Her right ear is ringing again, and it is scary and unsettling, but she decides not to tell anyone, in case they might want to cancel the trip to Iraq.

Slowly, she gets out of bed to fetch a glass of water. She does not need to turn on the light. Stretching her arms in front of her, she proceeds by touch in the dark. Her hands guide her, as if they possess a memory of their own. No sooner does she open the door than light pours in. A blend of sounds rises from the next room but she cannot discern what they are saying. Only when she inches much closer does she realize that the grown-ups have stayed up late, drinking tea, smoking, talking.

'You don't understand,' Uncle Elias is saying. 'I'm telling you, brother, this region is in big trouble. These jihadists are gaining power. No one knows what they are up to.'

'Yes, but they're in Syria . . . It doesn't affect us in any way.'

Narin lifts her head, thrilled by the timbre of her father's voice. She takes a step forward, eager to give him a hug. But what her uncle says next stops her mid-stride.

'I think you should urgently join us in Germany. It's not safe around here any more. Things are going from bad to worse. Hasankeyf will be flooded. All our memories gone – and just beyond the border is an army of bigots and fanatics. An army! They're dangerous.'

'He's right,' agrees Aunt Mona. 'It's terrifying. We don't even know who supplies ISIS with weapons. This doesn't bode well.'

'Calm down, you two. Otherwise you're going to make your-selves sick with worry.'

Narin gets closer. She struggles to hear higher pitches, but thankfully Father speaks in a low, measured tone. There is a gentle strength to his words as he carries on with conviction. 'You want us to leave everything and follow you to Hanover. Even if we agree, will Germany welcome us? How do we get a visa? Let's say we get past that hurdle, how would I find a job there?'

'Lots of people do it.'

'Yes, they do, but many can't. And those who do, at what cost? We all know how much you have sacrificed.'

'Life isn't easy in Germany,' says Uncle Elias. 'When we first moved to Hanover, the Germans hadn't even heard of the Yazidi faith. In their eyes we were all Turkish and that was it. And then they learnt a little more about the region, but this time they started calling us all Kurdish, and that was it. Again, we tried to explain. It took me years to be able to say openly and without fear, "I am Êzidî and I'd much rather you called me Êzidî instead of Yazidi, because it leads to a terrible misunderstanding." They think we are the descendants of Yazid, the Tyrant of Karbala, who killed the Prophet Muhammad's grandson, and they hate us. But we have nothing to do with any of that. Our name solely means "descendants of God". Our roots go all the way back to Ancient Mesopotamia.'

Uncle Elias pauses, his voice catching. 'Working in the factory is hard, too. Sometimes my back hurts so much, I can barely move. Almost every week I'm told by some random stranger to go back home. But Germany is my home now – and my children's only homeland! At least there I don't have to worry about police knocking on my door in the middle of the night. I don't have to fear being arrested and tortured.'

'I hear you, brother, but Mesopotamia is our motherland. This is our ancestral home. You want everyone to pack up and migrate? Look around, how many Yazidis are left in the region? It breaks my heart. There were hundreds of thousands of us once upon a time – and today we are just a handful. Only twelve Yazidis remain in this village – most of them not long for this world. When they, too, are gone, who will remember us? What will remain of us?'

'What can you do if there is no hope of things getting better? Be practical, I beg you.'

'There is hope. The Middle East is changing. I have faith in the new generation. The young do not approve of the old ways. They want freedom, dignity, democracy. And they demand the same opportunities as their peers in the West. As for the fanatics, no doubt, they are despicable, but they are here today, gone tomorrow. They cannot intimidate all of us. Why should we be the ones leaving and not our tormentors?'

'Khaled, you are naive. You don't understand,' says Uncle Elias. 'They'll never let us live in peace. There is no future for us in this region.'

'Maybe I am naive. But I'm a musician, brother. I was a kid when I discovered the *qanun* in the house. They said, "Children can't touch it, it's more than a hundred years old." I wouldn't stop crying unless they let me hold it. I didn't sleep properly until I learnt to play it. Now they invite me everywhere. Why? Because people need songs like they need bread and water. People need poetry, beauty, love! So long as the sun rises and rivers flow, there

will always be weddings and celebrations and music. Even fanatics cannot change that.'

Silence settles in the room, curling itself around the stove like
a listless cat that refuses to move. Gingerly, Narin inches closer.

'We hear you're planning to take Narin to Iraq?' asks Aunt Mona.

'Yes, I've been invited to sing at a few weddings in Mosul and
Baghdad. I'll also meet some friends. Narin and my mother-in-
law will come with me. They'll stay in the old village in Nineveh.
That's where my late wife's ancestors came from, as you know.'

'May her soul be on a higher plane.'

'After that we'll travel to the holy Valley of Lalish together. The
child should have been baptized long ago, but circumstances never
allowed. Already her left ear has mostly gone. We want to leave
before she loses her hearing completely. The doctor said the right
ear could hold on for another year –'

'She can't wear a hearing aid?'

'No, apparently they don't work for everyone. There are other
devices, I'm told, and I'm inquiring, but it's expensive and –'

He pauses, noticing Narin standing in the doorway.

'Daddy,' the girl exclaims, rushing towards him. 'When did you
get home? Why didn't you wake me up?'

Khaled takes her into his arms and kisses the top of her head.
'Sweetheart, you were sleeping, I didn't want to disturb you.'

'Dad, what's a fanatic?'

Khaled smooths away a strand of hair from his daughter's forehead. 'Have you been listening to us?'

'I'm sorry.' Words tumble out of her mouth. 'If those fanatics
arrive here, they'll be flooded. Water will protect us.'

'You mustn't worry about these things. Don't fill your beautiful
head with scary thoughts. Promise? Now go to sleep.'

Reluctantly, Narin nods. She walks to the kitchen and fills a
glass with water before returning to her room. All the while she
can sense the grown-ups are listening to her footsteps, waiting.

Lying in bed, unable to sleep, she notices a detail she missed earlier: during the entire conversation Grandma did not utter a single word. Her grandmother is the most talkative person she knows, and always has something wise to say, and when she speaks people listen. Of everything she has witnessed tonight, it is Grandma's silence that the child finds the most unsettling.

II

Mysteries of Water

—O—
ARTHUR

By the River Thames, 1854

I t is the last day of August – a sweltering afternoon. London is a greasy cauldron – fuming, fetid. Stinking odours rise from every quarter of the city – the tanneries, fellmongeries, piggeries, furnaces, factories, slaughterhouses, cesspools . . . The noxious fumes harbour all manner of disease. Early in the summer, the General Board of Health issued a warning that anything giving off a strong and unpleasant smell must be burned or otherwise disposed of – and that invariably means discharged into the Thames. Now the river, heaving with flotsam and jetsam, can barely flow; neither gushing nor rippling bright and blue, it simply slithers, sluggish and grey like a cold-blooded reptile.

Arthur does his best to protect himself and his family from the menace of miasma. By walking fast on his way to the office and back, he hopes that less of the dank air will enter his lungs. Despite the unbearable temperature, he covers his nose and mouth with a damp cloth. But as soon as he arrives home he asks his mother to keep the windows open to allow a light breeze to circulate around the basement, as a still, suffocating room is an even bigger danger. The ventilation in the flat they share with another family is dismal, and, in truth, it is not much better at the printing press. It makes him nervous to have to work in closed, stuffy spaces. Indoors and outdoors, he worries about catching diseases from the air.

★

Thursday afternoon, with the heat having reached an intolerable level, work has stopped early at the printing press. Arthur walks cautiously out of the office, mindful not to step in horse manure. He has read in a magazine somewhere that there are 300,000 horses across the capital. If one horse defecates between 4 and 13 times a day, he quickly calculates, it would amount to up to 12,000 tons of dung daily. Each day a huge hill of shit builds up in the city, and it is mostly boys like him who sweep it away.

Time and again, he has seen horses skid and flounder on the mud carpeting the streets. They slip as though on ice. Whenever a carriage topples over, a crowd gathers at the scene. The driver tries his best to keep thieves away, but often there is little he can do to stop them. In the blink of an eye, a carriage can be stripped down, all its upholstery peeled away and metal parts carried off. It is not only animals that fall down in the mire: humans, too, often lose their balance. People sprain ankles, break hips. Arthur knows he has to be extra careful, for, if something were to happen to him, his family would have nothing to eat.

He fingers the coins in his pocket – it's the money the late Mr Bradbury gave him. He has made it a habit to get treats for his family whenever he can. Eel pies and pickled oysters for his brothers, and, for his mother, an ivory button, a hairpin, a velvet ribbon . . . How she rejoices in these surprises! Yet today Arthur is going to buy her a proper gift. It may be sweltering hot, but his mother's hands are always cold. He will get her the gloves he saw for sale on Broad Street.

He could have forgotten about those gloves, as pretty as they were, but he hasn't. He does not forget anything.

Broad Street is lined with bright shops on both sides, customers sauntering in and out, murmurs of an easier life on their lips. Arthur passes by the house where the poet and printmaker William Blake was born, and the family hosiery where the artist once worked as a delivery boy. Blake – who saw trees with sinuous roots up in the sky, conversed with angels and spirits floating in his mind, and heard the calls of meadowlarks from Arcadia – has been widely considered a radical, if not a delusional eccentric, dying in obscurity, but Arthur has devoured his entire oeuvre and examined his engravings, and he wishes he had been his contemporary so they could have met.

With these thoughts in mind Arthur drops in to the haberdasher's on the corner. After spending a long time admiring the surfeit of silk ribbons, velvet buttons, flowing foulards and chenilles, and the reels of satin, moiré and taffeta fabrics of all colours, he leaves the place with a package under his arm. He cannot believe how much a pair of gloves costs! He has no money left to get something for his brothers. But, as he crosses the road, another idea occurs to him. He will bring them water – cold and fresh. Fortunately, he has his flask with him. That way his mother will not have to queue today in front of the lone fountain in the slum tenement, which is so clogged it merely trickles.

There is a cast-iron pump just around the corner. Not every source of water in London can be trusted. Some are so filthy no one dares to approach them, not even stray dogs. But this is one of the best on the east side, always reliable and very popular. Patiently, Arthur joins the people waiting in line. He fills his container, his mind as light as the day is bright and clear.

Once home he sets the water on the table. The family they live with have a tendency to help themselves to other people's things, which infuriates his mother, but Arthur does not mind. In his bag, he has a book he is looking forward to reading. He was there as it came off the press – *The Poetical Works of John Keats.*

> *We have imagined for the mighty dead;*
> *All lovely tales that we have heard or read:*
> *An endless fountain of immortal drink,*
> *Pouring unto us from the heaven's brink.*

The words flow over his tongue like warm honey, but, exhausted from the day's grind, his eyelids begin to droop. Maybe he should doze a little; there is no harm in having a nap.

In a few minutes, the twins tiptoe into the room, keeping a watchful eye on their elder brother snoring on the mattress. The rhythmic sound, a low rumbling, makes the children giggle. Sneaking up to him, they tousle his hair to see if he will wake. He does not.

That is when the little boys notice the package. Ripping open its pretty paper, they are thrilled to find a pair of lady's gloves! Each child puts one on, beaming.

After that, it is not long till they discover the flask on the table. One downs a cupful immediately as the other waits his turn. Outside on the street, a drunkard shouts profanities, furious at some slight – real or imaginary. His words are so salacious that the other child, who has just taken his first mouthful, bursts out laughing, spluttering and spraying water everywhere and soaking his clothes.

Arthur, disturbed by the noise, stirs in his sleep. The boys run out, laughing.

The next day, at dawn, one of the twins wakes up with stomach pains. He starts vomiting. The diarrhoea that follows is relentless, and even as hours pass it does not subside. They leave the only window in the room wide open, worried that particles of disease, airborne, have invaded the basement. But that does not explain why only one person in the family has been taken ill. As the day unfolds, a fearful silence descends over everything. The only sound that can be heard is the slow, rattling breath of the sick boy, like the wingbeat of a moth, vainly flapping against a lampshade.

Arthur does not go to work that day. He does not return the book he borrowed. The stench of death is so pervasive it enters through his nostrils and leaves an acrid taste at the back of his throat. Whenever he opens his mouth to say something, it is the same taste that coats his words. Tirelessly, he helps his mother with the cleaning and washing, and towards noon he manages to convince a doctor to make a house call for a small payment, although by the time the man arrives it is clear there is nothing anyone can do.

Meanwhile the other twin, quiet as a dropped stone, watches from a corner, in his gaze a blend of sorrow and bewilderment. Since the day they were born, the two boys were so alike that no one could tell one from the other – this included the neighbours, the vendors and, at times, even their own mother. Now the healthy one is silent, his mind snagged on a gnawing suspicion that he will still be grappling with in his loneliest hours, long after he is a grown man. He wonders whether it is he who was meant to catch the disease and suffer instead of his brother, and if death, too, has mistaken them.

Towards the evening, they carry the sick boy out on to the street and place him on a makeshift bed on the pavement. This way, they hope, he will not have to inhale the toxic vapours assailing their living quarters. It does not help. The child is losing strength, losing water. Horribly dehydrated, his face shrivels into a gruesome mask – eyes sunken, teeth protruding, cheeks hollowed, and his skin a scary shade of blue, the colour of a bruise.

Cholera, the *blue terror.*

Only a few streets away from where Arthur lives with his family, a doctor named John Snow is bent over his desk, taking notes by the light of a candle. On the open map in front of him he marks the neighbourhoods where the epidemic is raging. One by one, he circles the locations of the victims, and notices a definite pattern emerging. They all have consumed water from the same pump on Broad Street. People who lived around the area but somehow have not come into contact with the same source have not been affected. If his observations can be verified, it is proof that cholera has nothing to do with the quality of the air.

It is all in the water.

The doctor has already written to the city authorities explaining that they must urgently shut down the pump, either by removing it or breaking the handle. He is certain that the well is contaminated, probably through an underground sewer leak. But his letters have been met with ridicule and scorn from the General Board of Health. And so the pump on Broad Street continues to operate.

The maverick physician, refusing to give up, plots ways to disable the pump but cannot quite bring himself to damage public property. With patients waiting to see him, he is unable to spend whole days guarding this spot, trying to talk people out of using it. So, instead, he hangs up a sign warning passers-by about the peril and leaves.

That sign had disappeared by the time Arthur entered Broad Street. Perhaps it was carried away by the wind or stolen by an illiterate urchin who assumed it to be of some value. It does not matter. It is too late for those who have already ingested the water. Inside a drop, invisible to the eye, lies a curved, rod-shaped bacterium with a long tail that helps it to move with extraordinary agility.

People are dying so swiftly that disposal gangs start to patrol the streets, looking for corpses to collect. The bodies, horribly disfigured, are piled up and carted away, although some may still be breathing. Almost all of the victims reside within 250 yards of the crossroads where Broad Street meets Cambridge Street. The small number from outside this coordinate are from destinations where water was carried from the same pump.

As August gives way to September, hundreds of new cases erupt across London. Convinced that infections are caused by miasma and bad smells, the city officials spread tons of lime near the mouths of sewers to reduce toxic gases released into the air.

Queen Victoria complains about the 'evil odour'. In Parliament, MPs and civil servants walk around clutching handkerchiefs to their noses, deploring the stinking, Stygian pool that the once mighty Thames has become. More and more chalk lime and carbolic acid are poured into its slimy depths. Even cemeteries come under suspicion, and some will be relocated for fear that cadaverous emissions are causing all manner of ailments. None of these measures will have the slightest impact on slowing the pestilence.

By and by, as more evidence comes to the fore, the General Board of Health will have to concede that the dissenting doctor – and a few others who had arrived at the same conclusion – was right all along. Cholera is not transmitted by air but through water. Trying to banish the smell of raw sewage by dumping it in the River Thames, the main source of drinking water for thousands of families, has only exacerbated the spread of the pandemic.

Whilst the authorities grapple with this uncomfortable revelation, Arthur, who follows the news with horror and reads every scientific report published, is assailed by an insight of his own. For he now suspects, with a sinking horror, that the flask he brought home contained the deadly bacteria. It will take him time to piece together the truth, but, once he does, he cannot unknow it: it was water that was the cause of death in the family, and it was he who brought the water. He has killed his own brother.

What they call a river is actually multiple rivers flowing in one. Running deep within the same body of water are several currents, like layers of skin that remain hidden to the eye but are scarred by the same wound.

Between 1853 and the last months of 1854, more than 10,740 Londoners die from the blue terror. Death roams the alleys, its earthy breath snuggling in closer as it slips through cracks in the walls and slides under doors, like the low fog. To survive and to heal, the city must reform, and any meaningful change needs to start with the Thames. Now that more people recognize the consequences of dumping filth into the very water they drink from, it is urgent that a proper sewage system is built. For too long Londoners have been saying the river is a silent murderer. But Arthur understands that it is, actually, the other way round. It is humans who are killing the water.

—H

ZALEEKHAH

By the River Thames, 2018

When Zaleekhah enters the dining room, following Uncle Malek, she finds her aunt sitting at one end of the lacquered table, with her middle grandchild by her side. They have pieces of card littered all about them, immersed as they are in constructing a Victorian doll's house with pop-up furniture and lift-the-flap doors.

'Darling! Why are you standing over there?' Aunt Malek says, offering her cheek for an air kiss. 'Helen took the boys to tennis and let me keep Lily for the afternoon – aren't I lucky? She's just about to go and have a bath.'

'Hello, sweetheart.' Zaleekhah kisses the child.

'Hi, Auntie.'

'What is this amazing thing you two have been working on?'

The girl smiles. There is a yellow tinge to her skin that stands out beneath her neatly combed fringe. 'We're building a home for my dolls – it has a secret room!'

But there is no time to hear more, as the nanny appears then, collecting up the pieces and sweeping the girl upstairs.

'Come and sit with me,' Aunt Malek says to Zaleekhah, patting the now empty seat next to her invitingly.

'She'd better sit with me,' says Uncle Malek. 'We've things to discuss.'

Aunt Malek flicks a glance at her husband. 'You promised me you'd stay calm.'

'I am perfectly calm,' Uncle Malek retorts. 'If she has decided to end her marriage for no good reason, it's her choice. We're living in modern times.'

Quietly, Zaleekhah pulls out a chair in the middle of the table at an equal distance from each of them. She glances around. The place has had another makeover. The dining room is the most remodelled part of the Maleks' house. Every few months, it undergoes change, redecorated in a different colour scheme. Suspended above their heads is a chandelier adorned with white lilies and translucent green leaves of tinted glass.

'I haven't seen this before – is this new? It's beautiful.'

'New and very old,' replies Uncle Malek. 'It was displayed at the Great Exhibition, so it'd have been seen by Queen Victoria herself – and millions of others, of course.'

The chandelier is not the only antique in the room. Across from the entrance, an Art Deco cocktail cabinet houses crystal tumblers, aged malt whiskies and decanters of vintage port. In one corner there is a marquetry chest of drawers with the master carpenter's mark engraved on the frame – a hammer and anvil. Each piece has been meticulously selected by Uncle Malek. He is fond of collecting *objets d'art*, and he is fond of food, and it is here in this room that his twin passions come together and find their most perfect expression.

'Darling, we missed you,' says Aunt Malek, turning to Zaleekhah. 'Why don't you visit us more often?'

'I'm sorry, it's been a bit manic lately.'

The Maleks exchange glances but make no comment. Just then the maid walks in carrying a basket of bread. They wait silently as she sets a roll on each side plate.

'Well, I might need your expertise,' Aunt Malek says, laying her napkin across her lap. 'I'm putting in a Zen garden. It's a great way of reducing stress.'

Uncle snorts. 'Or transferring it to me.'

Zaleekhah suppresses a smile. 'I'd love to help but I don't know anything about Zen gardens.'

'Don't worry, I already have a landscape designer. You just help me with the water bit.'

'Water?'

'Yes, there's going to be a stream running through the garden and a rustic stone bridge . . . or maybe wooden, and miniature waterfalls, totally natural and relaxing. It's like having a spa in your own garden.'

'An expensive spa,' Uncle Malek says. 'The whole thing is going to cost a fortune.'

'You say that, but when it's done you'll be out there day and night. You're going to love it.' Aunt Malek cocks an eyebrow at her husband. 'As for the price, don't get me started. Your hobbies are more expensive than mine. I don't even know where we'll find space for that ancient piece you're bringing home.'

'Oh, here we go again. How many times do I have to tell you? It's a Mesopotamian tablet. It fits into the palm of your hand!'

'Right, I keep forgetting,' Aunt Malek mutters to herself. 'The price is high enough.'

They fall quiet as they wait for the maid to serve their first course – creamy asparagus soup topped with a poached egg and Brie croutons.

Her gaze fixed on her bowl, Zaleekhah breaks the yolk with her spoon, watching the amber liquid ooze out. Uncle's relationship with money has always puzzled her. He will not hesitate to spend a thousand pounds on a bottle of wine but baulks at what he regards as his wife's addiction to anti-ageing creams. He can make eye-watering bids for a rare whisky, delights in treating his family to luxury holidays and will foot the bill gladly for his friends on an evening out, yet will quibble over the monthly kitchen expenses. He is incredibly generous with presents for his loved ones, though not, Zaleekhah suspects, when his workers demand a pay rise.

'Is this the tablet you were telling me about?' asks Zaleekhah.

'It is indeed!' Uncle replies. 'A section of the *Epic of Gilgamesh*. We're talking about the oldest poem in the world. That alone is remarkable. But this one is all the more extraordinary. A blue tablet from the library of Ashurbanipal.'

'I thought things like that were kept in museums,' says Aunt Malek.

'Many are – but some end up in private hands.' Uncle butters his bread and pops a piece into his mouth. 'I've done my due diligence, of course. You can't trust anyone these days. Items looted from Iraq and Syria are all over London, New York, Paris, Tokyo . . . Relics from the ruins of Palmyra are displayed in antique shops in Europe. But, rest assured, my dears, this tablet came from a reputable dealer.'

'If it's that special, why are the owners selling it?' Aunt Malek asks.

'It happens. The locals are poor, ignorant folks. They own things whose value they don't fully grasp. When the elderly pass away, the young raise cash however they can. Can you blame them?'

Zaleekhah looks down at her plate. It is a source of endless contention between the couple: money. They both have it, except one was born into it, while the other made his own long and arduous journey towards it.

Aunt Malek, the daughter of an English family that amassed its fortune in textiles way back in the nineteenth century, finds it deeply distasteful when people prattle on about their finances, investments and profit. For his part, Uncle Malek never fails to get annoyed at those who are so privileged by birth that they have no idea what it is like to struggle to pay the bills. So when it comes to such matters, each despises the other in their own not so subtle way.

'You're too quiet, darling. Tell us about your life,' says Aunt Malek, after the fish has been served.

'Yes, tell us what's going on!'

Zaleekhah inhales. She knows they want to hear about her marriage but talking about work is easier than talking about her private life and so she says, 'You might remember, I'm part of this project – we're collaborating with scientists worldwide to help restore lost rivers.'

'Dodging the question,' murmurs Uncle Malek under his breath.

'If she wants to discuss lost rivers, we'll discuss lost rivers,' Aunt Malek says, frowning at her husband before turning back to Zaleekhah. 'Now, how does a river get lost?'

'Well, throughout the centuries humans have built cities on the shores of rivers. But when those cities expanded, the same rivers and tributaries were pushed away. Unwanted and culverted – hidden underground. At the moment we're working with a French team who are trying to revive the historic waterway of Paris.'

'The Seine!' Aunt Malek says with a dreamy smile. 'Isn't that the most romantic setting? We spent a summer in Paris when we got married. We have such fond memories, your uncle and I.'

'Actually, I meant another river,' Zaleekhah says. 'The Bièvre.'

'The what?' asks Aunt Malek.

'The Bièvre – it's buried under the French capital, and has been for a long time. It was an important waterway until the nineteenth century, when it became heavily polluted. They covered it over and basically forgot about it. The tourists who walk around Paris today admire the Seine, but they don't realize there's another river flowing beneath their feet.'

'We've quite a few of our own here in London,' says Uncle Malek.

'That's right,' says Zaleekhah. 'New York, Vienna, São Paulo, Sydney, Beijing, Moscow, Toronto . . . There are lost rivers almost everywhere on the planet. Not many foreigners are aware that Tokyo used to be a city of water. It's still an incredible place, of course, but more than a hundred streams and canals have been filled in and used as a base for roads or just hidden under pavements. Or take Athens. You two were there this summer. Now that city, despite its splendour, has no waterway running through it. But in fact, historically, Athens boasted not one, not two, but three rivers.'

'Oh, I had no idea,' says Aunt Malek. 'What happened to them?'

'They were buried.'

'Buried?'

'Yes, under layers of concrete. Just like elsewhere in the world. Roads are more profitable than rivers; you can sell more cars. The property market also prefers it this way. But remember in Ancient Greece rivers were sacred. Humans didn't always treat water like this.'

'Okay, now, let's not get carried away. There's no need to turn this into a rant against capitalism,' says Uncle Malek. 'If these rivers are dead, they must be for a reason. You yourself said they were extremely dirty. A threat to public health, I presume. They must have been spreading all kinds of diseases. It's not the wisest thing to hide them, but I imagine it was the best solution back then. The Victorians didn't have that many options available; let's not judge them too harshly.'

'I'm not judging the Victorians,' Zaleekhah says. She does not like to argue with her uncle, but nor can she keep quiet on an issue so close to her heart. 'I'm criticizing us. Here we are, more than a century later, and we need a new approach. Those culverts were built at a time when cities were smaller. Now, with the climate emergency, their flood capacities are danger-ously strained.'

'What can you do, my dear?' Uncle Malek steeples his fingers under his chin. 'Are you going to demolish private property to rescue your lost rivers? Aren't parts of Bucking-ham Palace built over one of those tributaries, now that I come to think of it? I hope you're not planning to knock down the Queen's walls.'

'All I'm saying is that if we don't find a new approach, we'll have worse floods in our cities every year. It's not an impossible task. They've done it in Seoul. It's called "daylighting" – returning a lost river to the open air.'

'Daylighting – that's a nice name,' chips in Aunt Malek.

'A nice name means nothing if the figures don't back it up,' says Uncle Malek. 'Now, I don't know what they've done in Seoul, but I do know there are limits to what can be done in London. As a general rule, ghosts are better left alone. Why try to raise them from the dead?'

'Because they're still there.' Zaleekhah lowers her eyes and pushes away her plate. 'Things don't disappear just because we wish them to. Even if we cover them with concrete and build over them and pretend they never existed, they're still part of us, all those ghosts that we thought we'd buried deep inside, and, if we don't face up to them, they'll continue to haunt us.'

When she lifts her head, she finds her uncle and aunt staring at her, their expressions changed.

'Darling, don't get upset. Let's not talk about heavy stuff.' Aunt Malek pats her hand. 'Tell me, did you enjoy the fish?'

Dessert is dark chocolate fondant with glazed cranberries. Declining her portion, Aunt Malek checks her watch. 'I must make my excuses. The chauffeur's waiting for us to take Lily home. I might actually spend the night there. Helen's husband is in Singapore, again, on a business trip.'

'Oh, please give them my love,' says Zaleekhah. 'I haven't seen Helen in a while.'

Aunt Malek pauses, her eyes trained on her husband for a second too long. Then she says, 'Well, I would if I were you.'

The comment, though made casually, prompts a silence that lasts after Aunt Malek has disappeared.

'I should get going as well,' says Zaleekhah. 'Thanks for having me. Everything was delicious.'

'Stay a little longer, my dear. We haven't had a chance to chat properly.'

Leaning on his cane, Uncle rises to his feet, gesturing to the butler, who has appeared at his elbow. 'We'll take our coffee in the library, Kareem.'

Upstairs, the fire has been lit even though it is not cold. A clock on the mantel ticks softly. It feels peaceful, the heady smells emanating from the flowers blending with the scent of books and old manuscripts.

'Is there something up with Helen?' asks Zaleekhah, once the coffees have been served.

'She hasn't been herself lately. Lily's not doing so well.'

'Lily? She seemed happy.' Even as she says this her mind drifts back to the child's unusual pallor. 'What's wrong with her?'

'We don't know yet; they're running tests.'

Zaleekhah's eyes widen, confusion instantly replaced by guilt. She has been so preoccupied by her own troubles lately that she hasn't stayed in touch with her cousin. 'I keep meaning to arrange to meet up with Helen.'

'Do it, my dear! She's your sister. No need to call first, just go. If not at the house, you can always pop into the gallery – she'll be there in work hours. You know how much Helen cares about you.'

'I care about her, too.'

Uncle stirs his coffee, the spoon clinking against the china. 'You sure you'll be all right in that gondola?'

'The houseboat? It'll be fine. Don't worry about me – please.'

Uncle shakes his head. 'When you told me about your plans, I was shocked, frankly. I'd have thought you'd want to keep your distance from waterside residences.'

Her throat tightening, Zaleekhah straightens her shoulders. They rarely talk about what happened to her parents.

'Must be an age thing,' says Uncle Malek. 'I've been thinking about them a lot lately.'

Zaleekhah watches his expression darken, his eyes glinting in the way she has grown to recognize. She does not tell him that she, too, thinks about them more often these days.

'Definitely an age thing,' Uncle Malek carries on. 'I've been thinking about my mother, too.'

Uncle was eight years old when he was sent to board at a prep school in England, the first in his family to get an education abroad. At that age he had no sense of how much his family had sacrificed to give him an opportunity that he saw as a penance. After three summers, when he was finally permitted to travel home, he was told that his mother had left his father for another man, bringing shame on the entire family. His persistent questions as to her whereabouts were met with cold silence. At the end of the holidays, the boy returned to boarding school to start preparations for the Winchester College entrance exams, and never asked about his mother again.

He excelled in his adopted country. At school he was known for his debating skills, sharp wit and sardonic humour. After university, he launched a fast-food restaurant and expanded it into a franchise, earning huge profits, not only because he was shrewd and inventive but also because it was an era when political influence and advancement could be bought with few questions. Donating large sums to political parties and campaigns, he befriended politicians and celebrities. His name regularly appeared in the newspapers; he advised the government and wrote opinion pieces in the financial press. Recently he achieved his dream of being appointed to the House of Lords.

Uncle likes to call himself a 'self-made man'. While that may be true, Zaleekhah suspects that the making of a new self requires the unmaking of an old one. It seems to her that her uncle has left a part of himself behind in Iraq – the part that was tender, trusting and optimistic. She believes that even after all these years he still has not forgiven his mother.

Zaleekhah's own mother – Uncle's elder sister by four years – was a kind, compassionate woman with an easy smile and warm eyes. She came to England much later and always carried with her the shadow of another land. She had no interest in titles or gains. What she loved was nature.

Both of her parents held a deep appreciation for the great outdoors. Most of her childhood memories feature vast landscapes. Her father, her mother and their camping in the middle of nowhere, hiking in the woods, admiring the arc of a rainbow stretching over a succession of cataracts . . . The crunch of pine needles under their boots, the powdery efflorescence coating the rocks, the blackthorn sloes they collected after frost spells, the silver flask that her father attached to his belt and let her drink from when she was thirsty . . . No other water ever tasted so good. Yet, in the end, it was water that killed them, leaving Zaleekhah all by herself.

'Before you go, my dear, can you put my reading glasses in that drawer?'

He wants her to reconsider her decision. It's his not-so-subtle way of reminding her of the envelope. But when Zaleekhah opens the drawer, what she sees is that book again: *Nineveh and Its Remains.*

This time she reads the subtitle: *An Inquiry into the Manners and Arts of the Ancient Assyrians and an Account of a Visit to the Chaldean Christians of Kurdistan and the Yazidis, or Devil-Worshippers.*

These last words intrigue her. She has heard in the news about the plight of the Yazidis when ISIS attacked and drove them out of their homes, though she knows little else.

'May I borrow this?' Zaleekhah asks, prompted by an impulse.

'The envelope?'

'The book. I'll bring it back when I'm done.'

Uncle Malek sighs. 'Take it, my dear.'

'Goodnight, Uncle.'

Kareem is waiting for her downstairs, holding her jacket. He opens the door for her. They stand side by side, inhaling the cool air.

'Thank you for everything,' Zaleekhah rushes to say. She wants suddenly to leave this house and the hold it has over her. 'I think I ate too much. I should walk a bit.'

'But your uncle called a cab for you.'

No sooner has he finished speaking than they hear a car pulling up to the kerb outside the gate.

Zaleekhah breathes out. 'I guess I'm not walking, then.'

Quietly, as if not to disturb the garden with its neat lawn and pretty plants, she makes her way towards the gate. As she passes the Andalusian fountain, she knows Uncle Malek will be watching her from the window, a grainy silhouette against the heavy, silk brocade curtains. She half turns to glance over her shoulder, about to wave goodbye, but to her surprise there is no one there, only a shadow from the Victorian lamp.

—o—

ARTHUR

By the River Thames, 1856

The year before Arthur turns sixteen, his family falls behind with the rent. The boy needs to work extra shifts. He wakes up before the pigeons start cooing, sleep oozing from his eyes. Always fastidious about hygiene, he still takes great care to wash as best he can, wiping himself with a flannel soaked in diluted vinegar or rinsing his body with water so cold that it pricks his skin like needles. He also uses, sparingly, a bottle of disinfectant and a bar of carbolic soap distributed by a charity. But the soap is of such poor quality that it barely lathers, no matter how hard he scrubs. Even so, he never fails to observe his daily rituals.

On some mornings when he leaves the building, he sees the silver beam of an argent moon glancing off the cobblestones. At so early an hour, the air in London has a peculiar tang, like copper on his tongue. He walks carefully, skirting round beggars, vagrants and opium addicts dozing on the pavement, those unable to afford even the two-penny bunks, or *coffins* – the cheapest sheltered accommodation available to the homeless. Once he stumbles on a man who has frozen to death – his beard encrusted with ice, his face softened into one final pleasant dream, his clothes stripped off, exposing a body as emaciated as a withered tree.

Hunger is a constant in his life – at times briefly assuaged but never absent for long. Most days his breakfast consists of a bread roll, which, if possible, he supplements with a scraping of butter. Sometimes he buys ale or coffee from a brightly lit stall with a charcoal brazier. The ale is watered down and the coffee tastes of nothing, but at least it is warm. He still picks up a treat for his mother and little brother whenever he can: hot-smoked eels, pickled whelks or kidney pudding. These, too, form part of his cherished rituals.

By the time he returns home, late at night, he is so exhausted that he must struggle to keep his eyes open, let alone read anything. He no longer dreams of Nineveh these days. So much arbitrary suffering has robbed him of hope for the future. The remorse he feels about his brother's death never abates. He misses his mentor and his champion, Mr Bradbury. He is not sure he will be able to survive another winter. Fleeting moments still have the power to make him smile – a gull song drifting over the rooftops, the sight of primroses in a flower-seller's basket or the smell of chestnuts roasting on a brazier . . . Only the small things can hearten him enough to hang on to a slender thread of existence.

One morning, Arthur is standing at a lectern in the office, reviewing a title the company is considering reprinting in English: *The Works of Rabelais.* The original book is illustrated by the French artist Gustave Doré. His drawings are full of ferocious elan. The boy studies them in admiration. It is his firm conviction that all books, whether fact or fiction, should have pictures. Images, like lanterns illuminating the path of a night-time traveller, should guide the reader through the realms of a narrative. But he no longer draws. He knows he does not have the skill of the French illustrator. He can observe the brash courtesans on the arms of wealthy gentlemen walking out of operettas on Drury Lane, or the dingy shops on Holywell Street selling pornographic books, or the railway travellers in Waterloo Station, or the milling pedestrians on Fleet Street, known as the 'Street of Ink', as it has become the heart of the newspaper publishing industry, and conjure up their likenesses on paper with vigour and finesse, but he cannot read a tale and come up with sketches that exceed the writer's imagination.

So engrossed is the boy in his thoughts that it startles him when the door bursts open and a visitor rushes in. Of medium height and build, he has a neatly defined, pointed beard. Below his eyebrows, set in an angular face, his dark eyes blaze bright and alert.

'Mr Evans, where is he? I need to talk to him urgently.'

'He has not arrived yet,' says Arthur.

'Hellfire, this cannot wait!'

'I am sure he will be here shortly, sir.'

'I am pressed for time,' the man murmurs as he consults his watch and tucks it back in his waistcoat pocket. Something about him is curiously familiar, although Arthur is certain he has not seen him before.

Still huffing, the visitor plants himself on the nearest armchair. Whether he is talking to himself or to Arthur is not clear.

'After much deliberation, I have decided this is the right company for me. My novels must be printed here!'

Arthur's eyes narrow into slits as he realizes who the man is.

'I must first get rid of that scoundrel of a publisher with whom I have had the misfortune to be saddled all these years. They think I cannot leave; they shall see. My mind is made up. Henceforth I shall be published by Bradbury & Evans.'

Arthur looks away. 'Mr Bradbury is gone, sir.'

The man pauses, turning his acute gaze on the boy. Whatever he sees in him, his expression mellows, and, when he speaks again, so does his voice. 'Yes, I know, a terrible loss. You must be his apprentice. I heard he was mentoring a boy from the slums.'

'That'd be me, sir.'

'I also heard you were very intelligent. A genius, they say.'

'I don't know about that, sir.'

The ensuing silence is brief. The man asks, slowly, 'Do you know who I am?'

'Yes, sir. You are the author – Mr Charles Dickens.'

The man nods his assent. His wandering eyes, ablaze with curiosity, scan the table. 'You like drawings. Do you wish to become an artist?'

'I like art very much, but I do not believe it to be my calling.'

'So what is your talent, then?'

Arthur considers. 'Mr Bradbury always told me I was good at seeing what others did not see – I am not sure whether that counts as a talent.'

The author smiles. 'It sounds like quite the gift to me. Perhaps you need time to discover how to use it. The sun is weak when it first rises, and gathers strength and courage as the day goes on.'

He seems to be about to say more, but the voice of Mr Evans pierces the air, followed mere seconds later by the man himself.

'Dickens, my dear fellow, what a surprise!'

Rising to his feet briskly, the author holds out his hands, as though he is the host and the proprietor his guest.

'If I had known you were here, I would have come in at once,' says Mr Evans. 'To what do we owe the honour of your visit?'

The two men stride towards the office at the back, their voices rising in intensity. Arthur can hear every word – especially after they have opened the drinks cabinet and enjoyed more than a few drams of Mr Evans's fine old brandy.

Dickens complains about his publishers. For far too long they have been taking advantage of him, he argues. The whole bunch of them are rapacious ruffians! Vulgarian exploiters hiding beneath a shiny veneer of erudition! All this time, on his own, he has been slogging away like a maid-of-all-work responsible for an entire mansion. It is he who has dreamt up all these stories, and it is he who has toiled by gaslight for long hours until his shoulders hunched forward and his eyesight was ruined, but it is they who reap the benefits. He has learnt the painful lesson that selling copyright to a publishing house does not serve a writer's best interests. Authors are no more than factory workers. But he has had enough. He will no longer tolerate the injustice. He will nail his principles to the mast of literature, and, like the good sailor he is, rather than abandon ship, he is ready to go down with it.

'I am therefore making you an offer.'

Dickens proposes to Evans that he should enter into a partnership with him. He will keep the copyright, but assign to the company the right to print and publish his works in exchange for a quarter of the royalties. The author himself will get the rest, as well as a hefty cash advance.

'My dear fellow, you drive a hard bargain!' says Mr Evans, wiping his brow. 'But how can I refuse the progenitor of *Oliver Twist*? We are in agreement.'

Arthur hears the hollow glug of more brandy being poured, the clinking of glasses, the nervous undercurrent to their laughter easing into a spirited harmony.

They publish four of Dickens's books: *Dombey and Son*, *David Copperfield*, *Bleak House*, *Little Dorrit*. Arthur reads them all, and, when they reprint his earlier novels, he rereads them as well.

The partnership proves so fruitful that they also decide to launch a national newspaper – the *Daily News*. Dickens, brimming with new ideas, convinces the company to endorse social reforms. It is their duty to aid the poor and the unfortunate, whose numbers are rising as more desperate families migrate from the countryside to the city in search of a living. London needs to set 'an example of humanity and justice to the whole Empire', not one of cruelty and inequality. Dickens is steered by passion, while everyone else is steered by him. Eight pages long, priced at five pence, in the very first issue they announce to friends and foes: *The principles advocated by the* Daily News *will be principles of progress and improvement; of education, civil and religious liberty and equal legislation.*

They lose a lot of money.

Dickens goes back to writing his novels.

Arthur does not see the author for several months, but then, one day in autumn, he appears again. It is too early in the morning, the sky still ink black. As the boy approaches the office, he notices a shadowy form by the door. Hearing him coming, the figure shifts towards the light under a street lamp. It is Dickens. He looks sleep-deprived and anguished, with stubble on his cheeks and dark rings under his eyes.

Like many others in this city, Arthur has heard the rumours spinning wild. The author is said to have fallen in love with a younger woman and purchased a bracelet for her, none of which would have been revealed had the present not been delivered to his own house by accident and ended up in the hands of his wife.

'Hello, sir.'

'Young Arthur,' says Dickens, tendering a smile that does not quite make it to his eyes. 'I am so pleased to see you.'

'I didn't know you woke so early.'

'Not always, boy. Only these days as I have got some domestic troubles.'

As soon as they enter the office, Dickens sinks down in an armchair, the knuckles of his hands white as he clenches its sides. He utters under his breath: 'The truth is, I couldn't sleep.'

Arthur notices he has more grey hairs now and the wrinkles around his eyes cut deeper.

Feeling the boy's scrutiny, Dickens straightens his shoulders. 'Look, I have brought us a treat – something to cheer up even the most miserable.'

Thus saying, he removes an elegant tin from his pocket and opens it. Inside, arranged in perfect lines, are pink, jellied cubes, dusted with sugar.

Arthur's eyes grow wide. 'What is it, sir?'

'They are lumps of delight,' Dickens replies with a lightness that belies his expression. 'Brought over from the Ottoman lands – a delicacy cherished by the rich and the not so rich alike. Come on, try one.'

Arthur leans forward and picks one up. It has an unusual taste, chewy, soft and perfumed.

'So, what do you think?' asks Dickens.

'It's strange . . . very tasty. Do they eat this every day?'

'I believe they do. I have heard the sultan is in the habit of distributing it amongst his *harem*.'

'What's a *harem*?'

'Oh, the most dreadful thing,' Dickens says, his voice intensifying. 'A horrid, demeaning institution that doesn't bear talking about. Although the late Miss Brontë clearly enjoyed reflecting on it. What a disreputable scene she conjured up for poor Jane Eyre! Remember what Rochester said? That he would not exchange this one little English girl for the Grand Turk's whole collection of women with their gazelle eyes, houri-forms and all! And then, what is the writer's intention, you might wonder, in causing dear drab Jane to imagine herself in Rochester's "pleasure villa", scantily covered in silks and flowers, awaiting a night of sensuous delights . . . What a fantasy to place in the mind of a reserved English lady.' Dickens pauses. 'Still, it is quite an erotic thought, I must say.'

Arthur has read *Jane Eyre* and, although he has not dwelt on this particular detail, he grasps enough now to make him blush.

Oblivious to the boy's discomfort, Dickens carries on. 'Even though the Brontës were raised in Yorkshire, their roots, let us not forget, were in the heart of Cornwall. Having lived by the sea, generations of their family must have grown up with tales of Ottoman corsairs raiding homes and kidnapping English women to take them back to their *harems*. That, I believe, inflames the literary imagination. Anyway, let's set aside that interesting, if somewhat sensational, detail.'

The author picks another lump of delight and holds it between his fingers. 'You must know that many cultures around the world are demonstrably inferior to our own – especially the Oriental race. It will take them a long time, if ever, to reach our level of civilization.'

Arthur arches his shoulders as a stark realization dawns on him. However passionate a supporter of the poor and downcast, however fervent a champion of the oppressed and downtrodden, the author takes a dim view of societies other than his own.

As if he has sensed the boy's disagreement, Dickens returns his gaze. 'It appears you hold a different opinion. Do you have in mind to go beyond our shores someday – are you ever tempted to travel to distant lands?'

Arthur nods wholeheartedly.

'To where?'

In lieu of a response, Arthur opens a drawer and pulls out the newspaper clipping he keeps under a pile of engravings.

Holding the paper to the light, Dickens reads it out loud. '*At the British Museum this afternoon, a large crowd greeted the arrival of colossal statues and other artefacts from Nineveh.*' He stops and peers at the boy over the page. 'Is this where you wish to go – Nineveh? That is a most singular interest of yours. Tell me, have you ever been inside the British Museum?'

'No, sir . . . A few times I went as far as the bottom of the stairs, but I did not dare to enter.'

'Why ever not?'

'I do not have the proper attire.'

Dickens's face softens. 'My boy, there is no need for that to be an obstacle.'

'It usually is,' says Arthur, resolutely. 'And, with all due respect, sir, you might not be in a position to know.'

In these words, the author detects another unspoken rebuke. He may once have laboured in a blacking factory, and ever since been a fervent advocate for the working classes and openly critical of the Poor Law Amendment Act, depicting in his novels the plight of the destitute, and making it plain that the blame for poverty is not to be laid at the door of those who endure it; but here in this room, compared with this boy, he is one of the privileged.

Dickens is pensive for a moment. 'Is it true what they say about you – that you never forget a thing?'

'I seem to spend a lot of time inside my memory,' Arthur admits. 'It's a useless thing.'

Dickens scratches his beard. 'No one is useless in this world who lightens the burdens of another.'

'I am not sure I have lightened anyone's burdens. Not my father's, certainly.'

'All fathers love their children after a fashion. Perhaps yours does not exactly know how to show his esteem for you.'

Arthur bites his lip. He does not want to challenge the famous novelist, but love that manifests only in a profound and bruising coldness, and leaves the other person hurting, can it ever be deemed love?

That same week a package arrives at the office for King Arthur of the Sewers and Slums. Inside he finds a tweed jacket, waistcoat and trousers, tailor-made and a perfect fit, together with a pair of brown leather boots exactly his size. Dickens has observed him remarkably well. There is a letter attached:

My dear Arthur,

I greatly enjoyed our exchange and I have subsequently given much thought to your words. You are a young man of considerable talent and commendable intelligence. I believe you must go to Nineveh and see the River Tigris for yourself. For reasons beyond your power, London has broken your heart. Perhaps when you arrive in the Orient, you will find it within yourself to forgive your home city, and its redoubtable river, the Thames. One always begins to forgive a place as soon as it is left behind.

Ever your affectionate friend,

Charles Dickens

After that, the author disappears once again, rushing headlong into the love affair and marital scandal that will usurp his energy and reputation in the months ahead. Arthur will write to him but not get the chance to thank him personally. Nor will he be able to tell him that he will eventually succeed in visiting the British Museum and the winged creatures of Nineveh, where he will find a surprise waiting for him that will change his life forever.

H—
NARIN

By the River Tigris, 2014

'Grandma, those winged giants that you said Leila saw in her youth, what happened to them?'

'The *lamassus*? They're gone.'

'Where?'

'Who knows – Europe, America . . . Now they're kept in big houses called museums. They're not in their native soil any more, although one or two might still be around, so keep an eye out. But all the others were borne away – tied to rafts and boats and ferried to rich countries. So I heard from my grandmother and now you heard from me.'

The child blinks in incredulity. It is hard to know what to make of Grandma's stories sometimes. As much as she adores the old woman, and loves listening to her, the idea of huge hybrid creatures sailing their way from Mesopotamia to America fails to convince her.

'I know you don't believe me, Narin, but a story is a flute through which truth breathes. And these are your family stories.'

'I understand, Grandma.'

'Remember, child, never look down upon anyone. You must treat everyone and everything with respect. We believe the earth is sacred. Don't trample on it carelessly. Our people never get married in April, because that's when the land is pregnant. You cannot dance and jump and stomp all over it. You have to treat it gently.

Do not ever pollute the soil, the air or the river. That's why I never spit on the ground. You shouldn't do it either.'

'What if I have to cough?'

'Well, cough into a handkerchief and fold it away. The earth is not a receptacle for our waste matter.'

Grandma says an elderly Yazidi woman, a dear neighbour of hers, migrated with her children to Germany, where the family settled in the 1990s. The woman was puzzled and saddened when she learnt that people over there filled a bathtub with water and then sat in it to soap themselves. She could not believe that anyone would be senseless enough to plunge into clean water without having first washed themselves.

Grandma says one should also pay homage to the sun and the moon, which are celestial siblings. Every morning at dawn she goes up to the roof to salute the first light, and when she prays she faces the sun. After dark she sends a prayer to the orb of night. One must always walk the earth with wonder, for it is full of miracles yet to be witnessed. Trees you must think of not only for what they are above ground but also for what remains invisible below. Birds, rocks, tussocks and thickets of gorse, even the tiniest insects are to be treasured. But as a water-dowser, it is the Tigris that the old woman holds in the highest esteem.

Narin watches Grandma sweep out the stove as she speaks, the old woman's slender fingers carefully collecting the ash gathered at the bottom on a tray. Ash is precious, essential for many cures. Sometimes Grandma dips a clove of garlic in the powdery residue and draws symbols on the forehead of an ailing patient. No one can touch that person until the mark completely wears off. At other times, Grandma takes a coin and bends it into a crescent. Then she drops the metal into a bowl of pellucid water, which she places under the bed of a sick person.

Numbers are important and Grandma's favourite is seven. In order to process an emotion, be it good or bad, you must allow seven days to pass. So if you fall in love, with a lightness to your moves like the speck of pollen on the wing of a butterfly, you have to wait seven days, and, if after that period you still feel the same way, then and only then can you trust your heart. Never make a major decision unless you have spent seven days contemplating it.

If you are cross with someone, or are on the verge of breaking ties with them, once again, you must delay any reaction for seven moons. This is the only way to ensure you will not be led astray by rage or revenge. A deal ought to brew for seven days before it is sealed; a house has to be blessed in seven corners before anyone moves in. You cannot bake a loaf of bread unless the yeast has rested for seven cycles. A newborn baby must be guarded from evil spirits for seven sunrises. There are seven days in a week, seven sages walking the earth, seven regions in the human body, seven sleepers in a cave escaping persecution, seven cardinal sins for which seven doors to hell have been reserved.

Of the seven days, Wednesdays are the most propitious. That is when Grandma prepares her balms, ointments and tinctures, because, as everyone knows, Melek Tawûs descended on this venerated day, making it the most auspicious time to do good. If you have a hidden wish, something too intimate to share, you may just as well whisper it to a flowing stream, preferably on a Wednesday. The current will take care of it. Equally, if you wake up from a nightmare in the middle of the night, turn on the tap and tell it to the water. It will soothe your pounding heart, wash away your fears.

Grandma says one should be kind to every living being, no matter how small or seemingly insignificant, for you can never know in what shape or form you or a loved one will be reborn.

'Yesterday I was a river. Tomorrow, I may return as a raindrop.'

Rivers have personalities. Some calm down with age, winding ponderously across fertile plains and meadows; others become bitter, surging with rage, tumbling through steep gorges; while yet others remain agitated and confused till the end. No two rivers are alike. The Tigris is, and has always been, 'the mad one', 'the swift one'. Not like its twin, the Euphrates, which, having a gentler disposition, courses at a slower pace, taking its time, absorbing its surroundings as it passes by. These two mighty currents – though both spring from the womb of the Taurus Mountains in Turkey and run parallel for most of their lengthy peregrinations until they perish together in the Persian Gulf – are strikingly dissimilar – much as two siblings can be very different, despite sharing the same parents.

'They speak to each other, you know, the Tigris and the Euphrates. When the wind blows this way, you can hear them.'

Narin scoffs. 'Really – can you hear them now?'

'I can, actually,' says the old woman, craning her neck. 'Listen, they're gossiping again, those two. They are very chatty. Euphrates is complaining. She says: "Why are you so restless, my Tigris? You're tiring everyone – and yourself. Why this endless rage of yours?"'

Narin draws closer. 'And what does Tigris say?'

'Tigris says, "Why're you asking, my Euphrates? Even if I were to explain, you'd never understand. You're blessed with calmness of spirit. I'm not like you. It's so hard to be me – it's hard to have to fight all the time."'

'And how does Euphrates reply?'

'Let me see . . .' Grandma says, her head bent in concentration. For a while she listens, nodding. 'Umm, hmm.'

'Tell me!'

'Oh, Euphrates says, "But you're mistaken about me. If you only knew how difficult it is to be calm and composed. If you only knew, it takes a fierce fight inside to remain peaceful on the outside."'

'What does that mean?'

'That tranquillity does not come easily.'

The child is silent for a moment, her lips compressed. 'Which river is wiser do you think, Grandma?'

'Well, if you promise not to mention it to our Tigris . . .'

'I promise,' Narin says instantly.

'Good, in that case I'll tell you. Actually, I agree with Euphrates. Better to be a gentle soul than one consumed by anger, resentment and vengeance. Anyone can wage war, but maintaining peace is a difficult thing. Because of this, I respect Euphrates more, but let's keep it from our grumpy old Tigris, eh? No need to enrage him any further.'

Inadvertently, the child casts a quick glance in the direction of the Tigris, splashing in the background – the waves breaking on the boulders, ripples and rapids imprinting the riverbed. By contrast, when Grandma speaks again, her voice comes in such a soft whisper that the girl almost misses what she says.

'Whether turbid or placid, in this land where the stones are ancient and the stories are spoken but rarely written down, it is the rivers that govern the days of our lives. Many kings have come and many kings have gone, and God knows most were ruthless, but here in Mesopotamia, my love, never forget the only true ruler is water.'

The room where the old woman and the girl sleep is sparsely furnished. At night they spread mattresses on the floor, unless it is very hot, in which case they go up to the roof. Two low divans sit opposite each other, piled with cushions stuffed with goat's hair – orange, scarlet, purple. A potted ivy climbs up by the window, reaching the ceiling and creeping along the cornice.

Every evening Narin sits on the floor so that Grandma can brush and braid her hair. As the old woman applies almond oil to the child's dark chestnut mane, she relates magical tales. She says one should never claim to *know* a story but merely to carry it. For that is where *chiroks* must be kept – cradled in the warmth of your breast, close to your beating heart.

'Grandma . . . does every sickness in this world have a cure?'

'It does, my love.'

'How can you be sure?'

'Because I trust God – He would not give us a stomach ache without growing mint nearby.'

'Then why can't you heal me?'

The wrinkles on Grandma's forehead deepen. 'Just because I do not know the remedy, does not mean there is none.'

'But you know everything.'

'I'm half as wise and twice the fool as everyone else.'

'That's not true!' exclaims Narin, appalled that anyone could say such a thing about her grandmother, even if it were the old woman herself.

'Wisdom is a mountain capped with snow. I've yet to meet the person who's given it a hug.'

'What does that mean?'

'It means no matter how much you know, there is far more that you don't. So you must always make an effort to keep learning. Did I not tell you the story of the angel Gibra'il?'

Her hair nicely braided and oiled, Narin shakes her head. 'You can tell me now.'

'All right, then. *In those days, in those far-off days, in olden times* . . . there lived a famous sheikh. One morning, he woke up and declared he'd studied everything worth knowing. He'd nothing left to learn! That same afternoon the angel Gibra'il appeared to him disguised as a dervish.'

'What's a dervish?'

'A humble seeker of truth,' replies Grandma. 'Now the dervish and the sheikh walked to the shores of the Tigris. When they reached the river, they watched a swallow swoop down, scoop up water and fly away. The dervish said to his companion, "Tell me, did the river sink any lower when the bird drank from it? Knowledge is a vast expanse of water, and you've managed to take in no more than the swallow's beakful." The sheikh understood his mistake and realized that no matter how much one knows there is a lot more one does not.'

Most of Grandma's stories feature water – surging, searching. She says, just like two drops of rain join on a windowpane, weaving their paths slowly and steadily, an invisible thread connects those who are destined to meet.

—O—

ARTHUR

By the River Thames, 1857

The first time King Arthur of the Sewers and Slums passes the grand portico of the British Museum, he feels so small and out of place that it takes every muscle in his body to stop himself from turning around and running away. Up close the building is far more majestic and imposing than he could ever have imagined. With its enormous stairs, concrete floors, four vast wings and Ionic columns, it rises above the surrounding terraced rooftops like a secular temple. Upon arrival, each visitor is greeted by a sculpture in the pediment depicting the progress of humankind – a linear journey, it seems, from its primitive state to one of glowing civilization.

The boy strides in, slowly and purposefully, even as his heartbeat quickens. This morning, clad in his new clothes, he has emerged from his house like a moth breaking out of its chrysalis, but now, as he tries to hold up his chin, he is awkwardly self-conscious. He mulls over all the answers he has prepared in case someone inquires where he is going. He wonders if the Keeper of Oriental Antiquities is still working here, and, if so, whether he will remember the exchange they'd had years back and perhaps be kind enough to show him around. Yet he cannot muster the courage to ask after the scholar, hoping he will appear of his own accord from behind one of the lofty columns.

Fortunately, just then, Arthur spots a group of students, more or less the same age as him, though clearly from another part of society altogether. He falls in step with the group. They do not seem to mind his presence; immersed in a sullen silence, they are shepherded around by a teacher who rarely glances over his shoulder to check who is following. For a while Arthur walks on their heels as they troop through the most popular sections in the museum – Ancient Greece, Ancient Rome, Ancient Egypt.

After a while, feeling emboldened, Arthur breaks away from the others and explores the building on his own. In the next room, he runs into a museum employee.

'Sir, I am looking for the *lamassus* from Nineveh – are they still here?'

'Where else would they be, lad?' says the man. 'Did you expect the winged creatures to have flown away?'

Arthur stutters. He does not belong in august institutions, and he worries that people can sense it. It occurs to him, in that moment, that poverty has its own scent, an odour that emanates from his pores, easily detected. It is an awful, debilitating thought. Drawing in a sharp breath, he turns around and hurries in the direction he assumes to be the exit. The man calls after him, perhaps in sympathy, but the boy does not wait.

The divisions that make up class are, in truth, the borders on a map. When you are born into wealth and privilege, you inherit a plan that outlines the paths ahead, indicating the short-cuts and byways available to reach your destination, informing you of the lush valleys where you may rest and the tricky terrain to avoid. If you enter the world without such a map, you are bereft of proper guidance. You lose your way more easily, trying to pass through what you thought were orchards and gardens, only to discover they are marshland and peat bogs.

Anxious to get out of the building, the boy quickens his pace. But the room he turns into does not lead to the exit, instead joining on to a long corridor. He scuttles down one passage after another, each sucking him deeper into the bowels of the museum, every hall opening on to another more baffling than the last. He is terrified that he may be trespassing into areas closed to visitors, but, having no better plan, he keeps going – until he finds himself in a chamber stacked high with wooden boxes and crates on all four sides.

There is an eerie quiet here, less an absence of noise than a stillness that absorbs everything and claims it for its own. Stored in vitrines and arranged on shelves are thousands of clay slabs. Broken, fractured. Some still bear traces of the earth from which they were extracted. Stepping closer, Arthur notices that they all have the same narrow, wedge-shaped impressions on their surface. Craning his head this way and that, he examines the mysterious signs, which are unlike anything his eyes have hitherto beheld.

'Are you looking for something?'

Snapped out of his reverie, Arthur turns around. It is another museum official, watching him curiously, though not unkindly.

'I'm terribly sorry, sir, I was just –'

'You're with the school, yes? Did you get lost?'

Arthur pauses. 'Umm, I am afraid I have.'

'Ah, I thought so. Your classmates are upstairs, with the Roman antiquities, boy – you are in the Nineveh section.'

'I'll go and join them,' says Arthur, but he cannot help asking, 'So all these bits of clay, they were brought over with the *lamassus*?'

'Well, we have thousands of tablets under this roof. They are not all from one single excavation, but, yes, they came from the same region as the *lamassus*, if that is your inquiry.'

Arthur nods thoughtfully. A spiderweb hangs suspended from one of the cases, and he watches it as it catches the light, dazzled by its geometry. He says, 'The marks on them – is it some ancient scripture?'

The man shrugs. 'Ancient bird tracks or chicken scratches, for all we know. Only a few can read them.'

'But there are patterns . . .' murmurs Arthur.

'You think so? Probably, yet many tablets are smashed, as you can see. Impossible to decipher this kind of gallimaufry.'

Their talk is interrupted by the sound of footsteps coming from the other side of the hallway. The schoolboys are back from their tour, looking bored.

'Are you not going to join your friends?' the man asks.

'Oh, yes, thank you, sir.'

With a final glance at the treasures of Nineveh, the boy hastens to leave the room. This he cannot explain to the man, not even to himself, but an odd excitement has taken hold of his heart. The signs on the tablets are not *bird tracks* or *chicken scratches*, random scribbles or decorative motifs. He is certain that what he has seen is a system of writing.

The next day Arthur is back at the British Museum, and the day after that. He has made a swift calculation in his head. His lunch break lasts fifty minutes, starting and ending at the same time every afternoon. From the printer's office to the treasures of Nineveh there are 2,103 steps, including the stairs of the museum, all of which takes him eighteen minutes to traverse one way and another eighteen minutes to return. This leaves him with fourteen minutes to spare. It is not much, but it is not nothing. In this way, provided he can walk fast enough and manage to consume his lunch on the move, he can study the marks on the tablets for fourteen minutes every day and get back to work before anyone notices his absence.

So it begins. Rain, snow or hail, Arthur abides by his new routine. Now more familiar with his surroundings and much less nervous, he rushes through the halls of the museum, an unbidden excitement growing deep inside of him. He crosses galleries where ancient artefacts are displayed on marble plinths, in glass cases or plan cabinets, but, being on a strict schedule, he gives them only a cursory glance, a silent salute. And then, like a lover late to an appointment with his sweetheart, he hastens to meet the Mesopotamian tablets.

Owning only one set of smart clothes, he has no choice but to wear the same suit every day, though he makes sure it is buffed with a brush and freshly aired. He is convinced that he has to be spotlessly dressed, his boots polished to a soldier's shine. His obsession with hygiene renders life difficult both for him and his mother. Once a week he asks her to help him to prepare a bath. Together they collect scraps of coal and wood dropped in the streets, light a brazier and heat water. Ordinarily, Arthur would have to wait for his father to have the first soak, his mother second, and only then would it be his turn, after which his brother might also use the same water. But his father rarely comes home any more, and his mother lets Arthur wash before anyone else. To save her trouble, the boy visits the local bath house, but the place is so squalid he regrets the decision.

For a person who sets great store by personal cleanliness, London is littered with traps. No matter how hard they work – the pure-finders collecting dog faeces to sell to tanners, the dustmen scraping up cinders and ashes to trade as fertilizers, the crossing-sweepers with their brooms – piles of mud and dung accumulate hither and thither, making it difficult to hasten from one place to the next on foot. Once, as Arthur is nearing Great Russell Street, he sees a carriage hurtling towards him, its wheels churning up muck, and, though he pulls back, he cannot avoid his clothes being splattered. Another day, distracted by a group of musicians playing barrel organs and hurdy-gurdies, he slips on a vegetable peel, falling sideways into a heap of refuse. On both occasions, he wastes precious time trying to clean himself with water trickling from a nearby pump, but he still turns up at the museum for the few minutes remaining to him.

The rules of etiquette, too, add to Arthur's challenges. Just as a lady ought to slightly raise her dress with her right hand when traversing the street, making sure to show nothing above her ankle, a gentleman must make way for a woman, and adolescents for the elderly. Such codes of behaviour inevitably slow him down.

Meanwhile, the staff at the British Museum are puzzled by this startled bird of a boy who comes every day, panting with exertion, his hair tousled by the wind. They watch him give a timid nod to the clerk at the entrance before he scampers to the Assyrian Gallery, where he stops in front of the tablets, stock-still, as if he were a statue himself, his face so close to the vitrines that his breath mists the surface of the glass. After precisely fourteen minutes he sprints out in indecent haste. They wonder if the lad is soft in the head, poor thing, and, if so, how they can gently deter him from his peculiar and increasingly irritating routine. A few of them debate whether they should inform the police and put an end to this unseemly spectacle. Eventually, they decide to notify their superiors. The matter is referred to the Keeper of Oriental Antiquities.

Thursday afternoon, at the usual hour, when the boy dashes into the Assyrian Gallery, he finds Dr Samuel Birch waiting for him, his eyes burning dark against the silver-white of his hair.

'Good afternoon, young man.'

Arthur's face brightens, though he registers the scholar has not recognized him. He returns the greeting with a tentative nod, torn between reminding him of the conversation they had had years back and, more practically, taking this exchange no further. He has barely thirteen minutes left and, as much as he would love to talk to the renowned antiquarian, a chat is a distraction he can ill afford.

'My staff have been telling me about you. They say you seem quite taken with the cuneiform – the markings on the clay tablets from Mesopotamia.'

'They are mesmerizing, sir.'

The man squints at Arthur as if trying to gauge the sincerity of these words, the skin around his eyes crinkling. 'I am intrigued by the intensity of your interest. Quite extraordinary, indeed, especially for a young person – although I fear you are arousing nervousness amongst my colleagues. Perhaps you would be so kind as to acquaint me with your intentions.'

'Why would that be?' Arthur asks, without tearing his eyes from the tablets.

'Excuse me?'

'Why do I make them nervous?'

'Oh, well . . . umm, because, as a general rule, people are afraid of those who are, or appear to be, *different*, and you, my boy, fall neatly under that description.'

Slowly, Arthur drags his gaze away from the vitrines and casts a searching glance at the older man. 'It was you who invited me to come over to see the stone beasts from Nineveh.'

'It was I?'

'Yes, sir, four years and fourteen weeks ago, plus one day – on the afternoon a pair of *lamassus* were borne in and towed up the stairs of the museum – that's when we spoke. The 26th of November – it was a Friday.'

The man is silent for what feels like an age. 'It had slipped my mind, but now I recollect that curious little boy.' He regards the youngster, taking in the fuzzy beginnings of a moustache on his upper lip and downy sideboards. 'You have grown much taller.'

Arthur shifts his weight from one foot to the other. 'I am sorry, I do not mean to be impolite, but I have only nine minutes left.'

Without waiting for the man's response, he switches his attention back to the tablets. They all exhibit the same wedge-shaped impressions – some horizontal, some vertical, others diagonal. Arthur is certain by now that this is a way of writing very distinct from an alphabet. It does not generally have letters representing single sounds or phonemes. Instead it has characters made up of several marks that divide the text into syllables, but, there being no visible gaps between the words, it is hard to establish where one finishes and another begins. Some signs, however, seem to stand for whole words, and that helps him to find their meaning. Leaning over the vitrine, he pores over the artefacts, all his senses quiveringly alert.

The Keeper of Oriental Antiquities watches Arthur, amazed to see that the boy's concentration is so profound that he has quite forgotten him. The boy's lips begin moving, and so does his finger, tracing the lines on the tablets through the barrier of glass. To the scholar's surprise, he is not just staring at the tablets but reading them. This gangling youth in ill-fitting clothes too light for the weather is deciphering what only a handful of privileged scholars have been able to decode before. Time stills. It feels as if nothing moves or breathes – or perhaps they all do in perfect harmony, the humans and the artefacts in the room, everything falling into a rare synchrony.

Arthur, back from his trance, straightens up his shoulders and sighs. His duty done for the day, he makes for the door.

'You are leaving?'

'Oh, I am terribly sorry,' says Arthur, startled to find the man still there when he turns around. 'I must return to my employer.'

'Wait, please. You were . . . were you really . . .' The man pauses, tries again. 'Can you read the tablets, boy?'

'Only a few words here and there, sir,' replies Arthur truthfully.

'Will you be kind enough to show me how you do that?'

The boy checks the clock. He will have to sprint to get back to the office on time, but he does not want to be rude. Besides, a part of him wishes to share his discovery, so he nods his agreement.

He begins by listing the experts he has studied in his free time. There is Edward Hincks, the Irish parson, and Jules Oppert, the French–German–Jewish scholar, and G. F. Grotefend, the grammar schoolteacher, but primarily he has benefited from the works of Sir Henry Rawlinson. He explains that by piecing together clues from their findings he has been able to draw his own conclusion: that the cuneiform is not an alphabet exactly but a collection of syllables.

Arthur takes a breath before continuing. 'I have come to realize that each group of strokes on the clay is a symbol and each symbol represents a particular sound, or, to be precise, a syllabic sound. And that may be purely phonetic, or it may stand for a thing. I have learnt, for example, how "King Ashurbanipal" is written – hence my interest in this tablet over here, which I believe was a letter.'

Together they lean over the glass case, peering inside.

'A letter composed by the king himself?'

'No, sir. Rather by someone close to him. Look at this cluster of signs over there. My guess is it is pronounced as *ub*, which, together with the next, *lugal*, could be read as "royal adviser". I have therefore reason to conclude that this letter was composed by the chief counsellor in the palace in Nineveh.'

His thick eyebrows raised in astonishment, the elderly scholar fumbles for words. 'And, umm, to whom might it have been sent?'

'Well, that is the part that confuses me. It seems to have been addressed to Ashurbanipal's brother, but I was not able to make further progress. Were the two brothers at cross purposes? Enemies, perhaps? Was the chief counsellor upset at Ashurbanipal? I would need to spend more time with the tablet to be sure.'

Interpreting the ensuing silence as an indication of the man's disbelief, the boy lowers his gaze. His mood shifts from pride to incipient panic. A sheen of sweat dampening his forehead, he walks towards the exit.

'I must get back to the office. Good day, sir.'

'No, wait – please.' The Keeper of Oriental Antiquities sheds his formality, hastening after him. 'It is remarkable, what you have just done.'

Arthur inhales sharply.

'We have been looking for someone to help us put the tablets in order. As you must have noticed, they are haphazardly organized, if at all. Some are still encrusted in earth. They need to be sorted and arranged – not that we have come up with a system yet. I was wondering, given your interest and your unusual talent, would you like to help us? We could offer you some emolument for your troubles.'

Slowly, the frown that has descended on Arthur's brow softens. He glances up at the scholar, his mouth slightly agape, trying to decide whether he is serious or teasing him, and, when he is convinced of the man's sincerity, a smile spreads over his face.

'Yes, sir, I'd like that very much.'

In his excitement, Arthur has accepted the offer without thinking it over properly. Only after he leaves the British Museum does he grasp the full implications of what he has agreed to. How will he manage to work two jobs at the same time? There is no question in his mind that he cannot afford to lose his apprenticeship at Bradbury & Evans, which, besides paying him a regular wage, is a good place to expand his knowledge. But, equally, he cannot decline the British Museum's offer and the chance to hold in his hands the tablets from Nineveh. The only solution he can think of is to give up his coffee breaks – one in the morning and one late in the afternoon – and request that the extra time be added to his lunch break. He will then have to forgo eating altogether and, at the appointed hour, sprint the distance from the office to the museum. This is the only way he can perform both his duties: he will run as fast as his legs can carry him. To test if it is doable, he times himself. It takes him eight minutes and twenty seconds to arrive at the museum gates and eight minutes and twenty-four seconds to race back – provided he manages to avoid any accidents or incidents on the way.

That spring, the pedestrians and pedlars in Covent Garden are surprised to see a youngster hurrying past them, darting across busy roadways and through dingy alleyways, bounding over piles of garbage, weaving past hawkers plying their trade on the pavements, gentlemen sauntering along dressed in top hats and breeches, and ladies in swelling crinoline skirts, tight bodices and dainty bonnets – apologizing profusely to whomever he has unwittingly bumped into as he hurtles along.

⊣H

ZALEEKHAH

By the River Thames, 2018

Inside the black cab that Uncle Malek arranged for her, Zaleekhah looks out of the window, watching the pedestrians, the cyclists, the restaurants flash past in a stream of blurred lights. London for her has never been a capital of solid, sturdy architecture and historical monuments and leafy public parks but rather a city carved by water, smoothed by tide and flow, an ever-expanding reservoir of fluvial memories, some obliterated, others repressed, still others forcefully gushing, like its many rivers and their tributaries.

They are everywhere – the ghost streams.

There is the mysterious River Fleet, for instance – the largest and most important of London's subterranean rivers, the 'hollow stream'. Once a broad tidal basin and an important artery bringing goods and business into the capital, it has repeatedly endured abuse at the hands of humans, choked and polluted with discarded carcasses and putrefying offal from the meat markets and tanneries lining its banks – next, all at once, it was deemed too filthy, too malodorous, too unpleasant to look at and therefore no longer of use. A solution was found to hide it from sight, cover its ugliness under stacks of bricks. It lay buried for about 250 years, until it was rediscovered and reopened – only to be buried again. A legendary river, then an open sewer, then an aimless canal, then an open sewer again and, eventually, forgotten by almost everyone. Still alive, though. A watery spectre that refuses to die.

Then there is the River Effra in South London, concealed and culverted, nowadays a conduit for drainage and waste matter, silently coursing under not only houses and offices but also cemeteries, whence it sometimes unearths and carries off buried coffins. There is also the Tyburn, a source of delicious fresh salmon in the distant past, though barely remembered these days, as it flows unseen and unheard underneath celebrated urban landmarks. The Walbrook, once a sapphire-blue river running through the Roman fort of Londinium into the Thames, shimmering like the wing of a dragonfly, provided residents with clean water; now it only feeds into a malodorous sewer.

Then there is the quaint and charming River Westbourne – 'the royal stream'. When Victorian engineers could not find a way to build a Tube station above the river, they made the river run through the station instead. Today, invisible to thousands of commuters, hidden in plain sight, it pours through a pipe above the platforms in Sloane Square Tube station, after being entombed in London clay to make way for the prosperous terraces of Chelsea and Belgravia above. It has survived storms, and even a bomb blast in the Second World War. They are all there, roiling beneath the cement pavements and the tarmacked streets, rumbling and rushing under strata of concrete and bricks, buried under sediments of history and the weight of amnesia.

Sitting back, Zaleekhah closes her eyes momentarily, as if hoping to hear the water through the noise of the traffic. On a sudden impulse, she leans forward and says to the driver, 'Excuse me!'

The man, busy chatting to someone on the phone, doesn't answer immediately.

'Sorry!' Zaleekhah says, louder. 'I've changed my mind. Can you take me somewhere else?'

Now she has his full attention. He looks at her through the rear-view mirror. 'The postcode was for the houseboats by the shore. So you're not going to Cheyne Walk?'

'Yes, I was, but I'm not now.' She gives him the name of a district in South-East London instead, a street of converted warehouses.

He nods, though in the driving mirror she can see his eyes tinged with a trace of suspicion.

The crepuscular light has drained into darkness by the time Zaleekhah arrives at a dull ochre, two-storey brick building in Bermondsey. A metal sign on the door reads *Centre for Ecology and Hydrology*. A not-for-profit, independent institute for research in biogeochemistry, water studies and biodiversity. Its flat roof, bland functionality and absence of ornament stands in stark contrast with the luxurious elegance of Uncle's house.

Opening the door, she steps into the corridor and inhales the familiar smell of disinfected floors. The entire space is divided economically into small rooms and modest cubicles, except for the larger common areas, which are reserved for team meetings. A few items are dotted around here and there: Post-it notes, inspirational quotes, postcards pinned to cork boards; mugs with funny sayings, succulents in ceramic pots . . . the universal simplicity of office objects. Zaleekhah does not find the effacement of individuality, if that is what it is, unappealing. It is a place designed for collective endeavour, not for personal gratification.

She walks slowly, her footsteps echoing in the empty building. The last door on the right displays her name – *Dr Zaleekhah Clarke*. For a moment she stares at the plaque. Upon getting married, she took her husband's surname. Now it will probably have to change again. Women are expected to be like rivers – readjusting, shapeshifting.

It is perhaps easier to justify the end of a relationship – both to yourself and to others – when there is a definite, tangible cause, no matter how painful. But it is harder to grasp the gradual evaporation of love, a loss so slow and subtle as to be barely detectable, until it is fully gone. Now she feels like a passenger on a sleeper train who awakens and draws back the curtains, only to find an unfamiliar landscape that had been there all along. She cannot pull the curtains closed again.

She is almost thirty-one years old. She has no children, no parents. This time last year she was certain that her husband was her family. Their colleagues always commented on how perfectly matched they were, which was meant as a compliment, and also the politest way of saying neither could have found anyone better. It was true, though: they seemed like a good couple, and there were times when they really were – *if only she'd had the capacity for happiness*. But she also knows that the fabric of their marriage had worn thin in many places. All it needed was one sharp tug for it to tear.

Zaleekhah lets herself into her office, which is small and spartan but clean. On the opposite wall there is a poster – a black-and-white picture of a single drop of water. At first glance, it seems to be plunging from a great height into a lake or an estuary, but it could equally be emerging from the depths of an ocean, ascending towards the skies.

Apart from this image, the walls are bare. Her research papers are arranged in folders on the desk, alongside a jar of pencils, all neatly sharpened. A fiddle-leaf fig droops listlessly by the window; it has stayed in its original, stunted form even though she has done her best to take care of it. On the left side is a slate-coloured sofa – also heaped with papers and folders. Good thing Uncle has never visited her workplace. He would have found it depressingly drab. But she loves her job, and cherishes this space she can call her own.

She moves aside the clutter on the sofa. Under a scratch pad, attached with a paperclip, as if it were an afterthought, she sees a note.

> *How to Bury a River*
> 1. Build concrete troughs along both sides of the riverbed.
> 2. Add a roof to the troughs.
> 3. Encase the river completely on three sides, turning it into one long, winding coffin.
> 4. Cover the roof with earth, making sure no trace is visible.
> 5. Build your city over it.
> 6. Forget that it was ever there.

Zaleekhah doesn't remember when she wrote this; she must have scribbled it in a moment of distraction. She crumples the paper and tosses it towards the bin, narrowly missing it.

On a shelf behind her desk, amid clusters of books stacked every which way, is an arrangement of photographs in silver frames. In the first she is with her husband, on their honeymoon in Marrakech. Sitting under a tree whose pomegranates droop ripe and rubicund above their heads, after a stroll through the souks in the medina, they look carelessly happy, spent and sunburnt. The next picture is a slimmer and younger version of herself, taken at her university graduation party. A palpable pride in her features, she leans over a sumptuous table, in the company of Uncle Malek, Aunt Malek and Helen, glasses held aloft in a toast. Beside that is a photo of her parents. Her father sports his customary charming smile, his eyes crinkling at the corners. Sitting by his side, her mother beams at the camera, her hair draped over one shoulder in a long, dark braid. She wears a green dress cinched at the waist, the soft curve of her belly suggesting the early months of pregnancy. This is how her mother would have looked, Zaleekhah assumes, had she ever appeared in her dreams.

The fourth frame – smaller in size – is tucked away at the back of the shelf, not easily visible. A photo of Zaleekhah at a conference in Dublin with a tall, slender man in his fifties. Her mentor, her colleague, her friend. Professor Berenberg was an eminent hydrologist, biochemist and climate scientist. Highly respected in his field, he was known not only for his brilliant intellect and contribution to the discipline but also for his kindness and generosity towards staff and students. They collaborated on various projects for long years – until he left the lab, alone and publicly disgraced.

Towards the end of his life, the professor became preoccupied with a hypothesis he referred to in his notes as 'aquatic memory'. He argued that, under certain circumstances, water – the universal solvent – retained evidence, or 'memory', of the solute particles that had dissolved in it, no matter how many times it was diluted or purified. Even if years passed, or centuries, and not a single original molecule remained, each droplet of water maintained a unique structure, distinguishable from the next, marked forever by what it once contained. Water, in other words, *remembered*.

Consumed by this hypothesis, Berenberg dropped all other research. Expanding and diversifying his team, he hired biologists, chemists and immunologists to work alongside hydrologists. He was convinced that if they could prove that water possessed some kind of memory, this would have groundbreaking implications, not only for hydrology and biology but also for medicine, homeopathy and conventional attitudes towards healing. Satisfied with his results, he submitted his findings to peer-reviewed scientific journals – and one agreed to publish his paper.

The backlash was almost instant. A tide of scepticism followed. His arguments were found to be weak, his conclusions insufficiently supported by evidence. It did not help the professor's case that independent researchers could not verify his results when they repeated his experiments under similar lab conditions. Scepticism gave way to disbelief, disbelief to rejection and rejection to ridicule. Berenberg did not back down, insisting on the validity of his method. The more he held his ground, the more he was lambasted. His reputation tarnished, he was forced to endure a swift downfall. Old friends stopped calling him. Young researchers distanced themselves. Shunned, he lost his lab and funding. Still he carried on doggedly, moving to the basement of his home; and when his last remaining grants ran out, he covered all the costs of his research out of his own pocket. There he worked with limited means and barely any staff – until one morning, two years ago, he was found dead on the floor, felled by a heart attack.

Ever since then, he has been a ghost river in Zaleekhah's life, pushed into the dark recesses of her past. She rarely, if ever, mentions his name, although she thinks about him often. Aquatic memory has been a contentious subject for her – professionally and personally. Her husband believed that the late professor, though well intentioned, was misled by his own unconscious confirmation bias, seeing in the findings what he simply wished to see. Whereas Zaleekhah is convinced that more studies are needed to understand water and its many anomalies, and until then it would be as absurd to conclude that Berenberg was deluded as it would be to suggest he was triumphant.

Following the death of the professor, without telling anyone, Zaleekhah continued his experiments for a while. The results were often confusing, neither stable nor clear. At times, she felt on the verge of proving the hypothesis. At others, the data were so weak she doubted the proposition altogether. With such wide variation, it was impossible to submit anything definitive to respected journals. Despite her disappointment, she carried on testing and tenaciously recording the results – until her husband found out.

'Are you out of your mind? Why are you wasting your time with a failed hypothesis?'

'I just want to see where the research will take me.'

'Isn't it obvious? It'll take you nowhere. It's poetic nonsense – not science.'

'Maybe they're not worlds apart – science and poetry, I mean.'

The glare in his eyes, the sudden withdrawal of his patience. 'I don't know what you're trying to do, but please stop it – for your own good. Unless you want to risk your job? I've never understood why you took the guy seriously. I'm sorry, but he was pathetic. He was clearly losing his mind.'

That is when Zaleekhah told her husband. Speaking slowly, she explained to him how much the deceased scientist meant to her and how she was not ready to let go of the theory of aquatic memory. She said she missed working with Berenberg and then she said something that she thought she would never voice out loud: Berenberg was her mentor at first, and a close colleague and a good friend, but, somewhere in between these stages, for a passing time, she had also been in love with him.

'In love?'

'Yes, but that was before I met you. Before we got married. I'd known him for a long time.'

Few things harden the human heart as fast as jealousy. Cold and commanding, it settles quickly in the warm spot left by affection, chilling it with its bitter touch.

'All these years you were working with your ex-boyfriend, and you didn't even think to tell me?'

'He was never my boyfriend!'

'What was he, then?'

'Nothing. He was just –'

'Special?'

'No, not like that. He was different – okay?'

'Different from me, you mean.'

'Brian, that's not what I'm saying –'

The silence that followed did not surprise her. But she was not ready for his anger, which felt too close to hatred.

'I can't believe you've kept this from me when you know how much I've given up for you.'

Once again, there it was, their one unresolvable debate, always ready to rear its head.

'Why are you bringing this up now? Because you knew when we got married I never planned to have children.'

'You never even *wanted* to want them!'

She looked at him, expecting him to hear the awkwardness in his own words. But in that moment, he lifted his chin and said, 'You wouldn't have my child, but I bet you would have had his.'

A few minutes later Zaleekhah packed a few belongings, put them in a cardboard box and left.

She will sleep in the lab tonight again. As long as she has her sleeping pills, she does not mind. With the water from a Thermos she swallows two pills. Then she rummages in the cupboard for a blanket that she keeps for times like this. She takes out the book she borrowed from Uncle Malek. She was planning to start reading it tonight, but her eyelids are closing. So instead she wraps her cardigan around it. *Nineveh and Its Remains* will be her pillow. Maybe she will dream of human-headed, bird-winged *lamassus* feathering earthwards from laden clouds.

She switches off the lights. In the dark, she is ambushed by a memory – unbidden and unexpected. They were packing his things, the two of them, the day Berenberg left the office. The temperature had fallen that morning, their breath condensing in front of their eyes. She asked him if he ever regretted studying 'aquatic memory', given the price he paid for choosing such a controversial subject.

'Not for one second. I wanted to research an unknown property of water, and I treasured every moment of it.'

'But it cost you so much.'

'True . . . but you and I both love the work we do and that love is beyond all personal success or failure. You'll pick up where I've left off, and, if you falter, someone else will take on your research. We do this to keep scientific inquiry going – with or without us.'

Thinking about these words now, Zaleekhah curls into herself and hugs her knees. The sofa is shorter than she is, but that's not the cause of her discomfort. She feels guilty for never having told Berenberg how much he meant to her and she feels guilty for telling her husband how much Berenberg meant to her. She was silent when she should have spoken; she spoke when she should have been silent. Either way, guilt is her most loyal companion.

And regret, too – not so much for her acts as for her failure to act. She was drawn to Berenberg's dedication and perseverance, a devotion so selfless as to seek only the good of its object, an unreasonable commitment perhaps more commonly observed in ancient mystics and ascetics than in the modern workplace.

As she closes her eyes, waiting to descend into a drugged sleep, she can hear a gentle lapping in the distance. They are all there. The lost rivers of time, out of sight and out of mind but notable in their absence, like phantom limbs that still have the power to cause pain. They are here and everywhere, eroding the solid structures on which we have built our careers, marriages, reputations and relationships, evermore flowing onwards – *with or without us.* Zaleekhah knows she may not be one of them, but she will always be attracted to people who are pulled towards something bigger and better than themselves, a passion that lasts a lifetime, even though it will consume them in the end.

—o—
ARTHUR

By the River Thames, 1857–8

The day King Arthur of the Sewers and Slums arrives at the British Museum, not as a casual visitor but as a member of staff, however junior and temporary, he walks into the grand building with a new sense of purpose. The Keeper of Oriental Antiquities is waiting for him at the entrance to the Nineveh collection. Beside him is another young man.

'Good morning, Arthur. This is my assistant, Edward.'

'It's a pleasure to meet the young genius at last!' says Edward, offering a handshake.

A flush creeps across Arthur's cheeks. He can never tell whether people mean what they say. For all his skill in deciphering words, he cannot detect sarcasm.

Edward and Arthur are only a few years apart, though the contrast between them is glaringly apparent. Athletic of build, trim and stylish, Edward comes from a moneyed family with an illustrious name and has recently graduated from Oxford University, where he read Classics. Next to him, beads of perspiration visible on his forehead, the scrawny Arthur does his best to ignore the flecks of mud and dung clinging to the hems of his trousers, his accent and his lack of proper schooling.

'Come, let us show you where you will work.'

The elder scholar and his assistant lead Arthur into the inner sanctums of the British Museum. Their footsteps echo along the marble corridors as they proceed through ornamented doors and lofty galleries and pass through storerooms lined floor to ceiling with shelves and cupboards packed with artefacts – numbered, catalogued and indexed. They end up in a room filled to capacity with wooden boxes. Inside, Arthur learns, there are more than thirty-five thousand tablets, excavated in Mesopotamia and shipped to England. Many of them are chipped or broken; and some so small, smashed and jumbled up that to reassemble them would be a jigsaw of inconceivable complexity.

This they will never say out loud, but both the Keeper of Oriental Antiquities and his assistant expect Arthur to last no more than a few days, his spirit shattered and his enthusiasm eroded by the scale of the challenge. The work asked of him is not only onerous and unrewarding, and the payment meagre, but impossible to accomplish: the assumption that order can be imposed on this chaos is close to madness.

Yet to their surprise, day after day, the boy from the slums keeps returning.

Where others see chaos, Arthur sees patterns. What is intimidatingly unfamiliar to them is to him an exhilarating puzzle to be solved. Every week he pulls another box from the shelves to find inside a new pile of damaged tablets. He strives to sort scores of fragments imprinted with unknown signs, searching for underlying narratives, a story that will bring him closer to the world of the Ancients. If he can find a window into the time of King Ashurbanipal, will he be able to hear the wind blowing through the hollow reeds of the Mesopotamian marshes, the sprinkle of water on the date palms, the sighs of another river, far away?

The more Arthur wrestles with the mysteries of the cuneiform, the more curious he becomes about the people who incised the signs. What were they like? Did the scribes-in-training simply record what was required of them, wishing nothing more than to perform their duties and obey the rules, or had they dared to add their own voice here and there, a personal touch, and, if so, what was their fate?

He imagines the pupils in tablet schools being scolded and beaten by masters no less strict than those he has known. Once he comes across a note on a piece of clay so small and smooth it resembles a pebble from a stream bed, something a river would make. It reads:

> *Wake me early in the morning.*
> *I must not be late or my teacher will cane me.*

Another time, he discovers a tablet with tooth marks in the corner. An exasperated student in Ancient Mesopotamia, upset at the mathematical problem he was set, has bitten into the clay surface. There it is, palpable even after thousands of years, his anger, his frustration, his silent rebellion.

Arthur also notices that most inscriptions end with the identical dedication, always to the same God:

> *Praise be to Nabu*

King Arthur of the Sewers and Slums is given a cramped room at the back of the British Museum, overlooking Russell Square. The windows rattle at the slightest breeze, and there is a draught gusting in from somewhere, but he never complains. He likes being here on his own. With every fractured tablet he pieces together, he meets new characters beyond his wildest imagination – Mesopotamian kings, gods and goddesses . . . priests, librarians and musicians . . . cup-bearers, tavern-owners and canal-builders . . . soothsayers, necromancers and interpreters of dreams . . . Their stories pile up on one another, like pebbles meeting at the bottom of a creek, tossed about by stronger currents. Arthur prefers to bury himself in the folds of distant history, anywhere but in the here and now. He feels closer to the people of the past than those of the present, more at peace with the ghosts than the living.

It doesn't occur to him that we are drawn to the kind of stories that are already present within us, germinating and pushing their way through to the surface, like seeds ready to sprout at the first hint of sun. His progress is painstakingly slow; it takes him weeks to plough through a tiny segment, though he is confident he can gain pace if he works harder. So far, most of the tablets he has deciphered have been about buying and selling. The one he is working on today records a merchant in Nineveh who demands immediate payment for a list of items – 33 jars of oil, 40 casks of wine, 25 sacks of barley. That is all there is to it. Arthur has no way of knowing whether the bill was settled. Still, no matter how trivial, every cuneiform script is extraordinary in his eyes. He finds it remarkable that, even though they have perished – all those high-ranking military officers, wealthy traders and mighty oracles – these simple clay slabs, made of earth and water, have survived. This, he believes, is nothing short of a miracle.

The staff at the British Museum, and the scholars who inhabit its commodious chambers, though used to his presence by now, treat him like the outsider he is. Even so, Arthur senses there may be unexplored opportunities for him. In every department across the museum, particularly in Classical Antiquity – the interlocking civilizations of Ancient Greece and Ancient Rome – there is an entrenched hierarchy, a strict pecking order. This is not the case in Mesopotamian studies. The field – relatively new and uncharted – is still amorphous, like liquid metal waiting to be poured into a mould. This can work to his advantage. He is aware that someone like him, without the prerogatives conferred by social connections and a private education, cannot advance in the other disciplines, where the doors are already closed and the posts mostly taken. But when it comes to reading the cuneiform, even the most eminent expert is but a beginner. Within the confines of the Assyrian

Gallery, it makes no difference whether you hold qualifications from a distinguished university or left school as a child – faced with a clay tablet, everyone is in the same field of ignorance. This realization only strengthens his dedication to the task at hand. For the first time in his life he is on an equal footing with those around him. Quietly, he revels in the delicious sense of self-confidence entering his veins, circulating in his blood, teetering on the threshold of a calling he'd never dared hope for.

If Arthur is going through a silent transformation, so, too, is the British Museum. Since its foundation, the institution has served as a repository of curios, an arbitrary collection of things eccentric, exotic or aesthetically pleasing, some on display, most in storage. Artefacts purchased or donated, dug up or stumbled across, spirited away or outright stolen. An inventory that was not always systematically catalogued. When the director of the National Museum of Denmark, Christian Jürgensen Thomsen, visited more than a decade ago, he was disappointed to find the galleries and storerooms in a state of chaos. His compatriot, leading archaeologist J. J. A. Worsaae, expressed his dismay in more vivid terms, decrying the museum as an 'utter shambles'.

Nowadays, however, the institution is changing. It is evolving into an intellectual hub, keen to become a fulcrum for the scientific study of civilizations. No longer simply a warehouse, it is actively taking part in determining what is worth preserving for posterity. Within its walls, history is not only being protected and displayed but also rewritten. Yet Arthur is too young to understand that, in deciding what will be remembered, a museum, any museum, is also deciding, in part, what will be forgotten.

Weeks become months. The Keeper of Oriental Antiquities continues to support him. He and his assistant have been wrestling with the tablets for so long, without any substantial progress, that the old antiquarian is relieved that someone else, however unlikely, has taken over the struggle. To this end, he obtains permission for Arthur to visit the museum outside its usual opening hours.

But there are more obstacles in Arthur's way than there are providers of support. One major hurdle, especially during the dreary days of winter, is the lack of light. The museum being full of precious objects and manuscripts, candles are hazardous. Gas lamps, though safer, are reserved for senior employees. Arthur is not entitled to one of his own. Thus restricted, he can study the cuneiform only under what slender rays of sun penetrate the dim interior. His eyesight slowly deteriorating, conscious of how little working time he has left as each hour passes, he sits as close to the window as possible, hunched over a tablet, until enveloped by a gloom so profound that it wraps itself around him like a stray spectre from its own world.

A few weeks into this, Arthur comes up with a practical solution. By pressing damp paper on to their surfaces, he creates exact replicas of the tablets, which he then takes home to work on late into the night. This gives him more time with the inscriptions. He has to be careful, though, for the impressions, fragile and friable, are often nibbled away by mice.

Yet the biggest hurdle arises when his parents receive an official notification of eviction. New railways are being built across London, and some of the tracks will cut through densely populated areas, including their own neighbourhood. In a matter of days hundreds of people lose their homes. The family now shares a single cramped room with three others, their walls stained by years of dirt and their windows patched with scraps of cloth to keep out the cold. Arthur starts to sleep in his clothes, worried that they might get stolen in the middle of the night. He still does his best to keep himself clean, but soap is limited and so is water. His mother attempts to help him, when she is feeling well enough that is, which happens less and less often with her grief over the loss of her young child, her frustration with her husband's drinking and spendthrift ways, and her endless worries as to how to put food on the table.

The decline in Arthur's appearance does not go unnoticed. Racing from the publishing company to the British Museum and back every single afternoon does not give him enough time to comb his hair or straighten his jacket, which is, by now, faded and fraying at the cuffs. It is not only his appearance that puts people off. His cryptic mutterings and eccentric manner also unnerve them, and the trustees have started to question whether they should continue to keep him in their employ. The Keeper of Oriental Antiquities feels obliged to tell the youngster, as soon and as gently as he possibly can, that they will no longer require his services.

That week it rains incessantly. The Thames swells up, surges forth. The frontier separating the earth and the sky blurs into a listless grey that covers everything, as a gauze would swathe a wound. The spires of the city glower like gibbets in the twilight. So forceful is the downpour that a primordial dread bestirs amongst Londoners, a fear deep down that they may have angered God – or a river-dwelling nymph or naiad. Gushing through the gutters, pounding on the windowpanes, the water demands to be seen and heard. London shivers and shrivels, folding into itself like a rose withering under the absence of sun.

On the third morning, the family's basement floods, and they find themselves up to their knees in murky, foul-smelling water. What little they have, they haul on to the street. While his father carries the mattress, his mother the stools and his younger brother the cooking utensils, Arthur rushes to save the impressions of Mesopotamian tablets.

'Look at you, stewing over a bunch of scribbles,' says his father under his breath.

Hours later, the rain having finally relented, the ground saturated, a defeated hush falls on the neighbourhood. A full moon hangs in the sky, so bright that Arthur can make out the maria on its surface. An arrangement of light and shade. So much in life is composed of recurrent designs. The zigzags traced by bolts of lightning, the rings inside a felled tree, the threads on a cobweb, the tessellations of a honeycomb, the twists of a conch shell, the petals of a chrysanthemum . . . A city also teems with fractal geometry. The catacombs beneath Camden Market, the arches of Paddington Station; the Neo-Gothic ornamentation of the Houses of Parliament . . . People, no less, are formed by repeated habits and conventions. The Mesopotamian tablets, too, embody a series of patterns whose meaning Arthur is determined to discover.

Wrapped in an old blanket for warmth, he places his finger on a line of cuneiform and reads out a mysterious name he has not come across before.

Gil-ga-mesh.

The following afternoon, Dr Samuel Birch enters the room where Arthur works, braced for a difficult conversation. He expects to see the young man poring over a tablet by the window, as is his wont. Instead he finds him pacing back and forth, his hair dishevelled, his collar askew, his tie unknotted, his shirt-tails hanging out and his eyes burning bright with excitement.

'Oh, sir, I am so glad to see you!' Arthur exclaims.

'Everything all right, Smyth?'

'I have news!' says Arthur, his voice trembling. 'I think I have stumbled on something important. More than that, fascinating!'

Thus saying, he picks up a tablet and translates these lines:

He Who Saw the Deep . . .
He came a far road, was weary, found peace,
And set all his labours on a tablet of stone.

Arthur lifts his head to find the scholar staring at him with undisguised astonishment. As their gazes lock, they both break into a smile, seized by the realization that they have encountered something mysterious and wholly unexpected. This tablet is unlike anything Arthur has read so far. This is not a merchant's grain inventory or a legal text or memorandum. It is poetry.

'How marvellous,' says the Keeper of Oriental Antiquities. 'The trustees are going to be delighted. Do you think you can carry on with the translation – if you can find more of it in this jumble?'

Arthur inhales a lungful. He has been waiting for this moment for so long. 'Should I be allowed to continue my labours, which I would be happy to do, it would be on one condition. Two, actually, if I may.'

'Tell me.'

'I'd need a gas lamp to be able to read when the light is poor.'

'That can be provided.'

'Also, a new jacket, sir. Mine is very old.'

A hint of affection in his gaze, the Keeper of Oriental Antiquities nods. 'You may most certainly have both.'

And thus Arthur starts to assemble an ancient story, piece by broken piece. Powerful and remorseless, Gilgamesh is a callous brute at the start of the epic. He deflowers newly married women on their wedding nights, attacks their humiliated husbands, tyrannizes entire communities. Deluded by hubris, infatuated by desire, blinded by ambition, he is ultimately debased and humbled by failure. This is something that puzzles Arthur. In all the books he has read, the heroes were apparent, clearly delineated. That they were superior to others in talent, courage, or intelligence was beyond doubt. But in the Mesopotamian imagination nothing is definite. The divine and the mundane, the good and the evil, the overworld and the netherworld – all are in a perpetual dance. *Gilgamesh*, the earliest recorded tale in the history of humanity, the oldest surviving poem, is also startlingly fluid and fluctuating, as its principal character shifts and pivots, repeatedly failing his trials. The-hero-that-is-no-hero matures only after multiple defeats. The narrative breaks apart and is restored again, like the sea that smashes against the jetty, destroying and renewing itself.

≈

That year in December, the boy whose life began by the River Thames is offered a full-time position at the Middle Eastern Collections of the British Museum. He takes his leave from the publishing house to dedicate himself fully to the Mesopotamian artefacts. He has just turned eighteen.

His salary is much lower than it was at Bradbury & Evans, and the hours are longer. Mr Evans warns him he is making a grave mistake in quitting; in another year or two he could have become a master printer. He has raised himself up this far but now he is foolishly abandoning his good fortune, and for what? The cotton famine has hit hard, mill workers in Lancashire have no job, and the tides of discontent and despair are lapping at the shores of London. Entire families have been left without food and shelter. There is so much hunger, penury and suffering all around, and here he is leaving a well-paid position to tinker with a heap of crumbling, smashed tablets.

His father is furious about the drop in his earnings; he curses and swears constantly, but there is not much the man can do to change the course of things. Arthur is now tall, and, though he has never been solidly built, he is strong enough to ward off blows. The sons of abusive fathers need to grow fast.

Around this time Arthur starts to keep a diary. His first entry reads:

> Thus it is that, in the winter of 1858, I, King Arthur Smyth of the Sewers and Slums, have entered into official life at the British Museum to regularly prosecute the study of the cuneiform tablets from the Library of Ashurbanipal in

Nineveh and, in particular, to pursue the translation of an epic poem, which seems to have been widely known and deeply cherished by the Ancients. I believe I have finally found my calling: it is my duty to piece together what has been broken, to help people to remember what has been consigned to oblivion throughout the centuries, and to retrieve what has been lost somewhere along the way.

I wish to be like the River Thames: I want to tend to what has been discarded, damaged and forgotten.

NARIN

By the River Tigris, 2014

'Tell me the story of the Flood . . .'

'What do you want to know about it, my heart?'

'How did it start?'

'With a single drop of water.'

Grandma cranes her head as if to see better through a keyhole into some other space. 'It fell from the infinite skies – a harbinger of what was to come. No one paid it any attention, of course. Then it started to rain in earnest, and it didn't stop for days and nights. The rivers rose, the land disappeared. Many died, but we Yazidis were saved thanks to a brave woman – her name was Pira-Fat.'

'Wait! What happened to Baba Noah and the Ark?'

'That was the first Flood, *Tofanê Nebî Noh* – it affected the children of Adam and Eve. As I told you before, we descend from Adam alone; Eve was not involved in our creation. The second Flood impacted the Yazidis, but we survived.'

'How?'

'Thanks to Mother Pira-Fat. She could float above the waters like a bird or a butterfly or an angel, you might also say. In her hands she held a glass jar. She put our seeds there, and after the waters retreated she planted our seeds, and so we grew back like plants and populated the earth again.'

'So there were two Floods, then?'

'At least two, for sure. But when I was a girl I heard community elders say, actually, there were three – if not more.'

Narin sighs. 'I just don't understand why God keeps doing this.'

'Doing what?'

'I mean, afflicting us with storms and torrents.'

'Well, others might say it is His way of punishing humans for going astray. The waves are sent down to clean the sins of mankind. But I don't believe that God in His benevolence and forgiveness is trying to hurt us. I believe the Deluge was an unavoidable calamity. You can also call it Fate. Also, don't forget, it takes a while for things to settle. This world, like goat's milk yogurt, will not solidify for quite some time.'

Narin smiles. 'You think the earth is a tub of yogurt?'

'Oh, definitely . . . It ferments, it thickens, and, although it is solid now, it can never forget that it was once liquid.'

'What does that mean?'

'It means it's still roiling inside. We don't hear it but there's water underneath, churning. There are cycles in nature, cycles in history. We call them *dewr*. Between the end of an era and the beginning of a new one, there's always a period of confusion, and those are the hardest times, may God help us all.'

'Are we now in one of those periods?'

'I think so, that's why we must carefully study the past. The stories of our ancestors are the roots that hold us up through tempests and high winds.'

Narin subtly touches her right ear: there is a buzzing inside, and it bothers her, but she doesn't want to mention it, as if saying it aloud will give it more power, more life. Instead she asks, 'So what happened after each Flood?'

'What happens after catastrophes? Those who survive nurse their broken hearts and start all over again, as one always does, as one always must.'

The only furniture of any value in the house is an oak chest painted in orange and green. Grandma keeps her dowry here, and all their valuables: crocheted doilies, embroidered towels, silk scarves, golden bracelets that were given to her as wedding gifts long ago . . . Narin has rummaged through its contents many times since she was little. Among the miscellaneous items that the chest guards is a *qanun*, carefully preserved. It is engraved with geometric motifs and covered with ivory, and there are tortoiseshell picks with which to pluck its strings. It is said to have been brought from Istanbul more than a century ago. This is the instrument that got Narin's father interested in music when he was a boy.

The *qanun* is very old but not as old as Narin's favourite object, which is trussed up like a baby, swaddled in white linen, wrapped with a red ribbon. A curious gift from the past. Searching the chest now, Narin takes out the bundle. Inside is a slab of clay with wedge-shaped symbols on both sides. It was given to her great-great-grandmother Leila, and she brought it with her when she left Nineveh and journeyed up the River Tigris, settling in Castrum Kefa. Ever since then it has been passed on to the next generation as a family heirloom. Narin knows that, though made of simple earth, it is very important. No one else in the village owns anything like it. Even though she cannot properly read either the Turkish or the Kurdish alphabet, Grandma has memorized quite a few of the arcane signs on its surface, thanks to her grandmother, and these she has taught to Narin. The child can thus intuit some of the shapes, though she has no idea of the story that the tablet holds.

'Tell me about your grandmother Leila.'

'My *dapir* . . .' says Grandma with a smile, and pauses as if she has said it all. 'She was so beautiful – eyes like a donkey's –'

'Hah!'

'Child, don't laugh. The donkey has the prettiest eyes. Leila's hair was long, black, silken – a patch of night sky. But, most importantly, she was a talented healer.'

Narin rests her chin on her palm. 'Same as you!'

'No, no. My gift, which, like hers, belongs to God alone, is piffling compared with my grandmother's. Your ancestor Leila was a diviner – a *faqra*.'

'What is that?'

'A seer who knows things that others do not. Remember, though, there are many in this world who claim to be augurs but are charlatans, in truth. My grandmother was one of the genuine ones.'

Narin leans forward to hear better. There are so many high-pitched sounds that she struggles to pick up, though she can still follow lower-frequency sounds, and her grandmother's voice, thankfully, is one of those.

'It's part of our tradition. *Koçek* or *faqra* for females, *chavron* for both men and women. They are all respectable, virtuous people. I still remember the famous ones from my childhood – Koçek Shamo, Koçek Silo, Koçek Hajo . . . Nowadays there are fewer. Since time immemorial our people have understood and respected this gift, and Leila undoubtedly had it.'

Narin presses her lips together, thinking. Grandma's next words take her by surprise.

'It can be painful, though, the gift. They go into a trance. Some fall to the ground, shaking like a leaf caught in a windstorm. You cannot touch them, the convulsions are that strong. Others start speaking in foreign tongues that no one can understand. Diviners are remarkable people – they can see what's coming, but that's not a small burden.'

'How can they speak other languages?'

Grandma sucks in a lungful of air. 'When they're in a half-conscious state, they change. In that moment even a slender *faqra* can lift a heavy sack as if it were a feather. Stranger things are known to have happened.'

Narin cannot imagine, however hard she tries, her great-great-grandmother balancing weighty sacks on the tips of her fingers.

'You may struggle to believe me. Remember, though, what defies comprehension isn't the mysteries of the world, but the cruelties that humans are capable of inflicting upon each other.'

The silence extends for seconds.

'Grandma, did you ever witness Leila making predictions?'

'No, I never did. By the time I was born she had long stopped.'

'But why?'

Grandma touches the tattoo on her face, as if to make sure that it is still there.

'Because Faqra Leila saw something . . . something terrible . . . and it happened exactly the way she had prophesied. It happened in a place called Nineveh. After that, she couldn't do this any more.'

The comment sends a jolt of alarm through Narin. 'What was it – that terrible thing?'

Grandma looks away, perhaps finding the question irrelevant or impossible to answer, but then she speaks, her voice mellow, though with an edge.

'They say when you have a vision that is too harrowing to put into words, it will leave you scarred forever. Leila gave up fore-casting the future and she wished her descendants to give up the practice, too – to save us the pain. Since then, we've become water-dowsers. We can find rivers and streams under the ground and we can also treat certain ailments, but the women of this family will not and do not divine any more.'

—O—
ARTHUR

·

By the River Thames, 1871

O
n a balmy day in June, Arthur turns into Piccadilly. He walks fast, with a vigilance that he cannot escape, his eyes on the pavement. He can hear a barrel organ in the distance, whistling the popular tune 'In the Sweet By and By'. Recently he has started to grow a beard, but his fingers, unused to finding so much hair on his face, keep straying back to touch the whiskery bristles. In his pocket, he carries a silk handkerchief scented with fragrance. These days the fashion is for musk and ambergris, a blend of aromas that he relishes, in spite of its exorbitant price. He has been reading tablets doggedly for many years now, and working without respite, but he has yet to be promoted.

The perfume he is wearing today is something he helped to compose. On a Mesopotamian tablet, thousands of years old, he came across a formula by a female parfumier called Tapputi. Without telling anyone in the British Museum, Arthur asked an embalmer on Regent Street to re-create the ancient concoction, using cane oil, myrrh, crushed almonds, horseradish, spices and sundry flowers. Tapputi's notes did not specify which flowers exactly and so Arthur chose violets, patchouli and almond blossom. The result was intoxicating, and this is what he has now applied judiciously to his handkerchief.

So much has changed in his life over the past few years, but the one thing that has remained constant is this acute loneliness, which he carries everywhere with him, a solitude that never leaves his side, the one companion that drives all others away. He misses his younger brother, who, after being sent to the countryside to live with an elderly aunt, settled down in Yorkshire, not wishing ever to return to London. He misses his mother, whom he hasn't seen in four years, not since she was confined to a sanatorium after spending a whole night ranting and wailing in the street. People complained she was not right in the head. Both the neighbours and his own father testified that Arabella was exhibiting symptoms of insanity and hysteria, and not long after she was whisked away. Although Arthur has repeatedly written to the directors of the institution, asking if he may come to see her, each time his request was declined, with the excuse that it would be too taxing for the patient. And as for his father, he has not seen him in a long while. It appears to Arthur that his entire family has unravelled, like the strands of a rope that has frayed over time. The only constant is his work – the tablets of Mesopotamia.

As he passes St James's Church, a torrent of sounds gushes by his side: hundreds of wheels from hansom cabs, carriages, calashes, barouches and drays spinning at once, vendors hawking their wares from their handcarts and children pushing barrows twice their size . . . Amidst the clatter and congestion, he catches the shout of a newspaper boy:

'The author is dead! Mr Dickens has gone to meet 'is Maker!'

Arthur gasps. He buys a newspaper and stares intently at the photo of the novelist, those eyes so familiar to him, penetrating and thoughtful but also faintly amused, absorbing the sheer absurdity of this world. He reads the article over and over. Accompanying the piece is a drawing of the author's study at Gads Hill Place, with an empty chair, slightly askew, as if only just that second vacated, its leather still warmed by the body that had spun so many stories in its embrace.

Sadness overtakes him. There are extraordinary people who appear unexpectedly on our paths, and, just as suddenly, they disappear, leaving their indelible marks and a sense of regret. Brief and bright, like a match striking a flame in the dark, they heat the damp kindling of our hearts and then they are gone.

As Arthur folds the paper, further down the page a small article catches his eye: a calf was born in London zoo. The hippopotamuses that were sent by an Ottoman pasha to England – Obaysch and Adhela – have finally produced a baby. It has been named Guy Fawkes. There it is, tucked into the same frame, one life coming to an end, another just beginning.

That day, as soon as Arthur arrives at the British Museum, he pulls from the shelves a random crate of broken tablets, finds a jar to use as a chamber pot and locks his door so that no one can enter and he cannot go out; and in this state he devotes himself fully to his work, for he knows that if he does not apply himself, the despondency in his heart will swallow him whole.

The following afternoon, his hair dishevelled, Arthur opens the door, his eyes brimming like the blue skies after a hard rain. Moving about briskly in the manner of someone who has just risen from a delirious sleep, he sends out word that he urgently needs to speak to everyone, including the trustees – especially them! His behaviour is baffling. All these years he has gone to great lengths to avoid even the most basic conversations, but now he cannot wait to gather everyone together. So they flock to his room – the trustees, the curators, the clerks and a few art students – impatient to know what Arthur might have to say. They are amazed to find him with his cheeks aglow, his tie loosened and his gaze burning fiercely, looking utterly deranged.

'Gentlemen, thank you for coming at once,' exclaims Arthur, opening his hands. 'I am so pleased to see you all!'

His audience exchange glances, and a few people roll their eyes, none of which Arthur notices.

'Something extraordinary has happened and I cannot wait to share it with you!' His heart skips a beat inside his chest as he adds, 'I've reason to believe we are on the brink of an astonishing discovery.'

His face a canvas of emotions, Arthur then translates a section from the *Epic of Gilgamesh*, reading out the lines he has deciphered.

> *Ever the river has risen and brought us the Flood,*
> *The mayfly floating on the water . . .*

He tells them that he chanced upon a highly interesting tablet: it offers an account of a deluge so catastrophic that it consumes kingdoms, and of a ship stranded on top of a mountain sheltering animals of all kinds. He describes how after days of drifting in tempestuous waters, those on board send out a bird to see if there is dry land nearby. The story is very familiar.

'Are you trying to say that you have found an ancient description of Noah's Ark?' asks one of the trustees.

Arthur rakes his fingers through his hair, smooths his moustache back into place, aware of the enormity of what he is about to say. 'Gentlemen, the *Epic of Gilgamesh* predates the Bible. Bear in mind that this poem was handed down orally for centuries before being recorded by scribes and kept in the library of King Ashurbanipal. This means that the Mesopotamian narrative of the Flood is actually much older than the Ark of Noah in the Holy Scriptures. I leave it to you to decide as to the implications of this finding.'

The silence that follows, though brief, feels suspended with tension – until the same trustee clears his throat and says, 'I must confess, my good fellow, that you have made a remarkable discovery.'

'Indeed, momentous!' another adds.

One by one, they walk up to him and shake his hand, commending him for his astonishing achievement. Last in line is the Keeper of Oriental Antiquities, the one person in this institution who has supported him from the beginning. And when Arthur, this introverted and bashful soul, sees Dr Birch there grinning with pride, he does something wholly unexpected. He runs to the old man and pulls him into a patchouli-scented embrace.

His excitement, though ungentlemanly, proves contagious. Spilling into the marble corridors like a breaking wave, it gushes through the panelled walls and arched doorways, washes over the Iron Age amphoras, Chinese bronzes, Egyptian mummies and human skeletal remains, Greek friezes, Roman relics, Byzantine coins, Renaissance engravings; it drenches the manuscripts of Galileo, Michelangelo, Newton, Washington, Cromwell . . . ultimately reaching the Assyrian section, where the *lamassus* are stationed, surges over their stone hooves and wings, and from there pours on to the streets of London.

The timing could not be more opportune. Darwin has recently published *The Descent of Man*, building on the immense success of his previous book, *On the Origin of Species*. Advances in geology, biology, botany and chemistry have deepened the schism between science and religion, academia and the Church. The latest findings in palaeontology, archaeology and geology all appear to overturn the traditional 4004 BC date of Creation taught by theologians. Suspicion is growing that the earth is in fact much, much older.

These days it is argued that humans, far from being unique and superior to other creatures, are just one amongst diverse species that inhabit the earth. The world, no longer preordained, seems to be in flux. It is against these shifting sentiments that Arthur has decoded the Flood Tablet. Some people interpret the discovery as a perfect illustration of the mythical nature of religion. Noah's Ark is clearly nothing more than a fable passed down generations. The similarities between the Mesopotamian narrative and the biblical account – a world-engulfing deluge, the construction of the coracle to help humankind and the animal kingdom survive the rising waters, the bird sent out to look for dry land – all indicate that the holy script is merely a retelling of made-up stories from days of yore.

But for others the reverse holds: Arthur's discovery is a confirmation of the veracity of the Good Book. Mesopotamia, they say, is the cradle of theological truth. Somewhere over there the Garden of Eden blossomed and burst into life; Abraham, the father of the faithful, was born; the Tower of Babel rose to heaven and then mouldered into pieces, dividing humankind into tribes that could never understand one another again. Daniel, the interpreter of dreams, was thrown into a lions' den, and his three friends walked through the fire unscathed. It is where everything begins, the tale of humankind, and at a time of spirited discussions on the origin of species, this remote land seems to hold the keys to the deepest questions as to the meaning of life and the existence of God.

The argument, by no means limited to England, reverberates across the European continent and ignites on the other side of the Atlantic. The *New York Times* publishes an article outlining the various narratives of the Flood side by side, and posits the theory that the biblical one is perhaps 'legendary like the rest'. A poem whose existence was unknown until yesterday – excavated in Nineveh, hauled on ships to London and now partially translated by a young man from the slums of Chelsea – is today the talk of millions of people around the globe.

Of all the new and unexpected things that happen to Arthur in the aftermath of his discovery of the Flood Tablet, the one that most astonishes him is the public's fascination with the subject. For years he had assumed that no one outside the narrow field of Assyrian studies would be remotely interested in his work. But the revelation that a story strikingly similar to Noah's Ark is depicted on an artefact from Mesopotamia has swiftly captured the collective imagination, sparking furious debate among conservatives and liberals alike.

All of a sudden, and much to his horror, Arthur finds himself –
just like the Flood Tablet itself – a curiosity. Every day strangers
come to the British Museum, asking about him. He takes the back
streets on the way to and from work, keeping his head bowed,
hoping to maintain a low profile. But that, apparently, will not be
possible for long.

'You have received an invitation,' says the Keeper of Oriental Antiquities one afternoon, waving a letter with an embossed,
gilded crest.

'Me?'

'Congratulations, you are invited to give a lecture at the Society of Biblical Archaeology.'

All the colour drains from Arthur's face. 'But I am no good at
that sort of thing. Could you not do it?'

The elderly scholar smiles. 'Oh, the members do not want
me, I can assure you. They want *you* – the prodigy from humble
beginnings! You will have the most esteemed audience – scholars,
diplomats, journalists, bishops . . . that's not all. The prime minister
himself is coming! This must be the first time a British prime minister will attend a lecture on Mesopotamia. Are you not excited?'

But Arthur, feeling overwhelmed and nauseous at the thought
of standing on a public stage, has already left the room.

The day before the lecture, anxious that he might not wake up
in time, Arthur Smyth asks a knocker-up to rouse him. But he
needn't have worried, for sleep is hardly possible. He tosses and
turns all night, alert at every little sound. When, shortly after
six, the man raps on his windowpane with a long stick Arthur is
already up and dressed.

Despite his pounding heart, he tries to remain composed.
He polishes his shoes, combs his moustache, pomades his hair
and dabs eau de cologne on his cuffs. A pricy blend for the special occasion – bergamot, lavender and lemon oil. Gestures that

usually calm him. Still, when he arrives at the Society of Biblical Archaeology, he takes the stairs two at a time.

The prime minister, William Ewart Gladstone, a man with both strong liberal views and a profound religious sense, a statesman of remarkable learning who is said to have read thousands of books in Modern and Classical languages, is seated in the front row. His expression is inscrutable.

Arthur bows to him and thanks the members of the Society of Biblical Archaeology for the opportunity to present his findings. No sooner does he say this, however, than his voice falters. All these people with their privileged education are here to listen to him – a novice with barely any schooling. The thought cuts into him like a scalpel into flesh. For a second, his throat closes up. What is he doing amongst them when anyone can see that he does not belong? The whole thing feels like a terrible mistake. Seized by a sudden urge to walk out, he almost steps out from behind the lectern. As he tries to steady his breathing, he glances at the piece of the Flood Tablet he brought with him. He has memorized it line by line. It is worn and cracked, like his mother's hands. He wants to make her proud.

'My lords, gentlemen, the story of humanity cannot be written without the story of water.' Arthur clutches the edge of the lectern to stop himself from trembling. 'Yet we hardly pay sufficient regard to this remarkable compound on which our lives and our futures depend. The findings that I intend to present to you today concern rivers and rainstorms, and the memory of an ancient flood. That memory, distressing as it was, has never left the people of the land that I will be talking about – Mesopotamia. As many here will already know, this word, in Greek, means "between rivers".'

Arthur begins by describing the region, for he has noticed that, captivated though they may be by the idea of 'biblical lands', not many in England can locate it on a map. It remains ambiguous in the public mind – faraway, foreign and largely fictitious. He goes on to set out how it has been home to myriad civilizations. He chronicles the extraordinary cities and temples its people have built, the enormous advances they have made in architecture, poetry, mathematics, warfare and, especially, irrigation.

His voice rising with excitement, he tells them that thousands of years ago, in Nineveh, there lived a remarkable king called Ashurbanipal. Unlike any other ruler, before or after, he was devoted to the pursuit of knowledge. To this end he amassed a monumental library, ordering his emissaries to gather tablets from far and wide. *Gilgamesh* is merely one of the many stories in this library – an important one nonetheless. It was an essential part of the oral tradition, central to the collective imagination long before it was written down on clay around 1800 BC, all of which sets the date of the epic almost a thousand years before the biblical story of Noah's Ark, nearly a millennium before the Book of Genesis.

A thin film of perspiration on his brow, Arthur explains how Ashurbanipal's library was burned when the city was attacked by its enemies. The destruction was total, palaces and temples reduced to naught. The inhabitants were slaughtered, treasures looted, buildings razed to the ground. But, being made of river mud and water, cuneiform tablets proved astonishingly resilient. While flames can easily consume papyrus and parchment, and devour rolls of paper, they cannot harm clay. Quite the opposite, in fact: the fire only baked and hardened them further. This is how they have survived under the earth while centuries have come and gone.

Arthur finishes his speech by detailing how for many years now he has lovingly devoted himself to the translation of the *Epic of Gilgamesh*. He is committed to the rendition of the Flood Tablet – the eleventh in a series of twelve. But it is imperative to remember that the narrative he has deciphered is by no means complete. He has been piecing together shards of words, in full awareness that there are lacunae in the poem. Seventeen lines in total are missing. It is his greatest wish, he concludes, to find them someday.

The applause that follows is hearty, genuine. Blushing as he bows, Arthur scans his audience. He catches sight of the Keeper of Oriental Antiquities perched on the edge of a row, clapping like the proud father he never had. To his surprise Mr Evans has also come. His previous employer must have joined the lecture late, slipping into an empty seat at the back. As he regards Arthur, there is nothing but warmth in his eyes. Arthur wishes Mr Bradbury could have been here, too. He wishes he could have summoned his mother and his brother and his deceased brother and the toshers to whom he owes his name. How gratifying it would have been to welcome them into this eminent crowd – all the people, dead or alive, he has come to love since he was a little boy, the people who shaped him, changed him, made him the man he is today.

The prime minister rises to his feet and walks to the lectern, only to launch into a lengthy speech. He offers his congratulations to Arthur, praising his hard work and highlighting the importance of the discovery. Ignoring the question as to whether it venerates or controverts the Bible, he goes on to praise Homer, whom he calls the friend of his youth, the companion of his middle age, 'from whom I hope never to part as long as I have any faculty of breath left in my body'. His talk has little to do with Mesopotamia and even less with the *Epic of Gilgamesh*, but no one seems to mind. For the audience is buzzing with questions for Arthur. Already so many people have raised their hands.

'Mr Smyth,' shouts a journalist. 'Would you be interested in going to Nineveh to seek the missing verses in the Flood Tablet?'

'Oh, that is my dream,' says Arthur, without a second of hesitation. 'Ever since I was a boy I have wanted to travel to Nineveh.'

'Are you saying you are ready to excavate in Ottoman territory, sir, under the sultan's dominion?' another journalist calls out.

Arthur falters. He hasn't given the logistics any thought. He says, 'If I could garner support for the endeavour, I'd happily attempt to do so.'

'Do I take it that you would like the government to provide the means for your expedition?' asks another journalist.

Before Arthur can reply, the prime minister deflects the comment. 'Gentlemen – if I may interpolate – I should not wish to encourage the dangerous notion that it is the duty of a government to engage in the patronage of archaeological initiatives. It has been the distinction and the pride of this great nation to do very many things by individual effort. A visit to Nineveh should be the child of private enterprise and not, I aver, that of the government.'

More questions ensue about politics and politicians, none of which interests Arthur in the least. He starts to sweat. His mouth is dry. He can no longer be certain that the lecture has gone well. In this moment all he wants is to leave this place and go back to work. But, just as he is plotting his escape, a journalist at the front raises his hand.

'Mr Smyth! Will you be celebrating your success with anyone special this evening?'

'No, sir, I shall not,' says Arthur.

'Could you tell us why you are not yet married? Our readers would like to know.'

Arthur gasps. The question is so unexpected that he struggles to find a response. It does not go unnoticed that a deep blush spreads from his neck to his forehead.

'I . . . just . . . do not have time for such things.'

'Are you saying love is trivial?' asks another journalist.

'I am not here to t-t-talk about love,' Arthur stammers, though his voice is now noticeably strained.

The next day he is in all the newspapers, with photographs and drawings of him splashed across the front pages. His expression is calm and serious, but, upon a closer look, his eyes are seen to stare in discomfort, unable to disguise that he cannot believe this is happening to him. Some of his words have been altered and twisted, whilst details from his life have been magnified and embellished.

One paper calls him an 'intellectual picklock', claiming that he is known as much for his eccentric ways as for his coruscating mind. Another paper embarrassingly mentions that he took off his clothes in excitement when he first discovered portions of the *Epic of Gilgamesh*. An editor expresses surprise at Arthur's humility and timidity, given the sensational role he is playing in the maelstrom of debate as to whether the Old Testament originated in Babylonian lore – and whether the earth was created by God or emerged as a random occurrence. Meanwhile, a women's magazine names him 'one of London's most eligible bachelors', urging young ladies not to overlook this rising star in archaeology. It is not only the lost portion of the Flood Tablet that he needs to find, the article proclaims, but what has clearly been missing in his life: love.

In his small room in the British Museum, Arthur reads all the press commentary, disconcerted both by their compliments and their carping. One newspaper has applied the phrase 'the genius from the slums' to him. That makes him pause. He has not forgotten what his old headmaster had said: *No genius ever came from the slums.* But Arthur feels neither gratified nor proud, only nervous.

He leaves his room and approaches a window overlooking the South Entrance on Great Russell Street. In front of his eyes the city flows, a rumbling of sounds, hordes of strangers gossiping about him, saying things he does not wish to hear.

—H

ZALEEKHAH

By the River Thames, 2018

Z aleekhah turns the corner into Great Russell Street, listening to the distant whirr of the rush hour traffic in the background. This morning she went to see Helen at the gallery that the Maleks have been subsidizing for their daughter. Located on one of the side streets surrounding the British Museum, the shop offers a range of art and collectibles, specializing in acquiring, authenticating and selling artefacts and works of art. But her cousin was not in, the receptionist told her, so she wrote a message and left.

On the way back, she walks fast, her mind full of thoughts she can neither ignore nor silence. A group of schoolchildren are jostling each other in front of the museum gates, making a joyful ruckus. As she steps aside to make way for a mother pushing a pram, she raises her head briefly to scan the shops on the opposite side. Only then does she remember what her neighbours had said about the owner of the houseboat. The tattoo parlour must be somewhere around here.

Slowing down, she scans her surroundings. To her surprise, the place is easy to spot. There, between a brasserie and a souvenir shop, is a tattoo parlour. On its window glows a sign in neon blue:

THE FORGOTTEN GODDESS

Being short-sighted, she moves closer to read the smaller inscription beneath, also in neon blue.

Our tattoos last longer than most marriages

After that, she cannot resist peeking inside.

Zaleekhah has never visited a tattoo parlour before and half expects to find a squalid dive, raucous music, shabby furniture, flickering bulbs and the obligatory contingent of unsavoury characters hanging around. Instead she sees an airy space with an elegant emerald-coloured velvet sofa, white armchairs and a floor laid with ceramic tiles in earthy tones. Bamboo pendant lamps, tall plants and plenty of flowers in terracotta pots give the place a homely air. Wooden shelves overflowing with books and magazines cover the opposite wall. It all looks warm, clean and quietly inviting.

Shading her eyes with her hands, she peers through the window. That is when she notices, to her slight embarrassment, that there is someone inside watching her every move with an amused smile. A tall, toned man with dark, wavy hair and wide eyes. As their gazes meet, Zaleekhah recoils, feeling like an intruder.

This has to be the owner of the houseboat – her landlord. He is still looking at her, still smiling. Now feeling obliged to present herself, Zaleekhah opens the door. A bell jingles.

'Hello? May I come in?'

'Sure!' the man replies breezily. His arms are decorated with tattoos. 'You made your mind up faster than I expected.'

'Pardon?'

'Tattoos. Are you not here for one?'

'Oh, no, no . . . I was just passing by.' Zaleekhah pushes her hair back. 'Actually, I was hoping to talk to you.'

'To me?'

'Yes, I'm your tenant. I'm renting the houseboat in Chelsea.'

His face, confused for a second, brightens. 'Ha! I wish . . . You're looking for Nen.'

'Oh, sorry, I thought you –'

'No worries. She's downstairs.'

She. Zaleekhah did not expect a woman to be the owner of the houseboat. Silently, she castigates herself for assuming it had to be a man.

'It's a lovely boat, isn't it?' he says. 'We've had a few staff get-togethers there.'

Zaleekhah nods, though the thought of them drinking, smoking and doing tattoos in the place she now calls home is a bit unsettling. Good thing Uncle need never know. She says, 'The view is amazing.'

'Even better when it rains, which is pretty much all the time. Please make yourself comfortable, and I'll go see if Nen is free.'

Alone in the room, Zaleekhah looks about, intrigued by the artwork on the walls. There are multiple drawings with detailed designs and mythic images, some framed, others pinned to a cork board. On the coffee table lies open a large notebook, crammed full of thank-you messages from happy customers. Next to it is an album with photos of people showing off their tattoos – people of every age, race and background. Many have their bodies inked with the same strange symbols. Zaleekhah tilts her head, trying to make sense of them.

'Hello!'

When Zaleekhah turns around she sees a woman dressed in a flowing blue dress with black leather ankle boots. Her hair, shoulder-length and honey brown, is wavy and slightly wild, as if mussed by a gust of wind that has blown her here. She possesses the same tall and lean physique as the man, although she seems older, perhaps mid-to-late thirties.

'Hi, I'm Nen. I heard you're going to take care of the houseboat – thank you!'

Her handshake is firm and steady.

Not expecting to be thanked for being a tenant, Zaleekhah says, 'Sorry for barging in unannounced. I was just passing by. I wasn't planning to come in, but one of your staff saw me peering in –'

'My brother,' Nen says, smiling. 'The youngest. I have four more.'

'You have five brothers?'

'Yup, all younger than me. We're a big clan.'

Always intrigued by large families, Zaleekhah can't help asking, 'What was that like growing up?'

'Depends which stage of growing up we're talking about. It was pretty terrible when I was little – the boys were loud, always quarrelling. And it was worse when we were teenagers. Dirty socks everywhere . . . Yet, somewhere along the way, it became an amazing blessing. How about you?'

'Oh, I'm an only child.'

'And what was that like growing up?'

'A bit lonely,' says Zaleekhah. 'But my cousin Helen was like a sister to me, if that counts.'

'Cousins, friends, books, songs, poems, trees . . . anything that brings meaning into our lives counts.'

Outside the window a group of tourists files past on their way to the British Museum, their chatter spilling into the shop.

'So is everything okay on the boat?' Nen asks.

'Yes, yes, all good,' Zaleekhah says. Feeling the need to justify a visit prompted by nothing more than idle curiosity, she then adds, 'Although the sink is leaking.'

'Which sink?'

'The one in the kitchen.'

'Oh, is it? I'm so sorry, I wasn't aware,' says Nen. 'That's no excuse, though. I should be up on these things.'

Zaleekhah hesitates. 'It's okay. Nothing major.'

'Still, we must get it fixed.' Nen tucks a strand of hair behind her ear. She has an easy smile, one that warms her whole face and lights up her fern-green eyes, which are framed with thick, long

238

eyelashes, coated in an indigo mascara. Responding to Zaleekhah's curious gaze with a beam, she asks, 'Would you like some coffee?'

'Oh, I shouldn't trouble you –'

'No trouble at all. Our coffee is rightly famous, if I say so myself.' She walks over to a machine on top of an Art Deco cabinet and lifts out the pot as if in proof. 'I've just brewed it.'

'Sure, thank you – black please. No sugar.' She realizes she hasn't introduced herself. 'I'm Zaleekhah, by the way.'

'Nice to meet you, Zaleekhah,' Nen says, pronouncing her name in three, clear syllables.

'A bit of a mouthful, I'm afraid. Don't worry if you get it wrong – most people do.'

'It's a lovely name,' Nen says and hands her a steaming mug. 'Mine is short for Brennen.'

'Irish?'

'Yup, from a "little drop of water".'

Zaleekhah nods, her fingers tightening around the mug. She says, almost by reflex, 'I study water for a living.'

'Really! That's impressive. A scientist has rented my boat. How brilliant!'

A small smile blooms on Zaleekhah's face, more out of awkwardness than pleasure. She does not expect to hear what Nen says next.

'Plus you're named after an extraordinary woman, the legendary Zuleikha – I think that's all very cool.'

Not knowing how to respond to that, Zaleekhah takes a quick sip of her coffee. Strong and rich but not bitter, with a hint of something she can't immediately identify.

'Lavender,' says Nen, watching her reaction. 'We put dried lavender flowers in our coffee. Balances out the caffeine, makes you calmly awake.'

'It's very good.' Zaleekhah glances around the room. 'The symbols on the walls, what are they?'

'Cuneiform – a thousands-of-years-old writing system from Mesopotamia. I tattoo in cuneiform – as one does.'

'That's very . . . interesting.' Zaleekhah falters. 'Umm, so what kind of things do people ask you to tattoo?'

'All kinds. Their names, their lovers' names, words that matter to them . . . or lines from a poem or a song. You can basically write anything in cuneiform. Here, let me show you.'

Setting her mug on a shelf, Nen takes out a pair of chopsticks and some modelling clay. 'So this is my practice dough. I make it myself – flour, water and a pinch of salt. Now look . . .' She presses the end of a chopstick into the soft surface, turning it this way and that. Her moves are deft, her concentration absolute. When she is done, a cluster of wedge-shaped marks is impressed neatly on the pale slab.

'What does it say?' Zaleekhah asks, craning her head.

'It's your name.'

Zaleekhah looks closer, inspecting the shapes, like arrowheads pointing the way. She says, 'Such a strange language.'

'Cuneiform is not a language, though,' says Nen, speaking softly. 'It's not exactly an alphabet either, since it doesn't have letters. It's more like a collection of syllables – a logo-syllabic script that was used by many civilizations – Sumerians, Akkadians, Babylonians, Assyrians, Elamites, Hittites . . .'

Her words are cut short as the front door opens with a jingle. A woman and a man, dressed head-to-toe in black, walk in hand in hand, grinning.

'Hello, Nen!'

'You two back already?' Nen says, returning the grin. 'I thought we'd agreed you'd not show your faces for at least three months.'

'Don't be heartless,' says the woman. 'We can't wait that long.'

'Yeah, we were wondering if you could write *Eat the Rich* in cuneiform?'

'Actually, he wants *Eat the Rich*,' says the woman. 'And I want *Eve was Framed*.'

Nen laughs, shaking her head. 'You guys are bonkers.'

Zaleekhah grabs her bag and rises to her feet. 'I'd best be going. Thank you for the coffee.' She leaves the dough on the table.

'Keep it, if you like, it's your name,' Nen says. Glancing over her shoulder, she gestures at the couple. 'How about you two go downstairs and wait for me? I'll be with you shortly.'

'Hooray!' exclaims the woman.

'About the kitchen sink . . .' says Nen, turning now towards Zaleekhah. In the changed light the green of her eyes deepens. 'You could have it fixed and send me the bill. Or I'm happy to pop in this weekend with a plumber and take a look.'

'I wouldn't want to bother you.'

'No bother at all. On Saturday mornings I go mudlarking by the river with my friends, so we'll be down your way anyway.'

'You go mudlarking?'

'Yes, at low tide,' Nen replies. 'Like in Victorian times – luckily with less sewage.'

'Have you found anything interesting?'

'Oh, heaps! Every time it's different – you never know what the river will offer each day. I've a pile of turtle bones at home – did you know the Victorians loved turtle soup? I also have shards of pottery, tobacco pipes, Neolithic plinths, Celtic coins . . . So many civilizations have left their mark on London. I once stumbled on a hand grenade from the Second World War. That was a bit of a hairy moment. We had to call the police and watch them detonate it.' Nen pauses, musing to herself. 'But I love rooting around in the river mud for things that have been lost or ditched.'

They walk towards the door and stop. Zaleekhah shifts on her feet. 'So I guess I'll see you on Saturday, then.'

'Sounds good.' Nen half turns, facing Zaleekhah, a directness to her gaze. 'Funny, when I saw you, I thought you didn't look like the person who'd want this kind of life, you know, "messing about in boats".'

Zaleekhah winces, recognizing the reference to a children's book her mother would read to her – *The Wind in the Willows*. Her face closes as she says, 'Yeah, I've never lived on water before.'

'It's really special,' says Nen. 'Once you wake up on a house-boat to a rainy morning or watch the sunset over the river, you'll probably never want to go back to dry land.'

'You think so?'

'Yes! So, yeah, welcome to the water tribe.'

That evening, hours after she leaves the tattoo parlour, the taste of dried lavender lingering in her mouth and a slab of dough marked with the cuneiform for her name cradled in her palm, Zaleekhah sits by the window in the houseboat. Outside the sky slides into darkness. On her lap rests the little porcelain *lamassu*. She glued the broken wing as best she could, but the tip is missing and, however tiny the piece, its absence is noticeable. Now she presses lightly on the mended edges, as if trying to gauge whether the join will hold. She knows she should stop, or it might come apart again, but her finger keeps returning to the crack, the fracture, as if testing how deep is the hurt.

III

Restless Rivers

—o—

ARTHUR

By the River Thames, 1871–2

The months following the lecture at the Society of Biblical Archaeology rush by in a blur. Arthur receives invitations to speak at educational societies, and his company is requested at gentlemen's clubs. They greet him politely, these men with silk cravats and suave manners, inviting him into their smoking rooms. He tastes delicacies he has never heard of, partaking in twelve-course meals served on fine porcelain. Roast goose, lobster salad, rabbit pudding, turtle soup, the last of which he struggles to eat once he learns it is cooked by removing the turtle's head and then dropping the rest of the animal into boiling water, complete with its shell.

In the houses of the wealthy he marvels at gilded mirrors, golden candelabra, solid-silver cutlery, and sips champagne served in opaline flutes . . . As he admires the paintings on the walls, he wonders how the old masters would have depicted the settings in which he now fortuitously finds himself. Meanwhile, keen to converse with him, people flock to his side. Neatly coiffed women in swathes of silk and satin smile when he stammers and blushes at their compliments – his shyness and awkwardness rendering him all the more endearing.

Week after week, Arthur raises toasts and shares desserts with bankers, lawyers, politicians and philanthropists, but, deep down, he feels increasingly frustrated. For, even though everyone pronounces his lecture a success and congratulates him for deciphering the cuneiform, his mind is on the missing portion of the Flood Tablet, lost somewhere in Nineveh.

It is on one of those evenings, at a house in The Boltons, that he is introduced to a fetching young woman. Mabel comes from a solid, well-to-do family, and, while she has had some education, she is not especially well read. But she seems intrigued by him, and curious about his work. Her smile is unaffected, and her flawless alabaster skin, flushed with warmth, makes her eyes sparkle. When she talks her speech is fast yet hesitant, and her hands idly touch her throat as if checking her words one last time before they leave her. Arthur is aware that his colleagues and friends are trying to matchmake, and does not question or resist it when he keeps running into her in different settings, by seeming coincidence, certain that she will soon tire of his eccentricities and reticence towards her, though she shows no sign of doing so.

As Arthur spends more time in middle-class circles, he becomes aware of something about them that he did not know previously: their preoccupation with marital bliss and domestic life. Neither the slum dwellers who struggle every day to keep body and soul together nor, he suspects, aristocrats, interested as they are in preserving their inheritance and fortunes, share this notion of marriage as a romantic ideal, almost to the point of holiness. Over and over he is told that the matrimonial home is an Englishman's personal fortress against the entire world. But Arthur has far more pressing matters on his mind. There is not a single day, not a single hour, that is not dominated by the Mesopotamian tablets.

He doesn't have words to convey that most marriages seem unhappy to him, and, if not unhappy, then tedious, bleak and repetitive. In any event the appeal of many women is a mystery to him. He has never tried to draw their attention, make himself special in their eyes. For the truth is, he has long accepted that this is the way with him; he could easily spend a whole life without touching another human being.

One gusty autumnal afternoon, as the church clock strikes two, Arthur receives a summons from the editor of the *Daily Telegraph*. He attends the meeting expecting yet another hour of empty prattle, planning to leave as early as he can. But, to his astonishment, the man informs him that the newspaper would like to sponsor an archaeological excavation. They are ready to offer a thousand guineas. To give others a fair chance, they will run an advertisement asking volunteers to come forward and then select the best candidate. This is a mere formality, as far as the editor is concerned, because he can think of no one more suitable for the task than Arthur himself.

All week long, Arthur waits for the advertisement to appear and, as soon as it does, he dashes off a letter. A few days later, the newspaper announces that 'the genius from the slums of Chelsea' has been chosen for the enterprise.

For the first time in his life Arthur feels like the Fates, the trio of capricious goddesses who weave the destinies of mortals, are smiling down on him. He takes a six-month leave of absence from the British Museum and starts making preparations. Only then, as he sets out to calculate the price of each item needed for the journey, does he realize that the funds offered, which sounded so generous at first, are actually rather limited. He must be careful with his personal budget, including his food expenses. But it does not matter. Intent on his goal, he is ready to set off for the land of Gilgamesh. King Arthur of the Sewers and Slums will finally reach the banks of the River Tigris.

Mabel's father is struck by the brilliance and potential of the young man his daughter is seeing. He expects Arthur to return from

Nineveh either with a considerable fortune or great fame, or, ideally, both. He contrives a separate meeting with him, urging him to propose to his daughter before he heads off for exotic lands. It is steadying, he says, for a young man on his travels to know that someone waits for him back home, an anchor of sorts, otherwise a fellow might simply drift. A woman needs this solidity, too, a course for the future securely mapped out. At his prompting, the couple take a boat trip on the Cherwell, with Mabel's younger brother playing gooseberry. Arthur watches as the sun dapples her dress under the frilled parasol, making patterns like water, swirling, dreamlike. At first they sit in a companionable silence that is only interrupted by polite remarks about the weather and the scenery. But soon Mabel starts peppering Arthur with questions. She sounds like she shares his passion for travel – a similar thirst for adventure, for the unknown, confined as she is to a world where everything feels too familiar. As they are disembarking, he holds her gloved hand as a courtesy and, to his surprise, she lets her fingers linger for a few moments. Slowly and without preamble, she draws closer, so close that Arthur can see the golden flecks in her blue irises. She gives him the smallest of kisses on his lips.

Arthur is stunned. He feels obliged to say something nice, but what that could be he has no idea. He stammers, 'Thank you for liking me, but I'm not very likeable.'

Mabel laughs, and, although her laughter has a tinkling quality like glass bells, Arthur loses the courage or the will to say anything else. When he replays this moment in his mind later, he convinces himself that it is healthy to forge a connection with another human, perhaps even start a family, just as riverside willows dipping their boughs into the current might feel less alone. And, though he cannot quite conjure up the image of himself as a doting spouse, and he fears he will fail to match Mabel's expectations, he yearns for a stable home life, a sense of belonging. An ideal engagement should last no more than twelve months, he is told, and in that time Arthur will be back from Nineveh.

Towards the end of the month, arrangements complete and goods packed, there is one more thing he needs to do before leaving London: he must visit his mother. Even though his requests to see her have been declined since she entered the sanatorium, now that he is famous, suddenly, he is allowed to visit her.

On Thursday morning he takes a carriage to the Middlesex County Lunatic Asylum at Hanwell, on the outskirts of London: an imposing red-brick building with two wings and sash windows, nestled in the middle of a barren garden behind high walls. Arthur presents himself to the gatekeeper, who records in a log-book the entrances and exits of every visitor. Once registered, he climbs down from the carriage and proceeds on foot. Over the past decades, there has been an increasing need for mental hospitals, accelerated by the spread of syphilis. More than sixty new facilities have been built. This is said to be one of the best in the country.

Inside he is greeted by the doctor in charge of the ward and a middle-aged nurse with lips so thin and brittle that her smile resembles a wound. Not that she smiles that often. But the doctor, a stout man, his face barnacled with moles, seems a jolly chap, perhaps too jolly given his location. He has heard that Arthur's lecture was attended by the prime minister and wished to meet him personally. But, for once, Arthur has no desire to discuss the Mesopotamian tablets. All he wants to talk about is his mother.

'Well, I'd say, it is a typical case of melancholy,' says the doctor.

'And how exactly would that be defined?'

The physician explains that in a recently published article on insanity by his esteemed colleague Dr Blandford, four different types of melancholy have been identified: gloomy, restless, mischievous and self-complacent. Each has a different root cause, and thus requires its own treatment.

'Which one afflicts my mother?' Arthur asks.

'Restless melancholy,' replies the man firmly.

'And is that very bad?'

'A rather precarious combination, I am afraid. The restlessness exhausts the mind, making it extremely hard to quieten down. Meanwhile the melancholy, an unreasonable sadness, paralyses the body. It is almost like being pulled in two opposing directions at the same time.'

Arthur wonders if sadness can ever be unreasonable. What if it has its own reasons, even if they may not be obvious to others? He asks tentatively, 'Has she shown no signs of improvement since she was admitted?'

'It will take time,' is all the doctor says.

They usher Arthur into the bowels of the building. He treads long, dimly lit corridors, hearing murmurs from behind the walls. He catches glimpses of the patients, some shuffling around, others confined to their beds or restrained by harnesses, more than a few with their heads shaved.

'Lice,' says the nurse. 'A terrible nuisance. There is no other way to deal with it.'

'But why are some chained up?' asks Arthur.

'They must be. Otherwise, they'd injure themselves.'

The same nurse warns him that his mother has tried this desperate path several times, cutting her fingers on broken glass and pulling her hair out in clumps. He should not be surprised to find straps around her ankles.

A claw of anxiety clutching at him, Arthur follows the nurse into a room with iron bars on the windows. He halts, barely breathing. There are eight patients in here, and he almost does not recognize her amongst them. It is not so much her body that has changed as her eyes. There is an emptiness in her gaze, the irises almost swallowed up by the darkness of her pupils. A brokenness to her expression, which reminds him of the cracks cutting deep into river mud. In front of her rests a tray topped with leaves plucked from a horse chestnut tree. One by one, she picks them up, smooths them out, sets them to one side. She seems immersed in the task, although she does look up when he approaches.

'Mother . . . It's me, Arthur. I have come to see you.'

Her face brightens a little.

'You seem well,' Arthur says. His brow crumples as he struggles to find the words. 'The doctor said you are doing fine. I attempted to visit you many times before, but they always told me to wait until you were feeling better . . . you must have improved a lot, because here I am.'

He wishes, with an excruciating yearning, for her to say something in response. But she doesn't. There is a sluggishness to her posture, a listlessness so palpable that he doubts whether the doctor has any right to call her state of mind *restless*. If anything, she looks quiescent, sedated.

He had planned to tell her about Mabel and their recent courting, if it can be called that. But instead he finds himself relating the story of Gilgamesh and his insatiable quest, his sense of disquietude, which carries him to the ends of the world. As he speaks, some of the other patients draw closer to listen. For a moment it feels as if they are sitting around a sparkling, popping fire in the open air, the wind laced with smoke and words, held together by a common thread of narrative. It feels ancient somehow.

'I will soon be travelling to find the missing lines of the poem,' Arthur says. 'I won't be able to visit you for a while. I'm going east – to Ottoman territory. They say the sultan's harem has four hundred and forty women.'

Someone chuckles. Not his mother.

'Wish me luck, will you? When I return to London, perhaps the British Museum will promote me. Then I will have a proper salary and I will get you out of here. You will have clean bedsheets, fresh bread every day. A scullery maid! She will light the fire in the mornings and your hands won't be cold any more.'

Outside the barred window a branch rustles, as if trying to break in – maybe the same horse chestnut tree whence the leaves came, demanding the return of its foliage. It starts to rain – a thin, sullen drizzle.

'I want you to be proud of me,' Arthur says. And, even though he can see his mother is slowly drifting off, her movements and gestures sluggish, he cannot help talking animatedly, as if words might have some power, an invigorating influence upon the soul.

'I remember when I first saw you, Mum. I remember the sound of the river, the freezing wind, the snow falling from the sky . . . You were so beautiful . . . you are always beautiful.'

From his pocket Arthur pulls a small, wooden object. He has whittled a tiny *lamassu*. A lovely, lively creature, though it does not match the craftsmanship of Mesopotamian artists. But it is a guardian spirit, and he will place it by his mother's side to protect her when he leaves London.

In three days he will be on his way to Nineveh.

H—
NARIN

By the River Tigris, 2014

'Three more days and we'll be on our way,' Grandma says. The old woman has been frantically preparing food for the road. This morning she stuffed vine leaves with rice, spices and currants, and now she is making *borek* – crispy pastry filled with spinach and feta cheese.

'I'm so excited!' Narin exclaims.

'Me, too, my heart. May *Khider* take care of us on the road.'

Khider is a protective spirit. He is also the patron of travellers, learners and lovers – which, Grandma says, often amounts to the same thing.

There are invisible beings all around that offer help and guidance without humans ever realizing, let alone appreciating, it. *Sore-Soran* controls the winds and sends a cool breeze when it gets unbearably hot. *Mama-Rasan* is in charge of harvests, doing her best to grow crops. *Xatuna-Farxa* is the patroness of pregnant women and toddlers. *Pira-Fat*, for her part, watches over younger babies, particularly in their first forty days. *Mama-Sivan* and *Garvane-Zarzan* protect shepherds and their flocks. And *Mama-Rasan* is the one who helps when water is scarce. That is why, during times of drought, when the earth is dry like cinders, Grandma takes a ritual cup and asks Narin to write these words inside: *Don't Forget Us, Mama-Rasan.* Then she holds up the cup to the skies and says, 'Fill it, God. Fill it with Thy mercy.'

There is also *Pira-Ster*, a benevolent spirit who appears in the shape of a grey-haired woman. During daytime she sleeps but as soon as night falls she starts roaming about the house, moving the furniture around. She is caring, if a little crazy and unpredictable. *Xudāne-Mālē*, 'master of the house', resides inside the fireplace and keeps the family safe. *Khalil-Ibrahim*, a 'friend of God', looks after larders and pantries. Then there is *Jin-Tayyar* – the 'flying djinni'. Full of mischief and not always well behaved, he likes playing tricks on people. But, while he delights in outwitting those who think they are smart, he is considerate with the weak and the vulnerable. Narin knows they are all here, somewhere. Invisible beings share the same space with the living, some outside and above the house, others much closer.

'Sometimes kindness comes from the least expected places,' says Grandma, as she sifts flour into a bowl. 'Have I told you the story of Ibrahim?'

'I don't think so.'

'Well, Ibrahim was God's beloved. That is why Nemrud hated him. He said to his henchmen: build a fire, cast Ibrahim into it. Turn him into charcoal, burn him to cinders.'

'Oh, he is cruel!'

'He was cruel. But it's also important to ask how everyone else behaved when calamity struck. Many just watched. Some even rushed to fetch wood, to add to the blaze. The lizard, for instance. Only a few good souls tried to save Ibrahim – like the frog. It filled its mouth with water and spat it into the flames, and kept doing this, until it was exhausted. The lizard laughed and said, "You are tiny, the fire is massive, what do you think you'll achieve with your itty-bitty water?" But the frog said, "If I were to do nothing, would I be any different from you?" Now that was a wise frog. We must always listen to our conscience and help those in need. We don't throw gasoline on a burning man. We carry him water.'

Narin contemplates. 'So when did this happen?'

'In olden times,' replies Grandma, as she cracks two eggs into the centre of the pile of flour.

'You always say that!'
'Because that's where stories live – in olden times.'

Grandma says time is a sentinel tree, marked with invisible rings inside, its straggly branches extending into the infinite sky, never perfect, never linear. In the span of a sentence a storyteller can jump back and forth centuries, as if a millennium could pass in the blink of an eye. But then it takes hours to describe a single event, every minute a stretch, an eternity.

'Remember, my heart. Story-time is different from clock-time.'

Clock-time, however punctual it may purport to be, is distorted and deceptive. It runs under the illusion that everything is moving steadily forward, and the future, therefore, will always be better than the past. Story-time understands the fragility of peace, the fickleness of circumstances, the dangers lurking in the night but also appreciates small acts of kindness. That is why minorities do not live in clock-time.

They live in story-time.

When the *borek* is baked, a delicious smell wafting throughout the house, Grandma cuts a generous portion for Narin. She sets a pitcher of cold, foamy yogurt drink by her plate and smiles fondly as she watches the child tuck in.

'When someone gives you the food they've prepared, they give you their heart.'

Grandma says that when she was little, there was a Muslim girl she loved to play with. The families were close and saw each other regularly. One day, on her way back from the shops, the girl's mother stopped by their house. It was a sweltering hot after-noon, and they served her freshly cut watermelon in their shady garden. The woman turned it down with a polite smile, saying she did not like the taste of the fruit. Nor would she accept the water offered, even though anyone could see she was sweating. So they brought her a jug of delicious lemonade. This time the woman reluctantly took a glass, but as soon as she thought no one was watching she poured it away behind a tree. They were shocked to find it there after she left. And that is when they realized something they had failed to notice all this time: that, even though the two families were neighbours, and they shared many a laugh and gossip together, the girl's parents refrained from eating their food because they regarded Yazidis as heathens.

'They thought our bread, even our water, was *haram*,' Grandma says. 'How can that be? We were children. We were friends.'

'I'm so sorry, Grandma.'

'I'm not telling this to upset you. I want to strengthen your resolve. Our ancestors were resilient and passed this resilience down through generations. But no matter how tall your grandfather, you have to do your own growing.'

'I understand, Grandma.'

'Remember, for all its pains and sorrows, the world is beautiful. How can it not be, when it is painted in the iridescent colours of the plumes of Melek Tawûs? If we know how to look, we can see beauty even with eyes closed.'

Narin sips her drink, a white moustache forming above her lips. When she puts down her glass, she asks, 'How long will we be staying in Iraq?'

'Two and a half months, my heart.'

'What if Hasankeyf gets flooded while we are away?'

'Don't worry. It'll take those bulldozers a while to build the dam.' Grandma wipes her forehead with the back of her hand. 'This trip will cheer us up. Blessed are those who get to visit the holy Lalish. Do you know the legend of how our sacred valley came into being? It is all in the "Hymn of the Thousand and One Names", "*Qewlê Hezar û Yek Nav*".'

'Tell me.'

'The hymn says that the earth rests on the head of a bull and the bull stands on the fins of a fish.'

'No way! How is that even possible?'

'You can't know what is possible unless you try to imagine it first,' says Grandma. 'Now when God created the angels, they floated above the seas for a long time. Upon arriving in Lalish, the angels exclaimed in unison: "This is the right place!" God threw leaven into the water to make it thicken. The earth turned solid. Lalish became a place of peace and safety. That is why, when you hear the name of our valley, you must say: "Oh my Home, my Home, you are my Home!"'

As Narin repeats these words, her gaze lovingly fixed on her grandmother, for a moment it feels as if she is addressing the old woman herself: 'Oh my Home, my Home, you are my Home!'

Home is where your loved ones are, but the reverse is also true. Those you love are your sanctuary, your shelter, your country and even, when it comes to that, your exile. Wherever they go, you will follow.

The night before they are to leave for Iraq, under a pale moonlight seeping from the open window, they curl up side by side on a mattress on the floor.

'Are you sleeping, Grandma?'

'Not yet, my heart.'

Narin sits up. 'There's something I don't understand. If Leila was born in Nineveh, why did she come here to Hasankeyf?'

'In the olden days both places were in the Ottoman Empire, but, more importantly, they were connected by water. The Tigris starts its journey in Turkey, flowing all the way into Iraq. It runs through mountains and valleys. People's lives and livelihoods depend on it. Our Leila was from a village downstream.'

'But why did she leave?'

Grandma heaves herself upright. Her long hair, hennaed and unbraided, spills on to her shoulders. 'She had no choice. Sometimes even trees have to uproot themselves – entire forests have been known to migrate.'

'What does that mean?'

'It means, as settled as we are in this land, the winds can blow so harshly at times that they can force us out.'

'You speak like a riddle.'

'Riddles are how Lady Truth cloaks herself.'

'Why would truth need to cloak herself?'

'Because if she were to walk about naked, people would stone her in the streets.'

Grandma waits as the child considers these words. Then she says: 'When Leila left home, she journeyed northwards, following the Tigris upstream. On horseback, all by herself. It was a difficult thing to do for a woman back then – it still is. But she made it. She settled in Castrum Kefa. This is where she got married and gave birth to her twelve children. Now, when my mother was born, it quickly became apparent that she had inherited some of Leila's talents. Then I was born, and they realized I had more of Leila's talents. Then my daughter – your mother – was born, may her return be easy. She had even more of Leila's talents, but your darling mother passed away far too young.' Grandma pauses. 'Do you understand what I'm saying?'

'No.'

'Pay more attention, then . . . Some of the women in our family have a gift. Although the nature of the gift may alter, in every generation since Leila left Nineveh it has been getting stronger. That means you, my heart, may possess even more of Leila's talents than your mother and me and my mother combined –'

'Me!' Narin exclaims.

'You, *dilê min*.'

The child frowns, seized by a surge of anger rising in her chest. 'How can you say that? The doctor said I'll go deaf.'

'What I'm talking about has nothing to do with your condition. Water-dowsing is an *awareness*. The gift is not constant – otherwise we would not be able to bear its strength. There are moments of illumination, and then it wanes. Leila used to call them "dreams". You must not be afraid of them. They may become more frequent as you get older. Be grateful, my child, be faithful. Always, honour your ancestry. There is a skill that runs in our family. We, the daughters of Leila, might have what she had, some of us a little less, others a bit more. It all depends on how you nurture what you've been given. It's a talent held in trust. No one owns it. We care for it before passing it on to the next generation.'

Through the open window, a languid breeze, saturated with the smell of reeds and peaty waters, creeps along from the shore. The river now feels imminent in the same way that tomorrow seems just around the corner.

'You said Leila foresaw that something terrible was going to happen and that's why she stopped divining. What was it? You still haven't explained.'

'It was a *firman*.'

'What is that?'

'*Firman* means authorization, sanction. A decree.'

'Why is that a bad thing?'

'Because it could also mean permission for massacre,' Grandma says.

Narin feels her heart accelerate.

'It was a long time ago. There was a pasha in Mosul, a greedy, selfish man who cared only about wealth and power. One of his eyes was brown, the other dull grey, like ash left over from a fire. He made a pact with a ruthless qadi to kill all Yazidi men and enslave the women. Ask the people in this region, do they remember what happened to our ancestors? Everyone has forgotten, everyone but us – and the Tigris.'

'Is that why Leila had to escape?'

'Yes, my heart.' Grandma smooths a strand of hair from Narin's face. 'But now let's get some sleep. Tomorrow we'll be travelling. When we arrive in Nineveh, I'll show you where it happened. Then you'll understand why sometimes even rivers have to migrate from their beds.'

—O—

ARTHUR

On the way to the River Tigris, 1872

K ing Arthur of the Sewers and Slums crosses the English
Channel for the first time on a blustery day in March. It
would have been easier to wait for less inclement weather,
but he feels bound by a sense of duty. He also fears that public
attention towards Mesopotamia – perhaps towards any subject –
is fickle. He needs to be on his way before people lose interest in
the *Epic of Gilgamesh*.

The sun is descending as his ship leaves British shores, and by
the time he is out in the open water it is dark all around. He can
hear the churning of the sea, feel its power, but see no further
than the crests of the waves lapping at the hull. A gibbous moon,
a day shy of fullness, glows between banks of clouds. Trying to
dispel his fears, he turns his attention to his companions. There is
a group of pilgrims on their way to the Holy Land: a surly theo-
logian who speaks to no one and a merchant who, conversely,
cannot keep quiet. Arthur wonders why his fellow passengers
have felt compelled to leave their warm beds to embark on such
a perilous journey in the middle of the night. He cannot explain
why he himself is here, for that matter. Why is he so obsessed with
unearthing ancient tablets that have lain broken and buried under
the ground for thousands of years? The question, once asked, sets
off a ripple of other questions, as a leaping carp leaves a trail of
watery wreaths in its wake. Sometimes he cannot tell whether

he has been hypnotized into seeking the River Tigris or is simply running away from the River Thames.

He is beset by memories of his visit to the asylum – the listlessness in his mother's moves, her slow, sluggardly slide into death, which has haunted him ever since. In leaving London to seek adventure in a far-off land, is he not abandoning her? He reminds himself that he cannot help her until he has advanced his career and earned decent money, but this kind of reasoning, rational and reassuring though it might be, does little to dispel his sense of remorse.

Halfway through the voyage, they are caught in a squall of hail – the waves rise to dizzying heights, the wind is unrelenting. The ship rocks from side to side, heaving with the swelling sea. It occurs to Arthur that he might perish here, sinking to the bottom of the water whilst dreaming of rescuing tablets from the bowels of the earth.

'First time crossin'?'

It is the merchant, watching him with curious eyes.

'First and last, if I can help it,' says Arthur.

Smiling, the merchant produces a silver flask out of his jacket. 'Take some – it helps.'

Although never much of a drinker, Arthur accepts the offer with gratitude. The liquid burns down his throat but sits warmly in his belly.

'It gets easier – you'll see.'

The merchant relates how he has traversed the Channel multiple times and intends to keep doing so until the end of his days. Once you have savoured the taste of travel, he says, your life will never be the same again.

Arthur arrives in Paris just as leaves are bursting out of their buds and daffodils are blooming in parks and gardens. He is excited to be in a city he has heard so much about. He feels like he already knows this place through stories, its many poor and destitute through his own experience, and its streets and alleys through his imagination. Above all, he wishes to see that legendary river – the Seine, and its younger sibling, the Bièvre. The latter, though smaller, has inspired poets and writers galore. Arthur has read Rabelais, and ever since wondered about the stream on whose banks they caught quails and fished for frogs and crayfish. He has read Victor Hugo, and remembers the descriptions of water in *Les Misérables*. Spurting forth from its source in Guyancourt, a fast-running and boulder-strewn torrent, the Bièvre has been flowing through the city for centuries, providing not only precious water but also ice supplies for Parisians.

On the way to the boarding house where he will stay overnight, he saunters with long, swinging strides, drinking in his surroundings. In London he never allows himself to relax, never taking a moment's respite to enjoy the songs of wandering artists or to smell the flowers straggling over high brick walls, but he can do that now that he is in a strange city and a stranger himself. He strolls through the *beaux quartiers* – neighbourhoods that abound in stylish boutiques, smart brasseries and gilded cafés with marble tables on the pavements where customers sit and sip absinthe, wine and lemonade, and laugh as if they have cast all their worries to the winds.

He recalls an essay – word for word – in which the French journalist and publisher Julien Lemer wrote that there is so much light spilling out from the shop windows from Rue Louis-le-Grand to Rue de Richelieu that one can read a newspaper as one ambles along. He observes the recently widened cobbled streets, bordered by tall trees and illuminated by gas lamps – a perfect execution of Haussmann's grand ambitions. As he meanders along the promenade, a feeling of lightness overcomes him, as though he were treading barefoot on moss. People, elegant and confident, stream by him on both sides, seemingly in no hurry. He has never before experienced this kind of easy assurance. The poverty and hardship of his upbringing have kept him from knowing such luxuries. He has no idea what it is like not to have to work every moment of each day, to go for a walk for no other reason than to see and to be seen.

But, before long, the cityscape begins to change. Colours fade, shadows deepen. Arthur strays into alleyways so narrow and sordid that if some upended carriage isn't blocking his way, then an unbearable stench is repelling him. There are cesspools everywhere. In the central arrondisements, many lanes, though visibly overcrowded, have no proper drainage. Stagnant water and raw sewage collect in murky puddles, appalling the senses. From the mills and tanneries, debris and carcasses are tossed into the Bièvre, as the river flows laboriously in sinuous curves before its confluence with the Seine.

Like London, the contrast between the neighbourhoods of the rich and the impoverished is so palpable it is hard to imagine they are all living in the same capital. But there is something else separating these communities, something less visible and tangible. It is their relationship with time. The wealthy do not have to rush after ticking clocks; they simply glide through each day, dandling the hours in their hands, wearing them like elegant gloves. For the poor, however, time is mere rags, tattered scraps that are never enough, no matter how much you pull and tug at them, neither covering goose-pimpled flesh nor providing any warmth.

Before Arthur leaves Paris, he visits the Louvre Museum to see the artefacts from Mesopotamia. He has read quite a bit about the famous building, originally constructed as a fortress, and changed and rebuilt time and again, like a poem in the making. But experiencing it up close leaves a deeper impression on him than he expected. If the Louvre were a poem, it is dedicated to unabashed beauty and passion and sensuality but also to power, materialism and possession. Inside, displayed behind glass cases, polished and pristine, he finds relics that by now have become familiar – cuneiform tablets, glazed bricks, pieces of lapis lazuli . . . There are also massive, human-headed, winged bulls from the palace of Ashurbanipal, solitary and displaced, just like the ones in the British Museum.

Two days later, early in the afternoon, Arthur is on board a new ship – a steamer with three masts and sails up, ready to embark on its journey across the Mediterranean. The vessel, not reliant on the direction of the wind, slices through the waves, leaving a pale trail in the water, hungrily swallowed by the deep. They follow old seafaring lanes, etched on maritime maps like whorls on fingertips. The harbour of Marseilles, the straits that divide Corsica from Sardinia, Sicily, Palermo, the Bay of Navarino, a spectacular sunrise over Etna . . .

The colour of his eyes changing with the light reflecting off the sea, Arthur spends many hours on deck, watching with wonder places he had never dreamt of. Everything he sees he commits to memory, despite his seasickness. His face pale, his stomach churning, and his hands grabbing the railings cold and clammy, he is nevertheless enthralled by the power of water.

An oddity of sea voyages is that they force even the most private of souls to converse with strangers. Amongst the various people he meets is one who makes an impression on him: a plant hunter from an island in the Caribbean, the grandson of Maroons who escaped slavery. The young botanist is on his way to Bhutan to find new species of flora and bring back seeds. In the course of their conversations Arthur learns that the man has never seen snow.

'Oh, it's magical,' says Arthur. 'The most stunning form of water.'

'Does it have a taste?'

And Arthur, without missing a heartbeat, replies, 'It tastes like mother's milk.'

Once he overcomes his seasickness, Arthur starts reading the books he has brought along. There is so much he wants to learn about the Levant – history, food, folklore, customs – though whether any of this will be of use to him in Nineveh he cannot possibly say. Deep inside, he feels worried. Never at ease around other people, he cannot imagine how he will ever manage to communicate with those from another culture. He suspects that his scholarly skills, whilst they may bring him some recognition in England, will not get him far in the eyes of the Ottoman authorities. Deep down he fears he is the wrong man for the task. He should have never left home, never ventured beyond the River Thames. Yet he knows of no one as obsessed as he is with the missing lines in the *Epic of Gilgamesh*, and perhaps that, in itself, makes him the right man for the task.

Doubt is corrosive for the traveller, and Arthur is full of it. But, as hours at sea evolve into days and he is still alive, both his fear and his uncertainty, though not entirely vanquished, give way to a new feeling, almost a thrill. He may not be a hero, but he is exhilarated to be setting out on an odyssey of his own. He yearns, with a force he cannot resist, to follow the siren call that has been summoning him since he was a boy.

Three magical syllables: *Ni-ne-veh*.

'Tomorrow, come on deck at the crack of dawn!' the captain says. 'The entrance to Constantinople by sea is a sight like no other. If you do not want to miss it, rise early!'

These words cause a tangible anticipation amongst the passengers. The children run around, the men chatter animatedly with each other, and the few women on board retreat to their cabins to get prepared. Even seasoned sailors seem invigorated. Leaning over the rails, Arthur peers into the horizon, trying to fathom what the excitement is about, but all he can see is a wall of fog.

The following day, before sunrise, he wakes to the sound of hurried footsteps. Groggily, he splashes his face with water, dresses and joins the others. Some passengers have brought telescopes, even though the sky is still pitch black. As the ship inches forward, the chill of the night wears off. In a little while, the thinnest sliver of crimson slashes open in the sky, light bleeding into the darkness. Nobody speaks a word, the silence complete and all-encompassing. In this state, they edge towards the mouth of the Bosporus, which divides two continents: on the one side lies the European coast; on the other, the Asian, though it is hard to tell where exactly one ends and the other begins.

The captain announces, 'We're almost there!'

His eyes adjusting to the dissolving gloom, Arthur stares into the distance, but he can discern no more than a few gauzy silhouettes. Then, as if a curtain is lifted from above, the fog dissipates precisely as dawn breaks above their heads in all its glory, with the sun's rays – purple, orange and the brightest fuchsia – revealing the crenellated walls, silvery cupolas and soaring minarets of a sprawling city. Arthur recognizes the dome of the Hagia Sophia from drawings he studied at the publishing press. He holds his breath, as miles and miles of settlement unfold before him, like a silken scarf. The palaces, the kiosks, the pavilions, the *konaks* and the trees – terebinths, spruces, cypresses – all come alive. The Golden Horn flows ahead in a glittering ribbon – more river than sea. The ship steers between the hill of the Seraglio on one side, and Kadıköy and Scutari on the other, until Galata and Pera heave into view, glowing with light. Arthur, stationed at the bow of the ship, turns around to take in the view, and then stands still, transfixed.

'Quite something, isn't it?' says the captain, appearing at his side.

'It is astounding.'

'Yes, indeed, but be careful.' The captain gives a chortle. 'It is a peculiar city, I have learnt to my cost.'

'Why do you say that?'

The captain leans closer, a whiff of spring onion on his breath. 'Well, because it has a greedy mouth, Constantinople – make sure it doesn't swallow you, like it has so many others.'

'I'm passing through,' says Arthur. 'I will be staying only a few days – and then I'll be on my way to Nineveh. I am not interested in Constantinople.'

'Sure,' says the captain, with a sidelong glance.

Arthur can feel his scepticism like a knife poking into his ribs.

It is well into the afternoon by the time Arthur disembarks, picks his way down the gangplank, bids farewell to the captain and is reunited with his luggage. He assumed the British Embassy would send someone, but there is not a single soul waiting for him.

Anxiously, he scans the port, which swarms with officials, merchants, sailors and stevedores bustling along the seafront. Ships of all sizes are moored along the dock – clippers, schooners, steamships and frigates – a thick forest of masts as far as the eye can see. Horses and carts deliver goods and cranes heave large crates of freight, swinging to and fro over the heads of passers-by. Hawkers circle around new arrivals, gabbling away. Over the din, Arthur can hear the slap of the waves against the hulls, the swelling of the water, the squawk of a seagull pecking at the litter nearby, the soughing of the wind through the rigging. Suddenly, he feels uncomfortable. He feels afraid.

'*Farangi*, welcome. Need help?'

Arthur spins around to find a weedy, short man with speckled skin and tired eyes. His callused hands, sunburnt face and hunched back indicate beyond doubt that he is a porter.

'How much?' Arthur asks, his voice rough with strain.

The man mumbles a few words in Turkish. Arthur accepts, trusting it is the right amount and he is not being taken for a fool.

'Do you know the way to the British Embassy?'

The porter gives a curt nod.

'Very well, let's go,' says Arthur, trying to sound confident. 'Do you have anyone to help you?'

But the man, having hauled one trunk under each arm and one on his back, is already trudging away.

'Wait for me,' Arthur yells.

A sonorous male voice cuts through the air, followed by others, the sounds reverberating from every direction. Arthur halts, confused. It takes him a moment to realize that the plaintive tones are the call for afternoon prayer spilling from the minarets nearby.

A wave crashes against the pier, spraying his face with mist. He is ambushed by the memory of a frigid day, so long ago it might have been a dream, the taste of snow on his tongue, the feel of his mother's hair, golden against the grey sky. The vision, for that is what it feels like, disappears as quickly as it appeared. Wiping his face, he hurries to follow the porter. He cannot have known, but the briny welcome that greets him in Constantinople on this afternoon in 1872 and the snowflake that melted in his mouth as a newborn in London in 1840 are one and the same.

—H
ZALEEKHAH

By the River Thames, 2018

Zaleekhah sits up in bed, roused from a troubled sleep. Her heart beats fast, as if sensing a creeping danger she is yet to comprehend. She doesn't need to check the clock to know what it will say: 3.34 a.m. She often wakes, to the minute, at this interstice between midnight and dawn. *Brahmamuhurtha*, the time of the Creator, when light energy is at its strongest, according to various faiths. The most opportune moment to burrow into your own soul and face your deepest fears, they say. For her, it is not about that. Not prayer, not meditation. It is the hour of melancholy – pure, unfiltered, restless.

Knowing she won't be able to go back to sleep easily, she turns on the laptop by her side. In the mechanical light her face takes on a bluish tinge. A raft of media pop-ups flash across the screen.

It catches her eye immediately – there, amid reports about the US president announcing that several ISIS leaders have been captured, a train collision in Germany and the latest preparations for the royal wedding, pushed to the bottom of the webpage, is a brief news item. Following a rare thunderstorm and flash floods in Egypt, thousands of death-stalker scorpions have invaded the city of Aswan, stinging more than five hundred people and killing several. Driven out of their dens, the arachnids have skittered into people's homes and yards, throwing everyone they encounter into a panic.

'It was only an hour of severe rain,' says an eyewitness. 'Then came the flood. It happened so fast we did not have time to run away and the creatures have gone mad . . .'

Zaleekhah draws in a breath, latching on to the words: *Then came the flood . . . so fast.'*

As she powers down the computer, her hand trembles slightly. She reaches down into her bag and extracts a bottle – sleeping pills. She will need them tonight. She shakes out all the tablets into her palm. She picks one, swallows it without water. Then she takes one more.

She turns off the alarm on her phone. Several WhatsApp messages await from colleagues with birthday greetings. Emojis of balloons and party streamers and cream cakes. There is also a message from her husband:

Hi Z, thinking of you. Sorry not to be with you on your birthday. I miss you more than I should, and I'm fighting the urge to call. So much is broken between us, I'm only beginning to accept, and I can't see how we can fix it . . . There's no easy way to say this: I'm filing for divorce. I thought you should hear it from me, not lawyers. Sorry things turned out this way. Hope you have a great birthday. I mean it.

Oddly, the first thing that comes to her mind is how she will tell her uncle. She rereads the message as if expecting some cryptic note to emerge. In the scope of one brief text Brian has apologized twice. She had liked this about him when they first met: a man who could easily admit his mistakes. She remembers the two of them, several cocktails in, the taste of his skin, sweet and salty at once, like the taste of summer, smooching by a fire escape behind a Chinese restaurant in Soho, until in their excitement they knocked down the rubbish bin and had to run away, scattering apologies in their wake. The memory makes her face hot. She wipes her eyes, unable to think of anything to write back.

A message pops up from Uncle Malek just then. She wonders why he is awake at this hour and if something is bothering him, but the message itself is cheerful.

> Did you think we'd forget your B-day, my dear? Dinner this evening. Helen will join. There'll be a proper cake and no fish – your aunt promised. It could still be a disaster! That is, of course, a joke. The food will be delicious and the company, too. Feel free to bring a plus one.

When Zaleekhah opens her eyes, her neck is stiff from sleeping in an awkward position. She checks the clock on her phone, realizing how terribly late it is. As she eases herself out of bed, a heaviness to her limbs, the sound of the doorbell pierces through the quiet of the houseboat. In the barely furnished space, the chime echoes loud enough to startle her.

Zaleekhah unlocks the door, sunlight flooding in. She finds herself face to face with Nen, dressed in vivid green overalls and yellow rubber boots, a rucksack on her back and a crocheted orange beanie pulled over her head. Behind her stands a tall, bald man carrying a toolbox.

'Oh dear, we woke you up!' Nen exclaims.

'It's okay.' Zaleekhah tugs at her collar, feeling self-conscious in her pyjamas. 'I should have been up.'

'Gosh, I feel terrible.' Nen smiles apologetically. 'We'll come back another time.'

'No, no, don't please. So, umm, have you been mudlarking?'

'Yes, the low tide was early this morning,' says Nen brightly. 'We stopped by to check the sink, but we can return later.'

'It's fine, there's no need. Now is a good time.'

'You sure?'

'Absolutely, please, come on in.'

Stepping back, Zaleekhah opens the door wider to allow them in.

Another smile spreads across Nen's face as soon as she enters. 'Wow, this place looks bigger when empty. It was all cluttered and messy when I lived here. I like your approach.'

'I haven't had a chance to buy any furniture yet.'

Nodding, Nen pulls a tin out of her rucksack. 'Here, I baked you some biscuits.'

'For me?' Surprised, Zaleekhah takes off the lid. Stacked inside are gingerbread biscuits shaped like miniature Mesopotamian tablets, each marked with different signs in cuneiform. 'Oh, wow. How did you make these?'

'Easy,' says Nen. 'Dough is like clay, as you saw the other day. I use a chopstick as my stylus. Each biscuit has its own word. Then I put them in the oven. Forty minutes, a hundred and eighty degrees and *voilà*! I bake them for all my friends.'

'So what does this one say?' asks Zaleekhah pointing to a biscuit with three vertical marks on its surface.

𒀀

'That's "Water",' says Nen. 'Try it!'

'Water –'

'Yes, the whole batch is designed for you.'

Zaleekhah pops the biscuit into her mouth, and a melange of flavours dissolves on her tongue – ginger, cinnamon, cardamom, honey and a touch of lemon. 'It's delicious.'

Nen cranes her head forward. 'And that one is "River". You should have that, too.'

Zaleekhah does not object. She has eaten so little this whole week that her stomach welcomes the unexpected treat.

Nen turns to the plumber. 'For my friend Rick, this one, the "Deluge". In honour of your plumbing skills!'

The man laughs as he accepts the offer and heads off to the kitchen with his toolbox.

'Would you like to sit down?' Zaleekhah asks. 'I've got a stool and an armchair. You're spoilt for choice.'

'Stool is good.'

Facing each other, they glance out of the window. A barge sails past in the distance, the water's surface a burnished silver. In the kitchen, the plumber, headphones in his ears, hums along to a tune only he can hear.

'I can't offer you tea or coffee, I'm afraid. I don't have a kettle.'

'Don't worry, I've already overdosed on caffeine.' Nen regards her kindly. 'You seem to be travelling light.'

Though the remark is made with a smile, Zaleekhah feels a tinge of embarrassment. 'I'm still sorting myself out.'

'That's how I feel every day.'

Zaleekhah runs her thumb over the edge of the armchair, startled by her words. There is such vim and briskness to the way Nen speaks and holds herself that she cannot imagine her feeling insecure or inadequate in any way.

'I forgot to ask: the name of your shop is intriguing – *The Forgotten Goddess*. What does it mean?'

'Her name was Nisaba.' Nen leans forward, as if to confide a secret. 'The goddess of writing and agriculture. They called her the "Lady coloured like the stars of heaven". She was the spark of inspiration behind every story and poem. The patron of storytellers, poets and bards.'

'Never heard of her.'

'That's because she's mostly forgotten.'

'Why?'

'You tell me.' Nen sits back, her eyes hardening. 'Why are women left out of history? Why do we have to piece their stories back together from fragments – like broken shards of pottery?'

It is not the question that takes Zaleekhah by surprise as much as the fervour in Nen's voice. It requires a different intensity, almost a passion, one that she suspects she does not have, to be so openly critical of the world and its innumerable inequalities. Slowly, she says, 'You seem to know a lot about ancient civilizations.'

'I know a little about a few, but I'm endlessly interested in history . . . ever since I was a child. At uni, I read Assyriology. I completed all the courses but didn't graduate. I was going through a rough patch at the time and I couldn't finish my degree. I failed.'

'Sorry to hear that –'

'Don't be,' says Nen. 'It all worked out – eventually.'

'And the tattoo parlour?'

'Oh, that's my saviour. I'm very gentle with the needle, everyone says. I had worked at a few parlours before, so, when I dropped out of uni, I realized I was only good at two things in life, and those two things had nothing in common. I knew how to tattoo and I knew how to write in cuneiform. It occurred to me that there is a whole cast of characters in the *Epic of Gilgamesh* that'd make great imagery. That sounded like a good idea – besides, I could ink in cuneiform. And, if no one wanted it, so be it, I had nothing to lose. That's the thing about failing: either it makes you super-afraid of failing again or, somehow, you learn to overcome fear.'

Zaleekhah sits still in thought.

'But, much to my delight, customers seemed to like the concept. They recommended me to others. The business picked up, and it's been doing well. I've done many versions of Gilgamesh, his friend-slash-boyfriend Enkidu, Humbaba the monster of the cedar forest, the temple prostitute Shamhat . . . they all make brilliant designs.'

'And words? What is the most memorable thing you've tattooed?'

Nen pauses as she considers. 'There was this guy – a talented athlete with a bright future. He had a terrible car accident, and was paralysed from the waist down. It crushed his soul. His career was over. He believed his life was over. He wound up in a very dark place. I think it was his wife's love that saved him in the end – and a brilliant therapist. By the time he visited my shop, he was determined to start over. He asked me to suggest a line that would always remind him of what he had been through. Something meaningful, empowering. He wanted it on the inside of his right arm – that way he'd see it every day. So we looked over the *Epic of Gilgamesh* together. I read him a few passages, and he chose.'

'What did he choose?'

'The first line of the poem; it was perfect for him. *There was a man who saw the deep.*'

'The name of this boat?'

'Yes, I bought the houseboat with the money I made that year – plus my lifetime's savings – so it felt right. That's for all the women who have gone through some shit of their own – *she who saw the deep.*'

Just then the plumber's voice rings out from the kitchen. 'Hey, Nen, I think I'm done here! Want to take a look?'

'Fabulous.' Nen jumps up.

She turns to Zaleekhah and says, 'People think a tattoo is an act of rebellion or something, but, actually, it's a form of storytelling. That's what most customers come in for – not just some random image or word in ink. They come because they have a story to tell.'

Seconds later the three of them stand side by side, watching the water gush into the sink without any leaks.

'All good?' asks the plumber.

'All good,' says Nen. 'Thank you, my friend. Send me the bill.'

'Will do, boss. All right, then, catch you later.'

He grabs his toolbox, puts his headphones back on and pads away.

'Right, I'd best get going too,' Nen says, touching two fingers to her forehead, as if doffing her hat. As she moves aside, she spots the ornament on the shelf. 'Oh, you have a *lamassu*!'

'Yes, it's a present from my uncle. He collects art and artefacts from all over the world. They have a gallery near your place, actually.'

Nen takes a step towards the *lamassu*. 'This is a Lladró. Looks like a limited edition. It must be worth quite a bit.'

Zaleekhah blushes slightly. She has never felt comfortable with the extravagance of Uncle's gifts. 'He's a bit old school, Uncle Malek; sometimes he can be a little over the top.'

Nen's eyes, when they meet Zaleekhah's again, are caring, and their green deeper, like a shadow at the bottom of a stream. 'Well, he seems to be important in your life. Was it he who encouraged you to study water?'

'Uncle Malek? No! He has zero interest in science. It was my decision, and I had to go against his wishes. And then, later on, it was a scientist who opened my eyes to the mysteries of water. If it weren't for him, I probably wouldn't have got anywhere near.' Zaleekhah pauses and breathes in slowly. 'I lost my parents when I was seven. They died in a flash flood – they were camping by a river.'

'I'm very sorry, that must have been so hard.' Nen's tone is gentle. 'This scientist, he must have been remarkable to bring you back to a positive relationship with water.'

Zaleekhah feels a tightness in her chest. 'He was, but he made a big mistake towards the end of his life. He became obsessed with a hypothesis he couldn't quite prove –'

'You mean he failed – like any other human being.'

'I guess you can put it that way. I was brought up to think differently, though. Uncle always says people like us cannot afford to fail. Immigrants, I mean.'

Nen jams her hands in her pockets. 'I don't know your uncle, but I respectfully disagree. I'd have thought especially an immigrant would understand what it feels like to meet loss and still not be defeated.'

They step out on to the deck. The Thames heaves in the background, moving so slowly it seems solid, a sheet of blue glass.

Zaleekhah asks, 'That couple I saw in your shop . . . did you really tattoo *Eat the Rich* in cuneiform?'

'Oh, I did! It looked pretty good.'

Zaleekhah shakes her head, incredulous. 'And how many tattoos do you have yourself – if it's not too personal?'

Nen flashes a smile. 'Zero.'

'What, really?'

'Yup, I'm terrified of needles. I'd probably faint if I saw one piercing my skin.'

They look at each other for a second and then burst into laughter.

'A tattoo artist who's scared of needles!' says Zaleekhah.

It is her first joyful moment in a long time. As though she senses this, Nen's eyes soften. There is a steady gentleness to her gaze as she says, 'No less strange than a hydrologist who is frightened of water. It happens.'

On the towpath a kingfisher calls. Since moving here, Zaleekhah has been noticing birds. She says, quietly, 'I guess you're right.'

'You should come mudlarking with us sometime.' Nen takes her hands out of her pockets. 'It's a good start to the day, peaceful, calming – especially for those of us *endowed with a restless heart*.'

A look of puzzlement crosses Zaleekhah's face.

'*Epic of Gilgamesh*,' says Nen. 'That's how Gilgamesh's mother complains to the gods: *Why did you endow my son with a restless heart? You have moved him to travel . . . face a battle unknown*' – Nen adjusts her rucksack and walks towards the gangway – 'bye, Zaleekhah. It was lovely to see you.'

Zaleekhah raises her hand and her voice. 'Thank you for getting the pipe fixed – and the biscuits!'

'Any time.' Nen steps off the deck and turns on her heel to wave back at her. 'You take care of yourself.'

From the corner of her eye, Zaleekhah senses a movement at the window of the adjacent houseboat. The couple next door are watching from behind their curtains. Embarrassed to be seen in her pyjamas, she's seized by a strong urge to go inside and close the door. But something impels her to resist, and she does the opposite. Stepping on to the gangway, she yells:

'Hey, Nen!'

'Yeah?' Nen stops mid-stride.

'Umm . . . There's a dinner at my uncle's house this evening for my birthday . . .' Another twitch of the curtains.

'It could be a bit boring – they're quite formal, and the food might not be to your liking – but I was wondering, you and Uncle seem to have interests in common, I mean, you're both fond of the *Epic of Gilgamesh*, and ancient history, and umm, yeah, so, would you like to come with me to meet the Maleks?'

—o—

ARTHUR

On the way to the River Tigris, 1872

T he British Embassy is in Constantinople's cosmopolitan Pera district. Designed to look like a miniature of Buckingham Palace, it is adorned with Grecian columns and large windows that overlook the Golden Horn. The massive chandeliers in the ballroom, originally intended for the British Embassy in Moscow, were installed here when the Crimean War broke out.

They put Arthur up in a small room tucked under the eaves. Exhausted, his eyelids begin to droop as he eats the dish in front of him – slow-cooked rabbit stew with barley. When he finally gets into bed, he pulls the blankets over himself and listens to the noises leaking through the window – Constantinople, stirring and susurrating in the dark, like a nocturnal creature snuffling around for prey.

In the morning, he is summoned to meet the ambassador. Climbing a curved marble staircase, Arthur enters a spacious, high-ceilinged chamber, richly furnished with bronze sculptures, antique cabinets, oil paintings, ceramic plates and vases of all sizes. Ornaments from India and East Africa are juxtaposed with paraphernalia from across the Ottoman Empire and displayed on étagères. In the midst of this grand collection stands the ambassador, square-jawed and broad-shouldered.

'Arthur Smyth! Welcome to Constantinople – or, as the Turks like to call it, the "city of a thousand domes".'

A scion of a long-established aristocratic family, educated at Eton and Cambridge, the ambassador is a man who has enjoyed a privileged route into the Foreign Office, and it reflects in the confident way he holds himself and the practised ease of his manner. As he extends his hand, he says, 'I have heard much about you. They say your speech made quite an impression on the prime minister.'

'When may I travel to Nineveh?'

The ambassador laughs at his guest's failure to adhere to the fine art of small talk.

'I'm sorry,' says Arthur, realizing his mistake. He tries to revert to the expected social niceties. 'This is such an impressive building you have here.'

'We are terribly grateful to have a little roof above our heads to accommodate visiting artists and eminent scholars like yourself.'

Arthur shifts uncomfortably from one foot to the other. He is not sure whether he should point out that this is not exactly a 'little roof' or whether he ought to pretend that it is.

Observing him, the ambassador says, 'These old tablets seem to have a hold on you. Such dedication. I admire it, I must say. There are those who'd never understand your passion, but I'm not one of them.'

Arthur swallows. As often, he is perplexed by the way the upper classes speak. They have a circuitous way of expressing themselves. He can never tell whether he is being genuinely praised or subtly mocked.

'When may I leave for Nineveh? I would like to set out at once.'

'Well, it's not a matter of what you want, my good man. It's what the sultan wants.'

'I thought all arrangements had been completed prior to my arrival.'

'You cannot excavate on Ottoman ground without a *firman*.'

'I beg your pardon?'

'A *firman* – an official permit. A seal of approval. A royal decree issued by the sultan or the authorities. Without that, you cannot dig at Nineveh, and, if you do, you will find yourself in a scrape – even I would not be able to come to your rescue.'

Arthur's face tightens. 'But surely I do not need to wait here? The authorization letter will arrive while I'm on my way. That will save me time.'

'Time . . .' repeats the ambassador, as though the word is new to him. 'It means different things in different parts of the world. The Turks have their own version, which can be painfully slow.'

Arthur shakes his head. 'I have been told that the sultan does not care about ancient clay tablets –'

'Oh, he doesn't, not at all, but then, suddenly, he does. The whims and fancies of the Sublime Porte . . .'

Arthur feels his stomach drop. In his desperation, he focuses on the patterns of the Turkish carpet, taking comfort in their regularity. He swiftly calculates there are 244 diamond-shaped motifs on its surface, including the halves and quarters along the edges. Whenever he looks again, it will still be the same number. This is something he can control.

'My dear fellow,' says the ambassador, 'I can see this news upsets you. I have something that might help.'

He strides over to a cabinet and pours a glass of colourless liquid. He offers the drink to Arthur and takes one for himself.

'Have you tried this before? They call it vodka – it was invented in a monastery by a Russian monk, God rest his jovial soul. He named it "bread wine", as it happens to be distilled from wheat. I must warn you, though, it is strong.'

Arthur takes a large sip. He coughs, turning bright red.

The ambassador smiles. 'I'd advise you to take things slowly in Constantinople. As they say, in this part of the world, if you run too fast, you will miss the safe place where you might have hidden yourself.'

Constantinople . . . such an elusive place, hard to grasp. An eel of a city – just when you think you have caught hold of it, it slips out of your hands.

A week goes by, then another. There is no news of his *firman*. Arthur sleeps fitfully at night and wakes up tired in the mornings, as if chased by beasts in his dreams. Several times he tries to engage with the Ottoman authorities, but, ricocheting from one official to the next, he gets nowhere. It does not help that he cannot speak the language. As a boy he showed a remarkable aptitude in learning Yiddish and Irish by eavesdropping on native speakers, and if he can only steady his nerves he will probably pick up Turkish just as fast, but he cannot shake off the feeling that even then he would not be able to make himself understood.

'Fish out of water,' says the senior clerk. 'You do not know how to grease palms, you do not understand *baksheesh*. You are too sensitive, impatient.'

If Arthur has a hard time with the Ottoman gentry, he does not fare any better with the British Embassy personnel. As well as the ambassador and his wife and their three children, settled comfortably on the premises, there are numerous clerks, attachés and secretaries. Merchants, too, come and go, even though the Levant Company surrendered its hold over trade across the region long ago. Arthur learns that, in the past, the residence offered a safe haven from the waves of bubonic plague that devastated Constantinople. But, despite its exquisite gardens and elegantly furnished spaces, he feels uncomfortable within these walls. The officials are suave and debonair, the guests full of swagger and bluster – men used to having their every whim indulged and every wish anticipated. Unable to match their conversational style and having little interest in the subjects discussed, each day after supper, instead of joining them for a drink around the fireplace, he seeks permission to retire to his room. He knows he should make more of an effort, and he senses they gossip behind his back, disparaging his uncouth manners and awkward ways, but he has neither the desire nor the ability to fit in.

On occasion, Arthur is invited to dine at the house of a local family. The kebabs, loaded with spices, upset his stomach. He finds the rice and mutton too fatty, though he enjoys the *hoshaf* they serve at the end – a bowl of sugary water with stewed fruits. Like Queen Victoria, the Turks have a sweet tooth and consume a dazzling variety of desserts, some with bewildering names – *Bottom of the Cauldron*, *Lips of the Belle*, *Wife's Belly*, *Floozy's Treat*, *Vizier's Finger* . . . But the one Arthur prefers is the *ashure* – Noah's Ark pudding, a recipe with forty ingredients, said to have been invented on the coracle to celebrate surviving the Flood. It is still alive, in this part of the world, still shaping everyday life, the memory of water.

Arthur likes the coffee-houses and makes it a habit to visit them often. With their dense covering of ivy, wainscoted walls and cushioned benches, they are charming and, unlike the streets, very clean. Perched under a pergola, he sips his coffee as he pores over a collection of poems. Sometimes he sketches his surroundings – children playing Knucklebones, men with fezzes and turbans, fruit-sellers bearing trays of figs . . . The first time he tries the water pipe, the *narghile*, he inhales too fast, spluttering and coughing so much that he makes the serving boy laugh. After that, he is careful. He observes the other customers, who hold themselves utterly still, as though they are not smoking but meditating on the ways of providence. Time slows down; the bubbling of water in the crystal bowl soothes.

A few yards from his favourite coffee-house in Ortaköy is a ramshackle hut frequented by a troupe of fishermen. Arthur watches them with admiration as they repair their nets or grill their daily catch. They invite him over one afternoon. Unlike the people at the embassy, the fishermen do not engage in small talk; they are content with silence. They sit in a circle around the fire, the neighbourhood cats forming another circle behind them. They offer him freshly caught, chargrilled bonito with flatbread and pickled turnips. Nothing he has had before has ever tasted this good.

At every opportunity, Arthur strolls along the Bosporus, watching the blue expanse, dazzling and unfathomable. Sparrows skim the water; seagulls swoop down to peck at scraps. He is surprised to learn that the Turks regard storks with great respect, believing that the birds make the pilgrimage to Mecca, and return each year, wiser and holier. There are fewer camels in this city than he expected, but once he sees two of them collide in a lane. The riders instantly find a solution: the camel with the lighter load sits while the other jumps over it. Unspoken agreements and unwritten rules govern daily life, and they must be obeyed by humans and animals alike.

It is the dogs that surprise him the most. They saunter around, bask in the sun, claiming the streets for themselves. A hundred years before, the reigning sultan ordered them to be bundled into sacks and exiled to an island in the Sea of Marmara, where many starved to death. The inhabitants of Constantinople, profoundly unhappy with the sovereign's cruelty, managed to bring back the surviving canines, and since then they have proliferated with a vengeance. No one can touch them now.

Going from one neighbourhood to the next feels as much a change as leaving one country and crossing over into another. Arthur cannot help but suspect that Constantinople is not a city but several hidden in one; not a singular entity, but a thousand broken shards. A wide array of languages is spoken here, depending on which street you happen to be on: Turkish, Greek, Armenian, Kurdish, Arabic, Persian, Ladino, French, English, Italian, Russian, Spanish, Bosnian, Bulgarian, Serbian, Croatian, Macedonian, Albanian . . . On his daily peregrinations, Arthur observes European diplomats with their distinctive attire, Jews in side curls, Albanians with black pistols and white petticoats, Tartars in sheepskins, Armenian porters doubled under the weight of the baskets on their backs, Georgians sporting metal belts around their waists . . . He runs into Dominican friars, Jesuits, priests, rabbis and imams. He sees Sufi dervishes with conical hats. He learns how to identify members of different communities:

Pomaks, Croats, Maronites, Romanis, Bedouins, Druzes, Syrians, Circassians, Egyptians, Cossacks . . . All kinds of accents bubble up in the gargantuan cauldron that is Constantinople. Some people wear watches with two dials, each showing a different time. The entire city runs on multiple time zones at once.

One major contrast between the streets of London and those of Constantinople is the scarcity of women in the latter. Once he glimpses a concubine leaving the sultan's harem for a rare outing, carried in a palanquin by liveried chairmen. A eunuch – most likely one of the many slaves kidnapped from Africa and viciously castrated as a boy – rides ahead of the group, berating anyone who dares to peek inside. Another day, whilst traipsing along the Golden Horn, he spots three Muslim women in a caïque, propped up against cushions, their laughter echoing off the surface of the water. He watches them until their boat skims out of sight.

In Scutari, he saunters along gravel paths bordered by birches and willows, until he finds himself in front of a military bar-racks: a huge, rectangular building with a parade ground at its centre. This is where thousands of casualties from the Crimean War – British, French and Turkish soldiers – were treated not that long ago. Arthur has heard so many stories about the Lady with the Lamp and her fellow nurses making their rounds, and the patients with gangrene and frostbite wailing in the dark, that he half expects to see them all here now. But there is no sign that they were ever here; only the rage of the wind – *lodos* – remains. It occurs to him that Constantinople, more than any other place he has seen or heard about, is a city of forgetting.

Three weeks into his stay, Arthur is taken to the Grand Bazaar by a dragoman who works as an interpreter for the embassy. They thread their way through arched alleys, pigeons darting in and out of the cupolas overhead. Walking in tandem with a steady flow of shoppers, they pass through carved columns and return the greetings of vendors sitting cross-legged on rugs, sipping tea as dark as their eyes.

Arthur discovers that each quarter of the bazaar specializes in a particular type of merchandise. One street sells only fabrics: brocade, cambric, muslin, silk, cashmere, velvet, damask . . . Another, decorative glass: ribbed, gilded, bubbled, engraved . . . The next is for smokers: bundles of *chibouks*, pipes of ivory, *narghiles* of crystal . . . In a different row, dedicated to perfumes, scents from countless bottles, powders, pomades and ointments mingle in the air. Arthur marvels at incense burners encrusted with stones, boxes of henna, pouches of musk, kohl to embellish the eyebrows and antimony for the eyes. This part of the bazaar is so packed that the crowd sucks him into a human slipstream like a tide dragging a boat under the water.

Turning a corner, Arthur finds himself in a passage glittering with gemstones: opals, agates, aquamarines, emeralds, sapphires, pearls, garnets . . . Arranged on stalls are piles of *tespih*, the worry beads that the Turks love to click. He stops to look at a blue cabochon.

'A fine choice,' says the storekeeper in fluent, if heavily accented, English. 'That's a special piece.'

'It's lapis lazuli.' Arthur smiles as Mr Bradbury's words ring in his ears. Lapis *from Latin, meaning 'stone'*; Lazuli *from Arabic and Persian, meaning 'heaven, sky, dark blue'* . . .

The celestial gem of the Ancient Mesopotamians. *Ancestors' Rock.* In his readings of the *Epic of Gilgamesh*, Arthur has come across mention of a blue tablet, but he always assumed this to be poetic licence. Yet now, as he holds the stone in his palm like a frightened bird, it feels wholly plausible that somewhere by the River Tigris, buried beneath the rubble, there might be just such an inscription in lapis lazuli.

'I give good discount. Just for you.'

Hardly has Arthur thought of a reply than he hears a commotion. Whoops, hollers and whistles – and then a cry of desperation.

'What in God's name is going on?' Arthur asks.

The dragoman cranes his head to see better. 'It looks like they are having a bit of fun with a devil-worshipper.'

Arthur rushes in that direction, still holding the stone – the shopkeeper and the dragoman on his heels.

A rabble of noisy youths has gathered nearby, their voices rising in waves. Chalk in hand, one of their number is drawing a circle around an elderly peasant. In the centre of the geometric shape, the man stands motionless, his shoulders hunched, his face etched with hurt.

'It's an oddity of the Orient,' says the dragoman, catching up with Arthur. 'Some people believe if you make a ring around a devil-worshipper they cannot get out – until a passer-by erases it. I'm not sure if it's true, but there is always someone willing to give it a try.'

Arthur pushes his way through the crowd. Upon reaching the front, he takes out the paisley handkerchief he purchased on Regent Street, a frippery. Slowly, he rubs out the circle. People fall silent as they watch him with amusement. The sight of a Yazidi being harassed is nothing exceptional, but a *farangi* on his hands and knees coming to the aid of one is something to behold in the Grand Bazaar.

Reluctantly, gradually, the rowdy youths disperse. All this time the old man has not taken his eyes off Arthur, but now he mutters something under his breath.

'What's he saying?' Arthur wants to know.

'He's thanking you.' The dragoman shrugs. 'The ravings of a dodderer. He says, you are a kind person, but you must be careful because you are endowed with a restless heart.'

Arthur's eyes widen as he recalls the line uttered by Gilgamesh's mother: *Why did you endow my son with a restless heart? You have moved him to travel* . . . Just as he wonders if the man might have heard of the epic, another stream of words follows.

'What is he saying now?'

'That there is a river running through you – whatever that means.'

Arthur studies the man, his skin wrinkled like leather, his nose majestic and broad at the bridge, his forehead wide and his dark hair abundant and curly, merging with the beard that rests on his chest. So alike is he to the images of the Ancient Mesopotamians that he might just as well have stepped out of an Assyrian bas-relief from the time of Ashurbanipal.

'Are you going to buy that stone or not?' says the shopkeeper.

By the time King Arthur of the Sewers and Slums leaves the four-hundred-year-old Grand Bazaar, holding a lapis lazuli piece in his palm, he is still thinking about the old Yazidi's words. What could he have possibly meant? In the *Epic of Gilgamesh*, the poem's troubled hero travels far away from home, making it to the mouth of the rivers at the end of the world – all for an adventure that is bound to end in failure. Maybe Arthur, too, suffers from the same malady. Maybe that is why he is incapable of settling down. All he knows is, if there is a river running through him, it seems always and in every way to flow towards melancholy.

H—
NARIN

By the River Tigris, 2014

'Did it ever happen to you, Grandma?'

'Not to me. But to my younger brother. He came home from school one day sobbing. The other boys had thrown him to the ground and drawn a circle around him.'

'But why?'

'Because people have fabricated all kinds of myths and lies about our culture.'

Narin glances at her father. She wants to ask him if he, too, has experienced anything similar, but Baba's eyes are on the road, his hands on the wheel. They are driving to Iraq, finally on their way to the holy Valley of Lalish. Narin sits in the front, which makes her feel grown up. Grandma is at the back, surrounded by suitcases full of presents for their relatives.

'If someone were to draw a circle around me, I'd hop over it!' Narin says.

'Of course you would, my heart,' says Grandma. 'But it's not some drawing in chalk that hurts. It is the intention behind it.'

When they reach Cizre, near the Turkish–Syrian border, and close to Iraq, Grandma tells Narin of a famous scientist who was born here.

'His name was Al-Jazari. A precocious child, born and raised in Upper Mesopotamia – like you, my heart.'

Grandma says Al-Jazari adored water. From an early age he was fascinated by the sweeping meanders of silted rivers, the movements of tides. He built exquisite fountains, irrigation devices and water-clocks. And one day he created something no one had ever seen before: a peacock machine.

If you pulled a lever hidden in the tail of the peacock, it released water from its beak so you could wash your hands. A few seconds later, the left door opened and a tiny doll appeared bringing soap. When you finished your ablutions, the right door opened and another doll emerged, carrying fresh towels.

'That's amazing!' remarks Narin.

Father joins the conversation now. 'Imagine, nine hundred years ago Al-Jazari invented impressive machines, far ahead of his time! They say many of his drawings are somewhere in America today. In a library or museum.'

'Oh, so they get to see them, but we don't,' says Grandma.

'Well, at least they'll keep them safe over there, Mama. Otherwise, God knows, they might have been destroyed or lost here.'

Grandma sighs. 'Safe for whom, though, Khaled? Westerners take our past, our memories. And then they say, "Don't worry, you can come and see them any time." But how do we even get there?'

'Those museums have millions of visitors from all over the world. Their doors are wide open.'

'Yes, but millions more cannot travel, can they? We're here, but our history is elsewhere. It's like they've severed our body into pieces, and they say, "Whenever you want, you can come visit your limbs." '

Khaled turns towards Narin and winks. 'Your grandma is very sensitive when it comes to this subject.'

Worried that the two people she loves the most are in disagreement, Narin chips in, 'That peacock clock . . . so was Al-Jazari a Yazidi, too?'

'Depends on whom you ask . . .' says Grandma. 'If you ask an Arab, he'll tell you Al-Jazari was an Arab. Iranians say he was Persian. Kurds say he was Kurdish. No one ever asks us.'

Father presses the accelerator, and they feel the flaws in the road. 'Arab, Iranian, Kurdish or Yazidi . . . what we do know is that Al-Jazari loved music. He built a mechanical band of musicians – tiny robots in a boat, playing songs for the guests as they sailed on the water.'

'No way!'

'It's true. He had such a fine mind,' Father says. 'And, like every genius born in this land, he's been forgotten.'

'But you didn't forget!' says Narin, eager to cheer him up. 'You remember Al-Jazari! And Grandma remembers!'

'Yes, sweetheart,' Father says, nodding. 'We are the memory tribe.'

Narin presses her forehead against the window, the reflection of her face merging with the yellowing fields. When she tires of watching the landscape, she turns back and glances at the box they are bringing with them.

'Why are we taking the *qanun*?'

Father replies. 'There is a master craftsman in Iraq. Very famous. I want him to take a look at it. The instrument needs repair, but I cannot entrust it to just anyone. It's very old, and it's a gift, so we must take good care of it.'

'A gift from whom?'

There is the briefest silence before Grandma says, 'The Englishman brought it with him from Istanbul and he gave it to my grandmother.'

'Why?'

'Well – it was his way of thanking her. Not only her, the whole village. He was grateful that they had allowed him to stay.'

'Let me guess,' says Narin, shrugging. 'And that, too, happened in olden times!'

After they cross the border into Iraq, they make their way steadily down the Tigris, the river their guide.

Grandma says that once upon a time this region was full of oryxes – large antelopes with long, straight horns, a blend of beauty and stamina. Their coats so bright that they reflected the rays of the sun like smooth mirrors, they could preserve water even in scorching temperatures. Capable of detecting scents from miles away, they could smell the promise of rain in the wind.

When Grandma was a girl, there were about five hundred oryxes in the region. By the time she got married only a handful had remained. The hunters arrived with their safari vehicles and automated weapons. Oil-company executives threw parties for their guests, driving them to the desert to give chase to these heavenly animals.

There were also lions along the Tigris once upon a time. Big cats so majestic and fearsome they inspired artists, who carved them into stone with astonishing detail. They lived alongside gazelles, foxes, lynxes, jackals, leopards and striped hyenas that

unleashed bloodcurdling sounds in the night. There were croco-
diles, too, though not as many in this part of the river. Once a
shark swam all the way from the Ganges in India to see the lights
of Baghdad, where it decided to stay for good. But now they are
all gone, the animals and the artists, all turned to dust. Only the
stones remain, and the stories, buried deep.

With one more pit stop, in three hours they reach the outskirts of
Mosul. From here they will drive to the village where Leila was
born. *Zêrav*, 'Golden Waters', is situated between the River Tigris
and its tributary the River Khosr.

'Imagine, Narin,' Father says. 'All this was once a momentous
empire. At its height, Assyria covered Iraq, Syria, Israel, Palestine,
Jordan, Lebanon, Egypt, Iran and parts of Turkey. It was powerful, not only because it was rich but also because it sowed fear.
When they conquered a new land, they forced the entire population to migrate. That was cruel. People lost their connection with
their birthplace.'

Father says thousands of years later, Yazidi settlements were
similarly wiped off the map when Saddam ordered that they be
destroyed to make way for the Mosul Dam. All at once the villagers
were left homeless. In their own motherland, they became refugees. Saddam also built reservoirs and dikes to divert water from
the marshlands – which used to be so green and fertile that many
believed them to be the original Garden of Eden. But the tyrant
wanted to teach the Marsh Arabs a lesson, and, in doing so, send
a message to all dissidents.

'You know, Marsh Arabs used to grow rice and cane reeds –
and scented cucumbers. Ah, that smell! But when the dictator
decimated the marshlands, the water became undrinkable, full of
salt. The buffalos were poisoned. The plants died. Twenty thousand square kilometres of bountiful soil, imagine, crumbled into
wasteland. People starved to death.'

Father says that, in the chaos following the American invasion, all the chemicals and rubble from fuel and weapons contaminated the Tigris. And the Mosul Dam, which Saddam in all his hubris had once named after himself, has now been declared the most perilous dam in the world, built on poor foundations of soluble rock that are dissolving by the day. At some point in the future it could collapse, and, if that happens, in only a matter of hours it will inundate Mosul and the surrounding area, engulfing houses and fields as well as thousands of years of history. He says that one ancient city in particular is in danger of being obliterated: Nineveh.

—o—

ARTHUR

On the way to the River Tigris, 1872

Weeks have gone by, and Arthur is still waiting for the *firman* that will allow him to travel to Nineveh. A nervous tension suffuses his every movement and gesture. Each day he asks the clerks if they have any news for him. Each day they advise him to be patient.

It is the same clerks who send for him one evening before supper. The dragoman who accompanied him to the Grand Bazaar is also in the room.

'We were talking about you, Smyth. We all concurred that you are in need of some diversion,' says the dragoman. 'You have been in Constantinople for weeks, but you have hardly seen anything.'

'I have seen quite a lot,' says Arthur. 'I go on walks.'

'Walks will only take you so far. Constantinople has many faces, but she only shows one in the daytime. You must meet her in moonlight. Tell us, what are your plans tonight?'

'I will be in my room – reading.'

'Forget your books, come with us.'

The three men insist so much that Arthur yields. He follows them out, intending to excuse himself from this unexpected engagement as soon as he can. But the next thing he knows he is hustled into a carriage, the seats soft and plush. After a short ride, they get out and make their way down a dimly lit street until they reach a house with a tall gate and a brass door handle.

The dragoman knocks twice, waits a few seconds and knocks once more.

A boy opens the door. Without a word, he ushers them into a room decorated with heavy curtains, silk cushions and soft rugs. Large trays have been set up in the centre, laden with drinks and delicacies.

Arthur glances around anxiously. 'What kind of a house is this?'

'The best kind,' says the dragoman. 'You would not want to leave Constantinople without a proper Oriental experience.'

Arthur flushes crimson. The memory returns, unbidden, of the day he went to the publishing house with his father, the eyes of the prostitute in St Giles still boring through him all these years later. He makes a move to leave, at the very moment that the door opens and a woman enters.

Prostitution in Constantinople is an acrobat, a skilled equilibrist. It walks a tightrope strung over and below the city walls, every step dangerous. Houses of ill repute, *kerhane*, operate in various locations, surviving in the aperture between what is regarded as sin and what is deemed to be permissible. Every now and then, some local constable, dissatisfied with his bribes or prodded by a burst of sanctimony, decides to close down a brothel and have all the women working there arrested. At other times, angry mobs, led by a zealous imam or a fiery preacher, march to an infamous address and attempt to torch the building with the residents still inside. On such occasions, the whole neighbourhood wakes up to the shouts and cries of terrified women and mortified clients escaping through the back windows into the shadowy night. Prostitutes banished from the capital are pardoned every few months, after which some remain in exile, while others return, only to be ousted again.

The public baths – *hammams* – can also be the setting for illicit encounters. Similarly, on the outskirts of the city, the caravanserai provide a discreet service of their own. For those who cannot rent a room, the *kayaks* gliding across the Golden Horn offer a bed of sorts – although this has its own risks. Should the boat capsize in a moment of passion, the couple will find themselves tumbling into the waters beneath. They will then have to swim ashore as silently as possible for, if caught, they will be punished. And those who can't even afford floating pleasure may visit the graveyards where the poorest streetwalkers ply their trade for the price of a sweetmeat.

Meanwhile, in slave markets across the empire, hundreds of women, many taken as trophies of war, are auctioned to the highest bidder. Stripped naked and shamelessly displayed, their teeth, breasts and genitals inspected, these captives are regarded as mere commodities. They will be sold and resold many times. If in the future they bear their master a child, they may earn the right to freedom – provided the man agrees to release them, which rarely happens. Although lately, with several reforms introduced, a few of these markets have been closed by imperial order, the trade continues to thrive underground. Sometimes a woman will be sold for one night and bought back the next morning, only to be peddled on to someone else, and this will not be regarded as immoral or sinful. And those who profit from this transaction need fear neither risk of legal penalty nor the wrath of pious mobs.

Arthur, who is not aware of any of this, stares at the woman who has just entered the room. Beads of sweat glistening on his forehead, he stumbles over his words: 'Terribly sorry, there has been a misunderstanding . . . I did not ask for this.'

'Of course you didn't,' the dragoman says. 'It is our gift to you.'

Arthur shakes his head. 'I don't want gifts. Please make my excuses to the lady –'

But to his surprise the woman seems to understand English. 'Don't go, my pasha. Why leave early?'

It is only then that Arthur realizes that this woman – stubby, full-necked and about his mother's age – must be the madam who runs the place.

She smiles, returning his gaze. 'You like music?'

As if on cue, three young women sashay into the room, carrying musical instruments. They sit on cushions and begin to play – a slow, sweet melody.

Despite himself, Arthur cannot take his eyes off the third woman, clad in a jade-green dress, with lustrous copper hair cascading over her shoulders; on her lap sits a flat wooden soundbox with horizontal strings.

'You seem to like what is before you?' asks the dragoman, his lip curling into a sneer.

'Beautiful,' says Arthur.

'Glad you think so.'

'And so ancient.'

'Pardon?'

'I have seen pictures,' says Arthur.

'Pictures!'

Arthur nods. 'I had read it was found in digs across Mesopotamia, but I never knew how heavenly it sounded.'

'Are you talking about the damned instrument?'

'Yes, the *qanun*,' says Arthur impatiently.

'The *qanun*!'

'Indeed, the word means "rule", "principle of life". From Greek, κανών, "kanōn". Also, "canon" in Latin. Quite fascinating.'

The dragoman shakes his head. 'What a waste of time bringing you here. One can only conclude that your tastes are on the other side. You should have told us your inclinations were *unconventional*.'

'But of course he likes women,' says the madam, pulling Arthur by the elbow. She fills a glass with a colourless drink that turns grey when mixed with water and offers it to him. 'Here, have some.'

Shaken by the hostility in the dragoman's voice, Arthur complies. The liquid burns his throat like fire. The smell of anise is overpowering. He drinks a bit more, takes a seat and closes his eyes, listening to the music.

A rare calm descends upon him. The vine motifs woven into the rugs, the inlaid gold and silver bracelet on the madam's wrist, the needlework on the damask curtains . . . every detail in the room takes on the lucent intensity of an illuminated medieval manuscript. Shapes and patterns blend into one harmonious swirl. His heartbeat slows, and he feels at peace.

The others, amused by how much he enjoys the music, tiptoe out, leaving him alone with the red-haired woman. She continues to strum, her fingers plucking the strings as though with a force of their own, until, suddenly, she stops.

Arthur opens his eyes. He finds her looking at him quizzically. 'Please carry on,' he says, gesturing. 'If you don't mind, that is.'

She does not object. Gradually, the songs take on a sadder tone. He wonders if the earlier melodies were for the clients, while the latter are for her ears only. As she plays, Arthur inspects the *qanun*. He marvels at its elephant ivory, tortoiseshell plectrum and taut strings stretched lengthwise. So this is 'the piano of the East', the soundbox capable of achieving the most sublime and haunting notes. This is what consoled the Ancient Mesopotamians when they were lonely or heartbroken, and lifted their spirits in times of need. And these are the strains that delighted King Ashurbanipal on many afternoons as he reclined on soft cushions in his library, reading poetry.

The *raqi* makes him drowsy, the music even more so. He dozes off on the low sofa, all the tension in his body fading away. He could have spent the night there, descending into a peaceful sleep, if it were not for a scream that pierces the air. It sounds like it is coming from the street, though it feels disturbingly close. Voices multiply, rebounding off the black dome of the night. Arthur realizes with horror that a crowd has gathered in front of the house.

'What's going on?'

But the woman has already darted out, without taking the instrument. When Arthur follows her on to the landing, he finds people scurrying up and down the stairs – prostitutes and clients in sheer panic.

'Oh, there you are!' The dragoman shouts over the din. 'Quick, we need to get out of here. There's a fire!'

Arthur pales. 'In the house?'

'The entire neighbourhood. We must leave now.'

'But what about the clerks? Shouldn't we look for them?'

'They know the way out. Hurry up.'

'Wait a moment!' Arthur rushes to the room. Grabbing the *qanun*, he charges back. 'We cannot abandon this!'

No sooner do they step outside than a wave of heat hits them in the face, acrid smoke stinging their nostrils. The sky is an open furnace. Dust and debris fly over their heads. A thick layer of ash coats everything. In the distance, they can hear glass smashing, someone wailing. People dart back and forth, hauling away pieces of furniture, trying to salvage what little they can from the flames.

A band of half-naked men, their faces painted and their hair covered in soot, charge towards a burning house. Slung across their shoulders are coils of ropes and water pumps.

'These are the firemen – *tulumbaci*,' says the dragoman. 'Some are quite mad, but they are incredibly brave.'

After what feels like an impossibly long wait, the firemen emerge, carrying boxes and trunks, the last of them holding a canary in a cage. They immediately go back in, sweat flowing down their necks, as the wooden beams crash and collapse around them, columns burning as easily as drawings on paper.

Two thirds of Pera goes up in smoke that night. The homes of Muslims, Jews, Christians are reduced to smouldering remains; 9,550 buildings are destroyed. More than 2,000 lives are extinguished. Only after the wind has died down and the fire has abated will the bewildered inhabitants begin to take in the awful destruction visited on their neighbourhood, days earlier a peaceful and prosperous quarter of Constantinople.

Hours later, Arthur arrives at the embassy premises, exhausted from the walk back.

He finds the senior clerk waiting for him.

'We've been looking for you, my dear fellow. The ambassador wants to see you urgently. We were worried the fire had consumed you.'

'I am all right,' says Arthur. 'What will these poor people do now? They have lost everything.'

'They will build again. Earthquakes and fires . . . Constantinople has been through it all. Wooden houses are burned; wooden houses are rebuilt.' The clerk drops his voice. 'You won't be here to see it, though. Your wait is over. The ambassador himself will give you the news, but you heard it from me first. Your *firman* has arrived. You will soon be on your way down the River Tigris.'

His heartbeat accelerating, Arthur lifts up the *qanun*. 'I need to return this.'

'Keep it, Smyth.' The man shrugs. 'The place where you got it has probably burned down. Take it with you. Maybe you'll learn to play it. It is a long way from Constantinople to Nineveh.'

After washing his face, combing his hair, and perfuming his collar and cuffs, Arthur climbs the marble staircase to say farewell to the ambassador.

'Smyth, good to see you. Please take a seat.'

Something in the man's tone alerts Arthur, but he doesn't dwell on it. 'I have heard the good news.'

'Pardon?'

'My *firman*. It has arrived, I believe.'

'Oh that . . . Yes, yes, I had forgotten.'

Arthur's heart constricts. 'Is that not why you wanted to see me?'

'No, I am afraid . . . We've received a letter for you. It's from your brother.' The ambassador averts his gaze. 'Your mother . . . she has gone the way of all flesh – my condolences.'

Arthur closes his eyes for a moment. The vein on his forehead pulsates. There is a pounding inside his head, which he doesn't yet recognize as pain. 'How . . . how did it happen?'

'I fear knowing the circumstances will not make the news easier to bear.'

'I do need to know. Pray, tell me.'

'Lately she had been improving, and the doctors had allowed her to go on walks around the grounds. She managed to get hold of a knife . . .'

Arthur rises to his feet. 'May I be excused? I would like to be alone.'

'Of course, I understand. Again, my condolences.'

Arthur stumbles towards the door, his legs heavy, as if he were wading through mud.

'Oh, Smyth . . . About your trip, we will do everything we can to make it easier, now that the *firman* is here and you have permission from the sultan to excavate for your poem – unless you have changed your mind and you would like to go back to England, which can also be arranged.'

Arthur shakes his head. He will not return to London now. He will finish what he started. He will go to Nineveh.

Outside in the courtyard, the pine trees tower over him, silvery and needle-sharp, as if a giant seamstress has used the green hillside as her pincushion. The scent of honeysuckle mingling with sea salt makes him feel nauseous. His eyes wander up towards the sky, which is riven by clouds. A seagull glides on the wind, but its choking call, a high-pitched whining caw, when it comes, sounds too close to keening at a funeral.

Home is where your absence is felt, the echo of your voice kept alive, no matter how long you have been away or how far you may have strayed, a place that still beats with the pulse of your heart. There is no one waiting for him in London – except perhaps Mabel. But in the light of their brief and superficial courtship, he does not expect her to miss him. As for his museum colleagues, they will simply absorb his duties. With no one left to regret his loss or to cherish his childhood memories, he no longer has a home.

⊣H
ZALEEKHAH

By the River Thames, 2018

After Nen has left, Zaleekhah sits by the window in the houseboat, her gaze following a seagull with something mysterious in its beak. When she can no longer see the bird, she takes out the box Nen has brought. She will have the cuneiform biscuits for breakfast.

The sky is murky and overcast, a hint of thunder in the air, an electric taste on her tongue. When she was little, she always wondered where fish sheltered in a storm. Did they carry on swimming even as the water raged and seethed, trusting it would not affect them, or did they flee at the slightest hint of disruption and, if so, where? Today she knows that her simple question is not an easy one to answer. Scientists understand how sensitive riparian, riverine and marine animals are to temperature and pressure and light, and can track their search for calmer waters, but they are still not entirely sure where fish go in a storm.

And if the river is polluted to such a degree that oxygen levels are low, fish cannot breathe properly. Their behaviour becomes erratic – at first they swim faster, moving frantically in search of pockets of air. Then they slow down, falling progressively into a lethal torpor. Massive die-offs can occur in a matter of minutes. Mother fish will exhaust themselves to bring oxygen to their eggs, even as the effort drains them. Still they will carry on fanning and ventilating to keep their offspring alive, until their own reserves of energy run out. Down in the murky depths, the glow from the eggs will fade away, one by one, tiny light bulbs flickering out, as darkness descends when a river dies.

After taking a shower, Zaleekhah scans the few items of clothing that she brought to the houseboat. None are suitable for the evening ahead. She knows that Uncle and Aunt will be elegant, and Helen, no doubt, fashionable. Next to them, as usual, she will feel drab. But then she remembers Nen is coming, too, and Nen wears whatever she wants. Her presence is strangely soothing.

She pulls out a shirt at random and puts it on, hating the way it feels – the fabric is coarse, the colour garish. She takes it off. This will go on and on, she knows. She will try on every single garment she owns and toss each of them to the floor, increasingly convinced that nothing looks good on her.

She remembers another birthday party, a long time ago. It must have been two years after her parents died and she had gone to live with Uncle's family. The house in The Boltons was decorated with fairy lights, streamers, paper lanterns – balloons, too. She had never seen balloons so pretty – with rose tassels and sparkling confetti. You didn't have to worry about accidentally popping them. Even if they burst, they would shower you with gold.

In the middle of the table sat a three-tiered, mermaid-themed cake, so pretty it felt wrong to mar its aquamarine perfection. There were children running around, gulping bubblegum-flavoured milkshakes. They were all Helen's guests. Zaleekhah hadn't yet made any friends in her new private school in Kensington and her old friends were in Manchester, unable to come even if they had been invited. And so her birthday party was attended mostly by strangers, in a house that was not her home, bearing a quiet sadness that disguised itself as merriment.

'Aren't you going to blow out the candles?' It was Helen asking, her eyes brimming with excitement. 'Make a wish!'

'I don't want to.'

'But we're going to sing "Happy Birthday".'

'You don't have to.'

'What's the problem?'

'I don't know . . . I don't like the decorations on the cake.'

'Dad!' Helen yelled at the top of her voice, her bottom lip jutting out.

Uncle Malek was calm when he appeared, video-camera in hand. Upon hearing Zaleekhah had developed a dislike for the mermaid, he picked it up by its fondant tail and put it on a side plate. 'Is that better?'

'Not really.' Zaleekhah pointed to the seahorses.

Uncle removed them, too, each leaving a breach in the smooth buttercream icing.

'But . . .' Helen protested, 'you're ruining the cake. It was so pretty.'

Uncle ignored her, his eyes fixed on Zaleekhah, 'Okay now?'

'No . . .'

The nine-year-old Zaleekhah did not want the marzipan fish, or the meringue octopus, or the golden shells, or the filigreed corals, or the chocolate treasure chest. And so Uncle extracted them one by one, piling them on top of one another, a marine disaster.

'Better, my dear?'

'Can you also scrape off the blue icing?'

They stuck nine candles into the mangled sponge that the cake had now become and summoned the children to sing, but, when Helen joined in, her face crumpled; she tried hard to fight back the tears, and her voice came out more like a wail.

Years later, Zaleekhah would find the video Uncle had shot that day. She did not look unhappy in the footage. Nor did Helen seem distressed. No one would be able to tell what had transpired. The only sign of something not being right was the broken mermaid in the background, her tiara crushed and her mouth hanging open, like a fish gasping for breath. Then, as now, Zaleekhah felt grateful to Uncle Malek for not getting upset with her, just as she appreciated the way he had taken care of everything after the accident that killed her parents – the funeral arrangements, the sale of the house . . . Uncle had set aside what little money remained after the mortgage was repaid and added a substantial sum from his own purse for Zaleekhah's education.

Uncle Malek . . . he was always reassuring, funny, supportive, strict in various ways but never towards her. Zaleekhah's biggest fear was being seen by him as a burden. A freeloader. A parasite. To honour her debt, she studied hard. While Helen was, and remained, mostly an average student, Zaleekhah excelled in every single course, sailing through exams and winning prizes both in and out of school. She knew that it was she, not Helen, that Uncle believed could follow in his footsteps. But, no matter how many years passed, every morning when she opened her eyes in The Boltons, she would remember that her room, her bed, her clothes, her shoes, her toys and even the books that she had read and reread . . . none of them belonged to her. She missed the small, terraced house she had shared with her parents, hearing their laughter through the hardboard wall at night-time in her bed. As soon as she could muster her strength, and before the hospitality of the Maleks ran out, she would have to leave. The house was less a home than a harbour where she had sheltered as if from a storm.

Zaleekhah recalls her parents, their easy smiles, their grace of speech, the way they loved watching old films together, and held hands on leisurely walks in Piccadilly Gardens. She remembers a placid afternoon, from a time so far away that her recollection of it laps at the edges of her memory, like the ripples from a coin dropped into a wishing well. A landscape buffeted by winds. A dusty trail fringed with clumps of heather and gorse. A silence disturbed only by the whirr of dragonflies and the tramp of hiking boots. Far ahead, rocks in fascinating colours, striped with layers, their shapes so unusual they could just as well have been sculpted by invisible hands.

Her father is walking briskly up the hill, humming a song. Every now and then he pauses to remark on a plant or an insect. He carries the heaviest backpack, and rivulets of sweat trickle down his neck. Periodically, he glances back over his shoulder to check on his wife and daughter. When he smiles, his eyes crinkle up against the sun, the skin pulled tight. Normally chestnut brown, the hair on his arms glows golden. Mother follows a few steps behind him, a burnt-orange bandana wound round her head. They move in tandem, their shadows blending into other shadows. The blue of water shimmers in the distance, its banks clouded with flies that resemble a spatter of ink drops from a fountain pen. As they approach their destination, her father trips over a root, almost falls. The flask slips out of his hand and the metal container bounces down the incline, clanking all the way.

Evening is descending, and Zaleekhah is still not dressed. She sits in the armchair by the window, touching the cold glass with her fingertips. She is wearing only her knickers and a bra, and she hopes that people in passing boats will not see her. They appear to be distant enough, and a part of her does not care that much. She has no wish to attend tonight's gathering. What would happen if she were to fail to show up at her own birthday dinner? What would happen if she were to stop showering, stop tweezing, stop waxing, stop washing, stop exercising, stop drinking, stop eating? Stop speaking again? Oddly, it is the idea of giving up work that makes her blood run cold.

The thought of death returns, like an intense dream that has found a passage from the realms of sleep to the waking world. Her limbs feel heavy, her chest constricted. Slowly, she stands up, begins hunting for something passable to wear. She will go to tonight's dinner. It is her birthday, after all.

—O—

ARTHUR

By the River Tigris, 1872

The distance from Constantinople to Mosul is almost 900 miles – four times the length of the River Thames. The journey is taxing, and Arthur is not the most well-equipped traveller. The longer he spends in Mesopotamia, the deeper his surprise at its complexities. Its many religions, creeds and sects bewilder him. People from the same area, even from the same town, can be stunningly different.

But there are also things that feel oddly familiar from his readings on ancient civilizations. He recognizes certain continuities: the irrigation canals, the unchanging landscape, the bullrushes on the riverbanks . . . Especially in the south, both houses and boats are made of reeds, and sometimes the same materials are used and reused – houses into boats, boats into houses. If he closes his eyes, he can easily imagine himself in the days of King Ashurbanipal. In some ways it is as though hardly any time has passed, and thousands of years were a mere puff of wind. The past, no matter how remote or unknown, is not bygone. It is alive. The past is a clay tablet, worn and chipped, but hardened by the heat of centuries.

He traverses forests and floodplains. After a while, nowhere feels foreign to someone who has woken, day after day, in unfamiliar rooms and unknown places. Closer to the River Tigris, he spends the night at a hostelry called Jacob's Inn, where he is served a meal of charred potatoes and a fowl so overcooked it crunches when he tries to bite into it. A Levantine merchant he has befriended on the way cranes his head and winks across the table.

'Congratulations, my friend, you have found your first antiquity – this poor bird must have been left behind by the Ancient Mesopotamians. Take it to a museum.'

The Orient. The term confuses him – where exactly does it start, where does it end? Arthur has read about Napoleon – the first, that is, the Little Corporal, the Nightmare of Europe, the Man of Destiny, the Corsican General – whose final wish was to be buried on the banks of the River Seine, though the British had him interred instead on the volcanic island of Saint Helena, until the body was exhumed and carried to France. What intrigues Arthur is how extensively Napoleon researched the Middle East. Modelling himself on Alexander the Great – the warrior who marched into battles with artists and philosophers by his side – Napoleon gathered painters, sculptors, linguists, writers, engravers, art historians, geographers, zoologists, geologists, engineers, botanists, cartographers, mathematicians, musicians . . . when he launched his expedition to Egypt. A hundred and fifty men of letters joined his military campaign. *The forces of the Enlightenment versus the benighted Orient.* The superiority of the West had to be established not only via warfare but also via science, art and literature. The French army consisted of thousands of soldiers, heavy artillery and horses, coupled with the latest technological equipment and navigational instruments. They brought along a printing press with Arabic type to communicate with the locals. Napoleon's massive flagship contained a spectacular library that specialized in volumes from the Ancient and Modern Middle East, and was given, aptly, the same name as the vessel it was borne on – *L'Orient.*

'We must go East. All the great men of the world have there acquired their celebrity.'

Just as a flame requires darkness to exist and expand, the idea of European supremacy needed its Orient imbued with deprivation and despair. Napoleon saw it as his mission to liberate the people of the region from their destiny and restore them to the grandeur of their ancestors. In this way everyone would benefit – the invader and the invaded. Emboldened by this conviction, he gave orders to amass antiquities. Taking them back to the Louvre, however, would not be easy. For they were not alone in their ambition. The British were also in the throes of Egyptomania.

On the first day of August 1798, *L'Orient*, weighing almost 3,000 tons and carrying 120 cannons, along with scores of soldiers, sailors and scholars, arrived at the mouth of the Nile. There were also a few women on board – wives, maids, laundresses and stowaways. At Aboukir Bay, the British and the French navies met in battle. As far as the eye could see, the water was covered with vessels of all sizes, their masts tall and proud. The river swirled, not used to this much blood. Those who witnessed the explosion of *L'Orient* say the sky and the sea fused into one brushstroke of orange from the ensuing blaze. The debris – wood, metal, canvas, ballast stones and human flesh – was hurled in all directions. And the ink from thousands of books and manuscripts dissolved in the Nile. It is still down there, the wreckage of the flagship. Bronze mortars, scientific instruments, gold coins and, somewhere in the silt and ooze, covered in moss and rearranged into new words by the undercurrents, consonants from a printing press with Arabic lettering.

Arthur knows the Tigris is a different river altogether, and it holds its secrets close. The Nile floods often but predictably, and thus its damage is less severe. The Tigris, however, in refusing to follow any patterns, mercurial all the way, takes everyone by surprise each time it rises, bringing disaster. If the clue to Ancient Egypt's secrets is in its great monuments, Ancient Mesopotamia's are woven into its silences – the gaps in stories. This, here, is the land of fragmented tablets and fractured poems.

The Tigris is an old river and like everything that has lived for that long, it is liquid memory. 'Fast-moving' in Old Persian, 'arrow-like' in its inexhaustible agility. The Ancients called it 'the tiger'. *Idigna* in Sumerian, *Hiddekel* in Hebrew, *Dijlah* in Arabic, *Ava Mezin* in Kurdish – 'the Great Water'. One of the four streams believed to have flowed out of the Garden of Eden, it gleams with unearthly light, frightening and beautiful and mysterious, nurturing life above and below the ground. Rising in the highlands of Anatolia, fed by fertile tributaries, falling rain and melting snow, it surges as if impatient to be somewhere else, and, at times, it swells with disastrous consequences. Bold and boisterous, if angered the tiger turns into a mortal enemy.

It scares Arthur, travelling by river. The vessel sways, its timbers creaking under the pressure, and it unsettles him, the velocity of the flow, foaming with wrath. Along the way he spots destitute villages. Poverty has a topography all of its own. It rises from the ribs of the earth, stretching its naked limbs against the sky, its features dry and gaunt, sore to the touch. Poverty is a nation with no borders, and he is no foreigner in it but a native son.

Downstream, on each side, he sees caves burrowed high up in the rocks. His guide tells him that for centuries persecuted communities have sought shelter in these hollows. Clouds of gnats swarm the boat, and the current carries them forward. Arthur has never experienced so much fear, thrill and anticipation, all at once. The mosquito bites on his legs itch and bleed. He can feel the skin on his face tightening in the wind and the sun, his features reshaped. He listens as the waves strike and retreat from the bow, admiring the resilience of the rough-hewn vessel as it withstands the might of the water.

If he closes his eyes he can imagine an utterly different view from thousands of years back and see his surroundings as if looking through cut glass: gardens lush as paradise, palms and grape vines, edible and ornamental plants; pine, olive, juniper, cypress, pomegranate and fig trees all around. Parrots gliding about amongst the branches, while tame lions roam below. Fruit of all kinds, luxurious orchards and, spreading far out into the distance, grain fields on four sides. All of it possible because thousands of slaves, their bodies tattooed with the identification marks of their owners, laboured with pickaxes carving channels to bring water into this barren landscape, diverting the river from the mountains all the way into Nineveh. They were here, the kings and the canal builders. It all happened here – the ambitious dream of King Sennacherib, continued and expanded by his grandson King Ashurbanipal.

Two days after he arrives in Mosul, Arthur is invited to a banquet by the pasha. The man has a full-jawed, fleshy face, and, sunk deep in their sockets, one of his eyes is brown and the other pale grey. He is visibly upset that the Englishman did not pay him a visit immediately upon arrival; and, by offering to host him nonetheless, he is indirectly chiding him for his lack of manners. But Arthur does not understand the coded message.

After dinner, the men smoke *narghiles* while Arthur shifts about on his cushion, yet to master the art of sitting cross-legged for long stretches of time. That is when a male dancer appears, a frilled skirt with brass bells wound around his waist. As Arthur watches the young man sway and twirl, he feels sad. He remembers a jewellery-box ballerina he saw on Regent Street, one of those figurines you encounter when you open the lid, instantly sprinting into a cheerful caper. He has always suspected that as soon as the lid is closed, the same figurine would sink back into the box, head down, shoulders hunched.

The pasha, observing him closely, says, 'You don't seem to be enjoying yourself, Mr Smyth.'

The clapping stops, a tense silence descending on the room.

The Levantine merchant coughs. 'My master, forgive him. He survived a fire in Constantinople. He is still quite shaken.'

The pasha nods, though his eyes remain cold. But Arthur does not glance at the man, powerful and assertive as he is. He looks only at the young dancer, who returns his gaze, and Arthur knows then without a doubt that he is not the only one wishing to be elsewhere.

After they leave the house, the merchant catches up with Arthur.

'The pasha is a dangerous man and you offended him – that's not good. He was already mistrustful of you.'

'Why so?'

'He thinks you are here to dig for gold. He suspects that is your real aim and archaeology is a pretext.'

'I am searching for the missing lines of a poem. Why is that so hard to understand?'

The merchant inhales sharply. 'My friend, maybe you are the one who doesn't understand. If you go to other people's lands to take their things, you cannot get upset at them for questioning your motives.'

The words, so unexpected, hit Arthur hard. Has he descended on other people's lands to carry off what is rightfully theirs? He firmly believes he is here to help excavate and preserve antiquities that will surely be better off in the hands of Europeans rather than the natives. He has seen nothing on his travels that can rival the grandeur of the British Museum, its cavernous and cool display rooms, its foreign treasures under the watchful eye of honest guards and subject to the expert scrutiny of diligent curators. This is not an issue of ownership, as far as he is concerned, but of who is in a better position to appreciate and protect historical heritage. Otherwise, he has never thought of the tablets of Nineveh as belonging to anyone other than the ghosts of the past.

Whatever doubt seizes him does not last long. His excitement is so great that he has no room in his heart for anything else. Finally, he is in the land of the Flood Tablet. This is the home of Gilgamesh. And this is the moment for which he has been waiting since he first saw the giant human-headed, bird-winged bulls being carried through the doors of the British Museum.

From Mosul to the ruins of Nineveh they ride in the dark on horseback. It is a short trip, but it is getting cold, and the wind is relentless. Arthur consults the map. It seems there is a village nearby. It is called Zêrav.

'We could break the journey there,' Arthur suggests.

The guide says, 'There's another village further down south.'

'What is wrong with the first one? It is much closer.'

'That place is no good. We should not go there.'

Arthur's expression hardens. 'Unless you provide an explanation, I must insist that we do. I am too exhausted for a longer journey.'

'As you wish,' says the guide, turning his face away. 'But don't say I didn't warn you. Zêrav is home to devil-worshippers.'

H—
NARIN

By the River Tigris, 2014

Ever since they arrived in Zêrav and moved in with their relatives, Grandma and Narin regularly leave the village to roam by the River Tigris.

Today, to catch their breath, they sit on a rock where the shoreline fans outwards in an arc. In the distance looms a huddle of low buildings. The villagers have told them that until not long ago these used to be popular eateries, neon lights casting rainbows that rippled on the expanse of water, succulent aromas drifting on the breeze. The menus displayed a range of meat and the daily catch – catfish, spiny eels, barbels. Saltwater species, too – gar, sea bream, anchovy. But the most coveted dish was the grilled carp, *masgouf.*

Narin, like her grandmother, does not consume fish, just as she does not consume pork or cockerel or gazelle or okra or cauliflower or pumpkin or cabbage or lettuce – all are discouraged by faith. Nor has she ever been to a fancy restaurant. But the sight of them in a state of disrepair makes her sad. She would have liked to know what they were like when they were bustling and full of life.

'Oh, we have a visitor,' says Grandma.

Upon tracing her grandmother's gaze, Narin sees a scorpion darting across the dry earth, having scurried from under a rock.

'Good day to you,' Grandma says. 'Go now, Godspeed. Keep your poison to yourself.'

Narin giggles. 'Why do you always do this? You talk to trees, rocks, running water.'

Grandma says everything in this world speaks all the time. Just as there is no such thing as absolute death, nor is there absolute silence, for silence, too, converses in its own language and dialect. Milk purrs while it churns into butter; mountains rumble as they crumble; mother goats recognize the bleats of their offspring long after weaning; wolves howl to find their way back home; crickets chirp by rubbing their wings together; and the human soul sighs as it leaves its bodily form and migrates on to the next one. Narin should not be sad that one day she won't be able to detect these sounds, because, once she follows the rhythms and cadences of life, she will always be able to move in tune with them. A deaf person can still hear the most enchanting music.

'Yes, but you even talk to dangerous animals –'

'Shush.' The old woman suddenly freezes, the furrow between her eyes deepening. 'There's something over there in the river.'

'What?'

'You stay here, my heart. I'll go and check.'

Narin does not like it when Grandma leaves her behind, so she silently follows her. As she approaches the Tigris, gathering the last of the light, the hair on the back of her neck stands up. A body is floating in the water.

'Is that man . . . is he dead?'

Grandma takes a moment to reply. 'Poor thing, he was someone's brother, someone's son. I'll see if I can pull him ashore.'

The girl pales. 'But you could fall in!'

'Don't worry. I'll be careful.'

Grandma removes her shoes and tucks her dress into her waistband. Grabbing her walking stick, she wades into the Tigris, step by cautious step. The water laps against her thighs in wavelets, the stones beneath her feet worn smooth from centuries of passage.

'Permission, *Ava Mezin*, I mean no disrespect. Allow me in.'

Thus saying, the old woman forges ahead. When the water reaches her chest, she stops. A brackish, vegetal smell assails her. Stretching out her cane as far as she can, she tries to haul the corpse towards the shallows. An impossible task, it quickly becomes clear. The current is too strong.

Panting, Grandma abandons the attempt. As she watches the corpse drift away, she mouths a prayer in his direction. 'Death is God's command – *Mirin a'mr ē Xwadēya*. The son of Adam is but a guest on earth, even if he has all the riches or lives a hundred years.'

The dead man is naked but for a pair of torn trousers. There are purple-red lesions across his chest – which Grandma knows are signs of torture and which she chooses not to point out to Narin. Sorrow colouring her features, the old woman turns around and trudges towards the shore.

'Do you think he drowned?' Narin asks, rushing to her side.

'Maybe.' Grandma runs her tongue over her lips. 'We'd better not tell anyone. They'll be worried, and there is nothing anyone can do.'

'All right, Grandma.'

Neither that evening nor the next do they mention this incident to their Iraqi relatives. Had they shared it with them, they would have heard the rumours about strange happenings. In recent weeks, all around Nineveh, locals have been disappearing, a shepherd here, a tinker there. Some emerge days later, refusing to speak about what they have gone through, while others never return.

This is why the restaurants have been closing one after another. The ancient river, once pellucid and silver under the sun, is now heavily polluted, not only with industrial waste, military detritus and oil residue but also with battered, bloated victims. So many corpses have been pulled out of the water lately that a Muslim cleric has issued a *fatwa* against the consumption of fish. The famous carp of Iraq have been nibbling at human flesh. When barriers are put up along the watercourse to trap the debris, it isn't only waste that they snare. Those tangled in the nets are buried hastily and without autopsy. As cemeteries of nameless souls expand along its banks, the Tigris has turned into a flowing graveyard.

Grandma converses with trees, rocks, running water. Everything, she says, speaks all the time. But this enemy – whomever it might be – stays silent.

—O—

ARTHUR

By the River Tigris, 1872

In the village of Zêrav the children greet him first. Giggling, wide-eyed, they scuttle out of their homes, curious to meet the unexpected visitor. Behind them walks a group of elderly men, long, thin plaits emerging from beneath their caps. The one in the middle, dressed head-to-toe in white, seems to be the sheikh. He carries a cane carved from alabaster, topped with a silver ornament – an emblem of a tree between two peacocks.

'Tell them who we are and ask them if we can spend the night here,' says Arthur to the guide. 'Would they be kind enough to put us up?'

'You are welcome here,' says the sheikh, after Arthur's words are translated. 'We believe every guest is God-sent.'

Ushered to the sheikh's house, they are first offered goat's milk and dried figs, and then a sumptuous dinner of rice with pomegranate syrup, chicken biryani, date cake and *kubba Mosul*, a rich meat pie made of bulgur dough, stuffed with ground lamb, raisins, pine nuts and almonds.

'Maybe there were some who advised you not to stop at our village. It is good that you did not listen to them,' says the sheikh.

Arthur blushes, trying not to glance at his guide, who is sitting by his side, arms folded across his chest. The man has not touched his meal and does not look anyone in the eye.

Sensing that he is deliberately refraining from consuming the food, Arthur, for the first time in his life, eats with a sharpened appetite.

'I am very sorry people say bad things about you,' says Arthur, between mouthfuls. 'That must be hurtful.'

The sheikh smiles, the wrinkles around his eyes crinkling. 'We are children of God, like everyone else. But people are unfair, and life has taught us to be strong, resilient. Otherwise we could never have survived.'

After dinner they are served coffee in tiny cups.

'You need to be careful,' says the sheikh. 'The Pasha of Mosul thinks you are here for gold. He is a powerful man.'

A shadow of surprise crosses Arthur's face as he understands that people across the region have been talking about him.

Pensively, he shakes his head. 'I am not interested in gold. I am looking for an ancient poem about the Great Flood.'

The sheikh lifts his chin. 'Well, then, you are in the right place because this is where it all happened – the Ark and the Deluge. We believe seven thousand years have passed since – every millennium one of the seven angels descended to earth to help humankind – not that humans have learnt much.'

Little by little, those present head home, leaving only a few men in the room. As the fire crackles in a brazier, the sheikh asks, 'Do you have a wife back in your country? Children?'

'No,' Arthur replies curtly.

'No one waiting for you?'

Arthur hesitates. 'I have a fiancée.'

'You love her?'

It is not bashfulness that prevents Arthur from speaking but an inexplicable sadness. For he has no language, even with a translator by his side, to explain how, ever since he was a boy, he has been pulled by a ghost river, a flow so strong it doesn't let him rest or take root. The current that carries him along is stronger than matters of the heart – or so he believes.

Still unsure how to respond, Arthur pivots on his heel, sensing a movement out of the corner of his eye. Someone has entered the room.

'That's my adopted daughter,' says the sheikh. 'Women do not join evening conversations – but she is different. She is a *faqra*.'

'A *faqra*?'

'Yes, Leila is a diviner.'

A *faqra*, they tell him, can detect things that others walk past without noticing. She knows the landscape in the way a reed warbler knows the ins and outs of marsh waters. She can tell a storm from the flight of herons, the shape of ant hills or the antics of spiders. A *faqra* learns things she wishes she never did and, once she does, she cannot unlearn them. This is why it is said that they die early, their hearts unable to carry the burden for too long. That first night in the village, Arthur learns that to be a Yazidi one must be born into the faith. Since no one can convert in or marry out, and since the community has been attacked and forcefully converted so many times, its population remains small in number in comparison with their neighbours. The sheikh's adopted daughter comes from a long line of seers. They recount the past and predict the future, unveil mysteries that remain shrouded from the rest of us. Although a gift, it is also an affliction that must be borne with dignity. The *faqrya* live in a temporal zone of their own, a cyclical history that spools back to the beginning of time. They understand the echoes through centuries, ride the waves of suffering, collect the remains of stories. They are the custodians of knowledge, the memory-keepers. In a culture where very little, if ever, is put into writing, they are the librarians.

The bed they offer him is soft and clean, and the sheets smell of rosemary. After the itchy mattress at Jacob's Inn, his body rejoices. He instantly falls asleep. Late in the night, he wakes up to a strange sound – a distant rustle. His heart racing, he opens the window and looks out.

There, under a moon so bright he could read by it, standing between clumps of heather, is a shadow. He instantly knows who it is – the sheikh's daughter. Leila wears a white robe that reaches her ankles. Her hair, long and dark, hangs loose over her shoulders. Her bare feet tread the ground as gently as if she were stepping on a lush carpet. Arthur can tell she is sleepwalking. It is such a curious sight that he can only watch, spellbound. But worried that he is intruding, he pulls his head back. When he returns to sleep, he has the most peculiar dream – he sees his mother, young and beautiful as she was, mudlarking by the River Thames in the same white robe, its hem dragging through the sludge.

Early in the morning, Arthur wakes to the sound of joyful laughter. About twenty children have gathered outside his window, jostling to get a better view of him. When they see him stir, they run away, laughing.

'How long have you been watching me?' Arthur says with a smile.

He searches everywhere for his guide, but it quickly becomes apparent that he has left in the dark without notice, refusing to accept Yazidi hospitality. Mortified by the man's behaviour, when Arthur sits at breakfast with everyone else, once again, he ends up eating for two. Not a difficult thing to do, as the food is delicious: crumbled white cheese with wild herbs, black honey from the bee hives of Sinjar, freshly baked flatbread and the most delectable butter. Arthur tucks in heartily, although with such haste to get to work that the villagers look on bemused. When he tries to explain why he is rushing, he falters.

It is the sheikh's middle son who comes to his aid. The young man – Dishan – has spent time in Constantinople and studied in Baghdad and can speak English and French, in addition to Kurdish, Arabic and Turkish. He gladly agrees to act as his new interpreter.

'Please tell them I must start excavating. I am very grateful for the kindness shown to me.'

'Go look for your poem,' the sheikh says when Arthur's words are translated. 'But there is no need for you to sleep in a tent. Our village is close to the site. It would make things easier for you to stay here. You can be our guest for as long as you'd like.'

'That is . . . that is very generous of you,' Arthur says. 'I would not want to be a burden.'

'Not a burden,' says the sheikh. 'We believe an onion shared with guests tastes better than roast lamb.'

Ni-ne-veh. The joy of being here at last! Arthur feels like a suitor reunited with a long-lost love.

There is something humbling about labouring at an archaeological excavation. You toil away in the heat and dust with your trowel and brush at the bottom of a pit, inching your way through the deposits of millennia. The border separating the present moment from the distant past dissolves and you find yourself tumbling into a vanished world that, though dead and buried, comes curiously to life. Your perceptions shift: you are made to realize the vulnerability of all that seems robust and majestic – palaces, aqueducts, temples – but, equally, the resilience of what appears small and insignificant – an ivory ring, a bronze coin, a wishbone . . . Nothing is trivial for an archaeologist. Even the most mundane finding is extraordinary.

They call it *Kouyunjik* – the mound covering the ruins of the North Palace. Located just on the opposite bank of the Tigris, 40 feet high, it is a hill with mysteries buried inside. This is where, one early-summer afternoon thousands of years ago, a tiny raindrop fell from the skies on the head of King Ashurbanipal, and this is where Arthur Smyth is now digging through layers of earth, layers of time.

IV
Memories of Water

—H

ZALEEKHAH

By the River Thames, 2018

As soon as Zaleekhah walks into Uncle Malek's house with Nen as her guest she has a pang of doubt that perhaps it is not such a good idea to introduce them after all – a pang that turns into full-scale worry after they sit down for dinner.

'So how much does a tattoo artist earn?' asks Uncle Malek, as they lay their napkins over their laps.

'Darling!' Aunt Malek raises her eyebrows.

'What? Can a man not make conversation in his own house?'

Nen looks amused. 'I earn enough to make a living.'

'And to own a houseboat in Chelsea Harbour, which can't come cheap, I'm guessing.'

'Darling!'

Uncle Malek leans back in his chair. It doesn't take him longer than a heartbeat to come up with a new question: 'Why don't you live there yourself, if you love being on water so much? Is there something wrong with it? Does the boat leak?'

Nen seems neither fazed nor surprised by this intrusive line of questioning. 'Nothing's wrong with *She Who Saw the Deep*, I can assure you, Mr Malek. It's just a while ago I moved in with my girlfriend – ex-girlfriend. Unfortunately, it didn't work out, and we broke up. By the time I was considering returning to the boat, it had already been rented out.'

Uncle Malek's eyebrows shoot up but he says nothing – until he takes a gulp of his wine. 'So you're gay?'

'Darling!'

'It's okay,' Nen says calmly.

Uncle nods. 'Of course it's okay! Why wouldn't it be? Everything is okay. Everyone is something these days –'

Aunt Malek interjects, 'Well any friend of Zaleekhah is welcome in this house.'

Nen throws her head back as she smiles at Zaleekhah. 'We're not exactly friends, though.' But no sooner has she spoken than she realizes the implication behind these words by the way Uncle Malek's face falls. So she rushes to add, 'I mean, we've just met. We are becoming friends.'

'Let's all raise a toast to friendship, then, shall we?' Aunt Malek chimes in. 'But, Nen, you're not drinking. May I offer you a different wine? I'm guessing this one isn't to your taste.'

'The wine is great, I'm sure,' replies Nen. 'I don't drink. I'm eight years sober this month.'

The silence that follows is brief but loaded. For a moment they all stare at her – Aunt Malek with undisguised curiosity, Uncle Malek with disapproval and Zaleekhah with something close to admiration. She has never met anyone so at ease with herself, scars and bruises and all.

Nen glances from one to the other. 'But if you'd still like to toast to friendship, I'm happy to join in with water.'

So they all raise their glasses.

The sound of hurried footsteps echoes down the hall. In a few seconds, Helen walks in, panting slightly. Clad in a designer jacket and a pleated midi dress, both in a powder blue that brings out her eyes, she looks glamorous.

'I know, I know! I'm late.'

She makes a beeline for Zaleekhah, an instant smile lifting the corners of her mouth. 'So how's the birthday girl? I haven't seen you in ages! Sorry I wasn't at the gallery when you stopped by. Let me look at you.'

Enveloped in a perfumed hug, and then held at arm's length for inspection, Zaleekhah awkwardly tucks a lock of hair behind her ear. In that second she cannot help seeing herself through her cousin's eyes – her shapeless clothes, the lack of make-up, but, mostly, the uncertainty that always clings to her when she is in this house. Discomfort is not an emotional state but a doorway she easily passes through several times a day. Lifting her chin, she says, 'I brought a friend – this is Nen.'

'Hello, Nen,' says Helen.

Zaleekhah watches the two of them shake hands. Only now does she notice that under the silver glitter eyeshadow, Helen's eyes look tired, troubled.

'How is dear Lily?' Zaleekhah asks.

A sudden pallor to her features, Helen pulls out a chair. 'They're still running tests.' There is a catch in her voice. 'It's been a tough week, I think I need a drink.'

Zaleekhah leans forward to stroke her hand. But she is a second too late. Unawares, Helen has already reached for her father. 'Thank you for coming with me to the hospital, Dad.'

Zaleekhah recognizes the expression that crosses Helen's face – a profound sense of gratitude. It is the feeling her uncle evokes in her all the time.

'Look at this table: I'm a blessed man,' remarks Uncle Malek. 'My wife sitting across from me, my two daughters at my side. And a delightful surprise guest joining us. If this doesn't call for a celebration, what does? Forget this bottle. Let's open a good Napa. Does anyone object to Screaming Eagle?'

That evening Uncle consumes more than usual. Ignoring his wife's interventions, he keeps filling his glass, not waiting for the maid. For some reason, after the third bottle is finished, all his words are directed at Nen. Steadily surrendering to Screaming Eagle, he launches into lengthy monologues, in which consistency is the first casualty, and coherence the second.

One minute he says: 'I am proud to be from the Middle East, Nen. Our region has always been misunderstood. Ask a Westerner, "Do you happen to know where Syria, Jordan, Iran, Iraq, Lebanon and Turkey are on a map?" They'd draw a total blank. In their eyes we're all from somewhere in the back of beyond. They don't even know that Mesopotamia was a fount of civilization. We invented cities, maths, writing, astronomy, even the bloody wheel! And the clock, too. How would they measure time without us? They have no idea how much they owe us.'

Nen nods. 'I agree, there are many negative stereotypes –'

Impatiently, Uncle cuts in, 'Our people, Nen, we are never the heroes. Always the villains in their stories! And, if not, the sidekicks. Sancho Panza to Don Quixote. Friday to Robinson Crusoe. Huckleberry Finn to Tom Sawyer.'

'Dr Watson to Sherlock Holmes . . .' Nen offers helpfully.

'Precisely! As long as we know our place in the background, it's fine. They might even tolerate some of us. I'm fed up.'

'I get it,' says Nen. 'You have every right to feel –'

'But don't get me wrong, I'm not Middle Eastern,' Uncle interrupts. 'I'm from the Levant! A proud descendant of Hellenistic culture. The Mediterranean and the Near East were one. No one talks about this any more, but it's a fact. Smyrna, Alexandria, Beirut – they were profoundly cosmopolitan. We weren't in separate boxes, the Greeks here, the Syrians over there. We constantly mingled. How would the Western classics have survived if they had not been translated into Arabic?'

'True, our debt to –' Nen tries.

But Uncle has already moved on. 'Yet nothing gives me more pride than being British. Did you know about my maiden speech in the House of Lords? It was passionate, a real tub-thumper. I said mingling as one is what makes us the great country we

330

are. In Britain difference lends us strength, and tolerance gives us unity.'

And so the night drags on.

By the time the passionfruit-and-mango birthday cake is served, Uncle has come to the end of his geographical tour. Now, as he swirls his wine, he squares his shoulders and says, 'Zaleekhah is very precious to us, Nen. No different from our own daughter. She has been through so much at a tender age. No child should have to endure that kind of loss and grief. And still she was always a delight. An exemplary student. Hard-working. Determined. Top of her class every year. Never a rebel . . . Even when she chose science against my wishes, I respected her decision. A part of me understood. That's fine, I said to myself. Not everyone has to study business or finance, although she clearly had the brain for that. But she was an idealist.'

Nen says, 'I understand.'

'You do? Because I don't!' says Uncle Malek. 'I don't understand how someone who has been so stable and solid all her life could end her marriage for no reason at all, leave her nice flat and move to a rickety boat on the Thames, which might be full of holes and leaking, for God's sake, and then show up with a new *friend* who turns out to be an alcoholic gay tattooist –'

'Darling!'

'Uncle!'

'Dad!'

Uncle Malek throws his hands in the air. 'We're all grown-ups here, are we not? I'm just stating facts. Am I offending anyone? Are you offended, Nen?'

'I'm fine,' says Nen, a flicker of amusement in her face.

Uncle takes another gulp of his wine, his mind drifting. Then, with a sigh, he looks sideways at Nen again. 'Zaleekhah tells me you like the *Epic of Gilgamesh*.'

'I do.'

'And you tattoo its characters?'

'I do.'

'Lord, heavens!' Another sigh. 'It's a great poem, though.'

Nen nods. 'It is – and it has fans from all over the world. You should see the tourists coming to my shop – from Japan, Norway, Canada . . . The ancient poem unites us across borders, but also, in some strange way, we can never seem to agree on how to interpret it. That's why it's been treasured by dictators and dissidents alike, the mighty and the weak. It can be read in multiple ways.'

'And how do you read it?' asks Uncle Malek.

Nen takes a second to reply. 'For me, the epic is primarily about both the fragility and resilience of being human, and, also, it is about the possibility for change. Learning to care for others, not just yourself. Gilgamesh, let's admit, is an awful person in the beginning, and it is only through love and friendship and loss that he becomes more humble and gentle. So it is a story in which there is no hero in the traditional sense, and everything is either fractured or fluid – like life itself.'

Uncle purses his lips. 'I beg to differ, my dear. I believe the poem is about the fear of death. We all must shuffle off this mortal coil, so to speak; we'll all push up the daisies. Can't be avoided. What is its moral lesson? Simple. The epic tells us that, since we cannot attain immortality, or even prolong youth, we must eat and drink and make merry and always prioritize family and friends. Our own people. That's its universal message. Family comes first.'

Nen sips water, puts the glass down. 'Why?'

'What do you mean, why?'

'Why should family be above everything?'

Uncle Malek frowns. 'Interesting question. I can only assume you haven't started a family of your own yet. You'll come to think differently when the time arrives.'

Nen stands her ground. Her tone is placid, but it now has an edge. 'Not everyone has to get married or have children.'

'Well, then, I'm sorry, you'll never know the kind of devotion that I'm talking about.'

'Darling!'

Uncle Malek turns to his wife, a hardness in his eyes. 'You keep berating me. You've been having a go at me all evening, but at least I'm honest. I speak my mind – unlike you! You make me do your dirty work for you, so your hands stay clean. You always act the saint, and turn me into the sinner.'

The comment, unexpected and audacious, drops in their midst, generating ripples of discomfort. For a moment no one speaks. Aunt Malek dabs her lips with her napkin and lifts her head.

'I think it's time for coffee. Some of us have clearly had enough wine.'

After coffee – and a pot of chamomile tea – is served in fine china, Zaleekhah glances apologetically at Nen, worried that her guest might be having a terrible time.

'So do you have a favourite quote from the *Epic of Gilgamesh*?'

Nen smiles, both because she likes the question and also because she knows Zaleekhah is trying to soften the tension.

'I have, actually. There's this line that Enkidu says to Gilgamesh just before they set out on the road. I think it's one of the most beautiful things you can say to a friend or spouse or lover.' Nen pauses for a second, her eyes sparkling in the light of the flickering candles, and then she recites:

> '*Where you have set your mind begin the journey*
> *Let your heart have no fear, keep your eyes on me.*'

'It's lovely,' says Zaleekhah.

And to everyone's surprise, Uncle agrees. 'Lovely, indeed!'

It somehow changes the mood, these twenty words from an ancient world, and the rest of the evening goes smoothly.

★

Before the evening is over, the Maleks hand Zaleekhah their joint birthday present. It's another large envelope – embossed with Uncle's letterhead. For an instant she fears it is the money she rejected earlier, and the thought makes her uncomfortable, but instead she finds a travel agent's voucher inside. Alongside is a cheerful birthday card in Aunt Malek's neat, cursive handwriting, the letters tilting slightly to the right.

They have given her a week's holiday for two to a destination of her choosing, at a time of her choosing, with business-class flights and five-star accommodation included. They say, as she is busy both at work and in her personal life right now, she can use it whenever is convenient.

'Oh, this is wonderful . . . but it is too much . . . Thank you,' says Zaleekhah, lowering her head lest they notice her discomfort.

On the way out, Zaleekhah and Nen walk together. Kareem waits by the door, holding their jackets and bags.

'He called a cab for you again.'

'Thank you, Kareem.'

A heady scent of earth and jasmine greets them when they step out into the garden.

Zaleekhah releases a long breath. 'I managed to convince Uncle not to send me anywhere in his private car, with a uniformed chauffeur. But I can't possibly stop him from arranging taxis for me. Can I drop you off on the way?'

Nen smiles. 'The Tube will be easier, but thank you.'

They pass by the Andalusian fountain, the water tinkling peacefully.

'Uncle can be difficult at times. He's very set in his ways – I think it's an age thing, too. He's becoming more rigid as he gets older.'

Nen listens without comment.

'I owe him so much, though. They raised me after my parents died. If it weren't for them – for him especially – my life would have been much harder,' says Zaleekhah. 'Anyway, I don't know why I'm telling you all this. I'm very sorry for his behaviour tonight.'

'Don't,' Nen says, softly. 'Don't apologize for others.'

They wait for the electronic gates to open, and when they do, they stand side by side on the pavement, watching a black cab enter the tree-lined street, driving slowly towards them.

'This was a lovely evening. Thank you for inviting me.' Nen takes a little box out of her bag. 'Didn't get a chance to give it to you earlier. Happy birthday!'

'Oh, you shouldn't have,' Zaleekhah says. 'Thank you!'

Nen tucks her hands into her pockets. 'If you have ten seconds for a story, I remembered something tonight.'

'Of course.'

'When I first moved to London, my brothers gave me a fish. A tetra. I called her Ki-ang. It means "to love" in Ancient Sumerian. I didn't know the noun for "love", so the verb had to do. Anyways Ki-ang was very cute, but I thought she must be lonely and so I bought another fish to keep her company – and for a while things were fine, and the second fish grew bigger, but one morning, when I checked, there was only one fish in the bowl. Love had disappeared.'

The cab pulls over in front of them, and the driver pokes his head out of the window, nodding in their direction.

'Was it an angelfish, the other one?' asks Zaleekhah.

'Yeah, you see, you know how these stories go. But I didn't. It turns out you can never keep the two together for too long, because the chances are the angelfish will gobble up the tetra.'

They stride towards the car. Nen opens the door for Zaleekhah.

'It's just it got me thinking tonight . . . I never gave the second fish a name, but if I could now, I'd call it "Gratitude".'

Zaleekhah gets into the cab. Through the open window she looks at Nen. 'You're saying Gratitude swallows Love.'

'Yes, if it gets too big.' Nen's gaze is unflinching. 'Forgive me, I don't mean to pry into your personal life. All I'm saying is, one needs to keep an eye on that Gratitude fish, I learnt to my cost.'

As the cab speeds towards the houseboat, Zaleekhah opens the box. Inside is a necklace made of a jagged, scratched piece of lapis lazuli, beautiful in its imperfection. There is also a note:

> *I found this celestial slice of blue buried in the river mud. Who knows how old it is, where it has come from. A mysterious time traveller in the water. I thought I should turn it into a necklace – for you.*
> *May it bring you joy, clarity and love.*
> *Nen*

—o—
ARTHUR

By the River Tigris, 1872

On a mound in Nineveh, shielding his eyes from the sun, Arthur takes a sip from a canteen fastened to a strap round his chest. The water is warm and tastes slightly bitter, but he does not mind. The earth, parched and pale, is pitted with trenches and holes dug by previous teams of archaeologists. Tons of rubble have been piled to one side, creating a second, artificial hill. From time to time, local people have demolished some of the ancient walls, using the pit as a quarry to obtain stone for their houses. As a result everything is in disarray. It is sheer madness to search in this jumble for a fragment of a poem.

There are thirty men under his supervision, some excavating, others clearing the debris. They start early in the morning, just as the sun is ascending. This is the time of the day that Arthur loves best. The rhythm of their shovels and pickaxes pierces the air, a steady sound that reminds him of the rattle of a speeding train. Save for a brief coffee break, they keep at it, sweat trickling down their tanned necks and sinewed arms. During lunch, Arthur retreats to a makeshift tent – which does little to protect him from the mosquitoes or the relentless heat – and studies the tablets. When the sun descends, work resumes. It is an exhausting rhythm, and he is worried that the money with which he has been provided to pay the labourers will soon run out. In the evenings, tired and thirsty, he returns to the Yazidi village.

Once, out of curiosity, Arthur peers into a burrow left by a fennec fox, only to find down below the remains of an ancient boat-yard. Underneath this arid landscape bleached of colour are the skeletons of sunken boats and hardy fishermen. Long-forgotten harbours are now covered by caravan routes, trodden by hooves and worn by dust storms. Ships that ferried cargoes of grain, figs and gems lie moored and motionless for the rest of time. Should you take a handful of sand and let it run through your fingers, you can hear the sighing of the sails and the singing of the sailors. Roiling under the bare desert, still alive, is the spirit of water.

When Ashurbanipal's palace was first discovered, with its hundreds of rooms, its walls adorned with scenes of lion-hunting and racing chariots, it was the statues and bas-reliefs that caught everyone's attention. The tablets attracted little public interest. Although a few scholars passionately argued that someday these broken slabs of clay would be prized more highly than even the sculptures, no one believed them. While pictures brought the past closer, an extinct writing system seemed of no value, and thus the library kept its secrets. It is those secrets that Arthur is now determined to unravel.

Yet he is also beginning to sense that unearthing a forgotten poem does not immediately mean saving it from oblivion. He is shocked and saddened to learn that many precious objects have been lost or destroyed accidentally in the past. The excavations of the earlier British teams have been chaotic at times. Artefacts have suffered unnecessary harm, and valuable specimens have gone missing, some of which have disappeared in Bombay en route to England. The tablets were not treated with proper care: tossed into baskets, they were sent down the river on rafts, sustaining irreparable damage.

For decades two European countries had excavated in the same area, side by side yet in fierce competition: the French to the south, the British to the north. When the wind shifted, it carried the sounds of one team to the other. If work came to a stop at one location, it was almost always bad news for the other. For they usually downed tools when they made an important discovery.

The groups sometimes ran into each other. A civil nod, a tense smile, an unconcealed animosity. For they were racing to be the first to carry off Mesopotamian antiquities to Europe. People in Paris and people in London were waiting. Interest was not limited to the public and newspapers. So taken was Queen Victoria with Assyrian artefacts that she commissioned a set of jewellery inspired by them. Her favourite was a blue piece, which she named her 'Nineveh brooch'. How she adored the colour, the way it reflected the light! On a visit to France, she gave it as a present to Empress Eugénie – a subtle message meaning the British were now rivals.

And so, on a day like this, the French team were rushing to send their spoils from Nineveh to Paris. The artefacts were loaded on to wooden barges, buoyed by inflated sheepskins, and dispatched from Mosul to Basra, where they were to be transferred to larger vessels. Among the precious cargo were four colossal statues: two genies and two *lamassus*. The latter were tied to rafts, travelling separately. Altogether, the rivercraft bore more than 235 crates, containing thirty tons of Mesopotamian spoils. But, between Baghdad and Al-Qurnah, they were attacked by bandits. One boat capsized. The marauders boarded the others, killing the crew. The bodies were tossed into the waters. The Tigris rose and roared, running faster. Meanwhile, seizing the helm, the raiders tried to steer the vessels in the opposite direction but lost control. And so the crates, full of priceless antiquities, sank to the bottom of the river. They are still there somewhere. The Tigris took them and never gave them back.

Now, as Arthur roams these shores, he wonders where they are, though he knows there is little point – they have been swept away by the currents and are impossible to locate, let alone salvage. In the depths of the Tigris are stone giants – human, bull and bird – resting on the silty riverbed, their eyes wide open as the waters wash over them.

Whilst many Western travellers have arrived in Nineveh with a sense of superiority, the place has the exact opposite impact on Arthur. He feels confused, humbled. Every morning, as he walks the distance from the Yazidi village to the mound that was once Nineveh, his mind is absorbed by the ruins beneath his feet. The remains. When we are gone – kings, slaves or scribes – what is left of us?

Empires have a way of deceiving themselves into believing that, being superior to others, they will last forever. A shared expectation that tomorrow the sun will rise again, the earth will remain fertile, and the waters will never run dry. A comforting delusion that, though we will all die, the buildings we erect and the poems we compose and the civilizations we create will survive.

Arthur knows they were frightened of death, even the mightiest rulers. It was the one thing they had no control over. He also knows that not far from here, on a day like this, thousands of years back, people of all ages lined the streets to watch the funeral of a Mesopotamian king. Leading the procession were the king's favourite wife, the king's youngest wife, the king's favourite son, the king's barber, the king's storyteller . . . Also accompanying them was a retinue of soldiers, servants, musicians bearing harps and lyres, and members of the court, clad in dazzling garments adorned with carnelian and lapis lazuli. They marched in silence, each carrying their own small cup.

When they arrived at the place designated for the royal grave, one by one, they drank the poison in their cups. They were all to be buried in the very same tomb, just so the king would still have his barber and his servants to serve him and his musicians to play him songs and his storyteller to tell him stories in the afterlife. That afternoon they all killed themselves as arranged, simply so that a man accustomed to power would not have to face his own mortality alone.

Arthur is beginning to suspect that civilization is the name we give to what little we have salvaged from a loss that no one wants to remember. Triumphs are erected upon the jerry-built scaffolding of brutalities untold, heroic legends spun from the thread of aggressions and atrocities. The irrigation system was Nineveh's glowing achievement – but how many lives were squandered in its construction? There is always another side, a forgotten side. Water was the city's greatest asset and defining feature, yet it was also what undermined it in the end. The large amounts of salt deposited by torrent and tide wrecked the soil. Rivers raised, rivers razed. Sometimes your biggest strength becomes your worst weakness.

Every night Arthur returns to the Yazidi village with more questions on his mind. He likes it there. The children and their trusting eyes, the sheikh and his quiet wisdom, Dishan and his quick wit, but, most of all, the *faqra*, with that deep and mysterious serenity flowing around her like a secret river . . . There are those who say the Yazidis are heretical Muslims or renegade Christians. Others claim they are apostate Jews, or an odd Zoroastrian sect lost in the folds of history. Some insist that their caste system must have been derived from Hinduism. There is a widespread assumption that the Yazidis are an ersatz version of an original creed, a stray offshoot. Arthur disagrees. More and more it seems to him that their lineage, as rooted in the soil as the native trees, can actually be traced back to the time of the Ancient Mesopotamians.

He wants to defend them against all slander and opprobrium. The vilification of Yazidis is not limited to the local Muslim tribes. Arthur finds out that an Anglican Church missionary who arrived here a few years back claimed 'a great lewdness secretly prevailed' amongst them. Arthur is certain the man had no idea what he was talking about, but the damage, once inflicted, cannot be undone.

Whenever he has free time, Arthur converses with the sheikh, or learns from Dishan how to drape skeins of newly dyed yarn over a wall, or helps an elderly woman to lay piles of fluffy sheep's wool to dry in the sun, or whittles wooden birds for the children. If his father were here, he would be pleased to see him employing his craft at long last. His own talents do not mean much to the villagers. They find him kind but odd, hunching over illegible markings. But, much though Arthur enjoys these activities, nothing compares with spending time with the *faqra*. Leila has a remarkable ability to play both wind instruments and percussion. Arthur shows her the *qanun* he brought from Constantinople, offering it to her as a present. At first she refuses it, too proud to accept gifts from a foreigner, and it is only when she sees how eager the children are to hear her play that she relents – after that, working in his room many days, Arthur listens to her gently strumming the strings, mesmerized by her ability to open up herself to music. Like one of those sunflowers that grows along the bank, tilting its head towards the first rays of light, Arthur cannot help but turn towards Leila whenever she is around. He admires her quiet resolve, smiles when he sees her smile. There is a delicateness in her strength, a gentleness in her movements. He watches her as she lovingly feeds mulberry leaves to caterpillars that one day soon will turn into butterflies.

Often in the evenings, the villagers gather to listen to the *faqra*. She tells stories from olden times, tales as ancient as the river itself. As moths flutter about the lanterns, she speaks softly but distinctly, this woman who hears voices from other realms. Try as he might to follow every word through the interpreter, Arthur is certain that he is missing important parts. What he does glean, however, leaves him craving to learn more. Most of the *faqra*'s stories are about water in some form. Curious to enter her liquid world, Arthur starts studying Kurdish, his boyhood ability to pick up languages fast now reinvigorated. For he wants to capture everything that Leila says. Having dedicated his life at first to the publishing of books and then to the translation of cuneiform, it fascinates Arthur that the Yazidis do not have a sacred scripture. He is endlessly baffled as to how a culture can sustain itself with the spoken word alone. Stories and poems and ballads seem to be the mortar that keeps them together, keeps them alive.

Many a night, as he is working on a tablet by the light of an oil lamp, a part of him anxiously waits to hear Leila's footsteps. She frequently wanders out in her sleep, though she never leaves the confines of the village. Always in these moments, Arthur is overcome by a sense of bliss, as if her presence were some kind of benediction. Even when his mind is busy deciphering the cuneiform, his senses are alert to the smallest signals – the crack of a twig under her feet fusing with the swishing tides of the Tigris in the distance. The sounds blend so seamlessly that he could almost believe she was walking into the river, that she herself was made of flowing water.

II—
NARIN

By the River Tigris, 2014

They kill the water first. In this land where rivers are sacred and every drop of rain is a blessing, they creep in at dead of night and poison all the wells, shafts and fountains in the village. The next morning the inhabitants of Zêrav wake up to a shocking sight. Slabs of concrete, metal debris and sacks of pesticides have been dumped into every source of water.

Several men volunteer to walk to the next Yazidi village to ask for help, only to find out that they, too, have suffered similar devastation and are in desperate need. The only drinkable water is kilometres away. The group, now larger, decide to go check on their Muslim neighbours. They are surprised to see that their fountains have been left untouched. It is only the water in the Yazidi settlements that has been tampered with. Some families take pity on them, but others shut the doors in their faces, saying they will not assist heathens. In the end they return with a few containers filled. Exhausted by the heat, on the way back they drink a little and save the remainder, knowing that their loved ones are counting on them.

The rest of the day goes by painfully slowly, the sun a ball of fury. Later in the afternoon, streaks of clouds needle the sky, but rain does not materialize. The villagers try to clear the fountains as best they can. Children move away stones, men haul out concrete slabs, and women use their scarves to filter out the debris.

In the past they had the river to fall back on, but the Tigris is also polluted. A melancholy fervour takes hold of everyone. There is something almost sacrilegious in witnessing clean water being deliberately soiled.

Two days later, the enemy returns, this time to kill the trees. Always at night, shrouding themselves in darkness, they set fire to olive groves, turning whole fields into wastelands of charred stumps. They break off branches, spoil the fruit; they torch the shrubs and uproot tender saplings.

A lone tree burning bright against the sky is a sorrowful sight. But entire groves going up in flames, once glimpsed, will be forever branded on your memory. As dawn breaks, Narin sits by the window, watching a bird outside. A swift is building a nest in a crevice on the wall. Doggedly, the tiny creature carries sticks and straw, sculpting a space of its own. Witnessing this makes Narin sadder than anything – the realization that, while they are dealing with such hatred and hostility, life goes on. In her mind she keeps coming back to the same fearful question, like a sore tooth she cannot help probing with the tip of her tongue: an enemy who poisons water and torches trees – what will they do to human beings?

It is a good thing her father is not here. He will be safer in Baghdad. But she also knows if something were to happen to her and Grandma, he would never forgive himself. The child is shivering, even though the day is so hot she can smell the crushed apricots mouldering in the garden, a cloying scent of decay.

Father calls the following afternoon. He says as he was driving north after performing at a wedding he was arrested at a checkpoint and held in custody without being charged. He sounds tired and listless – but that instantly changes when Narin tells him what is happening in the village.

'They poisoned the water?'

'Yes, they also burned the trees. Do you know who is doing this?'

'I don't know – must be a few fanatics.'

'Grandma is very worried. She keeps praying. When are you coming back?'

'I'm on my way.' Khaled pauses. 'I had no idea, I'm very sorry. I'll be there before you know it.' Another pause, this one longer. 'Maybe we should return to Hasankeyf.'

'But what about my baptism? We were going to visit the Valley of Lalish next week. I prepared my dress.'

'I know, sweetheart, but . . . this place doesn't feel safe.' He clears his throat, realizing he should not alarm the child unnecessarily. 'I don't expect these fanatics to do anything more extreme. They don't have that kind of power. They're just trying to intimidate us. That's what bullies do. But, don't forget, there are armed Kurdish forces guarding every Yazidi village. The *peshmerga* will protect you. So no need to worry – you'll be safe.'

'I'm not worried,' says Narin, lifting her chin with a bravado she does not entirely feel.

'That's my girl,' says her father.

Narin presses the phone against her right ear, her good one. 'I keep hearing a ringing noise. It's started hurting again.'

'Has it now? I'll come and kiss it better.'

'Grandma says it's bad luck to kiss your loved one on their eyes or their ears – it means farewell.'

'Grandma is a wise woman, but she's not always right.'

Narin holds her breath, sensing the undertone in her father's voice. Is he blaming her grandmother for insisting that they should travel to Iraq this summer?

'Do you regret coming here, Daddy?'

'No, no,' Khaled says quickly. 'But I think we'd better cut the trip short and return home. Anyway, we'll talk when I arrive. I'll be with you tomorrow.'

Her father cannot make it back the next day. Nor the one after that. The roads are blocked, and he is forced to take a long detour to reach Zêrav. He will have to stay a night or two in another Yazidi village. He needs to be careful, for there are rumours of abductions. But it is hard to gauge the true extent of the threat. Yazidis, Christians, Jews, Mandeans and Muslims who openly condemn the fanatics are all said to be in danger.

Meanwhile, sitting by the radio, Grandma listens to the news with a troubled expression. Ever since they contaminated the wells, she has not slept properly. She walks around the village at odd hours of the night, and by the singed trees in the daytime, her face turned towards the sun, attentive to the whistle of the wind through the reeds. Narin wonders what she hears and why she doesn't share it with her.

The next morning, Grandma is on the roof, as usual, performing the first prayer of the day. Her breath stalls in her chest as she senses something is wrong. And then she knows – the Kurdish forces protecting the village are nowhere to be seen. They are all gone! The *peshmerga* – 'those who face death' – have left, taking their weapons with them.

News arrives that eighteen thousand Kurdish troops in Nineveh alone have withdrawn in one night, leaving Yazidis completely defenceless. Fear, like a sander clamping a piece of wood, presses on their hearts, cold and heavy. In strained tones they debate what to do, but it is impossible to know in the absence of reliable information. What would be safer – stay or go? What if this is their last chance to run away? But, then, what if it is a trap to make them leave the village, so that others can appropriate their homes and lands? Families quarrel; friends fall into disagreement. In the end, they decide to put up white flags on the windows and wait.

347

In the village where Khaled is planning to stay overnight three trucks drive up the road, raising clouds of dust. The vehicles, mounted with machine guns and carrying militants clad in black fatigues, enter the main street, revving their engines, screeching their tyres. The militants have covered their faces with improvised balaclavas. All have semi-automatic rifles.

'Get out of your homes, now!'

A squat man with a close-clipped beard and hair the colour of straw seems to be the one giving orders. He does not speak Kurdish or Arabic. There is someone next to him translating his words.

Khaled, watching from the window, recognizes the person helping the fanatics. It is Hajji Amer. Khaled has welcomed this man at so many weddings and celebrations, broken bread with him, shared stories with him and considered him a trusted friend all these years – this man who is now shouting through a loudspeaker, 'Bring your money – and mobile phones.' His voice is brimming with something close to excitement. He seems to be enjoying his new-found power. 'Rings, bracelets, watches, necklaces, earrings . . . anything of value! Hand them all over!'

Behind closed doors, families are petrified, too frightened to move.

'If you do as we say, nothing will happen. You'll drop your things and go home. But if you hide anything we'll find it and we'll punish you all!'

One by one, doors open, fearful faces emerge. Men carry phones, money, even the gold bracelets given to their wives as wedding presents.

'Don't forget ID papers, credit cards, car keys . . . bring them all! Don't be afraid. Your safety is guaranteed by the Islamic State.'

Khaled drags himself out of the house with his mobile, wallet and passport. He has hidden his Turkish phone inside his sock and now he moves slowly, as though wading through water, never tearing his gaze from his old friend. Hajji Amer has not seen him yet; his back is turned to Khaled as he scurries this way and that, eagerly conveying the militants' instructions.

'I said everyone! Women and the children, too. Not a single person can stay behind. Get out, all of you!'

On a blanket spread on the ground the families drop their valuables and take a step back. Soon a large pile is amassed – a jumbled heap of documents and treasures, their glassy edges and metal surfaces catching the rays of the sun.

'Is this all? Liars! What else have you got?'

'This is everything,' says the *mukhtar*, the village leader. 'Can we return to our houses? The children are scared.'

'You'll leave when we tell you!' says Hajji Amer. 'First, we'll check if you're telling the truth.'

They ransack every house, smashing crockery, knocking over stools and cradles, making as much noise as possible. By contrast, back in the square, save for the cry of a baby and the hush of a mother, silence reigns. Fear marring their features, the villagers wait.

'All men and boys over twelve move to my right! Women and girls and younger children – you stay over there!'

Hajji Amer, the loudspeaker still in his hand, swivels his eyes around. His gaze, scanning the villagers, lands on Khaled, and for a second he looks startled, in the manner of someone stepping from bright sunlight into a dark room. But he quickly wipes any trace of recognition from his features.

'The Caliphate is being merciful towards you. We'll give you a chance to convert. If you agree, nothing will happen to you. But, if you refuse, we will expel you from your village. You have five minutes to decide.'

'We don't need time to decide.' Khaled steps forward, compelling the other man to look him in the eye. 'We'll never abandon our faith. But you must know this – as the *kreef* of two boys in this village. You've attended our weddings and circumcisions. Have you forgotten?'

Khaled will never know if any of this is translated to the leader of the militants. The armed group are already forcing all Yazidi men to march eastwards in single file. Now the silence is replaced by cries and screams.

'Move!'

'Where are you taking us?' asks Khaled.

'You're going on a walk.'

They trudge through fields, as yet unharvested, the militants behind them, prodding and pushing stragglers. Khaled glances down at the crops crushed beneath their feet – aubergines, peppers, barley, wheat, tomatoes . . . He has never been fond of aubergines, but if he survives this day he will eat them gladly.

They arrive at a water cistern where the militants order everyone to stop. Twenty metres wide and three metres tall, the underground reservoir must have once been used to irrigate the fields, but now it is empty.

'Move closer!'

'You want us to go down there?' Khaled asks. As he peers into the gaping concrete maw the terrifying thought crosses his mind that they will be forced together into that dark, confined, airless space and held prisoner.

'Stop asking questions and do as we say.'

All the captives, young and old, are forced to step up on to the concrete edge. A teenager with peach fuzz on his lip is trembling so uncontrollably that he can barely stand. Khaled grips the boy's arm to steady him. He tries to say something to comfort him, but his mouth is dry and all he can mutter is, 'Quiet, my child. This is our Fate. Trust in God.'

They hear a curse behind them, hurled in mindless rage. A word crackles in the air like shattered glass.

'Infidels!'

His heart pumping harder, Khaled lifts his chin. When he glances over his shoulder, he finds Hajji Amer staring straight at him. For a second their eyes meet. In the gaze of the man he once called a friend Khaled searches for a sign of shame or guilt or even pity, anything at all, but there is nothing there; it is as empty as the cistern below.

'Shoot!'

They open fire all at once. Shouting 'God is great' in Arabic, they gun down sixty-four Yazidi men and boys who have no weapons, no way of defending themselves. One after another the bodies fall into the void.

'Some are still alive!' a man yells. 'Aim for their heads!'

It takes only two and a half minutes to execute sixty-four human beings. The time for a drop of rain to reach the ground.

Inside the cistern it is very cold. A sour stench pervades the air – of cordite, blood, urine and something like rotting apples. Khaled draws a ragged breath. He knows he is dead, he must be, but how is it possible that he can still smell, he thinks to himself. His body feels numb, except for a burning pain boring into his thigh, where a bullet has pierced his flesh. Under and above him, warm and slippery, are corpses, crushing him from all sides. Fear has strangely disappeared, terror not yet sunk in. It is sadness that consumes his heart right now. It fills him with despair, the desolation of this place. The water reservoir has become a mass grave.

He can hear the militants laughing. Their voices are high-pitched, giddy with excitement, a thudding vibration that stifles all other sounds. Then comes the rumble of trucks driving away. He listens, attentive to the slightest rustle, trying to understand if anyone else might have survived. Not a single moan or whimper. He hears only the buzzing of a fly overhead. He can feel something wet running down his leg and he knows he is bleeding. He clenches his eyes shut, and would have kept them that way, if it were not for the thought of Narin. Somewhere out there, still part of this painful world, is his daughter and she needs him.

Inch by inch, Khaled levers himself out from under the tangle of twisted limbs and torsos. He notices he is still clutching the arm of the teenager, now lying motionless by his side, his eyes wide open. A howl escapes his lips.

Evening has descended by the time Khaled crawls out of the cistern. A sharp pain pulsates through him. He now understands there is a second bullet inside him, lodged somewhere close to his lower stomach. Gasping, he lies prone on the ground for some time, feeling the solid, warm earth. He rips a strip off his blood-soaked shirt and ties it around his thigh to slow the bleeding.

That is when he hears a ringing, the dancing jingle of a mobile phone. He has completely forgotten he still has it in his sock. His fingers shaking, he takes the phone out. It is his mother-in-law, Besma.

'Khaled!' The old woman wails as soon as he answers. 'Oh, bless your voice. I feared something terrible happened to you. Daesh is coming, everyone is saying. We hung white flags.'

'Mama – listen . . .' He tries to raise his voice, for she keeps talking over him. 'You must leave. You must run away now!'

'What? What are you saying? We have white flags –'

'Forget it. They don't care about that! They are murderers. They are slaughtering the innocent.'

Besma falls silent.

'You and Narin need to run. This moment. Tell others, please warn them, but do not stop to talk to everyone. Take my daughter – you must save her.'

'Son, where do you want us to go?'

'Go to the mountain,' he says, running his tongue over his dry lips. 'I'll find you there. Go to Sinjar!'

Far ahead down the dusty track is a desolate farm. The farmer – a middle-aged Sunni Muslim man – sees him coming and takes him to his house. He offers him water and food. He tries to clean his wounds. The second bullet is buried too deep, Khaled knows.

The farmer's aged mother watches from the corner, her lips moving in silent prayer, a string of beads in her hand. Tears run down her weathered face at the sight of his suffering. They do not speak. His head drooping, Khaled slumps on the floor, slipping in and out of consciousness, not sure whether they will shelter him or hand him over to the enemy.

Late at night, long before the sun rises, Khaled comes round and stirs. The farmer is waiting by the window, keeping an eye out. The man warns him Daesh have been threatening local families, saying that anyone found hiding Yazidis or Shias will be beheaded. He has prepared a bundle with some bread, yogurt and a bottle of water. His eyes are stricken with sorrow as he tells Khaled he cannot stay.

'Narin . . . my heart.'

Leaning over the sleeping child, Grandma shakes her gently. 'Wake up, my soul.'

The girl sits up. 'What's happening?'

'We must get out of here. It's not safe.'

'But we put up a white flag. You said they wouldn't harm us.'

'Your father says not to trust ISIS, and I trust your father.'

Wordlessly, Narin gets out of bed and follows the old woman.

Outside, their relatives are waiting in their cars, babies under their arms, children sitting on top of each other, bags of food and provisions jammed between the legs of the adults. Narin realizes Grandma has not slept at all, going from door to door trying to convince others to come with them. Only a few families agreed. Quietly, they drive in the dark with their headlights off.

'Where are we going?' Narin asks, once they have left the village behind.

'We're going to Mount Sinjar.'

And the child remembers then. Sinjar – the sacred mountain where the Ark came to rest, floodwaters seeping through a hole in the hull. That is where a big black snake appeared and plugged the breach, saving humankind.

'Like Baba Noah?'

'Like Baba Noah, my love.'

About two hours into the drive, as dawn is breaking, there is a bend in the road where an ISIS truck equipped with heavy machine guns lies in wait. Families fleeing do not suspect anything until it's too late. It's an ambush. Here, in this way, over a hundred Yazidis are killed. The handful who manage to slip past unharmed stagger away, carrying injured relatives. Some of the abandoned cars burst into flames; others, their engines still running, tyres flat, glint in the sun like metal coffins.

Only a few drivers, spotting the trap at the last minute, skid off the main road, rattling over the fissures in the scorched earth. By some unfathomable stroke of luck, theirs is one of them. No one talks. Their faces waxen, they keep going. Fifty metres later the car comes to a stop, smoke pouring from the bonnet. Quickly, they get out and run towards Sinjar.

In the foothills they are joined by thousands of others. Dust, there is so much dust. Narin walks, holding on to her grandmother's skirt. The ground starts to feel hot against the soles of her feet – cracked like a cast-off turtle shell. They are climbing the mountain – women, children, babies in arms. Above them, the sun, already high in the sky, burns fiercely. The temperature soars. There are no trees to offer shade, no springs to slake thirst, only dry, desolate earth. They all think the same thing, though no one will voice it out loud: how long can they possibly survive without water?

A human being needs about four litres of water every day. There are fifty thousand people under siege on Mount Sinjar.

—O—

ARTHUR

By the River Tigris, 1872

Çarşema Sor, 'Red Wednesday' – the festival that welcomes
spring and hails new beginnings. The day the universe was
created from a white pearl, and water and land were separated from each other. A time of rebirth and revival. April is 'the
bride of the year'. The villagers boil eggs and paint them in the
brightest colours, ready for the festive game *hekkane*. A mixture of
broken eggshells, wild flowers and clay is applied to the entrances
of homes. They decorate the graves, celebrating the arrival of the
new year with the living and the dead.

The whole week a frenzy of cleaning consumed the village
of Zêrav. Wherever Arthur turned, he saw people washing carpets, scrubbing stoves, sweeping compacted earth floors. Now
the sheikh knocks on each door to distribute a loaf of bread – and
yeast to use as leaven. Wealthier families slaughter sheep, sharing
the meat with those who cannot afford it. They melt the fat of
sacrificial animals to make candles – *çire*. The large candles will
be lit for God, the medium for the angels, the small for humans.
All these traditions are as old and unchanging as the mountains.

The children are puzzled when Arthur tells them that where
he comes from the new year takes place not when blossom gar-
lands the trees, chicks call from nests, lambs bounce around and
the earth is revived but in the midst of freezing winter. They smile
at him politely, displaying the gaps between their teeth. They do

not want to offend the Englishman with his blue eyes and bizarre customs.

On the seventh sunset, it is time to celebrate. They gather inside and around the sheikh's house, bringing food and flowers. Through the open windows wafts the smell of rosemary, honeysuckle, sage and wild garlic. Arranged neatly on a table are seven pieces of meat, seven loaves of bread and seven clusters of raisins. Arthur is invited to join, although it is unusual for an outsider to attend the ceremony. He is deeply moved. He understands they are making an exception for him. They see him as a friend. It occurs to him on that night that there is a side to friendship that resembles faith. Both are built on the fragility of trust.

A sherbet in his hand, Arthur retreats to a corner. Life feels blissful, and he hopes that the new year will bring joy to these people who have been so kind to him. In a little while, Leila enters the room – she is wearing a long white robe with red-and-black trim sewn across her chest. She carries a *daf*, every so often striking its edge. Tonight she will be divining. The children are escorted outside. This is not for them to see.

The *faqra*'s fingers move towards the centre of the *daf*, reaching its heart. As she plays the instrument, she slightly sways. The candles burn, shadows dance on the walls, and, outside the room, darkness gathers. Arthur does not dare to make a sound, let alone ask a question. He senses what he is about to witness is an arcane ritual. He will never know whether they have forgotten he is in the room, or whether they are allowing him into a sacred moment.

Leila starts to sing – a haunting melody, dirge-like. Her voice keeps rising and falling. One moment she is a young woman, but the next she sounds ageless, featureless, a creature of water and foam. When she speaks it is no longer in Kurdish. Arthur feels the hairs on the back of his neck stand up. The words pouring from her lips are remarkably similar to Akkadian, the ancient Semitic language of Mesopotamia. It enthrals him, the mirroring of the consonants. Yet again he finds himself wondering whether the

Yazidis could be the descendants of a civilization that flourished in this region thousands of years back. But there is no time for scholarly musings. The music accelerates, Leila's fingers rhythmically tapping the surface of the *daf*. And, just like that, she slides into a trance.

She starts spinning – fast, faster. Then, all of a sudden, she covers her face with both hands. Trembling, she releases a scream. Although it does not last long, the pain in her voice is so intense it reverberates across the room. Lines of worry appear on her forehead. Her face is waxen, as if drained of blood. She mutters something incomprehensible, but, between strange words, Arthur picks out one that he instantly recognizes.

'*Firman!*'

Bewildered, Arthur leans forward. Her use of this familiar word throws him. He whispers to the sheikh's son, 'What does she mean?'

'A massacre.'

'A massacre?'

'She is saying this will happen to our people. An enemy will come, some outsiders, others from around here. They will kill the men and abduct the women and the girls. She says their cruelty will know no limits.'

'But I don't understand. *Firman* means . . .' Arthur halts as it dawns on him that the same word – permission, order, authorization – can also stand for a licence to attack and kill. A licence for the decimation of a whole community.

Dropping the *daf*, Leila falls to her knees, shaking so fiercely that her teeth begin to chatter. Tears stream down her cheeks. Horrified, Arthur lurches forward as if to hold her, but the sheikh bars his way with his cane. There is a barrier, a line he cannot cross. Quietly, Arthur takes a step back. Whatever horror she is predicting must be heard.

When the *firman* strikes, the *faqra* says, the tomb of Nabi Yunus, the prophet Jonah, will be destroyed. Sacred sites will be reduced to ruins. Many will die; others will experience such brutality that they will wish they had.

> '*I see men, armed and trained, their hearts of stone*
> *I see my village burn, my home razed,*
> *Cries of the elderly, hills of bone.*'

Everyone in the room is silent. Some are weeping without a sound. No one dares to interrupt.

> '*The day they come to kill us*
> *run to the mountain.*
> *Do not go near the water,*
> *river, well nor fountain.*'

Leila falls quiet, having nothing else left to share. Exhausted and sapped of all emotion, she rises to her feet. Slowly, she walks out. Although she is still in a half-conscious state, when she comes to her senses, she will remember every word. Memory is a burden, and no one understands this better than Arthur.

As soon as the door opens, the children scamper back to the room, delighted to be allowed in again, eager to taste the food and join the evening. Their faces aglow, they clutch their parents' hands and ask what the *faqra* said, and whether it was good and joyful. The adults struggle to find their voices.

That night, Arthur is unable to fall asleep. His mind keeps circling back to the same question. So many civilizations and creeds have bloomed, thrived and withered across this region. But they must all have retained the belief that the future, *their* future, would somehow be better than the past, that tomorrow the sun would glow brighter and the shadows diminish. The Yazidis have a long-established tradition of divination. How does a people survive the painful realization that not only is their history full of oppression, persecution and massacres, but their future may also offer more of the same?

The next afternoon, Arthur sits by the River Tigris. The heat is insufferable, the mosquitoes even more so. The remains of Nineveh break his heart. This wasn't what he was expecting. When he arrived here, all he had imagined was that it was his responsibility to unearth antiquities and take them back to England. He wasn't prepared for the sadness that keeps pecking at his breast like a vulture at a carcass.

The *faqra*'s premonitions have bored into his soul. If they are true, does it really help a person, or a community, to learn what terrible fate lies ahead? All his life Arthur has made every effort to broaden his experience and expand his knowledge. He never thought there would come a day when he would wonder if it were preferable to live in innocence and die in ignorance instead.

Something is changing – he can sense it. It is in the orb of the sun, the swell of the river, the harsh trills and screams of starlings massing in billowing clouds – a gathering in the air like a premonition.

─H

ZALEEKHAH

By the River Thames, 2018

Friday afternoon, Zaleekhah leaves work early to see Helen. They meet in a café in the gardens of Russell Square. Surrounded by plane trees and flowers of a deep saturated yellow hue, she finds it peaceful in here, though the rumble of the city is impossible to ignore.

Helen looks distracted, tired. The lines on her face seem elongated as she tells Zaleekhah that the doctors now have a diagnosis for her daughter.

'It's her kidneys. She might need a transplant.'

Zaleekhah leans forward, holding her cousin's hand. 'Oh, no, poor love. I'm so sorry.'

'It's not easy to find a donor.' Helen's expression collapses.

'What does Uncle say?'

'He's sprung into action, of course, making calls everywhere. You know how he is. Extraordinarily supportive. I don't know what I'd do without him.'

For a long time, they discuss doctors and hospitals and dialysis treatments and the risks of complications, should a matching donor be found soon. Helen's husband is cutting his trip short and catching the first flight home. They talk, though briefly and with a feeling of unease, about other things, too, the gallery and the business, the Zen garden taking shape behind the Malek house, titbits of gossip, but every other subject brings them back to where they began: the kidney transplant.

Reaching for a napkin, Helen wipes her eyes. 'Forgive my selfishness. I haven't asked a single question about you, and it's not as if you haven't got your own troubles to deal with.'

'Don't worry about me,' says Zaleekhah. 'I'm fine.'

'I don't see you smile any more,' says Helen, studying her intently. 'I mean, a big smile. You don't look happy; it breaks my heart. There was a time when you were happy, wasn't there? I mean, despite everything. When we were younger, you did laugh, and, when you did, your laughter radiated through the room. Sometimes I wish we could go back to those days, that feeling of lightness.'

Zaleekhah recalls those years differently, but there is no point in disagreeing. She glances down at her hands, her nails bitten to the quick, the skin around them red and raw. She considers telling Helen that, for weeks now, she has been unable to sleep properly, even with pills, and that she wakes up tired every morning, carrying around a feeling of loss. But she decides not to share any of this. She does not want to add to her cousin's worries.

'It was lovely to meet your friend the other day,' says Helen suddenly. 'I hope Nen wasn't too shocked by my father.'

This is something they have in common, their mutual appreciation of Lord Malek in all his flawed but deeply human complexity, far removed from the public figure.

'I liked Nen,' Helen carries on. 'She seems very grounded – at peace with herself.'

'Yes.' Zaleekhah tilts her head, thinking. She nods, as if arriving at some conclusion. 'I like her, too.'

By the time Zaleekhah leaves the café, her head is teeming with thoughts. In the gusty wind, her hair blows about her face. For too long she has taken so little pleasure in life, invaded by a sickening, sinking feeling, even as she went through the motions of each new day, each piece of work. But now, as she sifts every word of her conversation with her cousin – how valiantly Helen is battling to help her little daughter recover – a part of her feels ashamed of her own ongoing depression, her habitual melancholy, her thoughts of suicide. People cling to life; small children fight for the privilege she has been willing, and silently planning, to throw away. Learning about what Helen and her family have been suffering leaves her confused and disorientated, her priorities upended. She wants to help them, she wants to be around for them, and, also, she wants to help herself.

The wish to rethink her life and the direction it is heading comes to Dr Zaleekhah Clarke not incrementally but in one sudden, inchoate rush. As she stumbles over a loose paving stone where rainwater has pooled underneath, she acknowledges, with a readiness that fills her with surprise, that she needs to change.

Half an hour later, Zaleekhah pushes open the door of the tattoo shop, making the bells jingle.

'She's not in, I'm afraid,' says Nen's brother.

'Oh, okay. I'll come back some other time.'

He regards her curiously, though not unkindly. 'Check the museum – you'll probably find her in the Nineveh section – that's her usual spot.'

From the tattoo shop to the British Museum it is only fifty-five steps. A few minutes later Zaleekhah enters the majestic building, the light from the glass above catching in her hair. Nen is easy to find. Ensconced on a bench with a notebook, she is sketching a *lamassu*.

'Hi!'

'Hi!'

Today she is wearing a red dress with tiny flowers and puffed sleeves, unbuttoned from the waist down, with a pair of ripped blue jeans underneath and black Dr Martens. The combination puzzles Zaleekhah. Her female colleagues at the lab mostly prefer formal shirts and baggy trousers, which is also her usual choice, whereas her aunt and Helen like elegant pencil skirts and tailored outfits. Somewhere in her mind, Zaleekhah has separated these two worlds – monochromes versus bright colours, dresses versus trousers. She has never known anyone who clashes colours and styles like Nen, delighting in mixing and contrasting without worrying what others might think.

'So you come here often, your brother says.'

'Well, yes, whenever I get the chance to slip away.'

Zaleekhah sits next to her, and for a moment she observes the ancient sculpture without speaking. 'I haven't looked at a full-sized *lamassu* in a while. I had forgotten how impressive they are.'

Nen gives a nod. 'I find them very therapeutic.'

'You do?'

'I doubt any therapists would send their patients to the British Museum, but when you're next to something so impossibly old, it kind of puts things in perspective. Whatever is troubling you in this moment means little in the sweep of time. I think everyone should hang out with a *lamassu* every now and then.'

A group of tourists walks by, moving from one gallery into the next, wonder and fatigue meeting in their faces.

Nen says, 'Did you know, when they were first discovered, Mesopotamian treasures were belittled in scholarly circles? They were deemed inferior compared with the Ancient Egyptian or Hellenic heritages. Their aesthetic power was denied, which I find utterly bonkers.'

Behind them on the wall are bas-reliefs from Nineveh, and now Zaleekhah turns in that direction. 'There aren't many women in these images. Is it always warfare and hunting?'

'Mostly but not always. Take a look at that one.' Nen points with her chin. 'That is King Ashurbanipal and his wife having a nice little picnic in the palace gardens. Very blissful, the whole scene. But check the trees: there's a surprise amid the branches. The royal couple are sitting beneath their enemy's severed head. That's what remains of the Elamite king Teumman.'

Zaleekhah studies the panel. 'So he was cruel, Ashurbanipal?'

'He was one of the most brutal Assyrian rulers. His destruction of Elam is regarded by many scholars as a genocide.'

'I kind of expected better from a man known for building an amazing library.'

'You're far from alone in that assumption. But it's actually a useful reminder that someone can be cultured and polished, generous, worldly, but still commit acts of startling cruelty.'

Behind them, they hear sibilant whispers as a group of students approaches.

Nen closes her notebook. 'Come, let me show you something.'

They walk towards the *lamassu* that Nen had been sketching. Only then does Zaleekhah notice one of its hooves is scorched and burned.

'I've been wondering how this happened,' says Nen. 'Did the giant sculpture survive a fire in Ashurbanipal's palace? Was it caused by a flaming arrow during the siege of Nineveh? Who knows. But I've a feeling something terrible happened and this stone creature witnessed it.'

The silence extends for a few seconds as Zaleekhah's eyes linger on Nen's face. Then she asks, 'Are people ever surprised by your interest in Ancient Mesopotamia?'

'All the time. Even my own brothers think it's a bit nuts. Correction. That I'm a bit nuts.'

Zaleekhah smiles.

'But how do we find our passions?' says Nen, as if debating with herself. 'I really haven't a clue. Most of the time it's pure coincidence – a book we encounter in the library, a teacher who leaves an impression, a film we can't forget . . . When I look back, I realize I'd have gone crazy if I didn't have other places to retreat to – the further away from my own reality the better.'

'And Ancient Mesopotamia was that place?'

'Exactly,' says Nen. 'I guess what water is to you, history is to me: an enigma too vast to comprehend, something far more important than my own little life, and yet, at some level, also deeply personal. Does that make sense?'

'It does, actually.'

'So, yes, Ancient Mesopotamia is my sanctuary. When I was young, I wrestled with mental health issues and it got worse later on.'

'Oh, I thought you grew up in a loving family –'

Nen returns her gaze. 'You can grow up in a loving family and still struggle.'

They walk out of the Assyrian Gallery, and pass by the gift shop with its shelves loaded with books and ornaments. The café in the Great Court is packed. They search for an empty table beneath the soaring glass roof, not an easy thing, as it is brimming with visitors, voices vibrating in the open space, like the sound of waves breaking against soft sand. They manage to find two chairs and sit side by side, their backs to the postcard racks.

Nen's face is at first unreadable, her features wholly concentrated. She says gently, 'I feel like you're struggling, too, Zaleekhah. I'm sorry for poking my nose in. I've been wanting to tell you . . . I think you're a lovely person. It's just so easy to feel lost when you feel low, like you're drifting alone in endless floodwaters. But you're not alone. There are many of us on this wooden Ark – sailing without knowing if there is land ahead. Sailing in hope nonetheless . . .'

If it were any other day, Zaleekhah might have changed the subject, uncomfortable with emotions that, like some unknown sea creature, rise from the deep. But not today. She won't look away. So she says, 'I think I've been depressed for so long that it became my normal.'

'Not very fond of that word myself – *normal*,' says Nen.

'The Ancient Mesopotamians – did they have a word for depression?'

'They did, but they viewed mental health differently, as if some outside force, a god or a demon, caused it. There are fascinating descriptions on clay tablets – incantations, rituals, fumigations and potions. There is *ashushtu*, which is more like distress. *Puluhtu*, used for people who are constantly worried or afraid, or have phobias. *Nissatu* means "grief". Gilgamesh says "grief enters my belly" when Enkidu dies. *Šinīt ṭēmiis* is the alteration of the mind, so that could be suicidal thoughts or severe panic attacks. And then there is *hip libbi*, the malady of melancholy – it literally means "shattering of the heart".'

'*Hip libbi*?'

'Yes,' says Nen, turning in the direction of the Assyrian Gallery. 'For a long time, my *hip libbi* lived inside a bottle of gin – like a djinni in a lamp. I would glimpse her in my drink – sometimes she would be floating on her back, utterly still, at other times swimming, but always there, at the bottom of each glass.'

Zaleekhah listens, appraising her with thoughtful eyes.

Nen says, 'In my twenties I prided myself on handling booze better than most. We'd go to pubs and all the girls would stop after a few shots, except for me – I could drink the men under the table and everyone thought that was pretty cool. In my early thirties, I was proud that I was a "high-functioning" drinker. I could easily go days and weeks without drinking. No problem! I loved proving that I had self-control, but I also knew there was a reward at the end. Drinking was how I motivated and calmed myself. Then things started to shift, but I still believed it was all fine. I had never been a mean drunk. Never argumentative. Never aggressive. I just got a lovely little buzz. Surely there was no harm in that. It was mild and mellow, except I could no longer have a good time without nursing a stiff drink. I had zero patience with people, unless I was tipsy enough, in which case I didn't care. It took me a long time to acknowledge something was off. I'm telling you all this because during those years of ups and downs, my interest in Mesopotamia never waned. It was a place so unlike my own reality that I could go there and rewire my brain. I could find refuge in that storyland between the two rivers – except it was real and it was amazing. Broken and bruised and beautiful and sad and yet surprisingly resilient and profoundly inspiring . . . that's what it means to me, Ancient Mesopotamia.'

From all corners seep the sounds of tourists, students, parents and children. An elderly woman carrying a tray with coffee and cake smiles at them and they smile back.

'You know, Nen, if I believed in reincarnation, I'd say you must have lived in Nineveh in another life.'

'Funny you should say that. One of my customers, she's very sweet but a bit mad, is into this stuff and she keeps trying to convince me that I was a scribe on Ashurbanipal's payroll.'

'Quite. Although I can also imagine you taming lions in the royal menagerie.'

Nen laughs. 'Maybe that's how I died, inside a lion's stomach.'

'And that's why you're afraid of needles – they remind you of claws.' Now Zaleekhah, too, laughs.

Nowhere does time slow down more gently than inside a museum, Zaleekhah thinks, appreciating how everything around them feels fluid, the borders between one region and another, one century and the next, turning porous. She says, 'Today I had coffee with my cousin Helen, whom you met the other day. Her daughter is very sick. She needs a kidney transplant.'

'Oh my God, that's awful. I'm so sorry. That must be very hard.'

'Yes, she's devastated. When I listened to her, my own depression seemed self-indulgent. I wanted to change. Does that make sense?'

'It does.'

The silence that follows is serene, peaceful.

'Nen?'

'Hmm?'

'If I were to come to your shop one day, as a customer, I mean, not as a friend . . . and ask for a tattoo, what would you say?'

Nen throws back her head, her eyes brimming with mischief. 'I'd be delighted – if that hypothetical day arrives, I'd ask you what you had in mind.'

'And I'd reply . . .' Zaleekhah looks away and back at her. 'That sign on the biscuit. I liked it so much. Simple, powerful.'

'Which one?' Nen says and instantly pauses. She doesn't need to ask more questions to know which sign Zaleekhah is talking about.

That evening Zaleekhah leaves the Forgotten Goddess, a slight, sizzling pain above her wrist. She could have had it anywhere, on her back, her upper arm, somewhere less visible where Uncle Malek would not notice it. But she chose this tender stretch of skin at the junction of her left hand and inner arm. It hurt a little, though not as badly as she'd thought it would. Now, as she walks to the Tube to get to her houseboat, she glances proudly at her tattoo.

Three marks in blue ink, the colour of lapis lazuli. The sign of water.

𒀀

ARTHUR

By the River Tigris, 1872

Early one morning, Leila accompanies Arthur to the excavation site. She likes to forage for herbs and plants, and occasionally they walk together. The air smells musky, earthy, and the entire landscape, carved by a relentless sweep and spill, wears the shape of the wind.

Leila explains that every Yazidi, wherever they might be in the world, should have a spiritual brother or sister. She uses the word *axiretê* – the 'next world'. This sibling – not by blood but by heart – has to be a trustworthy companion both in this life and the aftermath.

'So do you have a heavenly sister yourself?'

'I do.' Leila smiles placidly. 'My sister of the next world lives on the upper shores of the Tigris, close to Castrum Kefa. I live downstream. We always joke, whoever dies first will turn into a drop of water, and that way she can easily flow towards the other.'

Arthur tries to join her smile, but he cannot. It makes him uneasy to hear her talk of death, after her harrowing divination. He wants to reach for her hand, find a way to show her that he cares for her well-being. Yet the Yazidi codes of honour are strict. So, he pushes away even the thought of touching her.

'It is a good thing to have a spiritual companion,' says Leila. 'If something bad were to happen in my life, I would go to her for help.'

Arthur listens carefully. A part of him understands. Only those who have often felt unsafe would want to have such a bond with someone outside their immediate family, a kindred spirit that might offer help in one's hour of need.

Her eyes meet his as she asks, 'Do you have a heavenly brother yourself, your own *birayê axiretê*, back in your country?'

Arthur considers the question.

'I had a younger brother . . . Very sadly he died after drinking contaminated water. I have never been able to forgive myself. I was the one who brought the water home.'

And, even though they are talking about completely different things, Leila respects his need to speak about his loss. She listens without judgement, and somehow that is enough, that she attends to what he has to say, the compassion in her eyes, her readiness to share his sorrow.

An emissary storms into the excavation site the next week, bearing a message from the Pasha of Mosul. Wiping the mud from his hands, Arthur reads the letter. He is urgently expected at the pasha's house. It is clear that he has no choice but to attend. It is not so much an invitation as a summons.

'Look at you, Englishman, you have acquired a suntan,' says the pasha, an interpreter by his side.

'I must have. We work every day.'

'So I heard.'

A servant walks in carrying a tray loaded with pastries and coffee in tiny cups. After serving them, he retreats.

'Enjoy,' says the pasha.

Arthur takes a sip: the coffee is too sweet, too strong.

The pasha bites into a halva, watching his guest. 'It has reached my ears that you are spending too much time with heathens.'

Arthur knows he must tread carefully, if not for his sake, then for that of the *faqra* and her people. 'The village is close to the excavation site; it is convenient for me to stay there.'

'But you know they are devil-worshippers.'

'They are good people.' Arthur places his cup on the saucer, his hand slightly trembling.

'You speak Kurdish now, they say.'

'I am learning. It takes time. But I have the best teachers: the children in the village.'

'You are a strange man.' The pasha crams another halva in his mouth. 'About the excavation . . . the English and the French have taken away many statues over the years, small and large. Is it some kind of idolatry? Do your people worship them?'

A moth flies in through the open window. Flapping its wings, it bumps into a lamp, retreats, tries again, an incipient panic building.

'Those statues are displayed in museums,' says Arthur. 'As for me, the pasha knows I am looking for a poem.'

'A poem . . . You travelled all this way for that? Are you sure there is nothing more? You will get something out of it, though – power, money, fame, the admiration of women . . .'

Arthur reddens slightly.

'So it is not *only* a poem,' says the pasha, smiling as though he can see through him. He reaches out for another piece of halva. 'You are not eating?'

'I am known for my poor appetite.'

'But I heard you enjoyed the food of Yazidis.'

Arthur lowers his gaze, lest his face gives away his feelings. Before he can think of anything to say, they hear footsteps in the hall. In a few seconds, the door opens, and a tall, heavily built man with a puckered face and a thick beard marches in, sweeping past the servants.

'Oh, the venerable high qadi!' exclaims the pasha, rising to his feet. 'How generous of you to visit; you should have let me know you were coming, I'd have made preparations.'

'Stop the masquerade,' says the qadi. 'Is this the Englishman you were telling me about?'

Without waiting to be introduced, the judge takes a seat. There is a hardness to his expression that makes Arthur think of dungeons – hidden, closed and dangerous.

'We were talking about the devil-worshippers,' says the pasha. 'Our friend is rather fond of them.'

The qadi says nothing whilst his coffee is being poured. He doesn't pay attention to the sweets on the tray, but he seems keen on the coffee. When the servant leaves the room, the man gives Arthur a sidelong glance.

'Why do you like them? They are not people of the book. Muslims, Christians and Jews are people of the book. But the Yazidis are not.'

Arthur peers out into the garden, though in that moment he sees nothing. The two men's eyes trained on him, assessing his every gesture, he feels so strong an urge to run away that he has to clutch the cushion he is sitting on to suppress it.

The pasha smacks his lips over a mouthful of sugared pastry. 'Venerable qadi, I have a question I could use your advice on. Tell me, if I swore an oath to these Yazidis promising them peace, and in consequence thereof, believing their lives to be safe, they surrendered their arms and trusted me, how far am I bound to keep my word?'

'The Yazidis are *kaffirs*. Therefore you do not need to worry about lying to them. In the eyes of God, it is lawful to snare a heathen; you can deceive them into thinking you mean them no harm and then do with them as you please.'

Arthur feels his heart accelerating. His body reacts to these words faster than his mind can deal with them. He finds his feet, his head pounding.

'You are leaving?' asks the pasha.

'I must go – I am expected at the site.'

'Go, then, but if I were you I would stay away from infidels. I am sure you know the old adage, those who sleep with dogs will rise with fleas.'

That evening, like every other evening, Arthur returns to the village with newly excavated tablets. During dinner with the sheikh and his family, he considers telling them about what happened at the pasha's house, but he wants to refrain from worrying them. Distressed, confused, he eats little, toying with his food, for the first time since he arrived. When he lifts his head, he finds Leila watching him and he has the feeling that she already knows about his meeting with the pasha.

Later, in his room, he cleans the artefacts, brushing away layers of deposits. Then, by the light of an oil lamp, he begins to read one of the tablets. As soon as he deciphers the first line, his chest tightens. Placing a finger on the clay surface, he goes over the signs to make sure he is not imagining it. The wedge-shaped characters swim before his eyes, forming the words he has been yearning to see all this time: 'deluge', 'ark', 'waters on all sides' . . .

He has found the missing portion of the Flood Tablet!

A poem is a swallow in flight. You can watch it soar through the infinite sky, you can even feel the wind passing over its wings, but you can never catch it, let alone keep it in a cage. Poems belong to no one. Arthur has always feared that an epic of such significance, shared orally for millennia before it was written down and scattered over a landscape this vast, is bound to remain out of reach. Even as he embarked on a journey that would take him many miles away from home, setting off in search of the missing verses, he tried to prepare himself for his inevitable failure. But now the swallow has fortuitously alighted in his hands. He can cradle it inside his palms, listen to its heartbeat. He has the eleventh tablet of the *Epic of Gilgamesh* in its entirety.

Tomorrow at first light he will send word to the proprietors of the *Daily Telegraph* that he has succeeded. They will be delighted by the news and rush to publish it. People in England will hear about his 'Assyrian discoveries'. Maybe the prime minister will be interested again, and members of polite society, perhaps even Queen Victoria. There is a chance he may finally be offered a respectable contract by the British Museum. But Arthur is not keen to return home. All his thoughts keep circling, unable to settle, like seagulls when the water swells.

He opens the window and leans over the sill, peering out into the darkness. The smell of wild herbs is intoxicating, and there is a musky fragrance in the air that he cannot identify. Then he sees Leila, sleepwalking, silhouetted against the wall. The moon, a waxing crescent, is liquid tonight. It rains on her hair in silver drops. She threads her way through the garden, slipping in and out of the shadows.

'I found the missing section of the Flood poem tonight,' Arthur whispers, even though he knows she cannot hear him. 'I have to inform the sponsors of my trip, but I do not intend to return any time soon. I would like to stay here longer, studying the tablets, although I cannot pretend that is the only reason.

'Your divination, on Red Wednesday, concerned me. Since then, there hasn't been a day, a wakeful hour, that I haven't thought about it – about you.' He swallows, feeling light-headed. 'In Ancient Sumerian, *ki-ang* was "to love" – strangely, the word meant "to measure the earth". Love was not a feeling or an emotion as much as an anchor that rooted you to a place. All these years I have never yet found myself compelled *to measure the earth*.

'Recently, I came across a medical tablet from Ashurbanipal's library. It said if the patient keeps clearing his throat, and seems lost for words, or talks to himself even when clearly no one can hear him, he is probably suffering from lovesickness. It's interesting how the same word – *hip libbi* – could be used both for emotional and physical distress, a "shattering of the heart", though why that should be so, I cannot explain.' Arthur pauses.

'And, as I was reading this, I suddenly understood: that is what I do when you are around, Leila. I have the same symptoms when I am near you. That is when I knew I . . . love you.'

The silence extends. She tilts her head in his direction.

In that moment he has an uncanny feeling that she can hear him. He feels frightened then. But now that he has begun, he cannot stop speaking.

'I used to help publish books when I was younger. So I read many stories about love, and concluded early on in life that I am not, and never will be, the sort of person who experiences passion. This is not a complaint but a simple statement of truth. I try to approach life in full awareness of my limitations – by which I mean to say that I have no expectations and I shall never even dream of troubling or distressing you in any way.'

Arthur inhales the night air. Everything about him pulses: the river, the earth, the mountain. When he became enamoured of Mesopotamia he does not know, but it has happened and now cannot be undone. An ancient poem spools through his mind. In the distance glow a pair of gems. An oryx is watching him in the darkness. Such a beautiful creature! And, as he observes the animal move with grace, he feels he is glimpsing a remote future, an instant in someone else's life. A time he will no longer inhabit, but a time, nevertheless, that will be connected to this very *moment*, which is already fading, already gone.

He says, 'You and your people have treated me as a God-sent guest, and I am not ignorant of Yazidi codes of honour and modesty, which are absolute and strict, leaving me in no doubt that you are, and will always be, outside of my reach. So it is not with any hope, and it is certainly not with any expectation, that I tell you these things. No one ever needs to know how I feel about you. Not even you – especially not you, Leila.'

The breeze ruffles the loose tresses of her hair. She moves towards him, slowly and effortlessly, as people do in dreams. The shawl draped around her shoulders slips a little. Arthur no longer knows whether she is awake or still sleepwalking. She stands so close he can inhale the scent of her hair, and he thinks of jasmine, clove and geranium. Then she does something he would never have imagined her doing: she kisses him on the cheek – a touch so unselfconscious, it feels not like skin against skin but rather two drops of water finding their way to each other.

Then she is gone.

H—
NARIN

By the River Tigris, 2014

The Ancient Mesopotamians believed mountains to be alive. Borders connecting the terrestrial and the celestial, in-between spaces. The fingers of earth jutting out as though hoping to touch the skies. One of the oldest words found in archaeological excavations is *hursag* – 'mountain'.

In the same tradition, Sinjar is more than a mountain. The highest peak in a hundred-kilometre range, for centuries it has been a sanctuary for the persecuted and the oppressed. Countless people have taken refuge in its small caves and craggy gulleys. At its base nestles the Sharfadin Temple, eight hundred years old, built of pale yellow stone with two cones atop its roof. Every inch of this landscape is holy to the Yazidi faith.

Across the flat, barren expanse and up the rocky terrain moves an endless stream of human beings – raddled bodies push against gravity. Mothers clutch their babies; pregnant women try to protect the precious life within. Children, dazed and disorientated, trudge silently, too scared to cry. An elderly woman begs her family to leave her behind to die. They all keep climbing, hundreds and thousands, carrying their limbs like hollow reeds. Here, above the tree line, there is no shade to be found, and the sun beats down. The heat rising from the baked ground twists and writhes to form a ghostly calligraphy.

When they halt, no longer able to ascend, sweat trickling down their backs, Grandma takes out their only bottle of water. Using its plastic lid as a measure, she fills it carefully, making sure not to waste any, and gives it to Narin.

'I want some, too, please,' says a plaintive voice.

Grandma turns to see a girl of about five, her eyes sunken and sorrowful. She pours water into the lid, offers it to her. Immediately, a boy appears by her side, perhaps her brother.

'Me, too.'

Grandma's hand falters. This is their only bottle and she was planning to save it for Narin. But how can she deny water to any child? Smiling at the boy, she does her best to ration the life-giving liquid. More children line up before her, waiting patiently while their parents watch with doleful eyes. Grandma administers her paltry contribution, allotting a few kind words and a few drops to each, barely enough to moisten the lips and dampen the throat.

That night, on the slopes of Mount Sinjar, no one can sleep. Families huddle together. The temperature, which rose to 48°C during the day, plunges to 10°C. Grandma wraps Narin in her shawl to stop her from shivering. There is a fluency to her moves, a fierce determination.

'We will survive this, my heart.'

Narin's bottom lip sags. She tries very hard not to cry.

Grandma plants kisses on her fingertips, one by one, like she used to do when Narin was little.

'You must listen to me now. Whatever happens, tell it to the water. It will take away all the pain and fear. And, even if you cannot find a flowing stream, remember it is in you. You are made of water.'

Narin cannot stop trembling. Grandma pulls her towards her chest, holding her in a place other than where they are now.

As dawn breaks, a group of boys volunteer to walk to an old fountain at the base of the mountain. They take empty bottles and jugs, as many as they can possibly carry. Then they slowly start their descent.

Further down, where the track crosses a small clearing with clumps of bushes and shrubs, ISIS lie in wait. From their hiding place, the militants watch the youngsters break into a trot at the sight of water. They watch them drink hurriedly and fill their containers to the brim, their hands shaking from nervous haste. And then they watch them turn towards the mountain where their loved ones are waiting. Only then do they open fire. Bullets pierce the jugs, water mixes with blood. Of those who went to the fountain, no one comes back.

Up in the mountain, closer to the cloudless sky, another day goes by. Babies keep crying, though their voices are noticeably weaker. It is the elderly who succumb first, and the toddlers, dying of thirst and exhaustion, one after the other. The families do what they can to conceal the bodies, but the children see everything, even as they stare into the distance, a listlessness to their expressions, an inwardness. Their cheeks look hollow and waxy, as if sculpted out of old candles.

The next day rumours spread that the Americans are dropping caches of supplies. Some tins land on cushioning soil, others hit rocks, splitting and leaking their contents. The young rush to pick up the residues; mothers scrape up food with their fingernails and try to rub it inside their babies' mouths. People say the Americans are also supplying axes and shovels – for digging graves.

None of this largesse reaches their group. On the fourth morning, as death quickens its pace, Grandma gives the last of the water she has so carefully guarded to Narin. She places the drop from a plastic bottle with a blue lid on the girl's tongue as though it were a precious pearl.

She has no way of knowing, but this last drop on Mount Sinjar in August 2014 is the same one that fell on Nineveh one stormy afternoon, thousands of years back, settling in the hair of King Ashurbanipal.

'I must find water.'

Narin, lying down, sits up. 'No, don't go anywhere.'

'My heart . . . children are dying, I must help.'

Grandma removes a strand of hair from Narin's face. The girl's lips are cracked and swollen, and her pallor is so otherworldly that the old woman fears she has already passed the point of no return. 'You need to stay here with the others. Promise? I will ask a family to keep an eye on you.'

Narin lowers her gaze, and, though the day is scorching, she feels a shiver run down her spine. She simply says, 'Be careful, please.'

'I will, I promise. I'll be back soon. Remember, Narin, in the blackest sky there is a star glimmering high above, in the deepest night, a candle burning bright. Never despair. You must always look for the nearest source of life.'

Grandma is a water-dowser.

Grandma is a spring-finder.

Grandma takes out a forked branch that she picked up on the way and whittles it down with a knife. She would much rather use a branch from a willow tree for dowsing, but this will have to do. Should she locate a spring under the ground, it will not be possible to drill, but with the axes and shovels they can dig. There must be water somewhere nearby, and she believes she can find it.

Grandma trudges with heavy steps, her blood thick from dehydration. Even so, her concentration is fierce, her eyes focused on the ground, and in this way she proceeds, hearing nothing but the call of a hidden reservoir.

Time plods on as wearily as she. The wind whistles its songs. Ignoring the protests of her swollen feet and aching limbs, Grandma leaves the trail behind and keeps going. Thorns tear at her dress; thistles snag her ankles. She cannot stop blaming herself. She feels responsible for bringing Narin to Iraq. They should have never left Castrum Kefa, even though Castrum Kefa was leaving them. Her eyes well up and her vision blurs. Sweat runs down her neck. Yet she must carry on. She cannot return to her people empty-handed.

In a little while, her palms go cold, as if she has touched a block of ice. Her forehead furrows. It is never a pleasant experience, dowsing. She is spent, yet the pull she now feels is stronger than she is weak. The rod twitches. Here, under this parched earth, is the source. A tremor rises in her chest and spreads down to her fingertips. It is definitely here, she can sense it. Now she must go back and inform the others that she has found water.

Just as the old woman imagines imparting that news, her breath catches in her throat. Her gut clenches. For she has heard a sound that does not belong here. A low snide snigger. She half turns her head. No further away than the length of her shadow, staring at her from behind the barrel of a gun, is an ISIS militant watching her. She has strayed too close to the base of Sinjar.

'What are you doing, old crone?'

Someone chuckles. The man is not alone. They are patrolling the area, five of them, hunting down Yazidis searching for water.

Grandma clasps her hands to stop them shaking. She looks away. Even if she could speak Arabic, she would not respond. She will not give them the satisfaction of seeing fear on her face.

'You have nothing to say?' says the militant.

'Hey, look what I found here!' shouts another militant from behind sparse bushes nearby. As the men exclaim back and forth, their voices buffeted by the wind, Besma cannot follow what they are saying at first. But then, amid the clamour, she hears a beloved voice. Her entire body freezes.

'Grandma!'

Narin does not like it when her grandmother leaves her behind, so she has followed her.

V

Flood

—O—

ARTHUR

By the River Thames, 1872

Two things happen, almost simultaneously, after Arthur has telegraphed his employers to inform them that he has found the missing portion of the Flood Tablet. He tells the villagers that he has decided to extend his stay so he can keep working by the River Tigris; and yet, unbeknownst to him, his sponsors in England have already announced his imminent return to the River Thames.

A telegram arrives letting him know that his face is printed in newspapers in England, his victory announced to the public, and his travel home booked. His income suddenly cut off, Arthur feels outmanoeuvred, manipulated. Distressed by this turn of events, he tries repeatedly to persuade his employers of the benefit of spending more time in Nineveh, but, no matter how many messages he sends, and how pleading his tone, he cannot convince them.

After a month goes by in limbo, he has no other choice but to bid farewell to the people of Golden Waters and to make preparations for his return to England. Still, all is not lost, he hopes. He believes that, once in London, he will be able to get someone to finance a second expedition, which he would take up immediately.

The night before his departure, he watches Leila from his window one last time. He assumes she is sleepwalking, but, when she turns to face him, her eyes are open and alert. She carries a glass of water, which she splashes in his direction and smiles.

'What does that mean?' asks Arthur.

'We spill water for luck and protection. Go like water, come back like water – freely and easily.'

He takes out his pocketknife and through the open window reaches out to the pomegranate tree. He makes three vertical marks on its bark.

'That's the ancient sign of water,' he says. 'This mark is my pledge – I promise I will come back.'

'You will, I know,' she says. 'But you will return changed, and you will find things changed.'

He shakes his head, even though he senses she is probably right. He feels such a strong desire to hold her then that he has to cross his arms to stop himself. His voice weak, all he can do is to repeat himself.

'I will return. I promise, I will come back.'

In London he is greeted with excitement and elation. The *Daily Telegraph* hails his arrival:

Flood Tablet in England
Arthur Smyth a Hero!

He is a hero, suddenly, in a story written by others. His admirers are legion. They refer to him as an eminent scholar, a noted savant. They say he is not only remarkably intelligent but also brave to have embarked on such a dangerous voyage for the pursuit of knowledge. The extent of the attention takes Arthur aback. When strangers recognize him on the street and ply him with questions, he stammers his way through his replies. When smart gentlemen and elegant ladies demand his company, he fails to reciprocate their breathless enthusiasm. He even struggles to adjust to the weather – forgetting his umbrella, shivering beneath his overcoat, longing for the dry heat that his body has become accustomed to.

He has also acquired enemies. When he was poor, his only adversaries were hunger and cold. But now, as his reputation has grown, there are many who resent his success. The Religious Tract Society attack him, accusing him of producing fake tablets and publishing sham translations from a made-up language. Some go as far as claiming that actually he has never been to Mesopotamia but has instead been hiding in a farmhouse outside London.

Shaken by the response, both the praise and the opprobrium, Arthur has days when he does not wish to leave his temporary lodgings in Bloomsbury. Yet he keeps getting invitations to give talks and participate in colloquiums and conferences.

Then there is Mabel. His fiancée is happy that Arthur is home and even more famous now, and she tells him they must speed up their wedding plans. She draws up an extended guest list, befitting Arthur's improved status, and he cannot find it in him to protest. While he manages to remain outwardly composed and resume his work at the British Museum, where he is welcomed with plenty of admiration and no little envy, deep within he is unsettled. It seems to him that the different strands of his life and personality are unravelling. He has dedicated his life to words, but now, suddenly, words are not enough. He does not know how to articulate this feeling of extreme loneliness and rootlessness that has descended upon him amongst his fellow countrymen. Strangely, he feels like a foreigner in his own homeland.

A month later he receives an invitation to attend a party; it is from an earl renowned for his interest in the arts as well as for his stable of thoroughbred horses. Arthur and his fiancée are requested to be present at a reception at what is described as the peer's *country cottage.*

Mabel is delighted, though her excitement is supplanted by anxiety over appropriate attire. With his newly increased salary, Arthur takes her shopping. They purchase three silk dresses, and gloves, hats and a feather boa to go with them. Arthur is shocked that fabric can cost this much. As for Mabel, she now laments not having matching jewellery. For himself, Arthur rents a dark frock coat lined in rich satin and buys a wide ascot tie. He will have to return the coat later, but he doesn't mind. He doesn't expect to need it ever again.

The 'country cottage' turns out to be a sumptuous mansion. A clamour of laughter and conversation spills from the well-lit balconies and terraces into the manicured gardens. All of London's polite society seems to be here tonight. The gravelled courtyard crunches as carriages pull up, delivering more guests. The rooms abound with cherub statuettes, lacquered cabinets and heavy brocade curtains, their walls hung with silk. Despite the vastness of the residence and ceilings as high as some winter skies, Arthur feels confined, as if trapped inside a snow globe, which at any moment may be picked up and shaken.

Their hostess – an immaculately elegant and rosy-faced woman whose bosom heaves with pearls and a sapphire pendant – is a philanthropist and an art collector. She owns a miscellany of treasures, from Renaissance prints and drawings to Chinese Ming Dynasty porcelain, Japanese lacquer-ware and Mesopotamian antiquities, in which she has a special interest. She is said to have amassed a large number of objects through both family and business ties to British explorers who have visited the region.

'Mr Smyth, I am delighted you could attend our humble gathering,' she says. 'Would you do us the honour of joining some of our other guests in a tour of my little Nineveh?'

'Your little Nineveh, my Lady?'

Smiling, she threads her arm through his. 'Allow me to show you.'

And so while Mabel is escorted to the ballroom, where she sips champagne and smiles at portly, bewhiskered gentlemen,

Arthur follows the countess into an antechamber of the house. His breath catches in his chest the moment he steps in. It is Nineveh indeed! Displayed in profusion are bas-reliefs, wall panels, winged-animal statues and dozens of cuneiform tablets. The artefacts of Mesopotamia have resurfaced in an opulent house outside London.

'What do you think, Mr Smyth?' the countess asks. 'No doubt our modest assembly pales in comparison with the splendours you have seen.'

'Quite dazzling,' Arthur says, swallowing hard. 'But how did you –'

'Some are presents from dear friends. Others I have purchased –' She is distracted by another guest sweeping over to express his delight.

Arthur catches sight of his reflection in the French windows. Sorrow clings to his features. It feels wrong to find the artefacts of Nineveh displayed for the amusement of the wealthy and the powerful. The people of Mesopotamia, the descendants of the scribes who composed the tablets and the artisans who chiselled the statues, will never have a chance to see these pieces. Up until this moment, it had not troubled him that antiquities were to be brought to Europe to be lodged in major museums and institutions. To the contrary: he believed he was rescuing them from obscurity. But seeing them in a private home tonight makes his heart ache.

Slowly, he approaches his reflection and stares at his face. The eyes of the *faqra* look back at him. He misses Leila. The anguish that overcomes him is sharp. If he could only find a back door, he would flee this place and all its glitter.

'Are you coming, Mr Smyth?' the countess asks, glancing at him over her shoulder.

'Yes, my Lady.'

Arthur steps back from the window and follows the group out.

≈

At dinner he and his fiancée are seated on opposite sides of the table, and he finds himself next to an elderly dowager duchess. The lady is thrilled to be placed beside the famous Assyrian scholar just returned from the biblical lands. She watches him curiously from beneath her hooded eyelids. She observes how he barely touches the soup and takes only small bites of the main course – stuffed goose and stewed eel, cooked in nutmeg and port wine.

'You are very quiet, Mr Smyth. Tell us about your expedition. What was it like?'

'Yes, do tell us,' a man with a waxed moustache adds. 'Were you in danger at any point?'

A hush descends as several guests lean forward to hear his response. Arthur takes a sip of wine. He thinks about the horrific fire in Constantinople that swept through entire neighbourhoods, leaving thousands homeless overnight. He thinks about the poverty and destitution he encountered on the road to Mosul. And he thinks about the pasha and the qadi who, over a cup of coffee and a sweet treat, colluded in the harm of an entire community. Since returning home, he has been tormented by memories. He says, 'It was an uneventful journey.'

'You are too modest,' the duchess persists. 'Did you meet any marauders on the way? Did you witness any executions?'

'There were some difficult moments, but I can assure you my trip was no more treacherous than a ride on a Thames pleasure boat.'

Some people laugh; others sigh in disappointment. Arthur notices his fiancée is looking at him with something akin to concern.

At this point their hostess interjects, her voice cutting across the table. 'What about the devil-worshippers? Are they not to be found in those parts?'

Arthur feels himself tense up.

The man with the waxed moustache presses. 'I heard they are in the habit of looting passing caravans and they never wash! An utterly depraved people, and quite wanton, so they say. We are in polite society now – is that why you cannot tell us about the licentiousness of their behaviour?'

Arthur reddens. 'That is not only a lie, it is also a terrible insult.'

The man's face falls.

'The Yazidis are good people, madam, I can assure you.' Arthur turns to his hostess. 'They are generous, kind, protective of their customs and very clean. You may not even enter the sacred Valley of Lalish without first taking a bath and removing your shoes. Not that they would allow outsiders. I fear the Yazidis have been persecuted and horribly misunderstood, not only by many of their Muslim neighbours but also by Christians, including us Western travellers. This is most unfair.' He looks up, his voice rising with emotion. 'They are proud, respectable people and very modest. In truth, ever since I arrived in London I have been longing for their companionship and wanting to return to their homeland.'

It doesn't last long, the silence that descends. The same man chuckles loudly. 'This might come as a surprise for some but is actually quite common. Scholars lose their heads over their subjects; writers fall under the spell of their fictional characters; explorers become infatuated with the places they visit. Our dear friend has just confirmed for us a typical case of this unnatural and irrational attachment. And this proves that he is a good scholar!'

They nod and resume their conversations, the distraction over. The countess doesn't seem offended. But no one asks Arthur anything else for the rest of the evening. Whilst people on either side of him engage in lively chatter, he sits soundlessly, his forehead wrinkled in discomfort. His gaze falls on Mabel. His fiancée is smiling equably as she listens to the gentleman next to her. Unlike him, she is happy amongst these people. She is glowing. For a fleeting second she turns, and her eyes glance over him coldly.

You go to distant lands hoping to find something entirely different from what you had at home, never suspecting that you will return

391

a changed person. Arthur cannot say exactly when it happened, at what crossroads, but he is not the same man any more. Mesopotamia keeps calling him. In dream after dream, he is walking on liquid deserts, or sailing on shifting sands, only to wake up with a feeling of emptiness. He is worried that he has left something behind, a part of him that was fragile but genuine, mislaid in that region whose customs he does not always understand and whose myriad faiths and sects leave him perplexed, where even the water has its own distinctive taste; and yet, despite all that unfamiliarity, it has taken hold of his heart. The Tigris has seeped into his life and solidified, like dripping wax.

They get married in the summer. Mabel is a picture of beauty in her wedding gown with its satin fitted bodice and ostrich feathers, a long train she must take care not to trip over. She brings a dowry sufficient for them to rent a spacious first-floor flat in a Bayswater townhouse, with sash windows that are high and draughty, and a faint odour of mould that invades your senses after you walk in. They regret that an entire house with a large parlour, basement, attic and trellised garden is beyond their reach. Arthur may be celebrated around the country and respected in scholarly circles, but this does not translate into a high income. Most of his colleagues at the museum have private means, and do not have to rely on their salary alone. Even so, Arthur does not seem troubled by the arrangement. Compared with the squalor of his childhood home, these surroundings are palatial.

He starts to wear his hair longer. He also grows a beard. For years he maintained a clean-shaven look, except for a short spell with mutton-chop sideboards, following the fashion set by the late Prince Albert. He does not enjoy visiting barbers, although there is some pleasure to be found in sitting in a chair as hot towels are applied to his face and being shaved with a cut-throat razor over a fragrant bowl of steaming water. Fortunately, his new preference aligns with the latest vogue. Many men are sporting facial hair these days. He is still fastidious about grooming and personal hygiene – using almond oil and pomades. Bear's grease, though more durable, has an unappealing smell. Sometimes he outlines his eyes with kohl, an adornment learnt from villagers by the Tigris. But he never dares to go out like that.

These daily rituals are closely observed by Mabel. 'Wouldn't it be better if you were to shave properly? Wouldn't they respect you more?'

'But I like it like this,' Arthur says. 'I am tempted to have long locks hanging down my face, like Pterelaus, the Greek king. I hope no one will cut my hair in my sleep.'

She doesn't return his smile. She doesn't understand the reference. It is not the first time that Arthur feels keenly the gulf between them. He tells himself that she wants people to respect him because she loves him. The other possibility is too hurtful: that her focus on his reputation might have nothing to do with love and everything to do with their standing in the community, with his achievements chiefly a ladder to social advancement. Despite her comfortable upbringing, she is aware that the success of her husband's career is the only route to stability and fulfilment, that is if she wants to build a family, as she does.

He eats better these days. In the mornings they have bacon and eggs, smoked haddock, bread rolls, marmalade. Sometimes they get blanquettes of lamb, croquettes of fish for lunch. But Arthur always finds food a trial. That's the one thing he hasn't shaken off – the memory of hunger. The cramps shooting through his insides are still sitting in his stomach like stones. He feels the need to check daily whether they are out of provisions. He may have managed to lift up his head and change his prospects, but the ground beneath his feet never feels solid or secure.

Just as he used to hand over his earnings first to his father and then to his mother, he now gives his salary to his wife. He puts aside a small amount for his soaps and colognes, and the rest is for Mabel to apportion. He has asked her to save a bit, whenever she can, but Mabel likes the latest styles. The fashions of the day change fast, and each month their debts to the emporiums of Regent Street grow.

Arthur never complains about these shopping sprees that they can't really afford. He vows he will work harder to finish the book he has begun writing. That will bring in extra earnings. But soon Mabel will need new clothes. She is pregnant. Even though the manuals for sexual relations maintain that 'without an excitation of lust, or the enjoyment of leisure in the venereal act, conception cannot take place', this claim seems quite mistaken. Arthur and Mabel have separate rooms, and they have reached an agreement that he should visit her twice a month to fulfil his marital duties, on days of her choosing.

'Since we now have a child on the way – or perhaps two, as twins run in your family – isn't it about time you asked for a promotion?' Mabel asks. 'Have you not finished with those petti-fogging old tablets now? Really! Fiddling and fidgeting all day with dirty bits of clay.'

'But this is not some temporary work. It will take time,' Arthur says. 'The *Epic of Gilgamesh* is hugely important. This poem is even older than the Greek myths, imagine!'

Mabel holds herself rigid.

'Take Achilles and his companion Patroclus. That story, fabulous as it is, might very well be inspired by Gilgamesh and Enkidu –'

Mabel interrupts with a wave of her hand. 'If it is so import-ant, why don't you tell the museum to increase your salary to a decent amount? How do they expect us to raise a family on such a paltry allowance?'

'We shall manage somehow.'

'Somehow? Tell me how. You have your head in the clouds.'

Arthur's shoulders hunch forward. For a moment he seems lost for words. He hardly speaks for the rest of the day.

Still, every morning he wakes early, rushing to the office. He feels guilty for leaving Mabel on her own, though there is always

Florence, their domestic, who comes in daily to clean. As her pregnancy advances, he will have to be more present at home. He is determined to be a better father than his own father has been to him. And so for a while it seems enough – his book, his wife, the baby or babies on the way . . . and working doggedly on a poem as old as recorded time. He tells himself that he doesn't need much else. Yet there is something tugging at his heart, nesting deep in his chest. A trapped bird, it flaps its wings, beating hard against its cage, sinking its claws into his flesh. He is afraid of bringing it out, lest he cannot corral it again.

Last thing at night and first thing in the morning, when he retreats into the maze of memory, he thinks of the land and the river and the woman he left behind in Mesopotamia.

H

ZALEEKHAH

By the River Thames, 2018

O n Friday evening Zaleekhah is last to leave the Centre
for Ecology and Hydrology. She enjoys working late
hours. The lab transforms into a different place when
there is no one around, the silence in the building almost tangible.
It reminds her of a rock standing sentinel by a riverside, weighed
down by accretions of moss and the passage of time, a steady
observer of things that fade as all around it plants and smaller life
forms decompose and spring back to life.

Under the light of an angled desk lamp, Zaleekhah peers
into the microscope. On the glass slide, moving ceaselessly, are
thousands of unicellular microorganisms. The bacterium *Vibrio
cholerae*. Minuscule culprits capable of eradicating human lives.
Although it is easy to assume that cholera, widely eliminated
in industrialized societies, is no longer a threat, the deadly disease has never entirely disappeared, still cutting swathes through
populations in developing countries. With the destruction of the
environment and contamination of aquatic supplies, it is only a
matter of time before new cases erupt worldwide. In merely a
few decades, one in four children across the world will be living
in places where water is so polluted that drinking it will kill them.

She takes off her latex gloves, removes her safety goggles. Gestures she has repeated so many times that they have become daily
rituals. The tight straps have left a red weal around her eyes, as

they always do. She tidies the papers on her desk, then turns on her computer and enters the latest data from the files a researcher dropped in her in-tray earlier.

In the last six years, she and her team have studied over three hundred locations across the globe to see how climate change is affecting their signature characteristics, including flow volumes, silting and biodiversity. Every day they download data from gauging stations – from South America to Australia and eastern USA – noting the levels of water. The changes in hydroclimate come with an increasing risk of inundation. Zaleekhah knows there is no region in the world that is safe from flooding.

Today she enters the data from the River Tigris. She has been keen to work with scientists from the Fertile Crescent, a particularly vulnerable region, which in this very century will disappear completely. The arc sweeping from the Mediterranean to the Persian Gulf is fast drying up. Shared by Iraq, Iran, Syria and Turkey, the largest wetland ecosystem in the Middle East is dying.

Zaleekhah has always found it mystifying that Uncle has never shown any interest in going back to the region, not even for a holiday. He has cut all ties with his childhood, like a discarded toy that he has outgrown. She remembers a conversation they once had in her student days about how various types of salmon, born in fresh water but migrating to oceans, return to their birthplace to die. Uncle had listened, but a curtain had closed in his face. And, although they had talked about fish and nothing else that day, Zaleekhah knew they both thought the same thing: Uncle was not like that. He would never return to the waters where he was born. He had swum as far and as fast as he could – away from his motherland.

An hour later, Zaleekhah steps out of the building. As she closes the door, her phone rings. It's Helen.

'Sorry to call you so late, darling.'

'That's all right. Is everything okay?'

'I've incredible news, I couldn't wait to share. We found a donor!'

'Really?' Zaleekhah's face lights up. 'That's amazing.'

'Yes . . . yes . . . My father took care of everything.'

'Fantastic! I'm so happy for you – and all the family.'

'Oh, thank you! I'm still processing the news.'

Zaleekhah retrieves her keys from the bottom of her over-stuffed handbag. Switching the phone to her other hand, she locks the door. 'You must be so relieved.'

'I am . . . fingers crossed. I don't want to take anything for granted. Not any more. I'm so afraid that something will go wrong last minute.'

'Sweetheart, you can't think like that. It's all going to be fine. So which hospital will she be at? Guy's? Chelsea?'

'Neither. We're going to Istanbul – it's a top-notch clinic, Dad assures me. He knows the doctor in charge. We'll all travel together.'

'Istanbul? When?'

'In about three weeks. They'll let us know when to come.' Helen pauses. 'Could you maybe take some time off?'

'Definitely,' Zaleekhah says. 'I'll make sure I'm free. I want to be there.'

'Oh, that means the world to me. And, umm, Zaleekhah . . . my father can be overbearing at times, but he means well. Don't be too upset if he tries to dissuade you from going through with the divorce. He's been so preoccupied with Lily that he didn't have time to have a proper talk with you, but it's definitely been on his mind. I'm sure he'll now embark on his new campaign – SOZM, Save Our Zaleekhah's Marriage. You're aware that it's his way of showing how much he loves you. He'll move heaven and earth for the people he loves.'

'Yes, I know that.'

'Honestly, every daughter adores her father, but this whole ordeal made me realize what a special man he is. Incredibly giving, supportive. Same for me, same for you, there is no difference at all. He's always there for his family, any time we need him.'

'True,' says Zaleekhah. 'I never forget how lucky we are. I just need to gently break it to him I'm not going back to Brian. I don't see that happening.'

Helen sighs. 'All right, darling. It's your call. I love you. I'll book Istanbul tickets when the time comes.'

'Sounds good. I love you, too.'

The next evening Zaleekhah invites Nen for dinner. Since she is not a good cook and she doesn't have much by way of kitchenware in the houseboat, she orders food from a Lebanese restaurant nearby. *Baba ghanoush*, tabbouleh, falafel, pita chips, rice and lentils. She has used paper plates and wooden spoons, recycled and biodegradable, instead of proper ones, knowing that Nen wouldn't mind.

A little after seven, running a bit late, Nen turns up wearing a black-and-white handprinted blazer made of salvaged vintage fabrics and deadstock garments, flowing trousers and a long silver hoop hanging from one earlobe. She carries a backpack slung over one shoulder and has a wooden crate piled with oranges in her hands.

'What's this?'

'Your monthly stock of vitamin C.'

She opens the backpack and takes out a coffee-maker, a bag of coffee and a bunch of dried lavender. 'I had a spare machine at home, so I brought it with me, in case you'd like to keep it.'

'I would, very much. Thank you!'

Smiling, Nen tips the crate over by the armchair, the oranges rolling in all directions, like miniature fiery suns, brightening up the entire space.

'Now, do you have a tablecloth?' asks Nen.

'I have a shawl.'

'Perfect.'

They spread it over the upended crate, turning it into a little table. It looks charming, like something out of a children's book. It looks easy. Nen makes lots of things easy.

The food, much to Zaleekhah's relief, turns out to be delicious, and, slowly, she manages to relax. Maybe her simple dinner won't be a failure after all. A breeze wafts into the houseboat through the window – the faint scent of the river, full of promise. Zaleekhah finds herself talking about the latest data from the Tigris, the alarming drop in its water levels. Nen is a good listener, attentive and patient, and Zaleekhah realizes she enjoys telling her about her work.

'It's not only climate change,' Zaleekhah says. 'The construction of dams in Turkey, upstream, makes everything worse for Iraqis, downstream. It drastically reduces the flow of water. When one country builds massive dams, it has consequences for its neighbours.'

'It's so sad,' says Nen. 'These legendary rivers, the Tigris and the Euphrates . . . born from a woman's tears.'

'What's that?' asks Zaleekhah. 'I don't know that story.'

'Oh, it's quite a story.'

'Tell me.'

Nen pours herself a glass of water from the tap in the kitchen, checking whether the sink is leaking. She sits back on the floor, which she finds more comfortable than the stool or the armchair. Then she says:

'*In those days, in those far-off days . . . in olden times . . .* the sky and the land were one. The world was a blank tablet, waiting for the first words to form. Everything was in harmony – bitter waters and sweet waters blended seamlessly. *Tiamat* was the goddess of the sea – the saltwater – and *Apsu* was the god of springs – the fresh water. They were very different, but they fell in love.'

'Then what happened?'

'From their union rose other deities. When her beloved husband was killed, Tiamat wanted revenge. She was formidable, strong-willed. She assembled an army of mythical creatures and charged against the forces of *Marduk* – her arch-enemy. The war went on for a long time, but Marduk came up with a plan. He asked the wind to enter Tiamat's mouth. Her body grew as big as the world. He then easily killed her with an arrow. Earth was created from her decomposing body, and from her crying eyes sprang the two legendary rivers of Mesopotamia: Tigris and Euphrates.'

'That's brutal,' says Zaleekhah.

Nen takes an orange and starts peeling it. 'Compared with the Mesopotamian Creation story, Adam-and-Eve-and-the-forbidden-fruit is a walk in the park.'

'So both rivers were made from a woman's tears.' Zaleekhah pauses, and then hears herself saying, 'I'm so tired of feeling sad all the time.'

If Nen is surprised to hear this, she does not show it. She nods, a softness to her gaze.

'I envy happy people,' says Zaleekhah. 'Not in a jealous way – it's more that I'm puzzled by them. I want to study them – put them under a microscope like a specimen. How do they even do it? Whereas I'm always off-balance.'

Nen offers Zaleekhah half of her orange. She says when we look at a person all we see in that moment is a partial image of them, often subconsciously biased. They appear successful and content, and so we conclude there must be something wrong with us, since we cannot be more like *them*. But that image is not the full reality and nor are we that simple or static. 'We are all like clay tablets, chipped around the edges, hiding our little secrets and cracks.'

'Not everyone, though.'

'Everyone, I promise you. Is there such a thing as absolute happiness? Never-ending success? A perfect marriage? A quick fix to cure anxiety? We want to believe there is – just like Gilgamesh wanted to believe he could live forever. Then we're defeated, humbled. We learn to accept there'll always be something amiss, something broken, and unless we are kind to ourselves it won't change, this feeling of incompleteness.'

'I guess you're right. Although I can't imagine Uncle being like that . . . He's experienced many hardships, but he never lets them affect him.'

Nen shifts in her seat. 'I'm not so sure,' she says with conviction, as though this is something she has thought about before. 'Of everyone in your family, even though he seems the most successful, I think he might be the most damaged.'

Zaleekhah fills a glass of water and sits next to Nen, their shoulders touching. She takes a sip. There is a beat of silence as she puts her hand on Nen's. She says, 'I like talking to you.'

'I like talking to you, too.' Nen turns to look at her fully. Her face hovers only inches away.

Zaleekhah has never kissed a woman before, and, when she does, Nen tastes of oranges.

Sitting so close, Nen's body feels bigger than Zaleekhah had imagined it; her scent is intoxicating. Freckles spill across her chest, and there is a coppery tint to the hair on her arms, and her left ear is slightly longer than her right ear, or perhaps it is just a trick of the fading light; and all these details, trivial as they are, make Zaleekhah smile. She trails a tentative finger along Nen's lips, curved and deep crimson, a touch so hesitant that it exposes her disbelief at what she is doing. As though she can read Zaleekhah's mind, sense her uncertainty, Nen stays still, but holds her with a long and limpid gaze.

'You are so beautiful,' says Nen.

'I am not. I've never been pretty.'

'You serious?'

Zaleekhah shrugs.

'Look at me,' says Nen.

'I am.'

'No, honestly – look into my eyes. You don't see yourself in there?'

Zaleekhah peers closer. 'There's someone in there.'

'Use my eyes as a mirror to admire your own beauty.'

'Is that poetry?' Zaleekhah smiles. 'You write?'

'I wish I could. I'm just a devoted reader.'

Zaleekhah tilts her head, remembering their earlier conversation. 'The Forgotten Goddess – you said she was the patron of storytellers and poets. Will you tell me more about her?'

'Oh, I can talk about her forever – you need to stop me if I start rambling.'

'I like your rambling.'

'All right, then,' says Nen as she rises to her feet in one sinuous motion. 'But first let me make us coffee.'

They called her *Nisaba*, though, depending on the place and the era, she went by other names, too: *Nidaba, Naga, Se-Naga* . . . The goddess of grain and harvest, the one who holds sway over the rain, directing every drop that falls from the sky. In her pictures, she carries, in one hand, a stalk of wheat – the symbol of life, renewal and rebirth; in her other hand, she holds a gold stylus and a tablet of lapis lazuli. The roots of agriculture and the roots of literature are intertwined, and it is none other than Nisaba who braids them like a lock of her hair.

Nisaba is born of the union of heavens and earth, realms that seem so different and distant that it may not be clear what they have in common, and thus her gift – the art of writing – will always represent a desire to efface dualities, dissolve hierarchies and transcend boundaries.

As Mesopotamian cities burgeon and trade flourishes, the need for record-keeping increases. Each transaction must be noted with precision – goods, prices, debts . . . Yet human memory is fallible.

Mnemonic markers – scoring impressions into the bark of trees, scratching charcoal shapes on stones, painting lines on the bones of sheep – are no longer enough. A new method is called for. Something so versatile that it can link numbers and sounds not only to the inanimate but even to abstract ideas and intangible feelings. A more advanced form of script becomes imperative. Writing as a way to remember. But how?

The rivers help, as they always do. The Tigris and the Euphrates bring in huge amounts of silt. The fine-grained tilth, stiff and sticky, is ideal for moulding into tablets when wet, and strong when baked or left to dry in the sun. On these compact slabs the Ancient Mesopotamians enter the daily minutiae – the weight of a sack of barley, the price of beer, the number of workers on a construction site . . . As cuneiform, originating under the Sumerians, is inherited by the Babylonians and Assyrians, the scribes across the region discover that words, once impressed on stone, live longer than those who have imagined them. Stories venture beyond city walls, traverse deserts and span ravines. To write is to free yourself from the constraints of place and time. If the spoken word is a trick of the gods, the written word is the triumph of humans.

Thus Nisaba's fame grows. In cylinder seals she appears with her long, luxurious locks of hair carefully groomed into plaits, manifesting controlled, cultivated fecundity, and her eyes dark as the feathers of a starling. She wears a flounced robe, and the jewelled diadem on her head shines like moonlit waters. From her ears dangle stalks of wheat or clusters of dates, jingling with every step she takes. People incise her symbol on monuments and hang her image above the thresholds of their homes. Her name is carved on temple walls, inscribed on amulets. She is the patron of archivists and librarians; the one who whispers into the ears of balladeers and storytellers. They invoke her when in need of inspiration. She comes to their aid in moments of confusion. She is the chronicler of time, the collector of stories, the custodian of memories.

The goddess of writing documents the good and the bad: celebrations and lamentations, victories and defeats, beauties and atrocities, all that makes humans resilient and vulnerable in equal degree. In parts of Mesopotamia, she is so highly venerated that she is not only entrusted with recounting legends and tales but also with settling disputes and mending grievances. Justice, if it is to be at all meaningful, needs to be recorded.

When Mesopotamian bards recite ballads of heroism and heartbreak, it is Nisaba who plants a kiss on their lips. When students wake at the crack of dawn to practise their letters, it is Nisaba who guides their faltering fingers. The wedge-shaped script, advancing from city to city, becomes more elaborate with the years, as does the goddess herself. It is not just those whose task it is to catalogue merchandise and register transactions who refer to her in their writings; scholars, priests, mathematicians and astronomers do so as well. The temple at Eresh, dedicated to Nisaba, is known as *Esagin*, the 'House of Lapis Lazuli', for this is her stone and this is her colour. The goddess of knowledge and storytelling is imagined in the deepest shade of blue.

Centuries pass by; time leaves its traces like the bronze patina on a mirror's surface. The sun transcribes many a golden arc across the Mesopotamian skies, and Nisaba evolves into the goddess of literacy, literature and libraries. 'Glory be to my lady' is emblazoned on the walls of scribal schools. Clay tablets end with the same four words:

Praise be to Nisaba

Writing is a craft like any other. It must be learnt from the masters, pursued with dedication and practised daily, until your fingers blister, your back hunches, your eyesight starts to dim. Schools spring up far and wide. Rules are strict, mistakes not tolerated. Both male and female scribes study at these tablet houses, though the numbers of the latter are dwindling fast. Most of the remaining ones retreat to a cloister in Sippar, where they find the freedom to work, at the cost of becoming isolated from the rest of society. Enheduanna, the high priestess at Ur, a poet who breathes life into words and a devotee of Nisaba, senses things are deteriorating. She now has enemies everywhere. There are those who say that women should not be allowed to rule or counsel leaders, nor should they be allowed to write.

And so it begins, the slow death of the goddess of writing. There are still sanctuaries dedicated to her, and she is remembered and revered by some, but they keep their thoughts to themselves. Nisaba is a name to be uttered with caution.

In the time of Hammurabi of Babylon, a new fear enters hearts. The harshest punishments are set into laws, terror inscribed in stone. The code favours might, the code favours men – and therefore women, children, slaves, outsiders and men who do not have any power or wealth are all deemed inferior. Hammurabi's wrath is particularly reserved for those who transgress. A wife who accidentally hurts her husband's testicles is to be punished more severely than a habitual thief or even a cold-blooded murderer. Women accused of neglecting their homes are cast into the river. The Tigris, ever patient with the ways of humans, receives their bodies.

In the present order, the goddess of writing is stripped of her powers, all of which are now assigned to a male god – *Nabu*. From now on Nabu will be the patron of literacy and storytelling. Nabu will embody knowledge, memory and wisdom. And in hundreds of schools, young scribes are made to finish their assignments with these four words:

Praise be to Nabu

As for Nisaba, she is transmuted into 'the loving wife of Nabu' – faithful, giving and dutiful. Next she becomes his diligent secretary, helpfully hovering in the background. The only vestige of her glorious past is a lapis lazuli pendant in the shape of a stylus that hangs around her neck. Thus expunged not all at once but by degrees, Nisaba retreats into the shadows, from where she watches Nabu gather accolades and adulations. How fast he ascends! As Marduk is crowned the king of the gods, Nabu is declared the son of the king of the gods. He stands tall and proud by his father's throne, carrying in his hands the blue tablet that once belonged to Nisaba. By the time of the sixth king of the first dynasty of Babylonia, writing is no longer regarded as a suitable occupation for women.

Nabu's fame will continue to soar, spreading from Mesopotamia to the Mediterranean basin, where he is embraced by multiple civilizations – Greek, Roman and Christian. But the tradition of Nisaba will remain rooted in the very place where it was born, and it will also perish there, her tablets broken, her stylus buried by the banks of the Tigris. The transition complete, the goddess of writing will be erased – the lady of memory forgotten for eternity.

By the time Nen finishes telling the story, the light has faded in the houseboat, and the few possessions within it have transformed into shadows of themselves. Even though Zaleekhah has drunk nothing more intoxicating than Nen's coffee, her head is swimming.

'It's getting late,' says Nen, rising to her feet. 'I should make a move.'

'Wait.' Zaleekhah is not sure what she wants to say, or what she wants to do, but it feels important that Nen be around when she works it out. 'Would you like to stay here tonight? I have spare pyjamas I could lend you – if you'd like.'

Nen sits back, coughs a little.

'What?'

'Nothing. It's just I usually sleep naked, but I'll wear your pyjamas – gladly.'

Zaleekhah flushes – good thing it is too dark for Nen to notice. Or maybe she has already, for Nen now says, 'We can fall asleep holding hands, nothing else – we'll be like river otters.'

407

'I like otters,' says Zaleekhah. 'They link paws so they don't drift away from each other. That's how they survive.'

And that is what they do that night. Downstairs on the single bed, they lie down, fingers entwined, listening to the swishing of water against the hull.

'I can hear lost rivers,' Zaleekhah says.

'I can hear your heartbeat,' says Nen.

Zaleekhah does not expect to fall asleep easily, but she does, feeling a surprising sense of calm, almost at peace.

At 3.34 a.m. Zaleekhah wakes up with a start. She props herself up in bed, her chest tight. She stays still, listening to the gentle rhythmic breathing by her side. She inches away carefully, taking her time to relinquish Nen's hand. In the grid of moonlight from the shutters, Nen's body is a softly undulating silhouette. As quietly as she can, Zaleekhah leaves the bed and climbs the stairs.

Upstairs, she drops into the armchair and closes her eyes. Time stills.

'Zaleekhah?'

It is Nen. Her hair tousled, her feet bare.

'Are you all right? Why're you sitting in the dark?'

'It's bright enough.' Zaleekhah gestures at the moon.

'How long have you been here on your own?' Nen takes a step closer. 'Have you been crying?'

Zaleekhah wipes her eye with the back of her hand. 'I'm fine. I couldn't sleep; didn't mean to disturb you.'

Nen pulls up the stool and perches by her side. Then she says, tenderly, 'When will you tell me?'

'Tell you what?'

'You were there – I think.' Nen draws in a breath, releases it. 'You were with your parents on the night they died. I've been thinking about it – thinking about *you*. Your reaction to water, so visceral, and your sorrow so close to the surface, barely submerged. I think this is what happened. When they travelled to the Middle East, your parents didn't leave you in London. It was a family holiday. You were seven years old. Something terrible occurred on that trip. You survived; they didn't.'

A strange noise comes out of Zaleekhah's lips. Almost a scream but also so faint as to be nearly inaudible.

'My father loved being outdoors.' Zaleekhah shakes her head. 'He was always planning some trip – Hadrian's Wall, Isle of Skye, the Lake District, Yosemite . . . But my mother desperately wanted him to see the River Tigris. It was her dream to show him the land she came from. They saved up, skipped summer holidays so they could take time off in the autumn. The plan was to travel from Antalya to Antioch and from there to Mosul. My father was a cautious man. He'd never let us sleep on a dangerous site. This was a safe place to camp. There were cabins. He wanted to stay in one of those, but I insisted on a tent. I thought it'd be a nice adventure. We set up camp close to a stream. Too close. It was raining that evening, not much, though. The flood came so fast –'

'How did you escape?'

Zaleekhah throws her head back, tears streaming down her face. 'I woke up in the middle of the night needing the bathroom. I called for my mum, but she was too deeply asleep. I checked the time. It was 3.34 a.m. I couldn't possibly hold it till morning. I was scared to go to the campsite toilets, but I could pee behind the bushes. So I sneaked out. I was walking back when the flood came –'

Nen takes her hand. 'I'm so sorry.'

'I saw the torrent wash away the tent. My father's body turned up a few kilometres downstream, but they couldn't find my mother's until a day later, trapped in the reeds.' Zaleekhah lowers her chin. 'It's all my fault.'

'It is not,' whispers Nen. 'Tell me, if no help came until next morning . . . did you spend the night there alone?'

409

Zaleekhah does not answer. Nor does Nen push for a response. They sit silently for a moment, absorbing the weight of what has been left unsaid. Outside the window, the silvery currents of the Thames beat on.

Of the night at the campsite in Turkey, Zaleekhah can remember only traces. Her mind has deftly wiped the rest, leaving just smudges here and there. By contrast, she can recall the next day in minute detail: the column of police cars, a portly, florid-faced male officer chain-smoking, cigarettes piling up in the ashtray, a Turkish flag hanging at the entrance and the radio echoing tinnily from somewhere in the building, in a language so different from her own.

But what she most vividly remembers is Uncle Malek – how he strode into the police station, tall and solicitous, having just flown in from London, a suitcase in one hand and a gift purchased from the airport in the other – a pretty shawl, embroidered around the edges. He did not ask her any questions. He did not press her for an account of what happened. He draped the soft material around her shoulders, though the day was hot, and he told her she would survive this pain and would grow up to be a happy, successful woman. And, although his words were assertive, and his insistence on success disconcerting, the shawl felt comforting somehow; it was something she could disappear beneath, and she did not take it off until they arrived in England.

After that Zaleekhah did not talk for a long time. When she wanted to make herself understood, she would gesture or scribble on a piece of paper. The Maleks never forced her to speak, tiptoeing around her silence as if it were a sleeping baby not to be disturbed. A year later, one morning at breakfast, watching Helen struggle to open a jar of strawberry jam, Zaleekhah leant forward and said, 'Let me try.' That her first words should have been so commonplace caused Helen to gape in astonishment, but Uncle Malek pretended everything was normal, nonchalantly passing her the jar. She has no recollection of whether she managed to open the lid, but from that day on she communicated as most people do, in speech.

A couple of times Aunt Malek suggested the child should see a therapist, but Uncle was adamant that what she needed was a stable family environment and goals high enough to keep her mind busy. The family took good care of her. When they thought she was out of earshot, they spoke of her in whispers. She heard them sometimes.

ARTHUR

By the River Thames / Tigris, 1876

The next time Arthur travels to Nineveh, everything feels different. He does not have a private sponsor as before, no newspaper supporting him. Leaving his family behind proves difficult now that the twins are old enough to miss him. They line up by the door, their faces scrunched up with apprehension. He holds the girl in one arm, the boy in the other, promising to bring them presents.

His son has drawn a picture of him with a crown and a sword. 'Are you going to Messy-pota-mina, Papa?'

'Yes, Mesopotamia,' Arthur corrects, though a part of him wonders what the name means to a child who has never left his little corner of London. 'What's the sword for, young man?'

'To kill the barbarians,' pipes up the boy.

Arthur quails. 'They are not barbarians. They are people just like you and me. It is the land where civilization began.'

The boy purses his lips.

'One day, I'll take you with me, and you'll see for yourself.'

A smile, revealing missing teeth, blooms on the child's face.

'I'll treasure this and keep it with me all the time.' Arthur stows the picture inside his jacket. He looks towards his wife. But Mabel hangs back, holding herself ramrod straight. All week she has been markedly withdrawn. She wants him to know she has not forgiven him for deciding to travel again so soon, when the children are still young.

'I will return as fast as I can,' says Arthur.

'And when might that be?' says Mabel. 'You could have asked the museum to send someone else.'

'But I know the region and I can read the tablets. I am the most suitable candidate. I have worked on the poem for so long.'

'For too long! For the love of Christ! What kind of man neglects his family for a *poem*?' She lifts her chin. 'Or maybe you are deceiving me. You have an Oriental lover, and that's why you are so desperate to return.'

Arthur flushes red.

'Come with me, little ones! It's past your bedtime,' chirps the nursemaid, ushering the children inside.

They leave the couple standing in the doorway, eyes fixed on their shoes as if looking for scuffs.

'I do not wish to upset you,' says Arthur. 'I do not have a lover there – or anywhere. I'm duty-bound to go, but it is more than that . . . when I read the tablets, broken as they are, I feel complete.'

Mabel shakes her head.

'Ever since I saw the winged sculptures as a boy, I felt destined to go to Nineveh. There are men who are adept at politics, business, warfare . . . My father was gifted with his hands – he could carve exquisite woodwork. My talents do not lie in any of those directions, but, when I am alone with ancient tablets, it is as if they were written for me. I know how preposterous it sounds, but that is how I feel.'

'Pray, stop. You are embarrassing yourself,' Mabel says flatly. 'Such sentimentality. No gentleman would speak in this manner. It is unseemly – no wonder people find you effeminate, and surely you know that, with your foppish clothes and mawkish poems. I do not mind if you have a mistress. I might have cared once, but by now it is a matter of complete indifference to me. The plain truth is you love your job more than you love us.'

'But you knew what my work meant to me when you married me. Back then you regarded it fondly.'

'I did, true.' Her voice rises. 'I was even prepared to be interested in your old bits of clay. You seemed different from the other young men I met. I found your quirkiness rather endearing. But I am tired of it. I certainly didn't expect to have to spend long months on my own, worrying about money all the time. I thought your responsibilities as a husband and father would make you into a man.'

'I see,' says Arthur, and then there is nothing more to say.

Arthur Smyth arrives in Constantinople in the early summer of 1876. The city is a hive of frenzied activity, bedecked with bright purple, this being the season when the Judas trees are still in bloom. Against the blue of the Bosporus, the branches burst into a riot of ethereal blossoms. The colours, exquisite though they are, cannot mask the tension percolating in the air. There are uprisings in the Balkans, and discontent is spreading fast across the Ottoman Empire.

As he disembarks from the ship, the news has broken that the sultan has been found dead in a pool of blood, having slit his wrists. There are rumours that Abdulaziz might have been assassinated, his death made to look like a suicide. The city swarms with conspiracies.

'Delighted to see you again,' says the ambassador. 'This time your *firman* will be granted faster, I've every reason to believe. But, if I were you, I wouldn't rush.'

'You told me this before, sir: *As they say, in this part of the world, if you run too fast, you will miss the safe place where you might have hidden yourself.*'

The man's mouth hangs slightly open. 'Your memory is outstanding. But what I meant is that there are obstacles on the way.'

'Obstacles, sir?'

'Plague, for one thing . . . The last I heard it is ravaging the area south of the River Tigris. There is also cholera. And, in the north, several tribes are at war. It will be a perilous journey.'

'I need to be back in Nineveh, sir.'

As soon as Arthur receives his *firman*, he leaves Constantinople. At every place he sojourns, he makes sure to write to his family, describing the people he has met, the food he has sampled. He adds drawings, knowing how much his children will enjoy them. He depicts the landscape in detail – grassy pastures and fields of alfalfa, slopes tufted with copses of oak and birch, hidden waterfalls that take you by surprise, streams with water so fresh you would never wish to stop drinking. Always he finishes by saying how much he misses them, sending kisses to his 'little cherubs'. Repeatedly, he asks Mabel to write back, informing her of the towns he will be passing through so that she knows where to address letters. But his wife does not reply.

Her words keep ringing in his ears – *You have an Oriental lover* . . .

As Arthur approaches the Yazidi village, his heart starts to pound so loudly he worries his companions might hear it. He observes the small houses with flat roofs, the conical tombs, the fruit trees . . . they are all there, just as he remembers them. He will meet the *faqra* again, hear her sing. He will learn more Kurdish words from the children, and this time he is intent on teaching them some English. It has been four years, two months and sixteen days since he last spoke to Leila. He wonders if she has changed. She is probably married by now. He cannot help a twinge of jealousy, which he well knows is unbefitting in a family man with children.

His guide, a kind soul very different than his previous one, rides in front. Mahmoud repeatedly glances at him out of the corner of his eye. He has been silent on this final stretch of the journey. There is a nervousness in his manner that becomes more pronounced as they approach the Yazidi village.

'Is something wrong?' asks Arthur, slowing to a halt.

Mahmoud pulls on the reins. 'I didn't know how to tell you. This place is no longer what it was.'

'What do you mean?'

'Things happened while you were away. I am very sorry.' The young Arab's expression is so pained that it is clear Arthur will get nothing more from him.

Arthur dismounts from his horse. Zêrav appears through waves of heat rising from the scorched earth. A group of men are smoking in a corner. A woman ducks past carrying a jug of water. All these people around and not a single familiar face amongst them. For a moment he thinks he must be in the wrong place. Another village that looks eerily similar. It is only when he sees the pomegranate tree with the mark of water carved on the trunk that he stops doubting.

Several villagers walk towards him. The one in the middle, judging by his clothes, seems to be their leader.

'We heard you were coming,' the man says, waiting for his words to be translated. 'We heard you were a learned person. Welcome.'

Unable to respond with the appropriate pleasantry, Arthur says, 'Where are the people who used to live here?'

'Devil-worshippers? They are gone, good riddance.'

Trembling, Arthur spins round and strides towards Mahmoud. 'Where are my friends? Pray, tell me!'

Mahmoud lowers his eyes. 'The Pasha of Mosul and the qadi . . . they mustered an army and attacked. Not many survived. I am so sorry.'

A roaring fills his ears, a pounding like a drumbeat. Without a word, Arthur staggers away, his steps unsteady. No one stops him. No one calls him back.

★

What happened in the village of Golden Waters will never be mentioned in history books. Only the grandchildren of the survivors will remember. It will remain unvoiced in their unfinished sentences, uneasy silences, resurfacing nightmares. The memory of the massacre will be carefully handed down from one generation to the next, like passing someone a lit match protected from the wind in the shelter of your palm.

One day itinerant bards will sing about the *firman*. Luring the ghosts from their burial places, the ballads will tell how the pasha and the qadi, joining forces with the Beg of Rowanduz, known as Mir Kura, put hundreds of Yazidis to the sword in a matter of hours. Together they organized an army, instructing the soldiers to kill all the men and boys, and keep the women and girls as spoils of war.

The songs will lament how, outnumbered and outgunned, the villagers – women, men, children – tried to outrun their fate. Some fled towards Mount Judi and Tûr Abdin, others towards Mount Sinjar, but a larger group made for the River Tigris – the waters roiling and rising with melted snow. To their horror they found the makeshift bridge had disappeared. They searched for a boat, a raft, anything to help them cross, but there wasn't one to be found for miles. Unbeknownst to them, the qadi had had the bridge destroyed and the vessels removed. And so the people of Zêrav were trapped, the river rushing past in front of their eyes. Those who tried to swim were drowned. Paralysed by fear, they ran back to the mound of Nineveh. As the sun began to set, they were surrounded by troops. No one was left alive.

It happened here, in this soul-stirring land where thousands of years ago Assyrian kings built palaces, canals, gardens, and an enormous library with protective spirits at each entrance to make sure no harm would ever come to such a beautiful paradise. It happened here, by this archaeological site where Arthur now has permission to dig for the remaining lines of the *Epic of Gilgamesh*.

The name of the mound is Kouyunjik, 'little sheep', and some-day the bards will sing of how human beings were slaughtered here like sacrificial lambs.

Every day, Arthur sits by the mound, his eyes gritty and red-rimmed from lack of sleep. Like a cave holding the last vestiges of wind in its depths, not ready to let go of the encounter that hollowed it out, he carries the memory of his friends. He keens for them – the sheikh, the children, Dishan, the *faqra* . . . Leila once told him she was descended from the river and that is where she would like to return someday. She said she would become a raindrop or a snowflake, a vaporous nothingness in the ether before she alighted on this earth again. Now Arthur looks around, hoping for some sign, anything that will prove she is present, a watery spirit borne along by the currents.

Under a sky so vast it seems to stretch to infinity, Arthur observes the Tigris thunder past without pause, leaving stories in its wake like chalky sediment, oblivious to the suffering of humans. He feels a surge of anger inside his chest. It is this river that caused the death of innocents, forming an impassable barrier as they tried to flee. But, most of all, he is furious at himself. If he had stayed in the village longer or if he had returned earlier, might he have been able to do something to avert the calamity? Deep within he knows such thoughts to be as futile as they are arrogant. It is vanity to assume that our mere presence can alter the course of events. Heroes belong in myths, in which time stretches out dreamlike, and mortals blend with gods. He is no hero in any-one's story.

The sun etching imperfections in his skin, Arthur broods on how life has let him down and how he has let down others. What puzzles him most is that he had not heard about the bloodbath when he was back in England. He considers himself a voracious reader. Everyone says he is a cultured man. He is a scholar, a thinker, a researcher. An intellectual. But he has not encountered a single line in the newspapers or anywhere else about the slaughter of the Yazidis in the very place where British, French, German and Finnish archaeologists have been digging for the remnants of ancient Nineveh. Archaeology, for him, had always been about excavating past artefacts and unearthing the verses of an epic. Whenever he disinterred human remains, he regarded them dispassionately, as he assumed they were of antique origin. But now he finds himself faced with the idea of exhuming the fragments not of long-dead people but of those he has known and loved.

Days pass. Duty loses its urgency. It is as if a fog – dense and blinding like the ones he experienced in London as a boy – has descended over the Tigris, covering everything with its breath. To date he has perceived the world in clear-cut oppositions – West versus East, new versus old, science versus superstition, civilized versus unenlightened, and somehow, without putting it into as many words, he has also set the Thames against the Tigris . . . Such polarities have provided him with the certainty he needed to carry on. But his previous beliefs have been shattered, and all he is left with are splinters of doubt. In his fantasies the Tigris flows into the Thames and the Thames makes love to the Tigris, borders keep blurring into each other. For the first time in his life, Arthur is unable to apply himself and neglects his work. It has been weeks since he arrived in Nineveh, and he has yet to move a shovelful of earth. Nor has he been able to read a single new tablet. He feels submerged in sorrow, like a candle drowning in its own wax.

He fears he must be losing his mind, for he is aware of a presence by his side, the *faqra* watching over him. She speaks to him in that uncanny language she used when she was divining and he listens rapt, as if her words will soon reveal their meaning. Were his father to see him now, he would laugh. So this, then, is what he has become at the age of thirty-six – a man conversing with ghosts. He is indeed his mother's son.

It is an odd thing, to lose faith in the beliefs you once held firmly. How strange it is to have carried your convictions like a set of keys, only to realize they will not open any doors. Arthur no longer knows how he feels about excavating antiquities and carrying them off to England. He is unable to recall the thrill of discovery that once drove him. How will he continue to grub for buried relics when he is struggling to unearth his own sense of self? Has he, in his fervour for uncovering the library of Ashurbanipal, failed to give the same respect or attention to the living as he has to the dead? A sense of disquiet suffuses his every moment.

The heat is insufferable. If they do not break ground soon, it will be impossible to dig later in the summer. He is already behind schedule. Every day Mahmoud asks whether they can start hiring labourers. Every day Arthur responds with the same shake of the head. He feels hollowed out, outwardly the same but as empty inside as a blighted tree, its layers peeling back to dry heartwood.

A letter – short and dispassionate – arrives from his wife. Her tone is milder, as if she senses something is wrong. She tells him that the children miss him. She says they are keen to get a pair of canaries and asks him to suggest some names. *Lapis* and *Lazuli*, spring to Arthur's mind, but he cannot find the strength to put pen to paper.

Mabel inquires about the excavation, asking when he will be back home with 'his treasures'. Arthur wishes to respond in the same light, breezy tone, but his fingers are stiff as they grip the plume. He cannot collect his thoughts; and his sentences, when he finally manages to write, dangle awkwardly, like broken limbs that have yet to be set.

H—
NARIN

By the River Tigris, 2014

Hauled into a truck with dozens of women and children, Narin is transported in a convoy towards Mosul. Awash with anguish, she stands still, her face hard and rigid with fear. She has never felt so helpless, her loneliness so acute that it cuts through her ribcage. The wind rips at her hair, stings her face. She can detect the scent of wild herbs in the distance. Grandma has taught her how to distinguish them by smell – nettle, dandelion, mugwort . . . The familiar varieties tell her that they must not be too far from the shores of the River Tigris.

Narin knows two mighty streams flow through every human being: the good and the bad. Which course we choose to follow – through heart, spirit and mind – ultimately determines who we are. Some people will do everything they can to avoid hurting another person, even in the most desperate of situations, while others will inflict suffering as casually as if they were swatting away a fly.

In the stories Grandma narrated there were some reprehensible characters – callous kings who would marry a virgin each night, only to have them executed in the morning, greedy viziers plundering imperial coffers, marauders pouncing on travellers in the dark . . . but even the worst villains knew, deep down, that what they did was wrong. They did not pretend otherwise. They might try to justify their actions and even adopt the appearance of virtue to hoodwink others into thinking them good, but they did not, for a moment, imagine themselves to be virtuous. By contrast, the fanatics who slaughter the innocent and defenceless, pillaging villages, enslaving women and children, believe themselves to be holy. With every sorrow and suffering they rain on other humans, they expect to earn favour in the eyes of God, move closer to completing the bridge from this world to their exclusive paradise. How can anyone assume they will please the Creator by hurting His Creation? Nowhere in Grandma's tales did even the most depraved practise such self-delusion.

The old woman's words drift in the air, like the tail feather of a memory taking flight: *In the blackest sky there is a star glimmering high above, in the deepest night, a candle burning bright. Never despair. You must always look for the nearest source of life.* Narin lifts her chin, tears streaming down her cheeks. Where can she hope to find light when she is hemmed in by darkness?

Hours pass, and then the convoy pulls up in front of an imposing, historic building in Mosul that until recently was used for weddings and celebrations. Narin will only find out much later that this is where her father was scheduled to perform in about a week's time.

More trucks and buses arrive. Women and children abducted from Yazidi settlements far and wide – Kocho, Tal Banat, Qiniyeh, Tal Qasab . . . Only then does it become apparent that these are not random acts of violence but a calculated campaign of unmitigated hatred, the extermination of an entire culture. In just a matter of hours communities have been laid waste, populations decimated, and more than half a million people forced to leave. All over Iraq the destruction unfurls, even in hospitals with some doctors escorting ISIS to wards housing Yazidi patients. Though the militants come from across the world, and some do not speak Arabic, many are old neighbours, collaborating with the killers.

Inside the building, Narin is thrust into a large hall lit with naked, fluorescent lights. The place is packed. Every few minutes, the double doors burst open and the militants strut in, either to bring in more captives or to drag a woman away. Those who try to resist are beaten. Panic streams into every corner. A young mother with a baby begs for mercy and they kick her until she faints. The screams of those who are pulled away penetrate the walls, haunting the ones left waiting. A girl vomits in a corner, heaving and coughing up bile. A sour, nauseating stench pervades the air.

Narin crouches with her back against the wall – a tiny ball of fear. Her fists are clenched so tightly that her fingernails dig into her palms, making marks like partridge footprints on the banks of the Tigris.

'You all speak Arabic?' asks a militant – arms akimbo, legs apart.

Most of the girls do not move but a few nod slightly. He yanks the nearest one towards him. She has been selected to translate.

'Do you know why you're here? It's because your fathers are heathens,' says the man. 'Your mothers are *kaffirs*. All your ancestors are infidels and sinners. You and your people are devil-worshippers!'

Narin winces. She recalls the face of the bulldozer driver who interrupted her baptism, the cleaner at the hospital . . . All the people who have repeated the same awful words, over and again. How often in her young life has she heard this slander, and yet it still hurts like the very first time.

'But we are merciful,' says the militant. 'We'll give you a chance to repent. If you convert now, you may become lawful wives to our noble fighters. You can accompany a glorious army to *jihad*. I'm asking you for the first and last time: do you renounce your Godless ways?'

No one responds.

'You either join us and earn a place in heaven. Or you remain an infidel and deserve whatever suffering comes your way. You have sixty seconds to decide – starting from now.'

The hush that descends on the hall is so thick that not a single whisper can be heard: the baby whimpering in his mother's lap, the girl sobbing into a handkerchief, even the squeaking door hinges – all sound is momentarily suspended.

'Your time is running out,' shouts the man, enjoying the authority he finds himself invested with. 'Twenty-two seconds left – is anyone going to convert? This is your final chance.'

All of a sudden, Narin leaps to her feet and shouts with all her might, shattering the silence.

'Where is Grandma? What have you done to her?'

The child's question, so unexpected, baffles the man. His confusion visible in his face, he stops counting.

'My grandmother's name is Besma,' Narin screams in a voice that no longer sounds like hers. 'Those awful men took her away. Has anyone seen Grandma?'

'Shut the little bitch up!' says the man who was giving orders earlier. 'What is she – a simpleton or what?'

They seize Narin by the hair and drag her across the concrete floor like an empty sack. The pain, raking across her scalp, is so excruciating that she passes out. The din of the world fades.

When she comes to her senses, the hall is quieter. Most of the women and children have been taken away.

'The idiot girl is awake,' says one of the militants. He pokes the child with the top of his boot. 'Stand up! Speak, what's your name?'

'She doesn't understand Arabic,' says another militant. 'Only Turkish and Kurdish.'

'I heard her grandmother call her Narin,' says someone.

'Narin,' repeats the man as he writes her name down on a list. 'Tell us, how old are you?'

As they ask someone to translate the question into Kurmanji, all Narin can hear is the pounding of her heart. She doesn't know whether to reveal her actual age, or claim to be younger, or older, and what, if anything, would offer a chance of survival, if indeed there is one?

In the end she simply tells the truth. 'Nine.'

'Virgin,' says the man. 'She'd be a nice gift for the commander. He speaks Turkish. He'll know how to tame her.'

'You sure?' says the other man. 'She sounds like a trouble-maker.'

'Send her along with the others,' the first man replies, pointing to three young women crying in the corner.

'Fine,' the second man concedes. 'Three beautiful *sabaya* for the commander – and we'll throw in this morsel as well.'

A house in Mosul – a two-storey concrete dwelling with a satellite dish on the roof, an unkempt garden at the back, tomato plants in olive-oil tins arranged on the windowsills, the smell of heat baking into earth. This is where they are held prisoner: a family home, like any other, with children running around and chickens pecking in the yard.

A little boy watches from the hallway as the slaves are brought in, his dark eyes brimming with undisguised curiosity. He has a plaster on his forehead, just over his eyebrow, evidence of a recent accident. Narin looks at him and she wonders if the child has any idea what is happening under this roof.

'Move,' says a militant, nudging her with the butt of his rifle.

They are steered to a room upstairs with iron bars on the windows and locks on the door.

An hour goes by, perhaps more – they have no way of marking time. There is a bucket in the corner for when they need to relieve themselves. A constant shame, not of their own making, follows them wherever they go. Just outside, the light is a soft ochre, though further away the sky is darkening. They can hear people on the street going about their business. Somewhere nearby the clang of a pot on a burner suggests someone is cooking. A car passes beneath their window, music blasting. The familiar sounds of city life, usually so humdrum, serve only to intensify their feelings of helplessness.

A tall woman walks in without so much as glancing at them. She places a tray on the rug – flatbread with a bowl of yogurt, a jug of water. There are no spoons, no glasses. Even though they have not eaten anything all day, no one touches the food. But water they cannot refuse. As much as they try to drink in small sips, thirst takes over as they pass the jug around wordlessly.

In a little while the boy with the plaster comes in to pick up the tray. He also brings in a pile of brightly coloured garments – skimpy, lacy underwear. In a flat voice he tells them that his father wants them to put these on. As he says this, his stare falls on a floral bra, his expression betraying no understanding of the item, nor the implication behind his father's demand.

None of the women agree to wear the lingerie. All of them are beaten for their disobedience.

That night, they curl up on one mattress. Sleep is impossible. It is hard to believe that just a few days ago they were waking up next to their loved ones. How is it that lives so tenderly and painstakingly built, year after year, can be shattered in a matter of hours?

The next morning the militants bring in another captive – a woman with large, beautiful, black eyes set in a pale, oval face. Sorrow has left its traces on her features.

'Are you Besma's grandchild?' she says as soon as she sees Narin.

Gently, she walks towards the girl and sits by her side. 'I'm Salma, my darling. From the village of Kocho. I heard you shouting at that disgusting man. I knew your grandma.'

'You did?'

'Years ago, when I was pregnant with my first child, we were visiting our relatives in Hasankeyf, and I almost had a miscarriage – your grandma saved my life.'

The woman falters then, seeing the child's expression.

'They took her away,' says Narin. 'I don't know what they've done to her. I think they killed her.'

Salma leans back against the wall, steadying her breath. She will not tell Narin what ISIS is doing to the Yazidi women whom they regard as too old to serve as sexual slaves. Not wanting to waste a bullet, they bury them alive.

'I'm so sorry, child. I'll pray for her. I'll never forget her kindness,' says Salma. 'But how is it you're here? I thought your family were in Turkey.'

'Grandma wanted me to see the village where great-great-grandma Leila was born . . . I was going to be baptized in the holy Valley of Lalish. We travelled with my father –' Talking of her loved ones makes Narin's stomach clench. The tears she has been holding back come streaming down.

'You poor thing, let me hug you,' Salma says. 'May I?'

Narin wipes her eyes with the back of her hand. She nods, slowly.

Salma does not ask any more questions but continues to hold Narin until the girl falls asleep. She keeps close to the child at all times. She is compassionate, protective and loving.

It is Salma that the commander orders to his bedroom first, the following night.

Downstairs, there are three rooms and a kitchen where the commander lives with his family. The man is married with two young children and a baby still in the cradle. Every day a stream of ISIS militants come and go, collecting and passing on orders. Upstairs, next to where the captives are kept, is a large room with a balcony overlooking a busy street. This is where they hold their meetings.

Neither the commander's children nor the prisoners are allowed into this part of the house – except for Narin, whom they sometimes ask to bring tea and food.

The tall woman with heavy-lidded blue eyes turns out to be the commander's wife. She speaks Arabic with an American accent, barely looking up when she does so. Her voice is wispy, as if from disuse – except when she yells, which she does often. She instructs them to cook and do the laundry and clean up after the children. The harder they work, the more irritated she seems to become. The stew is too bland, the rice burned, the newly washed clothes still stained. She accuses them of stealing food from the kitchen and padlocks the fridge – and, a few days later, the bread bin, even though she must have smelt the hunger on their breath.

Every night the commander selects a *sabaya*, forcing her to put on make-up and lingerie. The next morning the same woman returns bruised and broken, without a word on her lips.

On the tenth day, the man sends for Narin.

'She's a child,' says Salma to the militant who brings the message.

'Seems old enough to me,' says the man, slowly running his eyes over Narin.

'She's a holy child. Tell him to leave her alone.'

'There's nothing holy about heathens,' says the man.

But Salma is adamant. 'Tell your boss she comes from a line of healers. Her grandmother had the gift. Her great-great-grandmother had the gift. Whoever touches the descendant of a *faqra* will be cursed.'

'Nonsense,' says the man. 'Don't waste our time with stupid lies.'

'You don't understand,' Salma insists without missing a beat. 'This girl's grandmother needed only to glance at a person once to divine what illness was eating them up. She could find water in dry soil. This is a family of seers.'

He laughs, but, all the same, he leaves without taking Narin and he does not return for her that day.

'I wish our fate had been like those in Halabja,' says Salma. 'Innocents were murdered by that brutal Saddam. They inhaled poison into their lungs, poor souls. What a horrific death it was, but one thing they did not lose was their dignity. If only we had been gassed at Halabja, it'd have been less painful.'

—o—

ARTHUR

By the River Tigris, 1876

N ow that he is unable to work, King Arthur of the Sewers
and Slums sends a telegram to the Trustees of the British Museum, informing them that he wishes to cut his
expedition short and return. He cites the plague and cholera that
are ravaging the region as the reason for his decision. The reply
is curt.

> Dear Smyth,
> We are sorry to learn from your most recent corres-
> pondence that the plague and cholera are increasing to
> so great an extent. Doubtless the situation requires the
> utmost precaution on your part as you proceed with the
> important mission with which you have been charged.
> Very truly yours,
> S. McAllister Jones
> Secretary to the British Museum

Arthur crumples the letter, trembling. He is now in a terrible bind.
In this state of mind, he cannot do his job, but his proprietors will
not allow him to leave Nineveh unless he makes a worthwhile discovery. As he struggles to find a solution, he turns his attention to
the debris left by previous archaeological teams. A massive heap
has been piled up: chipped tiles, fractured bricks and potsherds

430

that have been discarded without proper inspection. Patiently, he starts sifting through the jumble. The task suits him. He is used to seeing value in things others have been quick to discard.

And this is how one afternoon, rivulets of sweat running down his neck, he chances upon something unexpected. At first it is the colour that catches his eye – a flash of cobalt. A glaze so intense he blinks to make sure he is not hallucinating. Gingerly, he pulls it out from under the shards. Underneath the dirt and dust is a tablet. It is a deep, boundless blue. Arthur has examined thousands of Mesopotamian artefacts over the years, from small cylinder seals to large bas-reliefs, but he has never seen anything like this before.

That night in his tent, he sits wrapped in a blanket under an oil lamp, the breeze drawing symbols on the nape of his neck. He pores over the blue tablet. It is a segment of the *Epic of Gilgamesh*, but one he has not come across before. The hero, having lost everything – his friend/lover, his youth, his hubris – is returning home, a broken man. But it is not only the defeat of the central character that takes Arthur aback; there is a note at the bottom, only partially legible.

> *This is . . . a junior scribe,*
> *One of the many . . . storytellers . . .*
> *. . . weave poems . . . stories . . .*
> *. . . remember . . .*

Arthur is surprised to see that the tablet is dedicated not to Nabu, as usual, but to some unknown goddess called Nisaba.

When King Gilgamesh died, they interred his body under the river. Not inside, but under. To do this they had to divert the Euphrates, forcing it to flow in an unnatural direction; once the funeral was over, they returned the river to its original course. The workers who dug the hero's grave were all killed afterwards. That way, there would be no one left alive to reveal the burial place.

Mesopotamia is made of stories of water. Across its alluvial plains, the oldest tales are dedicated to streams, storms and floods. The Sumerian word for water, *a* – just like the Kurdish word *aw* – also means conception, semen, beginning.

Rivers are fluid bridges – channels of communication between separate worlds. They link one bank to the other, the past to the future, the spring to the delta, earthlings to celestial beings, the visible to the invisible, and, ultimately, the living to the dead. They carry the spirits of the departed into the netherworld, and occasionally bring them back. In the sweeping currents and tidal pools shelter the secrets of foregone ages. The ripples on the surface of water are the scars of a river. There are wounds in its shadowy depths that even time cannot heal.

The songs of this land, though seemingly about love or heartbreak, are actually about place – both the beauty and the sadness it embodies. The Ancient Mesopotamians are famed for inventing writing, mathematics, astronomy, irrigation and the wheel, but their biggest discovery has gone unrecognized. They are the first to experience the pain of losing a motherland.

The inhabitants of this region have always known that they rely on water for survival. Grateful for every drop of fresh water that graced their days, they thanked the rivers – and also feared them. When the levees break and the banks burst, they leave trauma behind – a story to be told from one generation to the next. Mesopotamian lore understands that water is the defining force of life. Trees are 'rooted water', streams are 'flowing water', birds are 'flying water', mountains are 'rising water', and, as for humans, they are, and will always be, 'warring water', never at peace.

Water has memory.

Rivers are especially good at remembering.

432

'Mr Arthur . . . sir?'

He lifts his head. These past weeks have prematurely aged him. His face is wan and tired, heavy from lack of sleep. There are crinkles around his eyes from squinting into the sun, and new lines have appeared on his forehead.

'I must tell you something,' says Mahmoud. 'This morning I met a tinker who travels up and down the Tigris, mending pots and pans. The man described some strange things he witnessed on the way here –'

Arthur is only half listening, but what Mahmoud says next has his full attention. 'He said, a while back, he saw a young Yazidi woman riding alone. He was worried for her and he wanted to understand why she had no one.'

'Did . . . did he say her name?'

'No. He tried to speak to her, but she would not talk to a stranger.'

'Did he describe what she looked like?'

'He said she had covered her face, but he could tell from her clothes that she was a Yazidi. Oddly, this woman had a *qanun* with her.'

Arthur staggers to his feet. 'It must be her! It's Leila!'

'I don't want to raise your hopes. But I thought I should tell you.'

His mind working fast, Arthur rakes his hands through his hair. 'How could I not think of this before? She had predicted the massacre years ago. She had warned everyone that night.

> *"The day they come to kill us*
> *run to the mountain.*
> *Do not go near the water,*
> *river, well nor fountain."*

'Do you understand, my friend? She did not go to the water. Of course not! She did not run to the river like the others – that's how she survived.'

433

Laughing a madman's laugh, Arthur grasps Mahmoud's hand and shakes it joyfully. 'Imagine, this morning I thought Leila was dead, but now I have learnt she may be alive.'

'We don't know for certain if it is her. I don't want you to be disappointed.'

Arthur is not listening. 'Life is full of the unexpected, my friend. As if we are walking in a river of mud, and we dare to dip our hands every now and then, searching for a button of hope, a coin of friendship, a ring of love. We are mudlarkers, all of us.'

Mahmoud has no idea what Arthur is ranting about, but he is glad he is smiling again – until he sees him hastily packing his belongings inside a canvas bag.

'Wait! Where are you going?'

'Castrum Kefa – that's where her *sister of the next world* lives. Leila's family are dead, so she must have gone to join her *axiretê*. I need to find her.'

'Pray calm down. That route is dangerous these days. The cholera . . .' Mahmoud pauses, realizing that, whatever he says, he will not be able to pierce the wall of Arthur's determination. 'Then I am coming with you.'

'Oh, no. I cannot ask you to do that.'

'I must accompany you,' Mahmoud says. 'I mean no offence, but I am not sure you would survive even a day on your own.'

Thus, in mid-August 1876, King Arthur of the Sewers and Slums sets out for the upper reaches of the River Tigris. Within his satchel he carries a flask of water, a bag of dates, a leather journal, and a tablet of lapis lazuli dedicated to a forgotten goddess. He bids farewell, for the second and last time, to his beloved Nineveh, forsaking a part of himself on a mound that hides artefacts from the palace of King Ashurbanipal and human remains from a forgotten genocide.

—H
ZALEEKHAH

By the River Thames, 2018

Early in the morning, the sun still low, Uncle Malek arrives at the houseboat unannounced. He strides on to the deck, and stares at the river for a moment before he rings the bell. He has never done anything like this before; paying a visit without calling is not his way.

'Uncle!'

'Hello, my dear. Did I surprise you? I was driving by, and I thought I should come to see this water dwelling of yours. Good thing I knew the name of the boat; it was rather easy to find.'

Her expression curdling to panic, Zaleekhah steals a glance at the road beyond the towpath, where Uncle's claret Bentley is parked, the chauffeur waiting inside. She turns towards him, casting about for a polite excuse to send him away. But something in his face gives her pause. Uncle Malek's eyes are bloodshot, as if he hasn't slept at all, and he has a hint of grey stubble. In all these years, she has only ever seen him immaculately shaved.

'Are . . . are you all right?'

Uncle Malek appears to be about to say something, but instead manages a flippant gesture, a perfunctory wave of his hand. Peering over Zaleekhah's shoulder, he assesses the houseboat.

'So this is your bolt-hole? Aren't you going to ask me in?'

And, just like that, Zaleekhah steps aside.

★

'Interesting,' Uncle remarks as soon as he walks in. 'Are you not planning to buy any furniture for your raft, my dear? Is this a trend now – empty home, empty mind, Nirvana on the river, that kind of thing?'

'I might get a few things eventually, I don't know. I'm trying to take each day as it comes.'

He regards her, bemused.

'Please have a seat.' Zaleekhah offers him the armchair and sits opposite him on the stool.

'The view is something, though, I must say.' Uncle looks about him, the fatigue in his eyes now deeper than his judgements are swift.

'Is everything all right? You seem a bit –'

'Cream-crackered? Probably. It's been stressful these past days with Lily's illness, as you know.' Uncle waves his hand. 'But that's not why I'm here. I came to address this muddle that you've created, which I hope to untangle so you can save your marriage.'

'That's not going to happen. Brian has filed for divorce,' says Zaleekhah.

'Is that right? Even so, if you make an effort I'm sure you two can find a way forward. Men are feeble creatures – he has to hear from you that you need him. Look, I know this isn't an easy subject. I'll tell you what. You probably don't have any food in that monastic kitchen. Let's leave this hermitage on the water and go somewhere nice for breakfast or brunch. Just you and me, a chinwag and good grub – like the old days.'

'I'd have loved that but –'

The sound of the toilet flushing downstairs invades the space between them.

Uncle's face crumples. 'Oh, you have a guest?'

It is not really a question, and Zaleekhah does not attempt to answer. She inhales sharply, her cheeks burning as though she were a teenager caught by a parent kissing on the street. She tries to say something that sounds casual, and fails.

'I'd better go, terribly sorry for disturbing, my dear.'

436

As Uncle leans on his cane, they are both startled by a cheerful greeting from downstairs.

'Is that you, Mr Malek?'

In a second Nen appears, wearing Zaleekhah's pyjamas. Her feet are bare, and her hair wet from the shower.

'Hello!' she says, beaming.

So many emotions pass across Uncle's face then: shock replaced by irritation replaced by something akin to anger and, finally, defeat. He sinks into the armchair again and mutters more to himself than to anyone else: 'I should have known it was you.'

'Did I intrude on something?' Nen drops her voice. 'Shall I leave?'

Zaleekhah says, 'No, please stay!'

Nen sits on the floor, cross-legged, her eyes jumping between the two of them.

For an awkward moment no one speaks, and the only sound in the houseboat is the slapping of waves against the hull.

'There is fresh coffee,' Zaleekhah says tentatively. 'Nen just made it. Would you like some, Uncle?'

Uncle Malek nods, too listless to decline. As Zaleekhah hands him a steaming mug, her sleeve rides up.

'You have a tattoo now? Don't tell me that's permanent, my dear.'

'It is. You like it?' Zaleekhah says. 'It means "water" in Ancient Sumerian.'

A sigh. Uncle takes a sip, sighs again. 'At least the coffee is good.'

'Dried lavender flowers,' says Zaleekhah. She cannot help smiling at Nen. 'Balances out the caffeine and it also smells divine.'

His certainty returning, Uncle stares at Nen. His expression is as ambiguous as his words are direct. 'You did all this.'

'I did what?' asks Nen, placidly.

'You confused our Zaleekhah. All her life she has been exemplary. Not even once did she upset me. But then you came along and swayed her and turned her into a tattooed beatnik with no furniture. It is a phase, I get it: when you are in the midst of

437

divorce and your husband does not want you any more, it makes you feel unloved and you hold on to the nearest person.'

'Uncle . . .' Zaleekhah speaks slowly but with conviction. 'I'm the one who invited Nen over. I asked her to stay. Why do you assume it was the other way round? Is it because you think I always do the right thing or is it because deep inside you find me timid and meek and incapable of doing anything . . . *unconventional*?'

Nen clears her throat. 'I can make myself scarce if you two need –'

'No, stay,' says Uncle Malek. He pushes his glasses up his nose before turning to Zaleekhah. 'I just don't recognize you now. Where is the little girl waiting for me in a police station in Turkey? The girl I wrapped in a shawl and took back to England? The girl who was top of her class and never caused me any trouble? At your parents' funeral, it was raining hard, so many umbrellas that when you stood under them it felt like the entire sky had turned black, and maybe my sister wouldn't have wanted to be buried in soggy England, we had never talked about it . . . That afternoon, I held your hand, and there was mud on your shoes, and I realized your shoes were mismatched – how was it that we hadn't noticed before leaving the house, neither your aunt nor I? They looked sad, those mismatched shoes, as if they were pulling you in opposite directions, and I promised myself I'd always be there to take care of you.'

'And you have been. I'm very grateful.'

'I don't want you to be grateful. I want you to be happy,' says Uncle. 'So do you have anything in that empty kitchen of yours to improve this coffee? A bottle of whisky somewhere? I had a terrible night and now this.'

'Why did you have a bad night? Is it Lily's surgery that's troubling you? You can tell me, you know.'

'No, no. That's all taken care of. Lily will be fine. We'll all be fine.' A crease appears between his eyes. 'I'd do anything for them. And for you, too, my dear. Anything.'

Zaleekhah tries to swallow the uneasiness that comes over her.

'You probably find me old school, a dinosaur frozen in time. Lord Brontosaurus . . .' Uncle breaks off, unable to develop the joke. His hand cradling the mug shakes a little. 'I only want to protect my loved ones. All my life I have fought for my family – unlike my mother, I would never abandon my own. Ever.'

Zaleekhah stares in astonishment, unable to believe he is crying. She has never seen him this emotional before and it takes her a few seconds to react. 'Uncle . . .'

But he is already on his feet, his chin up.

'I shouldn't have come unannounced. I apologize. Thank you, though, for the coffee. Dried lavender flowers, who knew.'

'Uncle, don't leave like this please –'

'Have things to do, my dear. Busy day ahead.' He pauses, but doesn't turn around, as though addressing his next words to the River Thames. 'Come to dinner. Bring your *friend* Nen. We'll continue our discussion of *Gilgamesh* over wine and water. Now, if you don't mind, I'm not going to mention any of this to your aunt. You think she is open-minded and totally *laissez-faire*, and I'm the old stick-in-the-mud, but, believe me, appearances can be deceptive.'

—o—

ARTHUR

By the River Tigris, 1876

August is the worst of times to travel from Nineveh to Castrum Kefa. It is less a month than an elegy for the vibrant songs of spring, a lament that floats through the desiccated stalks and brittle reeds bowed by the wind. Arthur eats little. It is hard to have an appetite when the sun is merciless. His diet consists of dates, flatbread, camel's milk. They sleep during the day and proceed at night. In the darkness, the landscape changes, transfigured as if by a master illusionist. Under a moon that seems so close you can rise up on your toes and reach it with your fingertips, the world acquires a rare stillness. The stars glimmer like tiny translucent pebbles on the bed of a river, each holding its own secrets.

His guide warns him it is dangerous to ride after sunset. But Arthur loves the serenity, the starlight, the silence so profound he can hear the earth breathe, fully alive. So they keep going, two nocturnal travellers retracing ancient caravan routes, chance acquaintances on a journey they can neither agree on nor abandon.

Arthur knows that the ground they are crossing was not always a desert. Deep beneath the sand dunes are the remains of what were once the most advanced cities – lush, opulent urban centres flourishing in the fluvial deltas. All across this region the soil was rich and the climate beneficent. It could have easily sustained many generations to come. But the abuse of natural resources, the lust for power and dominance, and endless rivalries led to the decline of cities, and then came famine, flood and drought. The greediest kings corralled the rivers and the bloodiest wars were fought over water.

When Arthur first started studying the tablets, he used to think of civilization as a solid edifice, elegantly expressed in marble, wood, glass and metal. A feat of engineering, planning, design and construction. The triumph of humankind over nature. But now, as he traverses this desolate landscape, it seems to him that what they call civilization is, in truth, a storm in waiting. Powerful, protean and perfectly destructive, sooner or later it will burst free of its barriers and engulf everything in its insatiable path.

In the villages they pass through, they see sick people lying listlessly, their skins an alarming shade of blue. The stench, seeping out from closed doors, is unbearable. Arthur recognizes the signs – it is cholera. The pestilence that emerged from the plains of the River Ganges and borne by water has spread far and wide. His infant brother's face appears in front of his eyes, the wound of his loss never healing.

'We must fetch a doctor for them!'

Mahmoud shakes his head sadly. 'No doctor will come here.'

Arthur watches the young guide raise his palms towards the skies and pray for the souls of the dead and the dying. Words in Arabic, rounded syllables strung together like beads on a rosary. It gives him comfort to see someone pleading with God for all those in need, regardless of race or creed, as this is an area where Muslims, Christians, Yazidis, Jews and Mandeans have for centuries lived side by side. If cholera does not pay heed to such differences, he feels, neither should the living. Yet, when he tries to join in the prayer, he cannot. He has witnessed too much hatred and bloodshed in the name of religion. A part of him still believes in a supreme being – the Creator of the universe and the source of moral authority. But a bigger part understands that he and God have long parted ways.

Faith is a bird, they say, and it cannot be kept locked up, however gilded you make its cage. Set it free, send it afar, and it may or may not return. Faith is a bird perhaps, but Arthur now regards it as a stuffed raven that stares down at him with its glassy eyes. It won't ever take wing again, and it is hard to imagine that it ever did.

He rides his horse like one possessed, impatient to reach Castrum Kefa and see Leila one more time. Feeling guilty about imposing this breakneck speed on the young guide, he says, 'You should return to your village, my friend.'

Mahmoud's forehead creases. 'You don't want me?'

'I can no longer pay you. I have run out of funds. Also, it is not safe. You should be back with your family.'

'You have a family, too.'

'Yes, and I will take every precaution to be united with them.'

Mahmoud draws a breath. 'I do not mean to be rude, but why go to such trouble for a woman who will never be yours?'

It is a question Arthur cannot immediately answer. He swallows painfully, the corners of his mouth cracked and sore from the heat. 'I just want to make sure she is safe and happy where she is.'

'You know you are behaving like Majnun.'

'Who is that?'

'It is a famous poem: *Layla and Majnun*. Qays was in love with Layla and she loved him back, but they could never be together. She was married off to another. Qays lost his mind and so he became *Majnun* – the "possessed". He turned into a poet and started wandering the desert, like a madman, consumed by thoughts of Layla, even though she was out of his reach forever – do you see the resemblance?'

Arthur smiles ruefully. 'But I am no poet, my friend. I am just a devoted reader.'

After much pleading, Arthur manages to convince Mahmoud to return to his people. Under a sickle moon he canters, determined to continue on his own. Across the desert to Aleppo is 350 miles on horseback. The next day, without a shelter or shade, the sun is fierce, and the wind refuses to cease, whistling profanities. Arthur listens, trying to decode the signs.

The Ancient Mesopotamians saw portents everywhere – in the glow of embers in the hearth, the murmurations of starlings in the skies, the swirls of smoke from incense burners, the fall of Knucklebones in the dust, the formations of the clouds . . . They read omens in the intestines of sacrificial animals, the contours of spilt flour, the patterns of oil on water . . . No one was indifferent to the auguries: kings and servants, all yearned for a glimpse of the unseen. Partly because they understood how fragile life is and how close the breath of death. And partly because they retained a naive hope that, despite the inequalities and injustices of this world, someone or something from another realm might give them counsel and assistance in their hour of need.

The sound of galloping interrupts Arthur's thoughts. Someone is following him. His pulse beats in his throat, his fingers tighten around the dagger in his belt. Not that he knows how to use it. The stranger keeps approaching, spurring his horse to full speed.

'Who's there?' Arthur yells. 'I am armed, I warn you!' It is foolish to shout in English, but he cannot help it.

A few seconds later, Arthur hears a familiar voice.

'It is me! Mahmoud.'

The young Arab has not left him.

Touched by his selflessness, Arthur bites the tender inside of his cheek and says, 'I told you to go back, my friend.'

'And I told you that you were not made for the desert. Someone needs to keep an eye on you.'

Illness creeps upon Arthur like a sucking louse, unnoticed until the damage is done. All this while he has managed to avoid dangers and diseases, but it seems his luck is coming to an end. His limbs feel heavy, and his mouth filled with salt. Nausea, belly cramps, fever. Dysentery is not deadly, provided it is treated quickly enough, and the patient gets enough rest and water. But he has lost precious time, and there are no doctors for many miles.

'You need to stop,' says Mahmoud. 'You cannot go on like this.'

'Not now. We are very close.'

The sun beats down. Sliding in and out of consciousness, Arthur clutches the reins.

The trail expands and stretches in front of him in dizzying cycles. Mahmoud keeps talking by his side, as if words have healing properties and silence would be life-threatening. When he runs out of things to say in English, he reverts to Arabic. Arthur listens to the cadence of his voice, finding a sense of peace in this language he does not understand.

'Castrum Kefa!' Mahmoud points at the ancient city appearing on the horizon, with its limestone cliffs and thousands of caves. 'We are almost there.'

Covered in dust and sweat, Arthur can barely stand. He slumps forward over the horse's neck. If it weren't for his guide, riding close by, he would have tumbled off.

A shepherd's hut is the only dwelling in sight. Mahmoud carries him inside. They lay Arthur on a straw mattress, where he shivers even as his body burns.

'I must get help.' Mahmoud rushes out the door. 'I'll be back as soon as I can.'

The shepherd watches over this unexpected guest for a while, but he must tend to his flock, and so he leaves.

★

Alone in the room, in the throes of fever, Arthur sees his mother, young and winsome even when bundled up in a thick, filthy coat with bulging pockets, and her feet encrusted with the effluent and mud of the Thames. It is snowing, the world is beautiful and cold and cruel. His children appear amidst the swirling flakes, playing by a pond, floating wooden toy boats. Smiling, he waves at them, though they do not seem to notice him. As he bends to splash his face with water, he catches a reflection in its mirrored surface. Two figures stand behind on each side of him, their elbows touching. His wife wears black widow's weeds. The *faqra*, by contrast, is clad in white.

Within seconds he starts to vomit.

It is in that moment that a shadow sidles into the room – a thief. Darting, soundless, he moves like a rodent. He flicks no more than a glance at the sick man in bed, moaning. Turning his back, he rifles through Arthur's jacket and empties the satchel – a notebook, a handkerchief, a child's drawing, a bag of dates . . . Upset by the meagreness of his findings, he curses. Then he grabs the leather boots dropped in a corner. Just as he is about to leave, he catches sight of the blue tablet. He revolves the artefact in his hand this way and that. It doesn't seem like anything of value, but he likes the colour. Perhaps he can smash it into pieces and use them to make rings. Or maybe he can sell it for a few coins. And so he also takes the lapis lazuli slab that a junior scribe has dedicated to a forgotten goddess, the stone still warm from Arthur's touch.

H—
NARIN

By the River Tigris, 2014

I n a nondescript cinderblock house with a satellite dish on the roof, Narin stands at a sink, her elbows covered in grease as she scrubs hard at a saucepan. There is a strained silence all around, punctuated by outbursts of angry shouting. The mood among the militants has soured as bad news trickles in from the battle lines. They are losing men and ammunition, forced to give up territorial gains.

The commander is in a foul temper, despite having recently acquired two more *sabaya*. He does to them what he did to the others. The younger Yazidi woman weeps all the time, sobbing even in her sleep, and the elder, mostly quiet, is found one morning with a noose made of bedsheets around her neck, barely breathing. The commander strips her naked from the waist up and whips her in front of the entire household. She is punished both for attempting suicide and for destroying the bedlinen.

'Hey, are you deaf?'

The little boy – the commander's son – has entered the kitchen. 'My father is calling you. They want tea! Go serve them.'

Carefully, Narin carries a tray loaded with glasses to the room upstairs. She taps on the door, waits. Assuming that they have responded, she pushes the door with her shoulder, just a tad. There are about twenty militants inside. The man sitting by the entrance has his back turned to her. He is holding an object in his hand. Narin looks closer, surprised to see that the signs impressed on its surface are similar to the ones on the clay tablet Grandma kept in her dowry chest.

Distracted, she takes a step forward, rattling the glasses. They all turn towards her and stop talking at once. Her throat closing in panic, the child walks through an intimidating silence.

She can barely stop her hands from trembling but she manages to pour tea for everyone. Just as she turns to withdraw, one of the militants mumbles something under his breath, seizes her from behind and starts to spin her in the air. Screaming, kicking, Narin tries to free herself, but her captor is much stronger than she is.

'Enough, Abu Muawaya!' It is the commander, a note of displeasure in his voice. 'That's my *sabaya* you're messing with.'

Vexed at being chided in front of everyone, the man drops Narin like a ragdoll. Too terrified to cry, she staggers out of the room.

Three days later, as Salma is heading downstairs to do the cooking, she overhears the commander's wife chatting with another woman in the kitchen.

'The girl is pure evil, I'm telling you. She put a curse on Abu Muawaya. Otherwise why would a healthy man like him die all of a sudden?'

'True. He wasn't sick or anything; it makes no sense,' the other woman agrees.

'It's because of her. The devil's child! I wish the little bitch would get lost. I keep begging my husband to sell her.'

'As he well should.'

'We feed and clothe her, but she shows no sign of gratitude. I don't want her under my roof. This is a devout house; we are pious people. She is Sheitan's servant, and she brings bad

447

luck, I can tell. If my husband doesn't get rid of her, I will do it myself.'

After Salma relates this to her, Narin tries to steer clear of the commander's wife, but, trapped as they are in the same house, it is almost impossible. Every time the girl enters the kitchen to wash the dishes or crosses the courtyard to hang out the laundry, she feels the woman's gaze trained on her. Even her children fall quiet when Narin approaches.

'I have decided to sell you,' says the commander. 'My wife is convinced you'll bring us bad luck. I'm not one to give credence to superstitions, but I don't like you. I don't want you around.' He regards the child for a moment, waiting for a reaction, and, when nothing comes, he adds: 'Your new owner will collect you in about a week's time. The man lives in Antep, so he'll take you back to Turkey to serve him.'

'Can Salma come with me?' asks Narin, her voice barely more than a whisper.

'Salma is going nowhere.'

He watches panic register on her face. He wants to break her, snap the tiny twigs of her resilience. 'Your new owner, I heard he's keen on unripe fruit. They say he likes his *sabaya* young. No older than twelve. He won't care about stupid superstitions – you won't get away with any of that nonsense with him.'

Narin is so petrified that she doesn't notice the commander has walked out.

Alone in the room, the child shivers, though the day is hot. This, she knows, is how she will die. She does not expect to survive the next house, or the next man. Her only chance is to run away, but, even if she were to manage to get out and started to knock on strangers' doors begging for help, how far could she go and who could she possibly trust, in a city where many will gladly betray a Yazidi girl in return for a bounty? She is aware of what happens to those who try and fail to escape – beaten, whipped and gang-raped while their owners watch.

Faint with fear, her knees give way. As she staggers, her fingers graze the lid of the trunk pushed up against the wall. She doesn't remember it ever being left open before, but it is now. Her hand, groping around for support, brushes against something inside. It is the clay tablet she saw earlier. Its surface is pitted with tightly packed marks – the same old script that she has studied with Grandma.

Carefully, she takes out the ancient object. Sitting on the carpet, she traces the lines with the tip of her finger, recognizing a few words: 'flood', 'water', 'the ark' . . . Despite herself, her lips curve into a smile as she remembers Grandma's stories. Glimpses of her previous life come to her, memories carried over the currents of the Tigris, like skimmed stones.

'You little whore! What do you think you're doing?'

A shriek escapes Narin's lips as she backs away in panic. She hasn't heard the man return.

The commander yanks the tablet away from the child's hands. 'How dare you rummage through my things?'

'I'm very sorry, I didn't mean –'

He punches her in the face. Narin falls flat on her back, winded. A trickle of blood drips from the corner of her mouth on to the rug. There is something brittle rolling on her tongue, like a seed rattling inside a gourd. It is a tooth – the one Grandma welcomed with laughter and love, in happier times. She coughs up blood, and for a confused moment she believes that the man has finished unleashing his rage – but it is only a temporary reprieve. He is putting the tablet away, swaddling it in cloth. The tenderness of the gesture contrasts sharply with his next move. He lunges back towards her and kicks her in the ribs.

Narin curls up in excruciating pain. It crosses her mind, swift as a swallow's flight, that if she dies now she will get to see

Grandma. A warm pool opens beneath her, and she slides into its liquid calm.

When she regains consciousness, every inch of her body is throbbing in agony. Her nose is clotted with blood, and her lips are swollen.

'She's coming round,' says a voice.

There is someone else in the room – a doctor. The man lifts Narin's head and tips a tasteless fluid down her throat.

'Can she understand what I'm saying?' the commander asks.

'She should. I've given her a stimulant.'

The commander sits down next to Narin on the sofa. 'Tell me, were you reading the tablet? How's that possible? Speak!'

'Grandma . . .' Narin rasps so low both men have to lean over her to hear. 'My grandmother . . . taught me.'

'An ignorant village woman?'

Narin does not offer an explanation. She will not tell them about Leila and how she arrived in Hasankeyf. She will not tell them about the Englishman. Her family's story is the only thing she owns that cannot be taken away from her.

The commander sighs. 'I don't expect you to understand. We're building a new world, laying the foundations, clearing away the rot. Future generations will thank us – the founders of the Caliphate.'

He pauses as if expecting praise.

'Listen,' he says, the dreamy tone gone. 'We have things from the Mosul Museum, and elsewhere. There are international buyers ready to pay big sums for this kind of stuff. But these tablets fetch more money if they contain poetry, I'm told. If someone could read these things, that'd help us assess their value.'

So, Narin thinks, this is why he has not killed her.

They not only murder, kidnap and rape. They have a sideline business: looting and trading antiquities. Despite the videos circulating of militants tearing down statues, vandalizing libraries and burning books, behind the display of indiscriminate destruction enormous profits are being made from smuggled artefacts. There are collectors across the world so eager to own pieces from Mesopotamia that they will blithely ignore their bloodstained provenance. Some items are openly auctioned; others quietly find their way into the hands of private buyers – in New York, Paris, Tokyo, Berlin and London.

It's nothing new – a repeating cycle. A decade ago, in the chaos following the American invasion, museums across Iraq were emptied. In a matter of days, thousands of artefacts disappeared – even those in the vaults of the Central Bank. Some curators tried to resist, barring the doors, risking their lives. Employees at the National Museum, in a last-ditch attempt to safeguard the exhibits, hung a sign warning that the building was under the protection of Western armed forces. A desperate lie. The American soldiers had no orders to save the museums or the libraries. When questioned about this later on, a military spokesman would simply say, 'Stuff happens.'

Now, as before, the security cameras capture how the looters seem to know where to go, what to steal first. Forcing open glass cases, they abscond with cylinder seals, statuettes, bronzes and tablets. They rip out the gems and precious metals from the finest of the Lyres of Ur – the gold, the carnelian, the mother-of-pearl, the lapis lazuli. Its pitiful remains will someday be found discarded in a car park, smashed to pieces. The statue of the Assyrian king Sargon II travels to London and New York, before it is finally returned to Iraq. A figurine of Entemena, the Sumerian king of Lagash, turns up in a warehouse in Queens. Inside elegant emporiums, stylish shops, respected auction houses, Mesopotamian artefacts await their next buyers, while others resurface in street stalls. Several treasures from Nineveh trade hands on London's Portobello Road. But the easiest targets are the tablets; those from the library of Ashurbanipal are much sought after. Especially the *Epic of Gilgamesh*. Light and portable, lines from the poem are spirited away to the four corners of the earth. While wealthy buyers may give the objects a safe home, it is a vicious cycle: demand increases theft, theft increases demand. The larger the sums offered, the more insatiable the looters' appetite.

'I brought you something,' says the commander.

He opens a bag and puts a tablet on the table. Instead of clay like the others, this one is brightest lapis lazuli.

'Is it true devil-worshippers have a thing about this colour?'

'We don't wear blue,' Narin says. She doesn't tell him that it is the colour of Melek Tawûs, a hue too holy for humans.

'Stupid, heathen ways.' He studies the child's face – the bridge of her nose is bruised and swollen, the cuts on her lips still unhealed. 'I want you to read this; it'll bring us a ton of money!'

Narin lowers her eyes. 'Only on one condition.'

'What did you say?'

The child swallows, a burning taste on her tongue, but she won't retract. 'You will not call Salma to your room any more. Nor any of the others.'

He stares at her for a moment. 'You halfwit. Start working. Don't ever tell me what to do.'

That same night he sends for Salma. When she returns the next morning, there are cigarette burns all over her chest. Everyone knows that ISIS has forbidden smoking. They have shut down tobacco shops, banning the sale and use of cigarettes. Those found in violation of the rule will be flogged or punished with a broken finger. Each wound on Salma's body is the commander's message to Narin that he can and will do as he pleases.

That is when the child loses all hope. She stops eating. She stops speaking. She knows that sooner or later he will sell her and the next man will be worse. But she can no longer feel anything – no fear, no sorrow, not even pain. Only numbness. She waits for death.

—o—

ARTHUR

By the River Tigris, 1876

As he lies dying in a shepherd's hut, Arthur's eyes flicker open briefly. He blinks, trying to understand where he is. An air of extreme poverty pervades the room. In one corner there is a pile of rags and a wooden bucket, and by his side a cup of tea gone cold. He reaches out from under the sheepskin. His fingertips brush the spine of his journal. He is surprised to find it tossed on the floor, its pages open at random. Breathing with difficulty, he gropes around for a stub of pencil, pulls the notebook over and manages to scrawl these lines:

> *Everyone in this world has some bent or inclination which,*
> *if fostered by favourable circumstances, will colour the rest*
> *of his life.*

His own life has been coloured by the love of poems and the pursuit of words. He has spent his youth arranging and printing them in books, and then deciphering, translating and studying them on tablets. He has devoted himself to an ancient epic, finding joy in piecing it together verse by verse.

Ever since he was a boy, people told him he had an extraordinary talent. His mother believed this wholeheartedly, his father only when it suited him. His colleagues concurred, though his own wife probably not. But Arthur is convinced that everyone has a gift. Given a chance and a modicum of support, anyone can elevate their skill. In the end, perhaps what separates one individual from another is not talent but passion. And what is passion if not a restlessness of the heart, an intense yearning to surpass your limits, like a river overflowing its banks?

Gilgamesh, the cruel and arrogant king who embarked on journeys, experienced loss and defeat, and learnt humility. Ashurbanipal, the remorseless and cultured king, prided himself on his magnificent capital, palace and library, all of which were razed to the ground. And he, Arthur, King of the Sewers and Slums, so named by a band of good-hearted toshers, miles away from home, has lost the certainty of his convictions.

Tears well up in his eyes. He would have liked to have been a better father to his children, to have spent more time with them, to have seen them grow up. His wife deserved a better husband. There is an immense loneliness in his heart, where there should have been intimacy. He carries within him desires suppressed, secrets withheld. Love is a puzzle in cuneiform, one he has not been able to solve. In truth, he has always been happiest when working on an ancient tablet. With a clarity that is almost painful, he recognizes that only when studying the past has he felt at home, only when sorting broken shards has he felt complete.

Time is a river that meanders, branching out into tributaries and rivulets, depositing sediments of stories along its shores in the hope that someday, someone, somewhere, will find them. The blue tablet is exceptional, but, as he ruminates about it, his own fallibility hits him. To whom does the object belong – the itinerant bards who recited the poem, travelling from city to city; the king who ordered it to be put in writing; the scribe who laboured in setting it down; the librarian who scrupulously stored it; the archaeologist who unearthed it centuries later; the museum that will keep it safe – or does it belong only to the people of this land, and, if so, will minorities like the Yazidis ever be counted amongst them? He has gifted Leila one of the tablets he found, but should he have given them all to her?

Arthur hopes that the *Epic of Gilgamesh* will be read, appreciated and studied by enthusiasts on every continent. They might not have much in common at first glance, except for an inexplicable pull towards a fragmentary tale in an extinct language. The lovers of the story will probably always be a curious bunch, walking under the spell of a poem three thousand lines long and more than three thousand years old. Incomplete and fractured, with its flawed hero, inherent uncertainties, shifting moods and refusal to offer easy optimism, it is a narrative that mirrors an imperfect world.

We carve our dreams into objects, large or small. The emotions we hold but fail to honour, we try to express through the things we create, trusting that they will outlive us when we are gone, trusting that they will carry something of us through the layers of time, like water seeping through rocks. It is our way of saying to the next generations, those we will never get to meet, 'Remember us.' It is our way of admitting we were weak and flawed, and that we made mistakes, some inevitable, others foolish, but deep within we appreciated beauty and poetry, too. Each historical artefact, therefore, is a silent plea from ancestors to descendants, 'Do not judge us too harshly.' We make art to leave a mark for the future, a slight kink in the river of stories, which flows too fast and too wildly for any of us to comprehend.

He closes his eyes, sinking back into a drowsy torpor. Unlike Gilgamesh, he is at peace with his mortality. The *faqra* taught him that death is less an end than a new beginning, an opening to the unknown, and Arthur, timid and shy though he has been all his life, is not afraid.

So it is that on this day in August 1876, King Arthur of the Sewers and Slums – the boy born on the banks of the River Thames into poverty and hardship, raised in the tenements of lower Chelsea; student in a ragged school; apprentice to a leading printer and publisher; decipherer of cuneiform tablets at the British Museum; a reluctant celebrity thrust into the centre of a fierce debate on religion versus science, Creation versus Evolution; scholar, explorer, archaeologist and savant; father and husband and a man with a secret love buried in his heart – breathes his last on the shores of the River Tigris, in the confines of a dilapidated mud hut, no different from those of the Ancient Mesopotamians, whose poetry and stories defined his life.

Mahmoud comes back with a doctor by his side. It is too late. They load the body on to a cart and take it to Castrum Kefa. A woman is waiting for them at the entrance to the ancient city. She wears a long, white dress. Leila now has a tiny tattoo on her forehead – the three wedge-shaped marks that Arthur once etched on the bark of a pomegranate tree. She has never forgotten him. She is the only person who has ever begun to understand his full being, both the boy and the man, his humanity, his courage, his solitariness, his fervour and his frailty . . . And he has kept his word. He has returned.

Arthur will be buried in the Castle of the Rock, one of the oldest continuous settlements in history, in a cemetery bordering the Yazidi village. On his tombstone they will write:

King Arthur of the Sewers and Slums
Born by the River Thames 1840
Died by the River Tigris 1876

—H
ZALEEKHAH

By the River Thames, 2018

In a chic enclave of Chelsea, Zaleekhah punches the code into a keypad set into the wall, waiting for the double gates to open. Inside, the garden smells sweet, of blossoms and fresh leaves and newly turned earth, and a hint of jasmine rising from the trellis. In the setting sun the waters of the Andalusian fountain shimmer, multiple shades of blue.

Kareem answers the door, a look of surprise on his face. 'How nice to see you! Was Mr Malek expecting you?'

The question rattles her a little. The niggling awareness that this is not, and never has been, her home. For a moment she considers telling him the truth: that she was so worried about Uncle that she had to come to check on him. But she dispels the thought, thinking of a less alarming-sounding reason instead. She pulls out of her bag a book – *Nineveh and Its Remains*.

'I'm returning this. Finally managed to read it.'

Uninterested, Kareem nods. 'Of course.'

Zaleekhah crosses the black-and-white chequerboard marble hallway and climbs the curved staircase, with its Chinese reverse-glass painted mirror at the entrance and portraits glaring down from both sides. She does not linger in front of her childhood bedroom; the door is closed and she leaves it like that.

Uncle's study, at the end of the hall, is empty. Zaleekhah steps in lightly, scanning the exquisite objects and artworks arranged on the walls and shelves. There is a mellowness to the light in the room, as if a gauzy tulle has been draped over a lamp, softening the edges. Through the open window she can hear the workers out the back, hammering in the Zen garden, not yet an oasis of calm. She approaches the window, peeks out.

Uncle and Aunt Malek are there, by the azaleas and rosebushes, crouching in the dirt in their Burberry wellies, with Lily between them, her skinny limbs pale in the cold. They all seem to be examining some tiny creature on a leaf – perhaps a snail or a caterpillar. Craning her neck to the side, Aunt Malek wets her finger and wipes a trace of mud from her granddaughter's forehead. Then she pulls the child close and gives her a hug. There is such tenderness in the gesture, such a total abandonment of formality and decorum rarely seen in her behaviour, that Zaleekhah draws back as if she has intruded on a private moment she was not meant to see.

Remembering why she is here, Zaleekhah abandons the window. She heads towards the coffee table to leave *Nineveh and Its Remains*. Instinctively, though, she glances at the chest of drawers, deciding, instead, to put the book in Uncle's original place for it. She opens the top drawer. The elegant silver paper knife is here, as is the money from the other day. Next to them lies another envelope, also in Uncle's monogrammed stationery, this one larger and unsealed. For a moment she stands still, staring at one corner, from which a photograph is poking out.

She pulls it out.

The photo shows a young girl, her slim, spectral shadow falling on the whitewashed wall behind her. It must have been taken indoors, in a place with cushions and carpets on the floor, and possibly at night, as the light is slanted, casting one side of her face into shade. The dress she is wearing is too big for her. She has a wide forehead, bow-lipped mouth and the most beautiful, saddest green eyes. She does not seem to look at the camera as much as through it, with such unmistakable pain in her face that she appears somehow older than her years.

Zaleekhah studies the image, not quite sure why it bothers her. It is so unexpected and unlike any portrait she has ever seen before. When she turns it over, she finds a note inscribed on the back in a neat, cursive hand, the letters tilting slightly to the right.

Girl X
Age: 13 years old
Blood type: AB+
Height: 1.52m
Weight: 42 kg
Organ-donor match: 96 per cent

Zaleekhah clasps her hand to her mouth in alarm. Her chest starts pounding rapidly. Trembling, she puts the photo back in the envelope, then changes her mind and takes it with her. She slams the drawer, but it is either stuck or in her panic she has trapped something in the runner, for it does not close properly. Leaving it like that, she hurries out of the room.

Downstairs, Kareem is busy giving instructions to the maid on how to dust the Victorian chandelier when he sees Zaleekhah racing towards the door.

'Are you leaving already? I just told your uncle you were here. He'll be with you shortly.'

'I . . . I have to go.'

Kareem's eyebrows shoot up. 'What shall I tell him?'

'Tell him I forgot an important appointment . . .' Zaleekhah stops. 'Actually, tell him I know what he's doing, and it's wrong.'

An hour later, Uncle's claret Bentley pulls up in front of Nen's tattoo shop, blocking the traffic trickling past the British Museum. The chauffeur rushes to open the door for him, watched closely by the drivers of the cars queueing behind. Uncle Malek gets out, reads the neon writing in the window.

He walks in, the bells on the door announcing his entrance. 'Where is she?'

Nen, busy cleaning and disinfecting her equipment, looks up, continues with her work.

'Where is she? She's not in the houseboat.'

'She doesn't want to see you, Mr Malek.'

Uncle sucks in a sharp breath. The pouches under his eyes seem swollen and darker today. 'What did she tell you?'

'Nothing. She doesn't speak.'

'Like when she was little.' Uncle sinks into the sofa. 'You don't have a drink, do you?'

'I have coffee.'

'Yes, your famous coffee!' Uncle's shoulders drop as he stares vacantly at the images on the walls. When he speaks again, it is in a low, slow rasp. 'There's been a terrible misunderstanding. Zaleekhah has got it all back to front. She jumped to conclusions without knowing the full story. I need to talk to her urgently.'

Nen stands still, her face unreadable, save for a telltale flicker of her eyes. Catching the change in her gaze, Uncle turns his head to find his niece staring at him, having just ascended the stairs.

'My dear . . .'

He leans forward as if to rise to his feet but sits back down again. 'Please, reserve judgement until you hear everything I've got to say. Allow me to explain.'

'I'm listening.'

'Right . . .' Uncle throws a curt glance at Nen. 'I'm afraid this is private.'

'I want her to stay,' says Zaleekhah.

'It's okay, don't worry.' Nen drops her needles and grabs her jacket. 'I'll be at the British Museum. I'd better finish sketching the *lamassu*.' Briefly touching Zaleekhah's shoulder, she smiles at her. 'Call me if you need anything.'

The door closes, the jingling echoing for too long in the tense silence. Uncle scans the room as if to make sure there is no one around.

'Our little Lily is very sick. You have no idea how serious it is. It might be months, if not years, before they find her a compatible donor on the NHS. Even if we go private, there are nation-wide shortages and huge waiting lists. I've searched everywhere, believe me. And then I came across something unexpected . . . a chance encounter. When I was making inquiries to buy the blue tablet, I was put in touch with some people who had heard of Yazidi girls in a dire situation. And one of them, it turns out, was a perfect match for our Lily.'

Zaleekhah shakes her head without looking at him.

'You must understand, no one cares about these girls; they've been completely forgotten. They are basically dead to the world. A few lucky ones get saved, but the rest? Not even their poor families can trace where they are.'

'So you think you're doing her a favour!'

Uncle lifts up his palms. 'In an ideal world none of this would happen, but we don't live in that world. Let's be realistic – if I hadn't found her, she'd remain captive forever, there is no doubt about that. She has no one.'

'That doesn't mean –'

'Please – think about it. Who would have rescued her, tell me. Who would have spent a penny to save her? This girl is deaf, I'm told. They don't want her. They see her as a burden. My under-standing is that she's already been sold on from a house in Mosul to a house in Antep . . . She's been starved, beaten, tortured and most probably raped.'

Zaleekhah presses her fingertips on the corners of her eyes, unable to open them for a moment.

'Her enslavers believe the girl is descended from a cursed line. They think she brings bad luck. Someone will kill her one way or another. But I can help. I can take care of her. Her whole life. She won't be abused any more. She won't be mistreated. She'll receive the best care. She'll go to school. I will provide.'

'You seriously believe you're saving her, don't you?'

'I'm making an arrangement that benefits all sides. If a deal leaves you better off, can it really be a bad thing? And the girl will definitely benefit. She will be free. She will have a new life, she is young, and she can start over. People live just fine with one kidney.'

'That doesn't make it right!' A gasp escapes Zaleekhah's lips. 'Don't you understand how unethical this is? The only reason you're interested in this girl is . . .' She stutters, struggling to find the right words. 'Organ-harvesting, that's what this is.'

'My dear, don't you care about Lily?'

'Of course I do!' Zaleekhah cannot stop her voice from breaking. 'Does Helen know?'

'No. Your sister doesn't know the particulars. She's just happy and relieved that a good donor has been found for her child.'

'Uncle, this is madness! I can't believe you're making it all sound so rational and logical. It's illegal!'

'Perhaps . . . but you're not the one taking that risk. I am.' Carefully and deliberately Uncle Malek reaches for his cane. 'I must go. Your aunt is expecting me home for dinner – she's trying out another fish recipe.'

An icy jolt runs through Zaleekhah's body then. 'You hate fish . . .' she murmurs, slowly. 'But you always listen to her, don't you? How did I not think of this before? It was the two of you. You used your connections in the region, but it was Aunt Malek who came up with this . . . *solution.*'

Shifting his cane from one hand to the other, Uncle stands and walks towards the door.

'It was her handwriting on the back of the photo,' says Zaleekhah. 'She insisted on this plan and you gave in, like you always do. But it bothered you, and still does – it nags at your conscience. That's why you've been in a terrible state lately. And that's why when you had a few drinks on my birthday you shouted at her. You said she never dirties her hands, always the saint, while you're stuck being the sinner.'

Uncle Malek stops, staring out at the street.

'You are clever, my dear. You always were. But does it really matter whose idea it was? We arranged everything together – the doctor, the hospital in Istanbul, the paperwork . . . we'll do this for our daughter and our granddaughter.'

Zaleekhah tries to hold back the tears. 'Of course – your family always comes first.'

'They are also *your* family, my dear – or have you forgotten?'

And there it is, contained in those few words, and in the constraint with which Uncle Malek utters them: the expectation of gratitude for everything he has done for her, the sum of her debt to him.

She starts crying. 'But now that I know your secret, how can you be sure I'll go along with your plan?'

'You will, my dear. We are all you have. We are your blood.'

—H₂O—
NARIN, ZALEEKHAH, ARTHUR

By the River Tigris, 2018

They are opening the floodgates today. The water will start pouring through the finished dam, a forceful, ceaseless flow – roaring, expanding, demanding its own quantum of space. The level of the reservoir will rise imperceptibly at first, but it will soon fill up. Each day the water will climb another 35 centimetres, reaching 20 metres in a couple of months. By the end of this year, Castrum Kefa will be completely inundated, the ancient walled city submerged for generations to come.

Watching her surroundings, Zaleekhah feels a swelling sadness wash over her, an acute awareness of things coming to an end. The landscape – barren, baked and treeless – resembles the underbelly of an animal fallen on its back, struggling to flip itself over, just as small and helpless.

'Are you all right?' asks Nen. 'What are you thinking?'

'Soft-shelled turtles . . .' Zaleekhah says with a distracted smile. 'They used to lay eggs by the Euphrates, but when the hydroelectric power stations destroyed the reed banks they were forced to migrate here to the Tigris. And now this refuge is also ruined . . . I wonder where they'll be able to go next?'

Nen listens, attentive as always. After a heartbeat, she asks gently, 'Did you manage to talk to your uncle?'

Zaleekhah shakes her head. 'He won't take my phone calls. Nor will my aunt. I don't think they'll forgive me for a long time, maybe ever. But I did manage to get through to Helen. It was the most difficult conversation I've had in my life. She was quite shaken, devastated. It had all been scheduled in and now they're back at the bottom of the waiting list. I feel awful.'

Nen removes a strand of hair from Zaleekhah's face. 'You did the right thing – the difficult thing.'

'Helen understands. She and I, we're looking for another donor – through official channels this time. I'll do everything I can to help her. I won't leave her and Lily alone.'

Nen nods. 'Ready to go see Narin?'

'Ready.'

They climb the steep hill, falling naturally into step. Past a broken splintered fence, the ancient cemetery stretches, its border blending with the horizon. The girl is there. She wished to spend time alone by her ancestors' graves, and, to give her privacy, Nen and Zaleekhah have been rambling around for the last half an hour, exploring the surroundings.

They bought Narin from a dealer who did business with a dealer who did business with ISIS. They paid $3,200 – the market price for a human being on that particular day. Most of the money came from the tattoo shop. They had assistance from locals, people who wanted to help. It was no secret that one more Yazidi slave was being held captive in a house in a busy suburb in a booming city in Turkey, just as thousands of others were still in family homes in Syria, Kuwait, Iraq, Saudi Arabia . . . prisoners in ordinary neighbourhoods where life went on as normal.

As the two women enter the old graveyard with its crumbling stones and tangled weeds, they fall silent. Further up the dust-ridden track, Narin's sylphlike frame is haloed by the baking sun. The girl has not heard them coming and will not notice their presence until they stand in front of her. So as not to scare her, Zaleekhah and Nen pause for a moment. Though they will not voice this out loud, they both wonder in that instant how long will it take for the child to recover. The other possibility is too harrowing to contemplate: that the wounds are so deep they might never heal, the heart might never forget. For now, they are glad they were able to bring her to her birthplace before it is lost forever.

Meanwhile, a few metres away, sitting on the scorched grass, Narin has withdrawn into her silent world. She has laid flowers by the graves of her mother and her great-great-grandmother Leila . . . Her beloved Grandma Besma is not here, buried in a mass grave in Iraq. The child has no idea whether her father is alive, but she clings fiercely to the prospect that someday they will find each other. In the afternoon she will speak to her relatives in Germany. When they found out she was alive, they were ecstatic. Maybe one day Narin will join them in Hanover. She is also aware that Zaleekhah and Nen want to bring her to London with them. What she doesn't know is how difficult it is to get the necessary permissions and paperwork for any such move. Nothing is clear yet. The only definite thing is that her old life is no more.

In a little while, Narin lifts her chin, as if to catch some scent from the riverbank, and sees the two women waiting for her – like figures hovering at the edge of a dream. Her face remains motionless. Neither relief nor recognition, only nothingness.

Slowly, the women approach the girl. Something unexpected happens then. As Zaleekhah proffers her hand to help her stand, her sleeve hitches up a little and Narin notices the tattoo on her wrist – identical to the deq on Grandma's forehead. Blinking back her tears, she stares at the image, the confusion and sorrow in her eyes joined by a new feeling – a tiny seed of trust that one day may or may not grow into something stronger.

The three of them pick their way through the scattered rocks and sparse undergrowth, heading back to the shabby hotel where they will spend the night. Before they leave the cemetery, Narin points out a tombstone, on which Nen and Zaleekhah are surprised to find an eccentric inscription in English: *King Arthur of the Sewers and Slums*. As they read, murmuring in puzzlement,

Narin, unbeknown to them, gives a subtle nod in its direction, a last goodbye to Arthur before the waters arrive.

It is only a matter of time now, and time, like an ancient tablet, is breaking apart, faster than anyone can reassemble it. Tomorrow, when the last remaining poems of Mesopotamia are submerged and all that was Hasankeyf has drowned, people will speak of the destruction of culture and environment and the memories of the land, though no one, not even the river itself, will remember that it all began with a single raindrop.

A droplet from the Tigris ascends ever so slowly, evaporating under the sun, a gauzy spiral of mist. An eternal cycle starts to repeat itself, from liquid to vapour to solid. Tears from the destroyed cities of Mesopotamia mingle with the haze of torrents yet to come. As the cloud passes over continents, it freezes into crystals. A snowflake falls over London, see-sawing rapidly towards a newborn baby lying on the icy ground. And the infant looks up at the mystery that is water, all flurry and movement, now silver, now blue, the most beautiful, deepest blue. And if we could only see the world through a baby's eyes, gazing up with innocent wonder, we could watch the rivers in the sky. Mighty rivers that never cease to flow.

The Journey of a Drop of Water	Residence Time
630 BCE, Nineveh, plummets as a raindrop and lands in King Ashurbanipal's hair	30 minutes
Evaporates into the atmosphere	5 to 15 days
Returns as a raindrop, seeps into the earth and reaches deep groundwater	1,500 years
Returns to the surface via a spring and travels to the open seas	970 years
Ascends to the atmosphere	5 to 15 days
1840, turns into a snowflake and falls into the mouth of a newborn baby by the River Thames in London	2 to 6 months
Melts into the river and is carried into the English Channel; driven by prevailing tides, it circulates around the Mediterranean ports	32 years
1872, splashes on Arthur's face when he arrives in Constantinople from a wave striking the quayside	5 seconds
Evaporates, rests on a cloud, falls as rain in the Taurus Mountains, sleeps in shallow groundwater and runs into the upper reaches of the River Tigris	142 years

2014, fills a bottle brought from
the Valley of Lalish   3 days

Dissolves into the atmosphere   5 to 15 days

Collected as rainwater,
distilled and bottled   1 month

Finds itself the last drop in a plastic
bottle of water on Mount Sinjar   12 hours

Evaporates, travels once round
the world eastwards   49 days

Falls as rain into an English reservoir
and stays there   2 to 3 years

2018, drunk as tap water in London   1 day

2018, turns into a teardrop in a
houseboat in London, falls into a sink   1 minute

Mixes with tap water and treated sewage,
and reaches the sea again   (still there)

This novel is the work of a junior scribe,
One of the many bards, balladeers and storytellers
    who walk the earth.
We weave poems, songs and stories out of every breath.
May you remember us.

Now and always,
Praise be to Nisaba

Note to the Reader

My maternal grandmother, the woman who raised me until I was ten years old, had never heard of the Greek philosopher and mathematician Thales of Miletus, but she, too, believed that water was the fundamental principle of life. She wished to teach me how to listen to gentle rain or murmuring streams, but, in my ignorance, I have been a rather poor student. In the end, as in many other things, it was literature that connected me with the realities and mysteries that had been in front of me all along. Holding a host of still-unknown properties, water remains a great mystery.

The stories and silences of Mesopotamia – current-day Iraq and parts of current-day Turkey, Iran, Syria and Kuwait – are shaped by rivers, past and present, dead and dying. Of the ten most water-stressed nations in the world, seven are in the Middle East and North Africa. The Tigris and the Euphrates, once the cradle of civilization, are at their lowest levels in history. As the Mesopotamian rivers dry up, day by day, thousand-year-old settlements emerge from beneath their receding shores.

King Arthur of the Sewers and Slums is a fictional character who lives inside my imagination, but I have loosely based him on an actual historical figure: George Smith – the working-class genius who decoded cuneiform, travelled to the Ottoman Empire and died on the way back in a village close to the border between Turkey and Syria. A self-taught pioneer Assyriologist who not only discovered and translated the *Epic of Gilgamesh*, he also dedicated his life to the ancient poem. Books by and about this remarkable character have been central to my research, such as his *Assyrian Discoveries: An Account of Explorations and Discoveries on the Site of Nineveh, during 1873 and 1874* and *The Chaldean Account of Genesis*.

I would especially like to highlight David Damrosch's fabulous masterpiece *The Buried Book: The Loss and Rediscovery of the Great Epic of Gilgamesh*. Irving Finkel's *The Ark before Noah: Decoding the Story of the Flood* offers illuminating and helpful insights. I have learnt a lot from *Myths from Mesopotamia: Creation, The Flood, Gilgamesh, and Others* (translated by Stephanie Dalley) and *The Epic of Gilgamesh* (translated by Andrew George). The lovers of the poem hail from all around the globe and I count myself amongst them. *Gilgamesh among Us: Modern Encounters with the Ancient Epic* by Theodore Ziolkowski is a fascinating source on the continuing influence and allure of the world's oldest work of literature.

Austen Henry Layard's groundbreaking work *Nineveh and Its Remains: With an Account of a Visit to the Chaldaean Christians of Kurdistan, and the Yezidis, or Devil-Worshippers; and an Enquiry into the Manners and Arts of the Ancient Assyrians* has been crucial in my research and attentive readers will notice that I have played with the word order in the original title. *Assyrian Palace Sculptures* by Paul Collins, *I am Ashurbanipal: king of the world, king of Assyria*, edited by Gareth Brereton, and *Winged Bull: The Extraordinary Life of Henry Layard, the Adventurer Who Discovered the Lost City of Nineveh* by Jeff Pearce have been precious sources. The scene where Arthur witnesses a *kadi*, a religious judge, grant permission to deceive and even slaughter the Yazidis on the grounds that they are not 'people of the book' is based on Layard's own accounts. It is real.

Many things in this book are inspired by actual events and historical characters – such as Obaysch the Hippo, sent as a present by an Ottoman pasha to England, or Tapputi, the Ancient Mesopotamian female perfume-maker . . . Gingerbread cuneiform biscuits also exist and they are delicious; you can find a recipe on the Penn Museum website. For other culinary traditions and rituals, you can consult Jean Bottéro's *The Oldest Cuisine in the World: Cooking in Mesopotamia*.

Charles Dickens was indeed published by Bradbury & Evans after he left Chapman & Hall in 1844. One can still chance upon first editions of *Bleak House* or *Little Dorrit* in the catalogues of antiquarian booksellers, though they are very expensive. Dickens broke up with the company in 1859, when they refused to print an advertisement in *Punch* magazine explaining why he was separating from his wife. For the purposes of the narrative, I have altered details or dates to suit the flow of the story. For instance, Layard's book was actually published by John Murray. *The Rubáiyát of Omar Khayyám* – the astronomer – poet of Persia – was printed by Quaritch. There was a famed Egyptologist in the British Museum by the name of Dr Samuel Birch who was employed as the Keeper of the Department of Oriental Antiquities, but I have made alterations to the time of his post. There was indeed a suicide that shook the English printing and publishing business, but it was that of the young Henry Bradbury, the son of William Bradbury. Dr John Snow is real, of course, and his discovery that cholera spread through drinking water rather than inhaling unpleasant odours contributed greatly to our understanding of pandemics. Steven Johnson's *The Ghost Map: The Story of London's Most Terrifying Epidemic – and How It Changed Science, Cities and the Modern World*; Peter Ackroyd's *Thames: Sacred River* (2 vols.) and *London Under*; Stephen Halliday's *The Great Stink of London: Sir Joseph Bazalgette and the Cleansing of the Victorian Metropolis*; Nicholas Barton's *The Lost Rivers of London*; Matthew Kneale's *Sweet Thames*; Jonathan Schneer's *The Thames: England's River*; Jerry White's *London in the Nineteenth Century*; Michelle Higgs's *A Visitor's Guide to Victorian England*; and Jonathon Shears's *The Great Exhibition, 1851* were all most valuable sources. The scene where Arthur sees Istanbul for the first time was inspired by the writings of the nineteenth-century novelist and poet Edmondo de Amicis, who vividly captured Constantinople through the eyes of a foreigner. The letter from the Secretary of the British Museum is real – I changed only a few words. I have also used bits and pieces from George Smith's diary, which, remarkably, he kept until his last moments.

Hasankeyf, a first-degree historical and preservation site included in the World Heritage List, is today erased. The place left a big mark on me when I visited it many moons ago, long before it was drowned by the controversial Ilisu Dam. The Arabs called it Hisn Kayfa; the Romans called it Kefa; but for consistency I have kept the Ancient Assyrian name *Castrum Kefa*. I must also point out that, although the *lamassus* at the British Museum are actually from both Nimrud and Khorsabad, I made small changes here and there, as I wanted to situate Nineveh at the centre of my narrative arc. The story of the King who was buried with his servants and storytellers is also true, though I moved the date of the archaeological discovery. The Library of Ashurbanipal, spread across four different locations, is not only fascinating of itself but also deeply relevant today, as libraries come increasingly under threat.

The scientist Berenberg, although an imaginary character, is loosely based on the French immunologist Jacques Benveniste, who developed the theory of 'water memory' at the cost of his career and professional reputation. I am interested in his work not from the standpoint of science or homoeopathy but simply as a novelist who is drawn to human stories. I loved and treasured all my readings about water, and, while I cannot do justice to the vast array of literature on the subject, I particularly would like to mention *Elixir: A Human History of Water* by Brian Fagan; *Blue Machine: How the Ocean Shapes Our World* by Helen Czerski; *When the Rivers Run Dry* by Fred Pearce; *How to Read Water: Clues, Signs and Patterns from Puddles to the Sea* by Tristan Gooley; and *The Flow: Rivers, Water and Wildness* by Amy-Jane Beer, where you will encounter the line that inspired the title of this novel.

The debate on museums and who owns cultural heritage is a complicated one, and there is no better space than literature, especially the novel as a literary genre, within which to freely explore the most complex issues of our time with nuance, depth, care and empathy. Fiction allows us to grasp important and sensitive subjects from multiple angles – a freedom we are steadily losing in the age of social media and unfeeling algorithms. *The Museum Makers: A Journey Backwards – from Old Boxes of Dark Family Secrets to a Golden*

Era of Museums by Rachel Morris explores the human instinct for collection. *From Nineveh to New York: The Strange Story of the Assyrian Reliefs in the Metropolitan Museum and the Hidden Masterpiece at Canford School* by John Malcolm Russell, based almost entirely on unpublished archives, offers a fascinating insight into Lady Charlotte Guest, 'the richest woman in England', who owned such a huge collection of artefacts from Mesopotamia that she had her own 'Nineveh Porch' at her country house, Canford Manor. Arthur stumbling across items from Nineveh in a wealthy house in England is inspired by this historical episode.

The research process for this novel has been intense, immense and interdisciplinary. I loved reading a diverse range of books and academic articles, from global environmental crisis and conservation hydrology to Ancient Akkadian funeral and libation rites, to the ethnomedicinal plants of Mesopotamia. *Rivers of the Sultan: The Tigris and Euphrates in the Ottoman Empire* by Faisal H. Husain; *Tigris and Euphrates Rivers: Their Environment from Headwaters to Mouth*, edited by Laith A. Jawad; and *Wounded Tigris: A Journey through the Cradle of Civilisation* by Leon McCarron helped me both from a historical and geographical perspective. Yet perhaps the greatest challenge arose when I delved into the richness and complexity of Yazidi culture and traditions. A collective identity that has been transmitted throughout the centuries mostly through songs, stories, lullabies and poems could not be understood solely by focusing on written texts. I have debated a lot which spelling to use, 'Yazidi', 'Yezidi' or 'Êzidi', and the only reason I chose the first was to maintain the continuity in the novel with the nineteenth-century script and Arthur's discovery of Layard's book.

Another challenge was that the practices of Yazidi communities differed, depending on place or period. Some tenets, such as not eating fish or believing in reincarnation, can vary widely between, for instance, Yazidis in Iraq and Yazidis in Armenia. I tried not to lose sight of this fascinating plurality and aimed to honour the significance of oral heritage. To this end, I examined songs, myths, legends and folk tales, as well as superstitions. *The Yezidi Religious Textual Tradition: From Oral to Written* by Khanna Omarkhali; *The Religion of the Peacock Angel: The Yezidis and Their Spirit World* by Garnik S. Asatrian and Victoria Arakelova; *God and Sheikh Adi are Perfect: Sacred Poems and Religious Narratives from the Yezidi Tradition* by Philip G. Kreyenbroek and Khalil Jindy Rashow; *The Yezidis* by Eszter Spät; *The Yezidi Oral Tradition in Iraqi Kurdistan* by Christine Allison; *The Role of Nature in Yezidism* by Rezan Shivan Aysif; *Yezidism in Europe: Different Generations Speak about Their Religion* by Philip G. Kreyenbroek; *Ezidiler: 73. Ferman* by Nurcan Baysal; and *The Yezidis: The History of a Community, Culture and Religion* by Birgül Açikyildiz have been most valuable and illuminating. I am profoundly grateful to people both from local communities and the diaspora who kindly and generously opened their hearts and memories to me, even when those memories were full of pain and suffering.

In my novel there is a genocide in the late nineteenth century by the shores of the Tigris, and this is based on historical facts. I have, however, changed the precise date and some relevant details for the narrative flow. Muhammad Pasha of Rawanduz, known as Mirê Kor, along with Bedir Khan Beg, massacred thousands of Yazidis in 1832. Those who ran towards the river were trapped, as, unbeknownst to them, all the boats had been destroyed. The genocide that took place in 2014 happened in front of the eyes of the entire world. *Sinjar: 14 Days that Saved the Yazidis from Islamic State* by Susan Shand; *The Yezidi Sunset: The Genocide by ISIS in Iraq* by Paul Martin Kingery; and *Shadow on the Mountain: A Yazidi Memoir of Terror, Resistance and Hope* by Shaker Jeffrey and Katharine Holstein are heartbreaking and powerful accounts. *State Responsibility and the Genocide of the Yazidis,* edited by Baroness Helena Kennedy, Aarif Abraham, Lord David Alton and Tatyana Eatwell, is a pivotal document, and I want to emphasize the meticulous investigations of the Yazidi Justice Committee (YJC). The comment in my novel by my fictional character Salma about her wish to have been gassed at Halabja rather than being captured and raped by ISIS is taken from the words of a survivor.

The memoirs and personal accounts of enslaved Yazidi women were extremely difficult to read at times but hugely important. Nadia Murad's *The Last Girl*; Farida Khalaf's *The Girl Who Beat ISIS*; Dunya Mikhail's *The Beekeeper of Sinjar: Rescuing the Stolen Women of Iraq*; and Christina Lamb's *Our Bodies, Their Battlefields: War through the Lives of Women* left a huge impact on me. I am deeply thankful to psychologist and trauma therapist Professor Dr Jan Kizilhan for his time and thoughts. For many years, Kizilhan and his team have carried out remarkable and selfless work to contribute both to individual and collective healing, helping the most vulnerable and traumatized. I also want to express my gratitude to Mona Kizilhan, Aarif Abraham, Leyla Ferman, Düzen Tekkal and her wise father, all of whom kindly and patiently answered my questions, no matter how foolish or small. Dr Leyla Ferman, the co-founder of the YJC and Director of Women for Justice, shared with me first-hand witness accounts from Sinjar, and thus I learnt about the way desperate families trapped on the mountain had tried to portion drops of water to keep their children alive. Leyla's family took this surname after a grandfather who was born during a time of *ferman/* genocide, so as to keep the memory of their history alive. I have read transcriptions of Yazidi ballads and songs that still to this day preserve the memory of past atrocities. I am immensely grateful to human rights lawyers, campaigners and survivors who have spoken with me either in person or through video conference. I have learnt so much from your courage, resilience of spirit and hard work for justice and recognition.

As I was writing this book, an influential Nigerian politician and his wife were jailed and found guilty by an Old Bailey jury under the Modern Slavery Act. This is the first organ-trafficking conviction in the UK. The couple had made arrangements with a doctor to lure a poor street vendor from Nigeria to the UK to harvest his kidney to help their sick daughter, who needed an organ transplant. I kept reading and researching about this extraordinary case, surprised to find out that Turkey, my motherland, appeared in such trial records as a key site for networks of illegal organ trafficking. While I followed this legal and ethical story, I was simultaneously studying the testimonies of Yazidi survivors and the two issues connected in my mind. Today around three thousand Yazidi women and girls are still missing, many of them held captive in typical family homes in cities and towns across the Middle East. One incident in particular shook me to the core. In 2021, a seven-year-old Yazidi girl was found in a horrible state in an ordinary neighbourhood in Ankara, not far from my maternal grandmother's house where I grew up, after an online auction to sell her to the highest bidder was foiled by the police. The Yazidi Genocide, horrific and harrowing though it has been, is not over yet.

I close my eyes and think of Thales of Miletus sitting on the banks of the winding Maeander River (the Great Menderes in present-day Turkey), which gave us the word 'meander' (from Greek *maiandros* and Latin *maeander*). I picture him there, watching the water with a sense of wonder and respect, observing its restless movement and renewal. Then I imagine a tiny drop splashing on to the philosopher's hand . . . the very drop that might have been inside my coffee this morning or perhaps inside yours, connecting us all beyond the borders of time, geography and identity.

Acknowledgements

There are some amazing souls who encouraged me to dream this novel into existence. People I am blessed to be working with. My unwavering gratitude to my UK editor Isabel Wall and my US editor John Freeman. Isabel, I don't know where to begin, honestly. Your meticulous, dedicated and insightful editing, your generous heart and the way you are always there advocating for your authors mean the world to me. John, I feel like we have known each other forever, and I deeply appreciate your mind and devotion as well as your great editorial and literary intuition. My special thanks to Jonny Geller for being a brilliant and thoughtful literary agent and for energizing and nurturing my ideas, even when they are merely half-baked, with such insight, clarity and precious friendship. I am grateful to the amazing Sophie Baker and Katie Harrison at Curtis Brown who represent my world rights with diligence and love. Edward (Edd) Kirke passionately and assiduously took care of every detail and design in this book. On each side of the Atlantic, I am indebted to Viking's Toye Oladinni, Samantha Fanaken, Anna Ridley, Jasmin Lindenmeir, Michael Bedo, Rosamund Hutchison and Chloe Davies (who is now on maternity leave); Atlanta Hatch, Ciara Finan and Viola Hayden; and the fabulous team at Knopf – Isabel Ribeiro, Laura Keefe, Erinn Hartman, Tricia Cave and Matthew Sciarappa. My heartfelt thanks to the wonderful and wise Reagan Arthur, not only for the support but also for the delicious ramen conversations.

I wish to express my profound appreciation to the one and only Lisa Babalis. Dear Lisa, I admire your generosity of spirit and signature kindness even as I was bombarding you with emails. You are the Greek sister to my Turkish heart and I thank you with all my soul. My dear friend Stephen Barber is an amazing Renaissance mind, and he has graciously responded to my multiple queries, from linguistic puzzles to Victorian aphorisms. My warm thanks to my whip-smart friend Catherine for her invaluable suggestions. Having a great copy editor is a treasure for an author and this is where the fantastic Donna Poppy comes in. The only problem is, Donna, I think I am now addicted to our long and stimulating conversations on the labyrinths of language. Thank you also to the brilliant Ellie Smith, who read everything with an eagle eye.

To all of you above I want to say this: all my life, literature has given me a sanctuary, a Storyland where I could breathe and feel free, and your presence helps me, an immigrant author writing in a language other than their native tongue, find a new home, a renewed sense of belonging.

A very special thank you to the remarkable scholar, and thoughtful and compassionate human being that is David Damrosch. I am so grateful to the *Epic of Gilgamesh* for making our paths cross, Professor, thank you. Dr Sebastien Rey, the Curator of Ancient Mesopotamia at the British Museum, has so patiently answered my frantic queries about archaeology, history, geography, Nineveh and much more. I am in awe of his generosity and dedication to his field. A huge and loving shout out to Francesca Stavrakopoulou for her splendid scholarly work on women who were left out of history, including the goddess Nisaba, as well as for her scribal sisterhood. I want to thank Dr Moudhy Al-Rashid for responding to my panicky queries with such warmth. Mary Beard, whose mind I deeply respect, was so gracious as to read this novel in its early form and offer valuable thoughts. The head of the Bodleian Library at Oxford, Richard Ovenden, is one of the most kind-hearted people I have ever known. When this book was only a glimmering of an idea inside my head I shared it with Richard and his encouraging words meant a lot to me. I have learnt so much from the aforementioned academics and experts, but any errors that remain in this novel are completely mine.

I must also express my indebtedness to two exceptional

women: Leyla Ferman and Mona Kizilhan, both of whom are among those rare individuals in life who combine goodness and gentleness with amazing toughness and resilience. As you say, *Those, who were seen as the weakest – turned out to be the strongest.* It is a gift to get to know you, thank you.

To my mother and my family, my deepest thanks for being who you are, for your love, support and inspiration, and also for putting up with my loud heavy-metal music. Thank you with all my being, Aurora, Zelda, Emir Z. and my beloved Eyup.

They say as a novelist you must not fall in love with your subject matter, but, as much as I admire the intellect and appreciate the realm of ideas, I do not believe you can write a novel solely from the rational mind. The heart must also be in it, and, once the heart is in it, who knows where it will take you.

This novel is where my heart led me.

This novel is my love song to rivers – those still living and those that are long gone.